THE

AN UNBOUNDED NOVEL

TAKEOVER

Books by Teyla Branton

Unbounded Series
The Change
The Cure
The Escape
The Reckoning
The Takeover

Unbounded Novellas
Ava's Revenge
Mortal Brother
Lethal Engagement

Under the Name Rachel Branton
Tell Me No Lies
Your Eyes Don't Lie

THE TAKEOVER

AN UNBOUNDED NOVEL

TEYLA BRANTON

WHITE STAR PRESS

This is a work of fiction, and the views expressed herein are the sole responsibility of the author. Likewise, certain characters, places, and incidents are the product of the author's imagination, and any resemblance to actual persons, living or dead, or actual events or locales, is entirely coincidental.

The Takeover (Unbounded Series #5)

Published by White Star Press
P.O. Box 353
American Fork, Utah 84003

Printed in the United States of America
ISBN: 978-1-939203-67-0
Year of first printing: 2015

To my readers, who have been so kind to spend a little time in my world and who have given me so much encouragement. Writing is like breathing to me, and the support of people like you, allows me to share my imaginings. I couldn't ask for more! I plan to have many more stories to share and journeys to complete together.

I

hope

you'll

come

along.

THANK YOU!

CHAPTER 1

THE CLICK OF MY RED STILETTOS ECHOED FAINTLY IN THE LONG hallway. The ridiculous shoes were completely unnecessary, in my opinion, but Stella was in charge of disguises, and she'd insisted.

"We want the guards looking at you, Erin, not at your credentials," she'd said, grinning as I tried to balance on what felt like stilts. I comforted myself with the very real possibility of using the pointed heels as a weapon.

Stella was right. The guards' eyes had been too busy with the curves of my legs under my tight skirt to do more than barely glance at my Homeland Security ID. A good thing, since the identification wasn't real. They should have called to verify, even though the main office had advised them of our upcoming arrival. Just in case they did check, Stella had tapped into their communications network and was ready to give them the fake approval code she'd provided when she'd set up the meeting yesterday.

I was more worried about running into an Emporium hit team than dealing with Homeland Security. Compared to the Emporium, getting the best of the US government was child's play.

We'd known we would have to pass through a full-body scanner when we'd entered this secret facility outside Dallas, so the weapons and communication devices we carried were disguised as ordinary items.

Not to mention my shoes.

If the Emporium showed up, Ritter, Dimitri, and I might need everything we'd brought to break Shadrach Azima out of here. He was a traitor to us, but leaving him in captivity any longer, now that he was finally out of Islamic hands, wasn't an option. He was still a Renegade, and we wouldn't leave him for the Emporium or the American government to experiment on.

Dimitri, our healer, was dressed as an aging, gray-haired doctor, complete with a white lab coat, a stethoscope, and a medical bag in hand. I didn't personally know any medical employees who wore white coats into a facility, rather than donning them there, but again Stella had insisted. The broad, normally dark-haired man fit easily into the role, and the guards had given even less attention to his forged credentials as a world-renowned geneticist than mine. At over a thousand years old, Dimitri had forgotten more about medicine than mortal doctors had time to learn.

Only Ritter, unconvincing in his nerdy, Clark Kent glasses and his long-sleeved, white dress shirt buttoned far too high, caused the Homeland Security agents nervousness. He towered over everyone, moving with an animal-like stealth. His longish dark hair was hidden under a light brown wig that slicked back behind his ears, and his black eyes were now blue with special contacts, all of which was supposed to hide his real identity but still couldn't mask the killer inside. This was probably why the guard accompanying us down the hallway tracked Ritter with an alert expression and his hand close to his weapon.

"Their ability to heal is miraculous," said our guide, Dr. Tina Hartley, a middle-aged woman in a white lab coat similar to Dimitri's. Her rich, brown hair was pulled into a thick bun at the base of her neck and was her one great beauty. Nothing else about her stood out—except her thoughts. In the mass of whirling emotions that filled her brain, she wondered if our visit would set her schedule back far enough that she would be allowed to work overtime. If so, she'd use the extra money to put toward her dream trip to Paris, where she'd meet a sexy man who wouldn't scorn her three college degrees and would write her poetry and run his fingers through her hair. The man in her thoughts looked a lot like Ritter, minus the shirt and glasses. Her imagination of him shirtless didn't begin to approach reality.

"I've read the reports," I said, though I hadn't—not the real ones. Despite Stella's technopathic abilities, we hadn't been able to hack into the reports, which weren't kept on any network connecting to the outside. Our Renegade cell's alliance with the US president had allowed us access to the official reports he'd received, but a note smuggled out of this facility had proven our suspicions that the president wasn't being told the entire story.

Either that or we were being set up—which could very well be the case. Our enemy, the Emporium, was as eager to get their hands on us as they would be to retrieve the so-called "patients" who were detained at this facility. Three months ago in mid-January, the president's announcement of Unbounded existence rocked the world, and things had been heating up ever since. We'd need to work harder to make sure the Emporium didn't end up on top when the dust finally settled. Succeeding was the only way Renegades could save mortals and humanity.

The doctor arched a brow, nothing of her scattered thoughts showing in her face. "The reports are not exaggerated. In the two weeks they've been here, they've pretty much decimated everything any of us know about medicine." Her voice took on a note of excitement. "They might even be the key to the problem of aging."

I glanced at Dimitri, whose only reaction was a slight pursing of his lips. His centuries-long study of the Unbounded gene had yielded no result in making mortals Unbounded. Theoretically, mortals who were direct descendants of Unbounded and had enough of the unique code in their genes could Change with scientific manipulation. But the theory had thus far remained unrealized, and other Unbounded researchers, also gifted in healing, agreed that mortals would remain just that—mortal.

"Good thing they live so long," I said, making my voice cold. "Plenty of time to figure it out."

"Yes. Two thousand years, and they age only two years for every century. It really is amazing." Hartley paused before a set of double doors in the hallway, swiping a card through a reader. "We have you scheduled with the Iranian, as requested. We've turned off the sound recordings, but we will, of course, leave video on during your interrogation." She pushed open one of the doors and motioned us into yet another generic corridor.

"Of course." I didn't for a minute believe they weren't recording, not after faking the reports to the president. At least Stella's faked request from Homeland Security to interview the Iranian could not be ignored. This facility was maintained by Homeland Security, and Homeland supposedly had oversight of the work these doctors had conducted this past month since retrieving the Unbounded detainees from the Moroccan government.

"Iranian, American, Russian," Dimitri said with indifference. "Doesn't matter to me. I'm just interested in examining any of them."

Hartley's eyes strayed to Dimitri. "With all your research

into human mutation, I expect you are especially interested in their limb regrowth and how we might transfer that ability to the general population."

Dimitri nodded and smiled. "Yes, indeed. I understand that all of them fully regenerated after the explosion in Morocco."

"They did regenerate beautifully. However, we have seen the need to experiment further."

A rush of silent emotion from Ritter caught me by surprise. His control was generally tight, even with our usual mental connection, but I understood the lapse because I shared his anger. We were accustomed to the Emporium Unbounded experimenting on other Unbounded, but this was the first time mortals were involved. Previously, Hunters, castoff descendants of the Emporium, were the only mortals aware of us, and they tended toward brief torture followed by hasty execution rather than experimentation and prolonged agony.

"Oh?" Dimitri's excitement sounded real. "Do you have a regrowth in progress now?"

Dr. Hartley shook her head. "Not at present. However, while you interview the Iranian for whatever information you feel he is withholding, I will talk to my supervisor. He might be able to arrange something for today." She gave him a smile that made her face slightly more attractive, but her mind registered guilt. Hartley may believe experimentation was necessary, but the morality behind it was another story.

"I don't believe I read about any regeneration experiments," I said.

"Some of our regenerations may not have been adequately detailed in the current reports," Hartley explained. "We have to be sure what we're seeing isn't just a fluke. So, naturally, we're repeating some experiments before we report our findings."

Someone was obviously keeping secrets about what was going on in this facility. No wonder Shadrach had been desperate enough to contact us. I only hoped the additional information he'd hinted about in his message was real and not a lie he'd concocted to make us come for him faster.

The doctor regarded me with expectant eyes, so I said, "I'm sure our superiors at Homeland Security would be grateful for a firsthand account of regeneration." *Our superiors,* meaning hers and mine. "That's why we employed Dr. Jude"—I dipped my head toward Dimitri—"to conduct his own brief examination of the patient and to give his opinion on the progress here. Anything you can do to facilitate that will be appreciated. Even if it takes us all evening."

Hartley's smile widened, and I didn't have to push to see the dollar signs in her mind. She thought her trip to Paris was almost a done deal, but after today, I could at least guarantee that she wouldn't be fantasizing about Ritter. She might even lose her job.

Pausing before the single door, Hartley swiped her key card again and pushed down on the handle, this time preceding us but stopping just inside the room, blocking our entry and our view of the occupant. "Hello, Mr. Azima," she called. "I hope now is a good time for the interview. The visitors I told you about yesterday have arrived."

Interview not interrogation—apparently the doctor knew how to spin a story.

"Would it matter if I said no?" Shadrach's English held more than a hint of accent, which told me he was under great stress. After four hundred years, he spoke many languages flawlessly.

My mind reached out to Shadrach's, but his barriers were in place, and much stronger than any I'd seen in a non-sensing Unbounded except for Ritter and Dimitri. No use expending energy to get through it—not yet.

"Now, now, Mr. Azima." Dr. Hartley gave an amused chuckle, and I felt irritated more by her patronizing tone than

I had by her fantasies of Ritter. "You know what we're doing here is for the good of all."

"The same has been said throughout history by all those who use human suffering to their advantage," Shadrach replied without emotion.

Hartley stiffened and more guilt filled her mind, but Shadrach's tone became conciliatory. "Never mind, dear. Of course I'll see them. I know you are just doing your job."

Dr. Hartley turned to us, her smile now fake, her eyes narrowed and upset. "Please, come in." She stepped farther into the room, holding the door open with one hand as we filed inside. The guard waited in the hallway. Ritter placed his hand next to Hartley's, giving her a smile to indicate that he'd hold the door. Hartley was so entranced, she didn't glance twice at his hand or see what looked like a piece of gray eraser that he pressed under the control pad outside the door.

Shadrach stood in front of a new-looking leather couch, his feet shoulder length apart, his arms hanging loosely at his sides. I'd expected to find him abused and underweight. But he was much as we'd seen him last—physically in his late thirties, more beautiful than handsome, and elegant with straight dark hair, deep brown eyes, and a sensuous mouth. His dark skin had a healthy glow that stood out clearly from the drab green scrubs he was wearing. Only in his eyes did I see a hardness that hadn't existed before, a hardness that four centuries hadn't succeeded in placing there before now. How much of his suffering came from witnessing his mortal son's murder by the Emporium in Morocco and how much derived from his internment here, I might never know.

He showed no signs of recognition, except for meeting Dimitri's eyes a fraction of a second longer than a stranger might. Shadrach was also a healer, and the two men had worked together in Africa years ago. Shadrach was one of the best, Dimitri had told me. Being a guinea pig for procedures that were far behind Unbounded advancements must have been particularly trying for the Iranian.

"Hello, Mr. Azima," I said for Dr. Hartley's benefit. "Thank you for meeting with us. I hope this won't take long, but the government does have a few questions about your involvement with the events in Morocco."

He sighed without meeting my gaze. "I don't suppose they'll ever get tired of asking, but my answers won't change. I had nothing to do with the attempt to sell plutonium to insurgents in my country."

That wasn't exactly true because Shadrach *had* tried to trade the recovered plutonium to the Emporium for his son's life. In true Emporium fashion, they'd murdered the son anyway. No thanks to Shadrach, we'd still managed to retrieve the package and save millions of lives.

"Well, enjoy your visit," Hartley chirped. "I'll come back when you give the signal to the camera." She indicated the guard. "Let Murphy know if you need any help. He'll be waiting in the corridor." She nodded at us, her eyes lingering too long on Ritter before escaping into the hallway.

For a brief moment, as the door closed between us, I felt a surge of unease, knowing that we were locked inside that room every bit as much as Shadrach had been for the past month.

Ritter went right to work, opening the laptop he carried. The device was supposed to record our interrogation but would actually connect wirelessly to the camera in the corner of the room. This would allow Stella, who was at our safe house in San Diego, to remotely follow the wires back to the computer and access not only that camera but the entire security system located on their internal network. Fortunately, this was the US government we were infiltrating, not the more advanced Emporium, so we'd been able to ascertain what technology they were using and didn't need to plug one of Stella's devices physically into their network. The laptop would suffice, but it would take some time.

Dimitri had already approached Shadrach, and both men were now seated on the couch, Dimitri listening to Shadrach's heart with his stethoscope. In reality, it was the hand on Shadrach's back that was doing the real work. Dimitri would be using his ability to see into Shadrach's body, to trace every vein and *feel* every organ.

I allowed my gaze to wander over the room, or suite, actually. On the wall was a flat screen television, and past this a bed sat next to a set of weights. A small kitchenette nestled in the far back corner, and the single door there must lead to a bathroom. Everything appeared clean and new.

Shadrach followed my gaze. "They let us into a common area twice a day to interact with each other."

"You mean the other patients?" I wanted to say Emporium agents, but I was sure the doctors were still recording.

"Prisoners," Shadrach corrected, distaste radiating from the word. He didn't say more, yet as he met my gaze, I saw recognition there. He knew me underneath the putty, the brunette wig, and the shiny red lipstick. He'd helped me once, healing my exhaustion when I'd needed rest, and despite his betrayal, I cared for Shadrach Azima. Trying to save his mortal son was a goal I understood, even if he'd let his desperation endanger us all. He should have known the Emporium better, that they wouldn't reward him as promised. Then there was the whole argument of whether or not the life of his son balanced out eight million lives being targeted in Israel. Or far, far more lives. Because the Emporium would not rest until they had complete control, no matter how many mortals died. Like Shadrach's son, mortals were only a subspecies to them. Expendable.

"Okay." Ritter stepped closer to the couch, placing the laptop on the coffee table. "It's working. You can talk freely now. Stella has control over the cameras and the sound."

Apparently satisfied with his examination of Shadrach, Dimitri shook out earbuds from a container in his medical bag and handed one to each of us. They looked like replacement tips for his stethoscope but in reality would connect us to Oliver, who was outside waiting for us in the van. I didn't actually need the earbud because I could use my ability to communicate directly to his mind, but Oliver hated me in his head, and I had to admit that his self-centered mental world was not one I had the least interest in visiting. Besides, if the Emporium happened to be near, it paid to keep our mental shields in place.

"This is the plan," Ritter continued for Shadrach's benefit. "There's a ventilation shaft in the hallway off the kitchen here, so we just have to make it there and follow the path to the roof. We've already dropped equipment there that will allow us to rappel down the building. Then it's only a matter of making it to the breach in the fence that we prepared last night. With Stella controlling the cameras, it should be easy to avoid being spotted. Your door lock is completely self-contained, but we have plans for that."

There was a touch of frustration in Ritter's manner at the simplicity of the plan, though he'd been responsible for the details. The Unbounded gene in our bodies made it so we preferred a head-on confrontation, and for someone with the combat ability like Ritter, skulking around in ventilation shafts went against all instinct. But he'd stick to the plan. Because getting Shadrach to safety and finding out what he knew was the most important thing. We might still run into problems, even with Ritter's close attention to detail, and that's why there were three of us—in case something went wrong.

"No," Shadrach said, his sharp tone stopping Ritter in mid-stride to the locked door. "We can't. Not yet."

I arched a brow. "Hey, you're the one who contacted us. Remember that cryptic email sent to our bogus chat group?"

"I meant we can't leave without the others," he said, coming to his feet.

We all stared. "You mean the Emporium agents? The people who tried to kill us in Morocco?" *The people who murdered your son.* But I didn't say that last part aloud.

"We can't leave them." Shadrach shook his head, his face looking suddenly ill. "You don't know what it's like here. They cut off my arm last week just to see how long it took to grow back. They put out one guy's eye. Oh, they're kind enough to give us morphine. Except for the guy they electrocuted to death. Yes, *electrocuted.* The guy they froze also didn't have any painkillers. They wanted to test his tolerance for cold." Shadrach swallowed noisily in the abrupt silence. "Those are only the highlights. They're far worse than the Moroccans— and they were nasty enough."

"Their people will come for them." Ritter's jaw clenched and unclenched like his fists.

"That's right. They will—and they'll murder every mortal here. But the doctors and staff are only under orders, for the most part, and they don't deserve that." Shadrach's dark eyes went to Dimitri in appeal. "In the past three months since the explosion on that rooftop, I've done what I can to help the Emporium agents heal, to ease their pain. They trust me, and since the announcement, they're different. They want to live in peace. They don't want to return to the Emporium."

"I find that hard to believe," Ritter said. "Maybe you have some other reason to want us to help them."

Shadrach grimaced. "I know what you think of me, and maybe I was wrong in Morocco—"

"You almost got us killed!" Ritter didn't take a step toward him, but the fury in his face made Shadrach step back until his calves hit the couch.

"I know," Shadrach said, his voice strangled. "But you're going to have to trust me on this one. Because you're not going to leave me here, so either you drag me kicking and screaming or you take them too."

The veins in Ritter's neck bulged. "Believe me, I won't have to take you screaming." For an instant, I thought Ritter was going to punch the healer out and throw him over his shoulder. I'd probably help him.

Dimitri stepped in. "Let's hear him out."

"Okay," I answered for Ritter, giving him time to calm down. "We'll listen. But we're going to make the final decision, Shadrach. Not you."

"Agreed," he said.

Ritter's fists relaxed. "This could be a plan on their part. Did you think of that?"

Shadrach scrubbed a hand over his face and into his black hair, causing it to fall out of place. "If so, it's an elaborate plan that started back in Morocco. Two of these agents hate the Emporium as much as I do, and the other has listened to us. I won't pretend that their courage doesn't come mostly from knowing Delia Vesey is dead. The fact that she can't hurt them or their families anymore if they don't do what she orders was a huge factor in their decision." He paused before adding, "Vesey caused some damages—perhaps permanent—in one man's mind, the one who took convincing. I fixed what I could, but he's not all there in the logic department. Reality is hard for him to understand. But the others, I'm sure of."

Now he made a direct appeal to Ritter. "They know where the Emporium strongholds are, at least five of them. The major ones. They're willing to share that information with us."

Ritter's head swung toward Dimitri and they shared a long, silent stare. I knew what it would mean to locate Emporium headquarters. They'd recently relocated many of their safe houses after we'd obtained intel on the locations from a thumb drive recovered in Mexico, and since then we'd made little headway on tracking their whereabouts. This intel could prove invaluable.

Shadrach's eyes fixed on me. "Erin can see that I'm telling the truth." The shield around his mind dropped—an invitation I immediately accepted. In the representation I created of his conscious mind, I stood on a sort of stage, and his thoughts fell from the darkness above me in a stream of what looked like sand, curving downward and disappearing again into the darkness at hip level. Each grain of sand represented a thought or memory, past or present. I would only see thoughts he was currently pondering or memories he recalled as I studied him, but it would be enough to get a feel about his truthfulness.

I stared deeper, more interested in searching for Emporium traps—the mental constructs Delia Vesey, a former Emporium Triad leader, had been so good at placing in people's minds. Mental traps could be fatal for the person carrying them and for any sensing Unbounded attempting to repair the damage. Delia's assistant had survived the encounter in Morocco, so he could have planted something in Shadrach's mind, and the Emporium had at least a few other sensing Unbounded, if the rumors were true. But Shadrach's mind was clean. Not a hint of Emporium meddling—or prefabrication on Shadrach's part. He believed what he was saying.

"He's telling the truth," I said, "and I don't see any Emporium constructs in his mind."

Ritter nodded once, his face grim. "Then we'll do it." His surface emotions radiated determination, but his mental shield was otherwise strong.

"Wait, wait, wait!" Oliver said in my earbud. "Are you guys sure about this? Because that's going to take longer, and I kind of feel like a sitting duck all alone out here in the van."

"Aren't you masking it?" I asked. His ability of illusion was the reason we'd let him come with us at all. Because while Oliver was a genius, his arrogance made us all pretty much want to kill him.

"Well, it was a fruit stand for a while, but people stopped and tried to buy some." He groaned. "I had to make the fruit appear moldy to get them to leave."

I bit my lip "So put up a closed sign!"

"Right."

Trust Oliver to take such pride in his illusions that his fake fruits looked and smelled great enough to make people stop to buy them even in this manufacturing area.

I caught a glimpse of irritation on Ritter's face before he said to Oliver, "We may need a distraction at the front of the building. Something with a lot of fireworks. Be prepared. And have Stella extend her satellite surveillance to a radius of three streets in case the Emporium decides to join our party. I want to know if there's anything unusual."

"Will do," Oliver said, sounding chastised. He didn't have a lot of respect for the rest of us, but his admiration of Ritter was almost as irritating as his know-it-all attitude. "The satellite we tasked here did go down for a few minutes. Could have been someone hacking our feed, but it's back up and running perfectly now, and we've detected no unusual activity so far."

"No other fruit stands?" Dimitri asked, a hint of a smile in his voice.

Oliver took offense at his gentle jibe. "As a matter of fact, there is a defunct one. That's what gave me the idea. There's an orchard only two miles from here, so it's completely logical for a fruit stand to be in this area."

"I was sure you had a reason, but that's good to know." Dimitri had more patience with Oliver than the rest of us. Probably because he considered himself the father of our cell. Biologically speaking, Dimitri *was* my father, but I'd only known him since my Change just over seven months ago. I'd come to terms with my uncertain beginning, and while I still considered the man who raised me to be my real father, Dimitri and I were closer in many ways.

Shadrach shifted nervously, his eyes going to the door. "So what now?"

Ritter's eyes narrowed at the healer. "Now we try not to get killed."

CHAPTER 2

"DO YOU KNOW WHERE THE OTHER MEN ARE LOCATED?" RITTER strode to the computer and brought up a map of the facility.

"Yes." Shadrach hurried over to Ritter, but his movements were regal, and I could easily imagine him in bright ceremonial robes, surrounded by women wearing burkas.

Shadrach showed us all the rooms where the other prisoners should be located. Two were in this corridor, but the third was apparently kept near the common rooms where they ate meals and conversed until the guards forced them back to their solitary quarters. That is, if the doctors' experiments permitted them to leave their rooms at all.

"We haven't seen one guy—Bedřich—for three days," Shadrach said. "Usually, that's as long as they keep us away."

Dimitri nodded. "Most casual regenerations can be completed in that time. Are they using a form of curequick?" That was our name for a mixture containing a heavy amount of sugar and proteins reduced to their most usable form. This mixture gave our bodies enough nutrition to speed up recovery by as much as five times. It was also addictive to us.

"Oh, yeah. Someone spilled that little piece of information the first week in Morocco." Shadrach made a face. "Can't blame them, though. We thought we were helping ourselves recover. We had no idea the doctors there would use the information to increase the frequency of their experiments. The supervising doctor here is even worse."

Dimitri stared at the screen, the tightening of his lips the only sign of his disapproval at the treatment. "We could stall until dinner and they're all in the common room."

"They have a guard there for each of us and a couple extra in the hall," Shadrach said. "It'd be a mess."

Ritter studied the map a few more seconds, committing it to memory. Combat Unbounded could remember plans and layouts and maps better than the average Unbounded. Unless I channeled his ability, I couldn't begin to approach his accuracy.

Ritter began typing on the keys. "Stella can control the feed from the security cameras, and there's only the one guard in this corridor, so getting to the first two prisoners without being seen won't be a problem. Unfortunately, Stella just sent a message saying that the corridors near the commons room have at least a half dozen people wandering around." He glanced at Dimitri. "You'll have to get the first two Emporium agents and Shadrach into the ventilation shaft while Erin and I go after the third one."

As Dimitri nodded, Ritter added, "We'll try to join you, but we might have to find another way out. I'll let you know if we need Oliver's distraction. You may have to coordinate that."

"He'll be ready." Dimitri sounded sure.

"Hey, guys, I'm still here," came Oliver's voice through the earbuds. "I can hear you. Of course I'll be ready." Everyone ignored him.

"Let's go." Ritter tapped a few more keys. "Once they come in here and someone presses a key on this computer, we'll have only two minutes before it self-destructs. Then we'll be live to the cameras again. It'll send a beep to our earbuds if we're in range when that happens."

Dimitri took out what appeared to be two inhalers from his medical bag and started toward the door. Several long sprays from each covered the lock in frost. Ritter put a hand in his pocket, and a surprisingly loud explosion sent the pieces of the doorknob to the floor. The next instant, Ritter pulled the door open and dragged the guard into the room.

"W-wha—" The guard struggled to reach his gun, but Ritter held him too tightly. The guard's confusion ended as Dimitri jabbed the end of a sleep dart into his neck. Ritter lowered the limp man to the carpet and then relieved him of his weapon and holster.

"All clear," I said, peering into the hallway.

We hurried, sprinting to the next door where the first Emporium agent was being held. Ritter flattened the last of his explosive on the control pad, a thin wire sticking out of the gray material.

"Only one person inside?" Ritter asked me.

"Yes." My ability to sense life forces wasn't fettered by walls. I couldn't tell if the person was Unbounded unless I could actually see him with my eyes, but the life force behind the door was blocking thoughts, which made the glow dimmer than the mortals we'd met here so far. Mortals could learn to block, but until they knew about our abilities, those here wouldn't have reason to. I was almost certain the person behind the door was Unbounded.

Dimitri used the rest of the spray in the small bottles to aid the destruction, but even after the detonation, Ritter still had to slam his foot into the door to force it open.

Inside, the Emporium agent was standing in a room identical to Shadrach's. He held a lamp in his hand, a frozen expression of dread etched on his face. Big as Ritter, but blond and pale, he looked vaguely familiar to me from Morocco, though far less imposing holding a lamp instead of a gun.

Shadrach pushed past us. "Come, Fenton," he said. "Now is your chance. We're leaving."

"Wait." I forced my mind against the Emporium agent's shield. "You know what this means, leaving with us this way, don't you?" Betraying the Emporium, I meant.

"Oh, I know." The man's jaw worked as he carefully set down the lamp.

Ah, there was the emotional crack I'd been waiting for. So much easier than breaking down a shield with no flaw. Gathering my energy, I forced my way inside his mind—just in time to see the hatred there. Not toward us but hatred of the Emporium who had ruled him for over a hundred years. Always promising advancements yet never quite delivering. Telling him he was a god to the lowly mortals, then treating him the same as the mortal guards.

His thoughts rushed at me, and I took them in as if they were my own. He didn't love the Renegades or mortals, but he was tired of working for the Emporium, of being their pawn in a war he no longer believed in. He wanted to find his own path—away from the killing and the intrigue.

I didn't blame him one bit. I longed for peace myself. For things to settle down. For Ritter and me to think about our future. Maybe even to consider that family he wanted so badly.

I nodded at Ritter, meeting his intent gaze, and the tension in his body eased. "Move," he said to Fenton. "If you try anything, I won't hesitate to kill you."

Fenton sneered in response. "I would expect no less from *you.*"

Ritter smirked, apparently finding it amusing Fenton had seen through his disguise and that his reputation had preceded him. Of course, most Emporium agents we ran into knew exactly who our prominent Renegades were—they studied us every bit as much as we studied them, and there were far fewer of us.

"Nobody is going to kill anyone!" Shadrach insisted.

Ritter took the lead, and I kept close to him. Shadrach and Fenton were in the middle, with Dimitri bringing up the rear, presumably to watch out for guards but more to keep an eye on Fenton.

"One life force," I confirmed for Ritter as we reached the next door. "How are we getting inside this one?"

His smile was almost tender. "Acid."

Dimitri was already taking out two more bottles. He handed one to Ritter, and they began spraying. The plastic buttons melted instantly, the metal soon beginning to run. These weren't ordinary acids, I knew, but something our scientist, Cort Bagley, had concocted.

Even after the bottles were emptied, it still wasn't enough. "What now?" Shadrach asked.

Ritter's hand went briefly to the guard's gun, but it didn't have a silencer, and we needed to save it as a last resort, especially since we had one more door to get through. "We do it the old-fashioned way." Taking several steps back, he ran at the door, slamming his shoulder into it. The door buckled slightly, but it didn't give. One more thrust and something in the weakened lock shattered. The door banged opened.

A woman jumped at us, a knife in her hand. Ritter sidestepped, his ability warning him of danger as the blade plunged toward him. He spun around, the guard's pistol in his hand.

"Eden, stop!" Shadrach ordered. "They're with me."

Her hand was already in motion, almost a blur that told me her ability was combat like Ritter, like most Emporium agents, but she stopped every bit as fast. Her breath left in a *whoosh*. She looked at us with wild eyes, her many freckles standing out in her pale face.

I'd used her distraction to push past her shields—not that much effort was required in her case. Eden was a beaten woman, one who'd lost nearly everyone she'd ever loved, including the grown daughter who hadn't Changed and who had been sent on a mission by the Emporium last year to seduce an intern at a hospital and steal their records. Her mission had supposedly ended in a shootout with police, but Eden learned her death had actually been caused by an Emporium sniper. She had another daughter growing up in an adoptive family where Eden had erroneously thought to place her out of Delia's reach. Instead, the child had been threatened and her existence used to coerce Eden. Oh, yes, she had good reason to hate the Emporium. Now, with Delia no longer threatening the child's safety, Eden wanted her freedom from all Unbounded. Her biggest hope was not that her daughter would Change, but that she would never know of her Unbounded connection.

The sadness in Eden's heart ate at me. I'd known Unbounded who'd left families, often faking their own deaths in order to keep those they loved out of the ongoing struggle between the Emporium and Renegades over the future of humanity. I personally hadn't made that choice, but it had cost my grand-mother's life and nearly my father's. Now I had to go to great subterfuge each time I visited my parents. My mortal older brother and his two children, who lived with our Renegade cell, were in constant danger if they left our Fortress in San Diego. It was a tough balance, and I still wasn't sure I'd made the right choice.

I met Ritter's eyes, but he already knew I approved Eden. The emotional connection that some sensing Unbounded shared with their chosen mate often traveled beyond any mental barrier. Ritter put out his hand for her knife, and Eden reluctantly gave it to him. I saw that she'd stolen the pocketknife from a guard when she'd pretended to come on to him. She'd been rebuffed—smart, since the cameras were always rolling—but no one had picked up on her sleight of hand.

Unlike most Unbounded I'd met, Eden was striking in a way that wasn't typical. Her myriad freckles, upturned nose, and full head of brown hair would have made her cute as a mortal, rather than gorgeously sexy, but the confidence of the Unbounded gene increased her certain something to make the unusualness compelling. Cuteness times ten. Hard to believe that she'd probably killed dozens of people for the Emporium.

"Let's go." This time I was the one to make the call. I didn't want to think about Eden or her daughters. The Emporium had caused so much heartache, but it didn't seem to affect their overall plan. Rarely did agents rebel, and the few that changed sides were on a kill list. Eden might be choosing us now, but if we didn't win this war, she'd become another victim.

At the end of the corridor, instead of splitting up, Ritter insisted on accompanying Dimitri and the others to the air shaft outside the kitchen. Two brightly glowing life forces called my attention, and I sent everyone back around the bend when two women approached from another direction.

We flattened ourselves against the wall as I peered through the two women's eyes and experienced their emotions. With unblocking mortals, it was more a matter of letting them past my shields than breaking into their minds. Their thoughts screamed out at me, as did their conversation. One looked much like Hartley in her white doctor's coat while the other wore a hairnet. They were talking about food.

"Just two milliliters in Fenton and Shadrach's food at dinner tonight," the doctor was saying.

The cook stopped in front of a door leading to the kitchen, her big hand closing around a bottle the doctor handed her. "What is it?" Suspicion filled her mind. She didn't like this doctor or working here, but she needed the money to support herself and her disabled husband.

"Nothing you need to concern yourself with. Just a test we need to conduct without their knowing." The doctor's mind told me that the neurotoxin would cause death within twenty-four hours in a regular mortal. An agonizing death as the toxins attacked nerves and caused paralysis, slowly shutting down all the organs in the body. There was no known antidote.

The cook was silently considering not placing the liquid in the food, but she knew she'd end up doing it because she had no choice. The doctors with their tests would know if she didn't. "All right. But if it tastes nasty, they'll know."

"Don't worry. We've made sure it's undetectable."

Poison wouldn't kill Unbounded, but the idea that the doctor would use it made me furious. And vindictive.

The cook opened the door to the kitchen and went inside, while the doctor continued down the hall in our direction. I moved past Ritter and met her as she came around the bend. Her eyes widened, taking in me and my companions with a single sweep. Panic filled her face, and she started to turn.

I debated sending a burst to the doctor's unprotected mind, but Ritter would disapprove of wasting energy I might need later. Besides, it wasn't nearly as satisfying. I balled my fist and punched hard. The doctor dropped to the ground, her chest heaving with fear.

"Who are you?" she asked. "What are you going to do?

Please don't hurt me!" Dimitri put a dart in her neck, and she lost consciousness.

Ritter lifted a brow, a question flickering in his eyes.

I shrugged. "I didn't like her thoughts."

"Find someplace to stash her," Ritter told me. "We'll get the shaft open. Shadrach, you and your friends keep watch."

While Ritter boosted Dimitri up to work on the shaft located at the top of the wall near where the women had been talking, I dragged the unconscious doctor to a door down the hall. It was locked, but with a regular keyed doorknob instead of one with a card reader. I slipped off my shoes. Touching spots on both heels, thin metal rods slid out. Time to test my breaking and entering skills.

Fortunately, it was a regular lock—one of the kind we'd practiced on almost daily in the past three months of down-time we'd had since the president's announcement—and in seconds, the lock clicked opened to reveal a simple broom closet. I dragged the doctor inside and dumped her unceremoniously. Kneeling briefly, I pushed my mind into her unconscious thoughts, represented by a lake of cool water and bubbles full of memories. I severed one of the bubbles, taking the memory of our faces, but not the hit. I wanted her to remember that. Satisfied, I stole her key card and left, shutting the door behind me. She wouldn't begin to wake for at least an hour. If they didn't find her before then.

The men had the shaft open, and Shadrach was already inside, helping Eden up as Dimitri boosted her. Fenton was next and then it was time for Dimitri. Ritter offered Dimitri the gun, but he shook his head, tapping his case. "I have one of those plastic printed ones in here. I'll put it together when I get in the vent. Don't worry. We'll be fine. Just make sure you and Erin get back here fast."

"Don't wait for us," I said.

Dimitri's eyes went to me. "Be safe."

"If Shadrach hesitates, throw him off the roof," I added.

Dimitri laughed. "For you, I will. With pleasure."

Ritter boosted Dimitri into the waiting arms of Shadrach and the others. Next, he lifted me up to secure the vent cover in place.

We hurried back down the corridor, passing the commons room where the detainees ate their meals and spent time together. Then came a set of locked double doors. I pulled out the key card I'd taken from the doctor.

Ritter's grin sent heat to my belly, but I shook my head. "There's company on the other side. Four."

"Unbounded?"

"No. Their life forces are bright. Not blocking. There's a fifth somewhere beyond them who might be."

"Probably the last Emporium agent."

"Yeah. It's strange though. Sometimes he's bright and sometimes dim."

"Shadrach said his mind was damaged." Ritter's warm hands closed over mine. "Show me." His mental shield had weakened, leaving a clear opening.

Ritter's mind was almost as familiar to me as my own. Not like a comfortable pair of pants, but more like a pool of hot, turbulent water that beckoned to me with a promise of adventure and delight, water that completely enveloped and consumed me. It was easy to lose myself in him. Once, that had scared me as much as his obsession with revenge, but now I trusted him more than anyone—with my life and with my heart.

I showed him the life forces from the outside: two bright glows close to the other side of the door and two farther along the hallway. Then I took us inside one of the minds, the one most familiar to me—Dr. Hartley. She was talking to a Jeffrey

Callas, who was obviously her superior. She wasn't attracted to his flaccid red face, or his thinning hair, but she respected the power Dr. Callas wielded and the list of initials behind his name.

Two guards waited down the hall, their gazes averted. Beyond them, the other life force, the one blinking bright and dim, beckoned to my curiosity from behind a doorway.

"When our visitors are finished interviewing Mr. Azima," Hartley said, "I'll let them know you have approved their request."

Callas made a deprecating sound in his throat. "They won't get anything from the man. He doesn't know anything or he would have told us by now."

"I don't know," Hartley said. "He still seems to avoid certain questions. Makes me think he's hiding something."

"You mean besides the fact that he acts as some kind of empath with the others."

Hartley wanted to correct him, to say that Shadrach Azima didn't so much as feel the others' pain as he did enhance their ability to heal faster, but Callas was sure to receive a promotion after they made history with their work here, and she had her eye on his job. She wouldn't jeopardize that—or her planned trip to the city of romance.

Hartley's eyes strayed down the hallway, past the guards to the room at the end where the Czech slept. "What about Bedřich?" she asked. "It's his turn, right?"

"For the amputation?" Dr. Callas shook his head. "It'll have to be one of the others instead. Bedřich's not well; you know that. I don't want headquarters to get any idea of pulling him from us. He's the only one we've been able to learn anything from about Unbounded."

"You believe him?" Hartley herself considered Bedřich a

raving lunatic, but she wouldn't let him know that. Most of what they had learned from the Czech had been during fits at night in his room. While in the grip of these outbursts, he destroyed everything inside his apartment and bashed holes in the walls, which was one of the reasons he was off in this wing by himself. The fits always included fearful rantings about an old woman named Delia.

"To a point," Callas said. "But they're all hiding something from us. Do the amputation on Eden—half a finger."

"But it's Mr. Azima's turn if we are skipping Bedřich."

"After interviewing Mr. Azima, they'll feel a connection to him, and it'll be better to do it on a stranger. Make sure you inject her with plenty of the new glutein concentrate, so they can witness their miracle in a couple hours. Don't want to be here all night."

Hartley joined his laugh without real mirth. She was glad not to do the procedure on Mr. Azima because she secretly liked the man. He was always polite, apologized when he upset her—even when he had a right to be upset—and she was sure he'd had something to do with ending her endometriosis pain. Though he'd touched her only on the arm since she'd been working with him, the pain had vanished completely. As for Eden, she didn't like the woman at all but wouldn't take pleasure in hurting her. Hartley had heard Eden crying over a daughter she'd lost, and Hartley pitied her.

Still, this amputation meant overtime and one step closer to Paris.

"I'll get the OR ready."

"Make sure Eden is already there and sedated before you allow them in. We don't want any of Eden's scenes. Oh, and double the guard."

Hartley had already planned to do that. Eden could easily

take out two guards, even partially sedated. So could Fenton, according to Moroccan officials, though he'd been calm enough here. Still, Hartley and her colleagues were always careful, and any time they moved either Fenton or Eden, they made sure they had a full complement of armed guards. Mostly, that had worked, except for the couple times Eden had sent guards to the infirmary with broken bones.

I found it interesting that the three Emporium agents were addressed by their first names, while Shadrach was called by his last, and usually with Mr. attached. Shadrach's elegance seemed to hold strong even among his jailers.

"I'll make sure everything goes smoothly," Hartley said. "I assume that means you approve the overtime?"

Callus frowned but nodded his assent. "Looks like we have no choice. I'll have to request additional funding. They can't expect us to accommodate these visitors without some recompense."

"I agree." Hartley noticed that Callas seemed to be waiting for her to leave, and again her eyes went past him down the hall. She wondered why Dr. Callas was here with the guards when he normally only supervised the experiments from his office. But she'd gone there and been redirected to this wing. Maybe his presence here explained the odd data that kept popping up in tests on the Czech prisoner. *No, they're patients,* she reminded herself.

But Hartley knew the truth.

Ritter and I were just as curious as to Callas's purpose, so I decided to peek into his mind, but it turned out he wasn't thinking anything about the Czech or about Eden's pending amputation. He was musing about his wife, Lilian, and about celebrating their twentieth anniversary. He wanted it to be amazing for her. He knew she would make it so for him—she'd wear that sheer pink nighty and drive him crazy with wanting before she finally let him take it off. Hearing his male colleagues talk, he knew he was a lucky man. His wife might not be as beautiful as his secretary, who had the best legs he'd ever glimpsed on a woman, but Lilian was a far sight better than Hartley, and he and Lilian were matched in the bedroom, which eliminated a world of possible frustration. He planned to work hard to make her comfortable and give her everything she could ever want. Whatever it took.

Callas nodded pointedly at Hartley. "Better get going then." He turned his back as she reached for the door.

The door where we waited on the other side.

CHAPTER 3

WE HAD ONLY SECONDS TO REACT. OUR MINDS ALREADY MELDED, Ritter and I instantly reached the only possible conclusion. Hartley couldn't be allowed to find that Eden wasn't there, but at the same time, we had to make sure she didn't alert Dr. Callas and his guards to our presence before the door completely closed.

We ran, retreating down the hall, with me channeling Ritter's combat ability, so I could be fast enough. Before Hartley got the door open, we reached another door, where I swiped the key card before we hurled ourselves inside.

Slightly too late. I could see in Hartley's mind that she'd spotted Ritter's backside and leg. "Who's there?" she called. "Seth? Is that you?" Dr. Seth Boulder, she meant, one of the doctors here and her main competition for future promotions.

Her heels clicked toward us in the hallway. Ritter, still linked to me, nodded when he was sure the door behind her had closed and the glow of Callas's life force was farther away. We stepped out to greet her.

"Oh, there you are," I said.

Hartley blinked in surprise, but anger replaced the surprise almost immediately. "How did you get—what are you doing here? This is a restricted area."

"Yeah, well . . ." Ritter moved fast, his arm a blur, jabbing the pen dart from his pocket into her neck. He caught her as she fell.

Seconds later, I was wearing her white jacket as we went through the double doors into the wing holding the Czech prisoner. Dr. Callas was no longer in the hallway and neither were the guards, which I'd expected would be waiting outside the captive's door.

He's doing something to the Czech, I told Ritter through our link. His agreement was more a feeling than words.

We sprinted over the tiled floor, Ritter reaching for the gun he'd taken from the guard. Three mortals weren't much of a challenge for him, but the Emporium agent was an unknown. We couldn't predict how he'd react, especially without Shadrach here to make nice for us.

We'll surprise them. Ritter's thoughts were easy to make out through our link, but I had to take them from his mind. He wouldn't know if I'd heard unless I responded, because even though he could feel if I was in danger from miles away, he couldn't see any thoughts I didn't share.

I showed him where the life forces were located inside the room. Two were near the door, and another farther into the room next to a prone life force. I slipped into Callas's head to find that he was sitting on the edge of a bed next to a sandy-haired man who had his hands clamped over his ears, shaking his head violently, his eyes squeezed tightly shut. "No, no, no. Please no. She'll hear. She'll hurt me." This must be Bedřich, the Czech Emporium agent.

I used the key card, and Ritter threw open the door.

The guards reacted immediately, but Ritter burst into

movement, punching one hard and sending him to the ground, before pointing his gun at the other's face. "Don't move."

Callas rose from the bed. "What is the meaning of this? Who are you?" He was shorter than I'd seen from Hartley's mind, but his green eyes were more compelling.

"I have better questions," I said, stepping around Ritter. "Who do you think you are, and what are you doing to this man?"

"Not that it's any of your business, but I'm a doctor and he's under my care. I'm going to have to ask you to leave. You're disturbing my patient." On the bed, Bedřich had begun to thrash, but he didn't open his eyes. I noticed two spent syringes lying on the bed.

"All Unbounded are my business." I crossed the room and took a syringe from Callas's unresisting hand. "What's this?" He didn't respond, but his thoughts told me it was a hallucinogen. "Well?"

"Nothing that will hurt him."

"Oh, good." I channeled Ritter's quickness and stepped toward the doctor, putting him into a headlock. "Then you won't mind taking it yourself." The needle slid easily into his neck before he could do more than strain against me.

He gasped, and I let him jerk away. "What have you done?" he asked.

"You said it wasn't harmful."

"I'm not Unbounded." His head twitched, but whether from a tick or a reaction from the injection, I couldn't say. Abruptly, he sat down on the ground and moaned, holding his head in his hands.

The mixture, at one-third the dose he'd been planning for Bedřich, if the two spent syringes told a correct tale, shouldn't kill him or cause lasting damage, but I was already having second thoughts. Even if I wanted him to suffer consequences for the extracurricular testing, I didn't like hurting him.

I turned toward Bedřich, who was sitting up now, his hands still to his ears. He looked crazy, with his dirty blond hair pointing in every direction and his brown eyes red and bulging. I tried pushing my way into his mind, but a hard barrier stood against me. It was a mottled, silvery black, strong but diseased, and had a signature that felt familiar. Delia's mark, I realized. She'd taught him this shielding, or maybe he'd learned it trying to protect himself from her.

I needed to see what was inside. Reaching for my talisman, a machete I'd been given in Mexico—or rather a mental version of the weapon that was now waiting for me in the van—I jabbed it into the tarnished barrier.

The guard who was still standing emitted a growl, our only warning before everything exploded into movement. He leapt at Ritter, pushing him backward. Ritter tripped over the fallen guard and landed on the floor, his gun flying from his hand and slamming against the wall. He was up in the next instant, foot lashing out to throw off the guard's aim as he pulled the trigger. The gun cracked deafening fire, and the bullet embedded in the headboard of the bed. Bedřich released an inhuman scream and launched through the air at me, uttering what sounded like obscenities in a language I didn't recognize.

Channeling Ritter, I stepped aside, chopping down at the Czech as he came to an impossibly graceful stop, like a cat finding its feet. The combat instinct made me jump away, even as he struck at me with a foot in a nearly successful effort to break my knee. His fists followed, one after another, and even using Ritter's ability, I was barely able to keep ahead of him, blocking or dodging his blows. His rapid attack and the precise placement of the punches told me his ability was also combat. Another part of me was aware of Ritter's fight through my mental link, but only vaguely since I'd learned to mute that connection in the midst of a battle. With two punches, Ritter sent the guard into unconsciousness, but the other guard had recovered and jumped on his back. Ritter pushed backward, slamming him against the wall.

Bedřich landed a blow on my shoulder and another on my ribs that stole my breath. The Emporium agent had seven inches on me and at least forty pounds. No way would I win in a fair fight, and playing dirty meant hurting him, which I didn't want to do, seeing as we were here to rescue him.

Even as I had the thought, his body crashed into me and we fell together to the bed. Somehow he had a knife in his hands, a jagged one that if plunged in deep enough would rip me apart on its way out. Who had he taken that from?

Maybe it was the desperation, but my machete finally carved a hole in his mental shield, and I arrowed inside him. His head was a mess. Destroyed bits of silvery gray construct littered his brain, obstructing the flow of the thought stream, disseminating it until thoughts and emotions careened around me like a sandstorm. Once again, I recognized Delia's touch. Why the bits of ruined construct hadn't disappeared when she'd died, I didn't know. The pieces she'd left inside me had disappeared, if not all her memories.

I sent a flash of mental light to the Czech's mind. Searing. Enough to cause unconsciousness, but hopefully not enough to cause more permanent damage. But he was too quick. The tip of his knife dug into my stomach, making it several inches past the thin body armor I wore like a second skin under my white blouse before he collapsed on top of me.

I rolled him off onto the bed. Ritter was already standing over me, murder screaming from his eyes.

"I'm fine." I pulled the knife out as I sat up, catching my breath as it tore my insides. I was glad that only a small portion of the jagged blade had made it past my protection. Biting down hard on my lip to stave off the pain, I used the knife to slice off a part of the sheet, which I balled and pushed through the hole in my armor to catch the blood. I felt sapped as I always did when I used my ability in that way, but there was no chance for rest now. "Let's get out of here."

Ritter nodded and grabbed the unconscious Czech. I stopped only to uncurl the wire from inside my bracelet to secure Dr. Callas to the bed. He was moaning and shaking, clutching his head, and I didn't want him wandering loose around the facility until the drug wore off. He pulled at my hands, but strength eluded him.

"Lilian," he moaned. "You are so beautiful."

"Too bad you're a toad," I said under my breath.

Ritter's mental shield was still at half strength, strong enough to keep most sensing Unbounded out but like an invitation to me. I made sure not to project the burning in my side. Even so, he knew there was no way we'd be able to make it through the air shafts before we were discovered, not with my wound and him dragging the big Czech.

"Oliver?" Ritter said, leaning down toward the microphone disguised as a pin in his tie. "We need that distraction."

"Coming right up," Oliver's voice came through, startling me with how calm he sounded. I also had a hidden microphone in my necklace, and he had to have heard our battle. "On your mark." Oliver hesitated several seconds before adding, "You guys okay?"

Ritter's gaze shifted to me. "We're good." Then he added, "Dimitri, we're going out the way we came in, or at least as far as possible. We'll meet you in the front. Cover us and have the van ready."

"I need three minutes." Dimitri's voice crackled, indicating that he was farther away than Oliver.

"Three minutes," Ritter confirmed.

I stumbled as we reached the double doors leading into the main wing. Ritter's lips hardened, but he didn't speak. Blood trickled down my side.

We hurried through the corridors, past the commons room, and finally the kitchen, backtracking the way we'd come in order to avoid a lab and an office area where small groups of life forces gathered. We had nearly reached Shadrach's wing when an alarm blared through the building.

I stopped and shook my head. "There're a dozen people heading to Shadrach's hallway. All mortals, but in formation."

"Homeland Security," Ritter said. His head jerked backward. "The offices."

"Eight there," I told him.

The alarm continued, grating on my nerves. Stella was in their system, thanks to the laptop, but obviously she hadn't found a way to remotely deal with what was probably a manually triggered alarm. I was glad Ritter was leading the way because the maps I'd studied jumbled together in my mind.

We reached the corridor leading to the offices, and I swiped the key card and held the door open for Ritter. His face was slightly flushed with the exertion, but I knew he'd slowed his pace for me. Every step was agony. Whatever I'd punctured dragging the knife from my stomach was worse than I expected. My Unbounded genes were rushing to heal the wound, and I knew the pain would soon ease, but until it did, I was next to useless.

In the office hallway, people looked uncertainly out at us from the doorways. "It's okay," I said. "We have it under control. This prisoner tried to escape, but we got him. Please notify Dr. Callas that he's been recaptured. Excuse me, we need to get this man to the infirmary."

Jaws dropped and people nodded. But one man said, "The infirmary's back that way."

"We're looking for Dr. Hartley," I said. "She needs to look at him now."

We hurried past without one person trying to stop us. Half a minute later, Ritter took an abrupt turn into a new corridor. *What's down here?* I asked silently.

Employee entrance.

He handed me a gun I hadn't seen him retrieve from Bedřich's room. "You up to it? Or should we dump the Czech?"

"I'm good. Only one guard."

A warning beep sounded in my earbud, signaling that someone had found Ritter's laptop. In two minutes the cameras would show our actual location.

The guard was standing in front of the door with his weapon drawn. "Help!" I cried. "I'm shot!" I'd thought the stain of red on my white blouse would convince him, but he didn't waver.

"Stop right there or I'll shoot!" he demanded.

I pushed light into his mind, and the effort of the mental flash momentarily blinded me. But I could see through Ritter's eyes, and I pushed forward past the fallen man. No use taking his memory when so many had already seen us. In seconds, I recovered my sight, much faster than in the past.

The outer door was locked. I stifled a moan of regret, knowing we should have fought the guard instead of rendering him unconscious, but Ritter bent to retrieve the guard's keys, and I used them to enter the narrow guard booth to find the door's release button.

We exited into a parking garage. In Ritter's mind, I saw his intention to find the exit and escape around to the front. "Wait," I said, holding up the guard's keys with the remote to his car. Ritter chuckled and unceremoniously dropped Bedřich onto the cement. Whatever bruises he might sustain would be long healed before he awoke.

Ritter raced through the garage while I waited, gun on the door behind me, mind alert for life forces. At the moment, they were concentrated near the closet where I'd stashed the first doctor, so someone must have found her prematurely, and that is what likely triggered the alarm. They were filtering outward from the closet, checking each room. It wouldn't be long before they discovered the missing prisoners and the drugged Dr. Callas.

A car engine revved somewhere, and then Ritter was screeching to a stop in front of me, driving a small two-door sedan that had seen better days. He jumped out and scooped up Bedřich while I pulled the seat forward to give him room to dump the man in the narrow back seat. Ritter sprinted around to the driver's side again before I could even slam my door.

There was no guard at the opening to the parking garage, and Ritter barely slowed as he exited, rounding the curb with a squeal of tires on concrete. He drove as if he'd been here before, but I knew he'd only studied the layout.

Our wheels squealed again as he curved around the building, where a scene straight from a movie set met our eyes. A tank decorated with the flag of the United States Army sat directly in front of the gates, a helmeted man peeking out of the top. An Army transport vehicle was parked nearby, and armed men hunkered behind both vehicles. A line of six Homeland Security guards stood uncertainly in front of the gated entry, staring with confusion at the challengers. I could imagine them wondering why they were being attacked by their own government.

Oliver had outdone himself.

All at once, the *rat-a-tat-tat* of machine gun fire burst

through the air, sending up curls of smoke. The facility guards dove for cover.

Ritter laughed and stomped on the gas, heading directly for the fence and the tank behind it.

"I hope it's you guys in that car," Oliver said in our earbuds. "The van's behind the transport, and Dimitri and the others are already here, but you'd better hurry. Helicopters are coming—and Stella's sure they aren't from Homeland Security."

The Emporium, I thought.

"Go now," Ritter barked at Oliver. "We'll continue in this car and meet you at the fallback location."

He didn't let off the gas as we crashed through the gates.

My heart didn't stop racing until we were on our private plane heading back to San Diego. My older mortal brother, Chris, was in the cockpit, and the Emporium agents were safe under Dimitri's watchful eyes. Oliver was still basking in the triumph of his successful illusion—Ritter and I'd both made the mistake of complimenting him on it—and his gloating was likely driving Shadrach and the others to consider ejecting him from the plane.

Ritter and I were in the rear of the plane behind the curtain that blocked the metal bunks we often used to transport unconscious Emporium agents to our prison facility in Mexico. For now, an unconscious Bedřich was the only occupant. Opposite the bunks, shoved up against the right side, were storage compartments that contained everything from emergency supplies to disguises.

Ritter unbuttoned my blouse and eased it off my arms. It took considerably more effort, and pain on my part, for him to finesse the tight, thin layer of body armor over my head. The tiny side zippers did little to help.

My breath still caught with pain whenever I breathed. Glancing down at the wound, I saw it was worse than I'd thought, or it wouldn't still be leaking blood. Ritter's jaw clenched, but he didn't say anything. The body armor was fitted and fully supportive, which meant I wasn't wearing a bra, but Ritter's eyes barely flicked over my bare skin as he mopped up my stomach and began injecting the area around my wound with anesthetic-laced curequick.

"It's fine," I told him, leaning back against the cargo locker behind me. The cool of the metal felt good in contrast to the heat of my wound. "No stitches." I hated needles, and while I needed the curequick, I drew the line at stitches that might help me heal but would bother me more than they were worth.

That made him angry. "You think I don't know how you feel? That you clench your teeth every time you take a breath, or that you move like something's broken? My instincts are screaming you're a liability, when normally they force me to admit you're the right person for the job. Not to mention this damn connection we have. So stop pretending."

I'd thought I was the only one who was annoyed at how the mental connection we shared sometimes seemed like too much information, but I understood now that it made him feel vulnerable. He took responsibility for everything that happened to everyone under his watch, but with me that went much deeper. He'd once lost his family and everyone he'd loved. He'd lived only for revenge.

Until me. Until us.

I reached out to him, pulling him close, glad the anesthetic was already taking affect. "I can't promise not to get hurt, but I can promise that I'll do everything I can to come back to you. Always."

"I know." His voice roughened on the words as his lips met mine, angling my head back as our kiss deepened. His mind shield vanished and his desire and frustration hit me, along with the thoughts: *I can promise not to prevent you from going into danger, but I can't promise to like it.*

Of course he wouldn't prevent me from battle, because taking that away from me would change everything between us. I kissed him harder. *You like this well enough.*

He laughed and the tension drained away. "I love you," he murmured, nibbling my neck.

"I love you too. But put a bandage on me and help me find a shirt before Oliver decides to come back here to brag some more about how he single-handedly extracted us from the jaws of death."

"No way," Ritter said. "I'm not finished yet." And he kissed me again.

For the moment, it was easy to forget that we'd almost gotten caught and that our cargo was possibly the most important we'd ever transported.

I only hoped that our Emporium captives really did have information we needed.

CHAPTER 4

"**N**OT EXACTLY THE QUIET IN-AND-OUT YOU PLANNED," AVA SAID dryly as Ritter and I walked into the conference room in our San Diego Fortress four hours later.

I shrugged. "I think you'll agree that the risk was worth it in light of what we returned with."

"Yes." Her steel gray eyes flickered over me with more than a cursory glance. Ava was not only the leader of our cell but also my fourth great-grandmother. Consequently, she was more concerned with my welfare than she might have been otherwise. But there was no outer sign of my wound, and by the end of our meeting, even the deeper internal damage would be only another memory.

Ava lifted a hand, inviting us to sit. I took the chair on the left side of the table, kitty-corner to where she stood, and Ritter settled next to me. Today Ava had her shoulder-length blond hair up, and she wore one of her customary suits. She looked younger than the thirty-six years she'd aged over the past three centuries. "I understand Dimitri sedated the third agent when he started coming to?"

"That's right." Ritter's gaze strayed briefly to me. "We couldn't risk him going nuts on us again."

Ava held my gaze. "You're sure it was Delia's work?"

I nodded. "I'd like to take another look at him. Her constructs were destroyed, but still lingering. I've never seen the like."

This brought a laugh, softening her gray eyes. "There seems to be a lot going on that we haven't seen lately. At any rate, we're going to take some flak for the rescue. In fact, the president felt the need to leave his special session of Congress in order to follow up on the disturbing reports he received from the facility."

"So, he didn't take it well," Ritter said, "our going behind his back."

"President Mann was very angry." One side of Ava's lips quirked up in a half smile. But there was something else lingering behind the levity. Something deep and dark, but though she shared my sensing ability, she didn't reach out to share it with me, so whatever it was, she wanted to tell us in her own way. "I think I made him understand that we had no choice, especially because he doesn't seem to be making much progress in Congress to protect either Unbounded or mortals."

"Oh, they'll approve DNA testing for members of Congress and term limits for Unbounded," Ritter said. "Because if they don't, in a hundred years, only Unbounded will be in Congress making decisions for all the world."

Ava finally sank into her seat. "I hope you're right—heaven help me for even agreeing that such testing is needed. I thought it would go more smoothly, but the voting has stagnated at every turn, even though not one of the five known Unbounded members of Congress has come forward to object publicly to the testing. At this point, the president is doubtful any of his new laws will pass in their current form."

"After today," I said, "I can't blame anyone for not wanting to admit to being Unbounded. The government was experimenting on them, remember?"

So far, only one Unbounded had announced his nature: Patrick Mann, the president's adopted son. He was the official face of the Unbounded—and a Renegade Unbounded. For his trouble, the Emporium had teamed up with Hunters to kill him, but fortunately, the four Renegades from our cell who were guarding him managed to save his life.

"The Emporium has obviously stepped up their plan." Ritter's frustration showed in the growl of his voice. "Their agents are popping out of the woodwork like termites. All they need is one Unbounded president and a change in presidential term limits, and they will have won. We'll have an overlord, not a president. Why can't the mortals in Congress—or anywhere else—see that?"

Mortals did seem to like making things worse for themselves. They either wanted to dismember us, experiment on us, or fall to their knees in worship. Despite Patrick's constant visits to groups all over the country, trying to show that we were just another race of humans, the mortal world was polarizing itself. The impending conflict promised to be long and bloody.

Ava must have caught my thought, because her eyes now seemed darker and haunted. I knew I wouldn't have to wait long for the blood. Something had happened.

Ava raised a monitor and keyboard embedded into the top of the table and began typing. "We've been working hard on this to see if we can find any connection between what's going on in Congress and the Emporium. There are precious few links, but what we have found all point to one man."

She finished typing, and a holographic image of a man in his fifties appeared over the table. His hair was mostly a light brown, the gray on the temples blending in to soften the hard lines of his face. Even as a hologram, his hazel eyes seemed to peer inside me. What I could see of his chest hinted that he was in great physical shape, and there was no sign of the belly that most politicians sported at his age.

"This is Ropte—Senator David Ropte, to be exact. Before a few years ago, he wasn't even in politics, but he has risen fast. According to intel on the thumb drive we recovered in Mexico, he received large amounts of money from the Emporium. All those records have been expunged in the past months, of course."

"He's Unbounded?" I asked.

"We don't yet know if he's Unbounded or a mortal sympathetic to the Emporium's cause. In the past few months he's increased his meeting schedule by four hundred percent. He's been seeing senators, representatives, and other political leaders—anyone and everyone with any kind of influence." Ava paused, letting that sink in before she continued. "He's come out strongly against the President's new proposals regarding Unbounded—both the testing and term limits as well as the bill that ensures protection from forced medical experiments."

I thought about it for a moment. "He could be just another power-hungry idiot trying to use the Emporium for his own advancement. The announcement about us changed everything."

"Whatever he is," Ritter said, "if he's not Emporium, they'll string him along until they gut him."

"Which might actually work in our favor," Ava agreed. "Until this afternoon, we didn't have anything solid on Ropte. However, there's been a new development we can't overlook."

Dread filled my stomach. This was what she'd been leading up to. The darkness.

Ava jabbed her finger at her screen, pulling up another

holograph that made my stomach churn. A family of four lay slaughtered, their blood seeping into the pale carpet underneath them. Ritter's fists clenched tightly on the table near the gruesome image. He'd seen many such scenes during his long life, but this one of an entire family must haunt him, must bring back the night he'd lost his own family. I reached out to his knee under the table, giving it a brief squeeze. He relaxed marginally.

"This is what separates Ropte from the other power-crazed politicians," Ava said. "The father of this family is Senator Burklap, and he's been vocal in his support of the president's new policies. He met with Ropte five times this month alone—and we're only two weeks into the month. Twice, Stella picked up residual chatter about them arguing so loudly the secretary called security. Yesterday they had another meeting, and Burklap's aide says he never returned to the office. Two hours ago, this slaughter is what that same aide discovered when he tracked down the senator at his DC residence."

Ava paused, turning off the image. I was grateful for the chance to let my brain catch up. Staring at those dismembered bodies reminded me of all the deaths the Emporium had been responsible for, and how many of my loved ones they still might murder.

"A group of Hunters is claiming responsibility," Ava added after several moments.

Ritter shook his head. "No way. They only kill Unbounded. And they never kill children."

"The rules surrounding Hunters have changed too," Ava reminded him. "At least with the new recruits who claim to be Hunters but are really just out for the sport."

From what I'd seen, Hunters were all pretty much out for the sport, for killing and asking questions later. Almost from the first day I learned I was Unbounded, they'd been trying to kill me. "Maybe the family has some Unbounded connection."

"No." Ritter leaned back, folding his arms against his chest. "Some Hunters are downright bloodthirsty bastards, but too many of them are descended from Unbounded for them to start murdering children who haven't reached the age of Change. They'd have to kill all their own children just for the possibility. And the attack against Senator Burklap's family was experienced. They were cut specifically in a way to sever focus points. No wasted strokes like you normally find with Hunters."

I really didn't want to see the image again, so I'd take his word for it.

Ava pondered a moment in silence before saying, "Ritter, I'd like you to contact Keene and have him get some feelers out to see what the *official* word is from the Hunters. He should have some insight into it. But I'm with you on this. I believe either Ropte or the Emporium, or both, are behind these murders. Unfortunately, it gets worse. When I talked to the president this afternoon, he told me four more supporters have indicated their intention to change their vote. Not just any men, but outspoken supporters like Burklap."

Fury built in Ritter's eyes. "Their families."

I could barely breathe at the idea. "Like Burklap."

Ava nodded. "We knew the fight was going to get worse. However, I'm still hoping we're wrong. Stella's been tracking the families of the four since the news came. We have to find them, even if we're only making sure they're safe."

I had the sinking feeling they weren't.

We all looked up as Stella Davis, our technopath, came into the room, her neural headset blinking, indicating that she was linked to the computer network. Her flowered dress fluttered behind her, accentuating her curves. She was half Irish and half Japanese, with the Japanese side taking precedence in her long, dark hair and mysterious brown eyes. Her Unbounded confidence was enhanced by nanites that made slight changes in her face and body, resulting in a combination that made most men stare.

"What is it?" Ava asked, taking the words from my lips because Stella's worry dripped from her surface emotions. "You locate the families?"

Stella came to a stop on the other side of Ava. I could barely detect the small mound of the baby boy growing inside her. He still had another five months before he was due to meet the world, but his life force was strong, and his thoughts radiated contentment.

"There's still no sign of any of them," Stella said with a frown. "The two families staying in DC have neighbors who say they were told the families were going back to their main residences, but they never arrived home. We're tracing down rumors of vacations for the other two families, supposedly to Idaho and Kansas. So far I've come up with nothing—no credit card receipts, no phone transactions, no bank transfers. I'll keep looking, but by the time I find them, it may be too late."

Ava nodded. "What about our new Emporium captives?"

"I questioned them about Senator Ropte," Stella said, "but every time I brought up Ropte, they froze."

"They wouldn't give you the information?" Ava's eyes narrowed.

"Not that, exactly." Stella blew out a breath of frustration. "They just seemed not to know anything. Except their reaction was odd, and I don't know what to make of it."

"Maybe they *can't* tell us," Ritter said.

I stood, grateful for anything that would take my mind off the slaughter Ava had shown us. "I didn't see any blocks in their thoughts back in Texas, but let's go find out."

Ava rose to follow me, pausing in the doorway to speak to Stella. "Start delving further into Senator Ropte, and see if there's a connection with the four families. Trace even the smallest lead. You should also monitor our progress with our prisoners. You might catch something we miss."

Stella had already pulled up a dozen holograms that flickered like twelve separate computer screens suspended in midair. She likely had another twenty connections open that we couldn't see. "I'll contact Patrick Mann as well. He's been hobnobbing with the rich and famous long enough to have heard something on Ropte. I could use his help tracing the information."

"If you need me, I'll help after I finish with the questioning," I told her. I couldn't approach Stella or Patrick's agility with computers, even when I channeled Stella's ability, but every second counted.

* * *

Outside the infirmary, two of our mortal security guards, Marco and George, stood at the open door with weapons ready. I nodded at them as we passed, glad to see them instead of Oliver, who was one of the few Unbounded I'd ever met that was inept at fighting. Of course, he *thought* he was great, which only made him more a liability.

Dimitri sat at a table inside a glass-walled isolation area in the left corner of the infirmary. Eden and Fenton sat with him, and Bedřich lay on the only hospital bed. He was awake now, so Dimitri had been at work on him, but the Czech's hands and feet were secured to the bed—a wise precaution. Shadrach was nowhere to be seen, and I hoped someone was keeping an eye on him. I believed he was sincere about helping us, but he'd acted on his own agenda before.

Feeling the need to check, I opened my mind, releasing the normal shields I kept in place to allow my colleagues privacy. I found Chris and my niece and nephew in the courtyard near the gardens located in the middle of our century-plus old mansion and the new walls we'd built so the children would have a protected place to play. It was those walls that had given our safe house the nickname of Fortress, resembling as it did the old forts from frontier days. Their nanny, Becka, wasn't with the kids, judging by the life form in her room on the third floor. On the main floor, our cook, Nina, was probably finishing up a dinner that I'd only eat in order to spend time with the kids.

I found the life forces that were Shadrach and Oliver together on a balcony on the second floor overlooking the courtyard. It stood to reason that Shadrach would be anxious to have time outside, but I was glad our upgraded security system meant he was under Stella's constant surveillance, and even Oliver's company would at least be some deterrent to any possible troublemaking.

Beyond the house and courtyard, I could sense nothing. The electronic grid running through the house and surrounding walls—even extending in a fine, almost invisible net high above the courtyard—prevented sensing Unbounded from seeing in or out. It also eliminated the possibility of shifters appearing without warning. We believed we had the only shifter, but the Emporium's continuous breeding program might have resulted in new Unbounded with abilities we weren't aware of.

The estate was sprawling, with large expanses of grass in the front and more extending far beyond the walls in the back. Weapons nestled in trees, under the ground, and on top of the mansion and the walls were at constant readiness. The Emporium had attacked us at a previous stronghold, and this time we were prepared.

I drew my mind back to the infirmary to see that Ritter and Ava had accompanied me into the isolation area. The three Emporium agents eyed us warily, but Dimitri smiled a greeting.

Weariness showed in his face, and I knew he'd expended a good amount of healing energy on at least one of the agents—probably Bedřich. Nice of Dimitri, considering Bedřich had tried to kill me.

"Hello," Ava said. "I'm Ava O'Hare, and I'm pleased to meet you."

"You're the leader here?" Fenton asked.

She inclined her head in agreement. "I apologize for the rush, but we need to ask you more questions about Senator David Ropte."

Fenton gave a snort. "We already told the Asian woman. We've heard the name, but we don't know anything more." The big man spoke confidently, but with no real conviction, as if he didn't believe what he was saying.

"If you're telling the truth, you won't mind dropping your shields and letting me see," I said. Fenton and Eden stared at me as if I had asked them to give me the number of their bank accounts and custody of their firstborn. Only Bedřich didn't meet my gaze, staring up at the ceiling, his body tense on the bed and his hands curled into fists below his restraints.

"I can do it without your consent," I added helpfully. I had recovered enough to force my way in if I had to.

When they didn't answer, Ava said, "She's the one who killed Delia Vesey."

The tension in the room tripled with that sentence. It sounded worse than it was. The lives of all my friends plus eight million people had hung in the balance. Not to mention that Delia had tried to transfer her consciousness and all her memories to my body. She'd planned to become me, and would have used my body to create potential hosts, essentially giving her true immortality. She'd deserved much more than death.

"Fine," Eden muttered. The resistance over her mind

vanished, and the sand stream of her thoughts came clear. She didn't know it, but Ava was also in her mind.

"What do you know about Senator Ropte?" Ava asked in the same casual tone she'd been using all along.

Eden shrugged. "Nothing. I remember a briefing on our agents that infiltrated the senate. But beyond that . . . nothing."

She was right. There was a literal nothing, a gap in the sands surrounding that thought.

As though someone removed it, Ava thought.

Yes, exactly as if someone had removed it as I had the doctor's memories at the government facility. I could easily imagine Delia and her assistant plundering her soldiers' minds. This meant Ropte was someone important enough for Delia to protect. Delia, who didn't care about anyone but herself.

I looked at Fenton, who glared but dropped his mind shield. "Think about Ropte," Ava directed. His sand stream shifted, revealing the same black spacing we'd found in Eden's mind.

I wanted to growl in frustration. "All missing," I told Ritter and Dimitri. To Eden and Fenton, I added, "The gap is big enough that you have to be aware something is missing."

"A blankness," Eden whispered. Her jaw worked with anger. "It's not the only time she did that to me."

"At least you have confirmation they're telling the truth." Dimitri's voice wasn't quite a chastisement, but close. Whatever conversations the three had shared, he was apparently leaning toward trusting them.

"I know who Ropte is," Bedřich said from the bed. We all turned to him, and I reached out instinctively, but his mind was shut tightly. Whatever mental damage had occurred in his brain, it wasn't affecting his shield now.

Bedřich laughed. "You won't get inside my head. I could shield against even *her.*"

"I did before." I took a step closer, pulling out my imaginary machete.

"You were lucky."

I slammed hard, summoning all my energy. Two hits, three. Concentrating on the place I'd hit before, though it seemed completely healed. I reached out to place a hand on his secured leg because touch enhanced my efforts. Desperation had fueled me at the facility, but now I worked with determination and skill. I felt Ritter's presence like a strength, as well as my friends around me. Finally the hole opened, and I was inside the maelstrom of Bedřich's mind. His thoughts still hurtled crazily around the bits of twisted construct, but the movement was far less volatile than at the facility now that the hallucinogen was out of his system.

I am always lucky, I told Bedřich.

He gasped and writhed on the bed, glaring hatefully at me.

Ava came to "stand" next to me in his mind. The bits of gray construct were falling toward the hole I'd made, slipping out, where they disappeared. *Why's it doing that?* I asked Ava. Though I was stronger mentally, she had centuries more experience.

Ava watched for a few more seconds before saying, *I think it's because he has such a tight control on his mind that the construct couldn't leave or disintegrate all the way when Delia died. Look, even now he's trying to block the hole.* Sure enough, the gray bits had ceased to flee his mind, though the hole wasn't repaired.

"Stop," I told Bedřich aloud. "I want to show you something." I sent him the images we were seeing. *This is what Delia left in your mind.* I used the machete to pound another hole in his shield, which was much easier from this side. *But Delia's dead now. You need to drop your shield and let them out. All of them.*

"What are they?" The anger in Bedřich's manner had disappeared. Fear had taken over.

"Constructs," Ava said. "Or parts of one that broke down after her death. It was likely hiding something you know from other people. Or preventing you from talking about it."

His shield dropped, but the bits didn't fly away. "More," Ava instructed, "You're still holding back." As she spoke, a clear inner shield I hadn't noticed before crumbled and the gray bits drifted away and disappeared. "That's it. You did it," Ava said.

His sand stream was still ragged, a sign of a diseased mind, but within moments, it settled into a more regular pattern. He breathed a sigh of relief. "I didn't know . . . that feels . . . better."

"What do you know about Senator Ropte?" I asked.

"Can you untie me?" he countered. "I'm not going to attack anyone. Not with you and *him* here." His chin angled at Ritter.

But my request had started the sands in his mind lurching and shifting to find the right memories. All at once I had the answer, the information Delia had been trying to hide: David Ropte was her descendant and next in line to ascend to her position in the Emporium Triad.

For the first time in Unbounded history, a member of the normally reclusive Triad was a public figure, someone who could be reached—and perhaps eliminated—before more people were murdered.

I reached over and set Bedřich's hands free.

CHAPTER 5

THE EMPORIUM TRIAD WAS THE RULING BODY OF THE EMPORIUM. The three members directed and controlled the bulk of Emporium business holdings and interests, employing hundreds of Unbounded agents and an unknown number of mortal offspring in each of their headquarters. Emporium businesses also employed thousands of unconnected mortals across the globe, who didn't suspect they were working for Unbounded.

The Emporium directed genetic experimentation on Unbounded and mortals alike and plotted to bring Unbounded to what they believed was their rightful place as leaders of the entire world. Upon the Triad's word people lived or died. Mortals, even their own offspring who didn't Change, were considered cattle or slaves, to be used and tossed aside. Millennia ago, Renegades had risen up against them to protect the mortals they loved, and we'd been fighting for that cause ever since.

We'd known Triad positions were passed down within the same three families, the successors groomed and chosen by the leaders, but any of their descendants could be chosen. Delia had lived seventeen hundred years, and she'd had ample progeny to choose from. We'd suspected her successor would remain hidden from the public eye, out of Renegade reach behind nameless corporations and numerous Unbounded soldiers. Not that we hadn't tried to find him. Together, Ava and I had spent copious amounts of time painstakingly searching the leftover bits of memories Delia had left in my mind, but they held no clue about her successor.

"So Ropte isn't just a supporter," Ritter said into the silence filling the infirmary. "All along he's been part of the Emporium. This explains a lot—why he's so against the president, and why he's probably responsible for the Burklap murders."

"Learning about him this late in the game makes me wonder how many other sleeper agents they have in place." I wanted to punch something—namely Senator Ropte, even if I broke my hand on his handsome, chiseled jaw. No wonder he looked so great in the hologram. I couldn't tell from an image if a person was Unbounded or not, but I should have guessed. "If we don't locate those families so the senators can vote without being influenced, the Emporium will succeed in blocking the president's new laws, and after that, who knows? By the time anyone pins those murders on Ropte, he'll be running this country."

"We *will* find them," Ava said quietly.

"What's Ropte's ability?" I asked Bedřich. "Is it sensing?" If he was anywhere near as powerful as Delia, we were in more trouble than we'd thought.

Bedřich hesitated two seconds before answering. "No. Delia's only real success in cultivating the sensing ability was in her assistant and a few others who weren't really suited for leadership. Probably a good thing for her or they might have destroyed her the way she destroyed her predecessor, or so the rumor goes. No, I believe he has another ability, but I don't know what it is. She never shared that information with me."

We threw out a few more questions, and I detected several more gaps in Fenton and Eden's memories, but I didn't remark on them. They didn't know anything more of value, and Eden looked like she needed to rest.

Ava finally called it quits. "In twenty minutes, I want everyone in the conference room." She started for the door.

Bedřich, now sitting on the bed where his legs were still tied, gave an unbalanced, mirthless laugh. "You'll never stop them. You know why? Because you care too much about mortals, while the Triad will sacrifice everything and anyone to get to the end—even each other."

Anger swept through me. "That's where you're wrong. We beat Delia because we worked together to protect mortals. I don't care what else they throw at us, we *will* beat the Emporium, even if we have to march into every facility they own and shoot them in their beds."

In two steps, I swooped up a pad of paper on the table in front of Dimitri and slammed it on Bedřich's stomach. "Now you start writing down every single Emporium headquarter location you can remember before the Emporium realizes we took you guys from the facility—if they haven't already figured it out from the scene we caused helping *you* escape."

The Czech glanced down at the pad, wrinkling his nose at what was already written there. "They're all here, at least the five big ones: San Francisco, New York, England, Germany, and Norway. They also have locations in France and Russia, but those are really just small affairs. Less than a dozen Unbounded at each. Maybe a couple dozen mortals. Oh, and the headquarters you uncovered in Venezuela. They probably moved survivors there to one of the other South American safe houses."

Eight in all? Plus extra safe houses? Our intel had indicated there were several hundred Emporium Unbounded, but even Keene had never been sure how many, and hearing it like this felt like a kick in the gut.

Ava stared at Bedřich from where she'd paused by the door to the isolation room. "How many Unbounded do the Emporium have? Dimitri asked your colleagues while you were unconscious, and they couldn't tell us. Maybe you can."

Fenton and Eden's minds once again showed a blackness that indicated a missing memory, but Bedřich nodded. "Over four hundred, last I knew. Not counting the mortal offspring who work for us." He lifted both shoulders and gave us an insincere smile. "But they are never counted."

"Of course not." I could barely get the words out past my disgust.

By contrast, the two largest Renegade cells were ours and the one in New York. We had others scattered throughout the world, including England, Italy, and the Mexican prison compound, but many of the cells were tiny, some consisting of only two or three members. With our newest Unbounded, Mari and Oliver, and Patrick, the president's son, plus four others who'd Changed in other cells, we only numbered ninety-seven Unbounded and even fewer mortals.

Ava's gaze swung over the room again. "Twenty minutes," she reminded us. "I'll need all of you. I'm sure our guests won't mind waiting in their quarters."

I left Ritter, Dimitri, and our mortal guards to secure our guests in the holding room, which resembled an elaborate hotel suite—except there was no way to leave. Multiple hidden cameras and microphones were everywhere, including the bathrooms and bedrooms. One portion of Stella's mind would monitor those feeds with little additional effort. Marco and George would stand outside the only entrance with their machine guns, but they wouldn't be needed.

"We should find out what Patrick Mann knows about Senator Ropte," I told Ava as we headed for the front staircase, which led down to the mansion's entryway on the main floor. Being in DC so much of the time, the president's son might have even met Ropte.

Ava touched her ear, which I hadn't realized before hid an earbud. "I'm already receiving a report from Stella. She's also alerting the New York cell. We'll need their help on this."

"Four hundred Unbounded." I heaved a sigh.

"That we know of," Ava corrected.

We'd reached the landing midway to the main floor. "I'd hoped maybe two or three hundred," I said. "Especially since so many went to prison after Morocco."

"They've been force-breeding a long time."

"There's got to be a way. Even if we can overtake them, four hundred is a lot of people to . . ."

To kill. Mostly scared, disenchanted people like Eden and Fenton, or those who would soon become scared and disenchanted. Or the ones who were blindly loyal, who felt they were destined to be gods by the simple accident of their genes. I didn't want to hurt any of them, but if it came down to them versus all mortals, there could be no other choice.

"Killing them is—"

An excited bark interrupted whatever Ava was going to say. At the base of the carpeted stairs, Max, a crossbreed of lab and collie, bounced toward us, his nails skittering on the rock floor of the entryway. I didn't much like the mutt, but he adored me, and his presence meant my niece and nephew weren't far behind. I felt my mood lighten.

"Go say hi to the kids," Ava said. "They'll miss you."

Meaning she suspected I'd soon be going on a difficult mission. "I can't. I promised to help Stella."

"She and Patrick have it covered for now, so take a few minutes." At the bottom of the stairs as we parted ways, she added, "Oh, and Erin, don't be late to the meeting."

As if I'd even dare.

I was petting Max when the kids came running into sight, Kathy, my twelve-year-old niece, in the lead. She had grown taller these past months, suddenly becoming a young woman, with softening angles and bouncing emotions. Her blond hair was pulled back into a ponytail, her blue eyes framed with mascaraed lashes. She came to an abrupt stop at seeing me, and her brother, Spencer, barely avoided crashing into her.

"Aunt Erin, you're back already!" Spencer shouted, throwing himself at me and making Max bark wildly. At ten, Spencer was still very much a little boy, all bony enthusiasm except for his freckled face that had somehow managed to hold onto a bit of baby fat.

"Shut up!" I ordered the dog, who rewarded my sternness with a wet lick of his rough tongue. I wiped my hand on my pants.

Spencer let go of me and launched himself at Max, burying his face in his golden fur. "You know she hates that, dummy. Better quit or you'll be out in the doghouse." He laughed because we didn't have a doghouse, and Max spent his nights in Spencer's bedroom. The setup was fortunate, because I wasn't about to share my space with the dog, though Ritter had a soft spot for the creature.

Kathy looked at me, her eagerness contained but still bright in her eyes. "Dad says you guys got three Emporium agents! And that you got stabbed. What happened?"

"One of the agents didn't realize I was there to help him,

that's all." My hand went instinctively to my side, though only a twinge reminded me of what had happened.

"I can't wait until I can be a Renegade," Kathy said with a sigh. "And go on ops and meet exciting people."

"Me too!" Spencer looked up from the dog and grabbed my hand. "We're going to eat. Come tell us all about it, okay?"

I let him pull me along, glad for a moment that neither child was paying attention to my face, which felt rigid. I didn't want either of them to become Renegade agents. At eight generations removed from an Unbounded ancestor, Changing was next to an impossibility for them. Except as an extremely rare fluke, Changes didn't occur after six generations.

So Kathy and Spencer could easily be killed. A wound like I'd received today, or a nick of a poisoned blade, could mean death—would eventually mean death. Luck never held out forever. No, what I wanted was a world where they wouldn't have to fight the Emporium. Where they could attend a normal school instead of being locked behind tall walls in a mansion, and where no machine guns and rocket launchers were mounted on the roof.

A world where I could give Ritter the baby he wanted without fear that the Emporium would try to take the child for their own purposes. Even with sperm manipulation and oral supplements, there was still a fifty percent chance that any child we had together would be mortal, but I was growing accustomed to the idea of having a child who might not Change. Maybe I could deal with it, when and if the time came. We'd have over thirty years of hope before we knew for sure, and maybe that would be enough. Every day mortals lived and died, reconciled to the short seventy or eighty years allotted them. Ava had adjusted to losing her children and had gone on to have hope in her posterity. Stella was taking that risk now.

Ritter was ready to move forward. Maybe I was almost there.

But first we had to deal with the Emporium, and especially this new threat.

My older brother Chris was in the dining room when we entered, already at the counter where the cook was setting out the food buffet style. Chris's hair, grown out to his collar, surprised me as it always did, even after several months. He'd worn it short before we'd joined the Renegades, before his wife, Lorrie, had been murdered by the Emporium.

"I see you kids found more than just the dog," Chris said, throwing a smile in my direction. It was good seeing him smile again. For a long time, I'd wondered if he would ever get over losing Lorrie.

"We didn't let Max go bug anyone," Spencer said. "He just missed Erin."

Said dog was snuffling at my jeans, looking for nonexistent food. I sat on a chair at the long banquet table and scratched his neck. A small clump of hair came out, and I held it out to Spencer without comment. He was responsible for combing the dog, who shed like crazy in the spring.

"Aren't you going to eat?" Spencer asked me, shoving the knot of hair into his pocket and heading toward the food at the serving counter across the room. "And where is everyone anyway?"

"Things are a little busy tonight, that's all." I didn't answer his question about eating. He knew Unbounded didn't need to eat, but he couldn't imagine not wanting to. To be honest, the grilled pork chops inside the domed warmer smelled amazing, and they'd taste even better, but my stomach was tight with worry, so it was better not to bother. Instead, I upped my absorption of the molecules in the air, tasting a hint of pork on my tongue and reveling in the subsequent energy coming through my skin.

Chris came to sit beside me as the children loaded their plates. He didn't remind them to wash their hands like Lorrie would have. "So," he said, sitting close to me. "What's up?"

"A senator and his family were murdered."

His fork sat by his plate, forgotten. "Stella told me about the Burklaps and the missing families. What else do you know? Is that why Ava called the meeting?"

"We think the man behind the murders replaced Delia Vesey."

His jaw tightened. "Stella has to stay out of this. The baby—"

"No one will risk Stella, so don't worry about that."

The tightness eased. "Good. We can't lose this baby." Chris was the father of Stella's lab-created child, but I knew their relationship had gone far beyond the lab. He was totally and completely in love with her, and despite Stella's ongoing grief at losing her mortal husband, I suspected she was starting to feel the same for him.

"Yeah . . . uh, about that. When are you going to tell the children? Stella's already showing. Kathy will guess soon enough that she's expecting, and then what? It's getting harder to keep the secret from them. Every time I open my mouth, I'm afraid I'm going to blow it."

"I know. I just worry about how they'll react."

"They love Stella."

"They miss their mom." He ran a hand through his hair, the wrinkles around his eyes reminding me that he was mortal, and I would lose him before I physically aged another year. The thought didn't hit me with as much agony as it once had. It just was.

"They'll love the baby. It'll be okay."

He nodded. "I just . . . things aren't decided between Stella and me. I-I love her. I have for a long time. I think Lorrie would understand."

"Tell them."

The kids came back then, with heaping plates they would devour almost completely. The cook had given up baking or boiling vegetables for them and instead had a constant variety of raw choices available. Spencer particularly liked the sweet peas, shells and all.

I watched them begin eating, joking and laughing together. It was peaceful, this slice of time where the horrors we experienced often didn't seem quite real.

Until I thought of Senator Burklap and his family, who would never be eating again. On that lovely note, it was probably time to head up to the meeting.

"Aunt Erin, I—"

I held up a hand, silencing whatever Kathy had been going to say. I sensed a distinct change in the air, one that triggered all my awareness. It took me a few precious seconds to understand what was different, to realize that I was receiving a jumble of thoughts from *beyond* the mansion. And if I could sense thoughts and life forces outside the electronic grid that protected us from mental assault, we were vulnerable. Unless Ava was holding some kind of unprecedented drill, only the Emporium could have wiggled through our mental protections.

"Down!" I said to the kids, reaching for my gun.

Immediately, Spencer and Kathy dived under the table, no questions asked. The weeks of training and subsequent grounding and household chores had seen to that. Max followed them, his tail between his legs, and Chris shot to his feet, his own gun ready. I faced the door; he faced the window that overlooked the garden.

I felt someone trying to get inside my mind—someone I recognized. Ava. I let her in. *Erin, we're about to have a visitor. She wanted to surprise you, but I didn't know if . . . Look, don't shoot anyone in the next two minutes, okay?*

I blew out a sigh of relief, but I didn't put down my gun and I didn't tell Chris to lower his weapon.

"Who is it, Ava?" I said aloud for Chris's benefit. "Why shouldn't we shoot?"

Just don't.

A soft *pop!* sounded in my ears, and a woman who appeared to be our friend Mari Jorgenson materialized in the dining room—Mari with her black hair dyed red for her undercover job protecting Patrick Mann. She wasn't alone. The two men with her appeared to be Keene McIntyre and my younger brother, Jace. Keene's piercing green eyes, framed by his red hair and beard—also dye jobs—were as mocking as his smile. Jace had let his blond hair grow shaggy, but it looked good with his black leather jacket.

At the same moment, I became aware of Ritter bursting into the dining room, a sword in one hand and a gun in the other, looking rather like an avenging angel.

"Don't shoot!" Mari said, standing between us and the men.

"I knew we shouldn't have surprised her," muttered Jace, holding up hands that were nearly as deadly as Ritter's. "Erin, it's me, Jace. You're not going to shoot, right? It really is us. No illusions or nanite tricks, I promise. Come on, put the gun down." Even as he spoke the electric grid came back to life, shutting out the world beyond the mansion.

I stared, my heartbeat slowing. "You guys are supposed to be in DC." But it was them, and their mind shields were down—a wise choice if they didn't want to be shot.

"We were until a second ago." Mari gave an excited laugh and took several steps toward us. "That's the surprise! Or part of it. As you've noticed, I'm not here alone. Ava's known about this for weeks, but I begged her to let me surprise you."

Now I understood. As I folded Mari in my arms for a hug, I had to admit it was a fantastic surprise. "Oh, Mari, this is great!" Before, she could only shift to a place she could see or to a location within a city or two range that she'd already visited. Or, if they were near enough, she could find people she'd connected with and shift to their location. But she'd only been able to shift herself—or with me when I channeled her ability. Now it appeared that not only could she fold space clear from the other side of the country, but she could bring others with her. It was a long-awaited break-through.

"I couldn't target you from so far away," Mari explained, "but the Fortress was easy to find, and once I began shifting, DC and San Diego touched, and I could see you were here in the dining room, so I switched arrival points at the last moment and here we are."

"Gotta admit, it's pretty cool," Jace said, now hugging Chris. "She'll probably be able to go anywhere in the world with more practice. I bet you can't wait to try it."

That was exactly what I was thinking: channeling Mari's ability. "Smart alec," I muttered as I took my turn hugging Jace.

"I've been all over the world," Mari said. "Well, at least to locations I've already visited. Like Venezuela. It was Keene who helped me figure it out." Her voice had an odd note now, which made me look at her and Keene sharply. Their hands were at their sides, but they might as well be gripping one another with the amount of sensual energy pouring off them. Looks like he'd finally told her about his Change.

Keene's ability was synergy, and not only could he change the reaction in atoms, but he could also intensify the abilities of others, exciting their powers, helping them reach new heights that might otherwise take years to achieve. He'd worried experimentation could mean blowing everyone into clouds of dust, but apparently he'd overcome his fear at least enough to practice with Mari.

I hugged Keene, though not as tightly as the others. Being this close to him made me hyperaware of Ritter as he came across the room toward us, his sword already returned to his back sheath. Keene smelled faintly of his familiar spicy cologne and memories we were both better off forgetting. I was glad for him and Mari.

"We were very responsible about experimenting," Mari said, as if to further allay Keene's fears.

I laughed. "Like I believe that." Once, as an accountant, Mari's life had been orderly, full of planning before leaping. But that was before her Change. Now she was as driven by her impulsive, confident Unbounded genes as my brother Jace.

"No, seriously," she insisted, shaking her auburn head and sending the long hair rippling. "We took short distances at first and then, well, we sort of got into a couple jams—"

"I almost blew us up," Keene drawled.

"Now that sounds like a lot more fun," I said.

Jace erupted with a laugh. "It's been an adventure keeping Patrick alive. You missed a lot." He paused before offering a sweeping gesture toward the table. "Um, shouldn't you do something about them?"

I turned to see the children still under the table, staring at us and hugging the dog. I had to admire Spencer; his staying put showed an extraordinary amount of patience.

Chris sighed. "You can come out now."

"We won't be grounded?" Spencer asked, his brow creasing.

"Of course not!" Chris growled. "I only grounded you before because you messed up in training."

"You grounded me like five times," Spencer mumbled.

"That's because you acted like it was a game five times."

"Well, it was, wasn't it?"

Before Chris could respond, Ritter said, "No, Spencer. Training is *never* a game. If this had been a real invasion, you'd be glad you'd stayed under that lead-lined table." His gaze met mine, before he fist-bumped the new arrivals, accompanying the welcome with a slight dip of his head. On him, the greeting looked rather ancient and full of ceremony—as it had probably been intended before mortals began using their own more casual version.

"Well, it's just Jace. And Keene and Mari with red hair," Spencer said. "*Ugly* red hair, by the way, if anyone cares what I think. I liked their old hair."

"We could have been an Emporium hit team in disguise." Jace caught the boy up in his arms.

Spencer gave him a flat smile, his eyes drifting briefly to me. "Nope. Aunt Erin would have shot you, and dad would've fired when she did. Hey, you bring me anything?" He began checking Jace's pockets for something of interest.

"It's not like I knew we were coming until about ten minutes ago," Jace said, pushing Spencer's hands away. "I'll bring you something next time."

Spencer rolled his eyes and went back to his food, the dog begging at his side. With a smile that was too adult, Kathy joined Spencer.

"I guess you're here for the meeting," I said to the newcomers with an internal sigh of regret. So much for my few minutes with the kids.

"Yep," Jace answered.

"Speaking of which," Mari said. "We have about thirty seconds before Ava wants us all in the conference room."

Having Mari around was like having the most accurate watch in the world at your fingertips. When it came to time or anything to do with math, Mari was queen. I could do the same to some extent when channeling her, but I didn't understand any of it when we weren't linked.

"Already?" Chris muttered. "Guess we'll see you in a bit, kids."

As a group, we started for the door. My last glimpse was of Spencer extending a hand overflowing with food to Max, and the dog's tail thumping the rock-tiled floor with anticipation. Neither seemed disturbed by their time under the table, but *I* was disturbed. Children should never have to hide under a table, or worry that someone might kill their remaining parent. No kid should grow up thinking that dangerous ops were a fact of life.

Of course, Kathy and Spencer weren't the only children caught in the crossfire. If we didn't find the senators' families in time, the power might shift once and for all toward the Emporium, and if they controlled the world, no child—or adult, for that matter—would be safe.

CHAPTER 6

HAVE WE LOCATED ANY OF THE OTHER FAMILIES?" JACE SAID FROM his seat at the foot of the conference table. His black high-backed chair leaned at an angle, his feet thrown up on the table. He looked comfortable in jeans and the leather jacket that fit snugly, as if it'd grown there instead of being purchased from a sale at his favorite Costco.

"I've tracked two of the families with an eighty percent chance of accuracy," Stella said from her usual place midway down the table opposite where Ritter and I sat. "There are still a few variables before I can say for sure, but one family appears to be at a house in Virginia and the other in Maryland. We also have possible leads that put a third family somewhere in Idaho. Fifty percent chance. But there's nothing from the fourth family yet, and we can't risk them for only a fifty percent probability of finding the third family."

"I'd take fifty percent from you over a hundred percent from anyone else," said Mari, who sat between Stella and Keene near the end of their side of the table. Mari's hands fidgeted as they always did when she wanted to be moving instead of talking. I could imagine that now with the entire world open to her, the feeling of being closed inside this room was even more intense.

"Even if it were a hundred percent accuracy, we can't move on those three until we know about the fourth." Ritter spoke with an authority no one questioned. None of us had lost more than he because of the Emporium—or knew them as well. "Once they know we're onto them, they'll cut their losses and slaughter those we haven't saved. We must save all of them."

"I'll find them," Stella said. "Patrick and I are following up on some leads right now." I'd already guessed that from the furious way her neural receiver was flashing, but something inside me relaxed at the words. Stella was my best friend, closer than a sister, and if anyone could find a needle in the proverbial haystack, she could.

"What we need is to meet with Senator Ropte," I said. "He's Delia's heir and the prime suspect, so what's stopping us? All we'd need is a good connection to his network and a few minutes, and I bet we'd discover the families' locations. I volunteer for the job."

Stella looked thoughtful. "It could work, if Patrick or I am close enough so you can channel our ability. Or if you can get me into his network remotely. It'll depend, of course, on how well Ropte keeps his information guarded." She looked at Ava for guidance.

Ava stood at the head of the table, leaning over slightly, her hands resting on the mahogany surface, her gray eyes missing nothing. "With Erin and Mari working together, and the rest of you for distraction, that may very well be our best chance. Patrick should have the connections to make such a meeting happen."

Stella's attention faltered slightly as she conferred over her electronic connection with Patrick. I imagined her mind flashing questions up on a screen faster than any human could type and Patrick answering in kind. In seconds, she had an answer.

"Patrick says Ropte talked to him at a party last week and suggested another meeting, which Patrick didn't take him up on at the time. Apparently, Ropte encouraged Patrick to speak out against his father's proposals. He suggested that Patrick needed to think more of his own kind."

"Who is with Patrick now?" Ritter asked, tensing with the question.

Stella gave him a smile. "Don't worry. Cort has him on lockdown at the safe house where they've stashed him. In case you didn't notice, Cort didn't come back with the others."

"I noticed, but I want to be sure that Patrick doesn't get any ideas about going to see Ropte on his own. Especially without Mari around to shift him out."

"The stronghold is completely secret," Mari told him. "We drove to it once so I could fix its location, but from then on, we've only shifted in and out. He's perfectly safe."

Ritter didn't appear satisfied until Keene held up something from his pocket—a handful of keys. "I had the same thought, so I made sure there wasn't any way to drive out. He'd have to walk miles first or blow the cover by calling in a taxi—if he could find one willing to go out that far."

Ritter's laugh surprised me, and I realized that was because I'd heard it so rarely. The others also relaxed at the sound, grinning, Jace's smirk the biggest of all.

"Keep looking, Stella," Ava said. "But the possibility of meeting directly with Ropte is promising, especially if he has no idea we've learned who he is. Naturally, he'll suspect Patrick because of his nature and his refusal to join the Emporium, but he can't know about Mari and Keene working undercover. The backgrounds we created for them are solid."

I caught a glance between Mari and Keene and again felt

the connection between them. With Mari posing as Patrick's mortal fiancée and Keene as her brother, they wouldn't have found much free time this past month, but there was definitely something going on between them.

"What's the news from the Hunters?" Ritter asked Keene. "Have you heard from your sources?"

Keene made the jumble of keys disappear. "The official word from the Hunters is that they aren't responsible for what happened to Burklap. Or rather, the kill order didn't go out from their leaders. But as you expected, they can't vouch for all the new members who've joined in the past three months."

"It's terrible what happened to Burklap," Mari said. "We met him last week at an event. Such a vibrant man, and now he's just . . . gone."

This interested Dimitri, who sat on my right side. "Can you recall anything odd from that night?"

Mari hesitated. "No, not really, other than I'm pretty sure that was the same night Ropte approached Patrick. Well, he was there, at least. But a lot of politicians were. Quite a few of them really seem to love Ropte."

"Well, think about it and let us know."

"Okay," Mari agreed.

"A few of the leads we're following come from the White House," Stella said into the sudden silence. "They're busy working the case too. Patrick's father doesn't want any more families to end up like Burklap's, and at the same time he needs the votes of those senators."

"Taking the families was a smart move by the Emporium," Jace said, his jaw tight. "If you can't find the families, there's no chance of rescue and those senators will have to do their bidding."

"There will be more victims before it's over." Twin lines appeared between Keene's eyes. "We're going to have to do more than find these families and protect all the others who might go missing. Eventually, we're going to have to hit the Emporium hard enough that they'll stop. For good."

A shiver rolled through me at the certainty in his voice. Keene had grown up in the heart of the Emporium, as a then-mortal son of Triad member Tihalt McIntyre, and had experienced firsthand their cruelty. He'd tried everything to be one of them—impossible when he didn't Change as expected. Then he'd made a choice that saved my life and helped Chris and his children escape from the Emporium. Yet even after leaving the Emporium and facing the truth, joining us hadn't been easy for him.

"We have to stop these kidnappings first," Ava said. "We can't second-guess ourselves. But at least Stella has been able to verify that they're the only families currently missing."

Ritter nodded. "I agree, but Keene's right that they'll up the ante, even if they wait until after we save these families. We have to prepare for worse. Unless we decide to take the offensive."

We all pondered his comment for a few seconds, and then Ava nodded. "I want to hear ideas on that. I think we all agree that the time is coming when we'll have to face them directly."

"With the information from our new guests, we know where they are," Dimitri said quietly.

Ava turned to him, an unreadable expression on her face. "I don't know how we could survive taking the fight to them, not with our low numbers, but we may have to." They shared a long stare, and I caught a sense of fire and burning and fighting and dying. Dimitri at least had survived a similar battle with the Emporium, and it hadn't ended well.

In the next second, the impression was gone, and Ava turned to Stella. "Let me talk to Patrick."

Patrick appeared over the table in 3D. Or at least his top

half did. He was facing Ava so I was looking at his profile, but it was easy to identify him. He had dark brown hair and blue eyes that looked out from a pleasant, average sort of face—or a face that would have been average if he were mortal.

"Patrick, Stella's been keeping you apprised of our discussion, I assume?" Ava asked.

His generous mouth curved in his customary smile. "Yes, and I'll set up a meeting with Senator Ropte. All I need is a good connection to his network and a few minutes."

Ava frowned, her face unyielding. "Not a meeting at his office. We want a social situation at his home. You'll go in with Mari and Keene and Erin. The others will be outside for backup. Your job will be to keep Ropte distracted so they can get the information. I won't be sending Stella because we need her here, which means Erin will have to channel your ability."

Patrick's smile turned sheepish. "All right. I'll send out a few feelers. He's popular, so I think I just need to show up wherever he's going to be. Shouldn't take me more than a few hours to pinpoint an event he'll be attending. Then when I run into him, I can suggest that I'm willing to hear more in a casual setting. Assuming I can get an invitation to his house, it still might not happen for a few days."

"We don't have a few days," I said. "There's got to be another way."

Mari snapped her fingers. "What about that senator who wears her hair up in that huge gray bun? I seem to remember her hanging around Ropte and flirting with him to the point of ridiculousness. Well, when she wasn't flirting with you."

Patrick gave a short, mirthless laugh. "Oh, you mean Beatrice Shumway. Yep, she courts everyone, despite her age, and is actually more successful than most. She might be a good one to plant a suggestion on because she was there at that party when Ropte approached me last week. If I dropped a hint that

I was amiable to hearing more from Ropte, she might work to arrange something in an effort to please us both."

"It has to be at his place, though," Ava reminded him.

"Leave it to me," Patrick said. "I know how to work the system. Ropte has a very nice townhouse in DC, and it shouldn't be too hard to get him to throw a party. Guess it depends on how much he wants to meet with me."

I looked at Ritter, and I could see my own worry reflected in the set of his jaw. If Ropte suspected anything, Patrick would be in danger. Big danger. At the same time, if Ropte's ego was big enough that he believed Patrick might be swayed to his side, it could work.

When no one voiced opposition, Ava spoke. "Okay, then. Erin and Ritter, you will accompany Keene and Mari back to DC. You will be responsible for retrieving the families held in Virginia and Maryland." She hesitated a second before asking, "You can shift them all, can't you?"

"Easy," Mari said with confidence.

"Man, does that mean I'm out of a job?" Chris spoke for the first time from his seat on Ritter's other side. We all laughed.

"Not on your life," Ava said. "In fact, you need to get to the airport and ready the plane. When we do find those families, we're going to have to act fast—and at the same time. I'm banking that Stella's hunch about Idaho is right, so Jace and I will take a team and wait there for a final location. Dimitri and Oliver can take the smaller plane to wherever the fourth family is once we've got a lead for them. Everything will go through Stella, who will remain here to coordinate." Ava stood, signaling that the meeting was over, and the holo of Patrick vanished.

Nodding at me, Ritter headed to the door with a gleam in his eyes that told me he was heading to our weapons arsenal to choose what we would need for our op. He didn't hurry, but his movements were fast compared to a non-combat Unbounded. Dimitri hurried after him, no doubt worried about what our guests might be up to in the holding suite. I'd risen to follow them out the door when Jace's hand landed on my shoulder. "Can I talk to you for a few minutes?" he asked.

Jace had always been my favorite brother because he and I were only two years apart, and since discovering our nature, we'd grown even closer during our many ops together. Unlike with Chris, our conceptions had been manipulated in a fertility clinic by Ava and the others when my parents had difficulty conceiving and requested a sperm donor. Without that intervention, neither of us would have Changed. I was grateful, but I still dreaded telling Jace the truth about his biological father. He'd been asking, and I knew he wouldn't leave it alone.

"Sure," I said, sinking back into my seat.

He settled in Ritter's vacated chair as the others filed past us. When they were all out of earshot he said, "About my father. It's time I knew."

I wanted to tell him that he should *never* have to deal with that knowledge, but Jace wasn't the same boy who'd Changed last year. He listened to orders, he'd begun to think before acting, and he could fight like a demon. He'd become a vital member of our team, someone to rely on. Maybe he could handle the fact that his father was an egotistic megalomaniac with delusions of godhood and a plan to enslave mortals. That he'd tried to kill our family, including Jace, to achieve those ends. Just thinking about it brought back the fear.

"I'm sorry we haven't talked before now," I began hesitantly. "But Jace . . . it's not good."

My brother grimaced. "Don't you think I've guessed that? Look, I'm not going off the deep end just because some guy donated sperm to start my existence. Our dad, the guy who raised us, is my father, but I need to know the rest."

"Let's go up to my room then."

Jace grinned and bounced to his feet like he had as a child when I'd invited him to see a movie with me and my friends. My heart ached that he'd have to shoulder the burden of his heritage. I knew only too well how it felt.

Ava and Mari were waiting for us outside the door to the conference room. "I need you to get to the infirmary," Ava said, "so Dimitri can give you a large dose of nanites."

There was only one reason for that. Newer nanites made it possible for technopaths to mask—or change—their identities completely. That meant if I channeled Patrick or Stella, I could make myself look like anyone in the world. "Who am I going in as?"

"Still working that out with Patrick, but we'll definitely be using the nanites for your disguise. We can't have the Emporium catching wind of you anywhere near Ropte. They'd be all over you in an instant. It's going to be dangerous enough as it is."

I glanced at Jace before replying. "I'll go up in a bit."

"Now," Ava said. "Dimitri is waiting."

I looked at Jace, who shrugged, hiding his disappointment. That alone showed how far he'd come. "I'll catch you later," he said. "Before you leave."

"All right." I watched him go, aware of Ava's eyes on me instead of on Jace. She hadn't given me permission to tell my brother about his conception, but I wasn't going to ask for her blessing. Maybe I was still annoyed that she hadn't been up front with me about Dimitri and my own beginning.

"I'll walk you up to the infirmary," Mari said, her voice bright with eagerness. "Or I can give you a ride."

Ava surprised me with a laugh. "Yes, show us how you do it. I'm going upstairs to talk to our guests while I wait for a phone call from our Mexican compound."

I frowned. "Problem there?"

"No," Ava said. "It's rather a good thing, actually. The new batch of reformed prisoners we've let work at the compound are ready to transfer to the village we created for the others we released from the prison. They're doing quite well—keeping all the rules and working with the natives. No sign of wanting to run back to the Emporium. Of course, we've been really careful to make sure they're ready."

I knew that much. I'd been down there several times in the past three months, interviewing the reformed prisoners and testing their minds for deceit. It was a relief to find something going right for a change. "That's great."

Ava smiled and turned back to Mari. "Okay, let's go."

Mari reached out and gripped our shoulders. "There are two ways I can shift now. Before, I always went to a gray area I call the *in between*. Keene's power showed me another way. I try not to use it when I'm taking others with me, though, because it eats more energy. But look what it does."

Her shield dropped as it always did during shifts, and her thoughts tumbled into my mind. Almost immediately, the air shimmered in front of us, rippling and cracking until I could see the corridor outside the infirmary.

"You can see where you're going," I breathed. The tactical advantages were limitless.

"Well, I always feel where I'm going, even when I use the gray," Mari said, "and I know just how it is in my mind, but, yeah, this is different because I can see if something's there waiting for me that wasn't there the last time I visited—like people or a wall. But for some reason shifting using this method takes more effort. It's like I'm dragging the place to me instead of slipping sideways through the gray."

"Very useful to check out who might be waiting for you," Ava said with approval in her voice.

Mari's smile widened. "Yeah, it has been." She wrapped the image around us, and instantly we were upstairs.

"I'd like to try that out later," I told Mari.

Ava started down the hallway toward Dimitri, who was just exiting the holding quarters. "Remember, if you stop channeling Patrick for too long," she said over her shoulder, "your body will nullify the nanites, and you'll look like you again."

"Got it." I hadn't used nanites on an official op before, but I knew the drill. Ever since my marriage to Ritter, I'd been channeling Stella's ability daily to assure that I wouldn't ovulate and become pregnant. The Unbounded gene was programmed to survive, and that included repairing tied tubes and going around—or through—any birth control method. This rampant fertility, and our Renegade commitment to following our posterity for six generations, made relationships complicated, but I'd found a way around that. For now. As long as I didn't miss a day.

Mari leaned over and whispered as Ava drew away, "Can you believe Stella and Chris?"

"Yeah, it's crazy. At first I wasn't sure about the two of them, but Chris has taken it slow. I'm hopeful."

"She seems so happy. I'm glad she's getting her baby. Losing her last one . . ." Mari sighed and shook her head. "I wondered if she'd ever recover."

"She's tougher than she looks."

"So I guess I'm going to be a . . . what do they call it when your fifth great-aunt has a baby?"

"I have no idea." I let my gaze slide past her to where Ava and Dimitri had paused as they reached each other in the hallway. "So," I added, "you and Keene, huh?"

Mari's smile grew wider and more secretive. I noticed that her mind shield was firmly back in place. "*That* we'll have to save for another day."

After my injections with Dimitri, I did a mental search for Jace, but he was no longer in the Fortress. That probably meant Ava had sent him on an errand. I didn't think she'd done it on purpose, but I had to admit to feeling relief. Instead, I went up to my room to pack a bag. Besides my weapons and my meta-materials bodysuit, I threw in a couple of dress choices for the swanky affair we would have to attend at Ropte's—provided we could get him to invite Patrick.

My bed beckoned to me with seductive promises of oblivion, but I wasn't really tired anymore, and I didn't want to be alone in that bed. I didn't have to push out my senses to know Ritter was downstairs in the basement workout room, because this close I always knew where he was. There was no word from Ava or Stella yet, so maybe he was working off the frustrations he'd felt in Texas.

Minutes later, I entered the workout room, skirting several large duffel bags full of weapons Ritter had taken from our stores. His back was toward me, but he turned and threw a sword as I approached, tossing it before he could have seen me completely.

I caught the katana, being careful not to touch the blade because it looked old and expensive. "It's beautiful."

He reached me, sliding his arms around my body and pulling my back against his hard chest. "It's for you."

"Looks old."

He chuckled. "Actually, it's not. An Unbounded guy in Italy makes them. He likes to mimic ancient swords, but they're far stronger than anything you would find anywhere in the world—ancient or modern. He studied sword-making in Japan, of course, but his ability allows him to enhance the strength of the metal. He's created many Renegade swords. I ordered this one three years ago."

I started to hand it back. "Then it isn't mine."

His arms tightened around me. "Everything I have ever done is for you, even before I knew you."

My body kicked into high awareness at the rough emotion in his voice. Giving me this weapon was his way of courting— all combat Unbounded gave weapons in courting—and to refuse would mean more than refusing an expensive, one-of-a-kind sword. I had to hand it to him. Maybe it was his centuries of living and his old-world courtesy, but this man of mine somehow kept making me fall for him.

"Thank you," I said.

He moved around to my front, still holding me, but avoiding the sharp katana, now pointed toward the ground. "Oh, I'm sure you can do better than that."

I was about to show him just how much better when Mari materialized with her customary soft *pop*. "Patrick did it! Ropte must want him bad because Stella has already picked up rumors that Ropte's people might be throwing an impromptu get-together for supporters in DC. No official invitations have been sent out, but at least two other private events have been canceled. Stella's tracing phones now to see if there were any calls between Senator Ropte's residence and the people who were putting on the cancelled events."

I stepped back from Ritter. "And the rumor says this party will be when?"

"Tomorrow afternoon at Senator Ropte's residence."

I exchanged an uneasy glance with Ritter. Was it too convenient? Or did Ropte just want to seduce Patrick that badly after hearing that Patrick might be amenable? Either way didn't bode well for us.

"Ava says we should leave now," Mari added. "She wants you to have time there to prepare for your alias."

"I'm already packed," I said.

Less than a half hour later, we met in the conference room. Ava and Dimitri were present as Keene, Ritter, and I grabbed hands and let Mari take us into the gray. It was only as we appeared at the safe house some miles outside DC that I remembered I still hadn't talked to Jace.

CHAPTER 7

PATRICK WAS WAITING FOR US AT THE SAFE HOUSE, BUT HE WASN'T alone. With him was Noahthea Westmoreland, or Noah for short. Noah was a member of the New York Renegades who had been helping Patrick in his duties as the face of the Unbounded. She was a beautiful woman with very dark skin and tightly curled ebony hair that cascaded halfway down her back. Her slender torso and long legs were emphasized by an ample bustline and rounded backside. Today her perfect figure was set off by a snug black dress, but as usual it was her voice that held people mesmerized.

Unlike most Unbounded, Noah's gift was what I considered one of the beautiful abilities. It wasn't meant for battle but for splendor and inspiration, and she had regaled music lovers all over the world for over a hundred years under several different identities. Her audience *felt* words when she sang them. Her joy raised listeners to new heights, and her sorrows made them shed bitter tears. Ava had told me that gifts like Noah's had once been envied among Unbounded, but that was before we began battling the Emporium. Now Noah and those like her were a weakness we had to protect. Most of us did so willingly.

"Noah!" I hadn't seen her for months except in the occasional holo when Mari reported in. I set my duffel on the carpet and moved toward her. "It's good to see you."

"You too!" She hugged me and added in a whisper, "Especially with Patrick going to Ropte's. I feel so much better with more backup." She withdrew from me and bumped fists with Ritter in greeting. "Never thought I'd see you settle down," she added to him.

"Ha. We don't have time for settled. Dangerous or explosive, maybe—a lot more fun." His eyes swept over me, conveying a heat that enveloped my entire body. Three months of marriage, and a single look still set my stomach doing frenzied somersaults.

"Where's Jace?" Patrick asked, glancing past us in search of my brother.

"He's going to be on one of the other strike teams," I said. "With Ritter and me here, we should have enough for Maryland and Virginia."

"If not, we can ask for help from our Renegades," Noah said. "I put them on notice. Right now they are coordinating with Ava and Stella to protect the families of the other senators who are supporting the president."

"So, did you get an official invite from Ropte?" Keene asked.

"It just came in," Noah said.

"Come on," Patrick added. "Cort will explain the setup." I barely had time to note the plush off-white couches that looked as beautiful and seductive as Noah herself before they motioned us from the living room and into the hall.

Noah led the way to a spacious sitting room where four couches, this time a light brown, stretched in a semi-circle in front of a monitor that took up half a wall. Along another wall was a long row of counters, and a small kitchen took up the back portion of the room. Only the counters looked used, their surfaces full of instruments, beakers, microscopes, and several contraptions I didn't recognize. Cort Bagley sat nestled in among the experiments, but he put down a circular object and came to his feet when he saw us, his blue eyes as piercing as Keene's green ones. Besides the eyes and the brown hair—or at least the hair before Keene's disguise—the half brothers didn't look much alike. Cort was bookish serious while Keene was more witty bad boy.

"Good to see you guys." Cort extended his fist, but I bypassed it and hugged him. Cort was one of the people who'd shown me the most kindness after my Change, and I looked at him as a friend and mentor. He was surprisingly awkward for a man who'd lived five hundred years and had buried several wives and many of their children.

Ritter walked over and, after exchanging a greeting with his old buddy, picked up the device Cort was working on. "Security bypass?"

Cort nodded. "We'll have to actually tap in before Stella can overlay with fake feeds, but it should do the job once we're inside Ropte's. Most times we don't care if the Emporium knows we stole something from them, but this time, we need to keep them in the dark."

"Why don't you give us a feel for what we'll find at Ropte's?" Ritter said. "Any information will help me set up the details."

Cort motioned for us to sit, and I made way to the nearest couch, sighing as the cushions cradled my body. Maybe I could use a little sleep. I looked up when Ritter dropped the duffle he was still carrying and sat next to me, his eyes shuttered. I knew what that look meant—he was trying to get his emotions under control. I'd be in danger at Ropte's townhouse, and his instinct was to protect me. He'd have to deal with his own demons. I refocused on Cort, who had settled on the next couch with Patrick and Noah.

". . . like any other political gathering," Cort was saying. "That actually works to our advantage to have so many powerful mortals there. If it were a more intimate gathering, I'd be concerned that their agenda was to capture Patrick. I think it's safe to say that Ropte would prefer to convince Patrick to join him willingly."

"Well, yeah," Keene said with a snort, sitting next to Mari on the third couch. "If he can get Patrick to change his stance, many of those following him will fall into line. Particularly some of the politicians still supporting the president. Once they're out of the way, the term limits will be struck down, and all the protections for humans will be out the window. I'd say Patrick is first on his list."

That made me feel better about the entire situation because Patrick was a born politician, having been raised by the man who was now in the White House. "So Patrick just has to double-talk him and make Ropte think he's being swayed."

Cort nodded. "If Ropte's anything like the rest of us, he'll be patient only to an extent. Once the families are rescued, all bets are off."

Great. Now the uneasiness was back. "And what's my cover?"

It was Noah who answered as she settled on the couch next to Patrick. "We thought you could go in as me. My own face is known to the Emporium, of course, but not my current alias, Felicia West. I'll show you the disguise I've been using, and you'll copy it using Patrick's ability and your nanites. Lately, I've been to all the events with Patrick and Mari, so my presence won't be questioned."

"Everyone always asks her to sing," Mari added.

"Wait. What if they ask *me* to sing?" The idea was horrifying. I'd done a stint in school choir as a teen—long enough to know I didn't belong there. I wasn't bad, exactly, just not good.

Ritter's eyes gleamed as though the idea of me up on a stage appealed to him. "Noah will be with me," he said, "and we'll be close enough for you to channel if you need to."

I relaxed. Channeling was something I could do. "But I won't sound like Noah, even if I'm any good."

"Close enough," Noah said. "I have a recording of my newest song, and if you listen to it, you should be able to copy my style sufficiently. One ability that most singers have is to mimic, and it'll be easy when you're channeling me."

"You should hear all the impressions Noah does." Patrick flashed her a look of admiration. "Dionne Warwick, Karen Carpenter, Whitney Houston, Barbra Streisand, and Taylor Swift. And that's just in pop music. She really excels in her opera impersonations."

Noah laughed. "I went through a phase fifty years ago. Everything I sang was opera. Now I'm going through what I call my modern phase. Well, modern chic, mostly."

"You have your own style," Mari said. "And everyone loves it."

Noah looked down, and a wave of embarrassment came from her surface emotions. Not because she didn't have confidence and pride in her ability, but because her singing was a part of her like her hair or skin, and she had no control over how others reacted to it. "Anyway," Noah said. "It's a new song, and no one has heard me sing it besides those living here, so your impersonation will be close enough. You'll give the debut public performance." She laughed, letting me know the idea didn't bother her. I suppose after launching so many songs under different aliases, she didn't mind sitting this one out.

"What's Ropte's perimeter security like?" Ritter asked Cort. Next to mine, his leg tensed briefly, the only sign of worry I could detect.

"That's the best part." Grinning, Cort leaned farther back on his couch, crossing one knee over the other. "It's a townhouse smack dab in the middle of other townhouses. It's big and expensive and elaborate inside, but the front meets the street where anyone can walk practically up to it. So no scaling walls and taking out surveillance cameras. Sorry to disappoint you. There's a garden area, but it's not even a fourth of an acre. You'll be well within Erin's range so she can channel you or so you can swoop in for the rescue." Cort held a hand up against my protest. "Not that anyone will need rescuing. But those of us remaining outside will be loaded to the teeth because we don't have any idea how many Unbounded hit teams Ropte has at his disposal. There are bound to be some. This is a Triad member we're talking about."

"We have to know before we go in," Ritter said. "If I were him, I'd have snipers in place, and agents among the help."

Cort cleared his throat. "And he may have all those. But with the most prominent people in Washington DC assembled at his private residence, the last thing he's going to want is a bloodbath. Killing off his supporters, even as collateral damage, isn't going to put him in the White House. Besides, Patrick has Secret Service flanking him wherever he goes, and after what happened at that school last month, they'll have someone on every roof in the near vicinity and half a dozen more on Ropte's roof watching for windows that shouldn't have movement. So, if something happens, it'll be either after Patrick leaves Ropte's—and Mari makes sure that's impossible by shifting him here—or inside wherever Ropte has his computer."

Inside where I was stealing his information, Cort meant.

"So where is the Secret Service anyway?" I asked. "Shouldn't there be at least four agents breathing down our throats here?"

Keene laughed. "We discovered early on that we need to be the only ones who know where Patrick is staying. They don't like it, but we'll meet them somewhere in DC right before we go to Ropte's. We have alerted them, and they'll be scoping out the area now."

"I'd feel better if Erin did that." Ritter looked at me.

"We need to be there early," I agreed. "There's too much they could miss." I hesitated as my gaze landed on Keene. "I could use help if you think you'd be able to boost my range." I felt odd asking. We'd worked together before, and while our teamwork had saved many lives, his role in the matter had also caused the death of several innocents. I believed I was equally responsible for their loss, but Keene didn't see it that way, and I knew he still agonized over what he could have done differently.

He hesitated only an instant. "I can do that. Mari and I've worked out a system. I think it'll work for you."

"We'd all better get some sleep then," Ritter said, standing. "It's after midnight local time, and we need to be sharp tomorrow. We'll finalize our assignments in the morning."

I nodded, giving a yawn that wasn't faked, but Noah was already slipping into the empty seat next to me. "Here's the recording," she said, placing a tiny MP3 player into my hand.

I put in one of the earbuds but didn't turn it on. "If you wouldn't mind," I said, pushing aside thoughts of sleep, "before we turn in, I'd like to see what happened at the party where Ropte talked to Patrick. Were you there that night? Did he talk to you? It would be good to see any interaction you had with him, so I know what to expect."

"I was there." She tilted her head to think, her black curls gliding over her bare arm and shoulder. "I don't remember if we talked, though. There were so many people. But you're welcome to take a look." Her mind shield lowered and I slipped inside. "How does it work?" she asked.

I was acutely aware of everyone watching us. "Think back to that night. What happened? Just start talking. I'll let you know when I see it."

Noah concentrated. "I was wearing a green dress that night. I have some stuff that makes my skin even darker, and that's what I've been using for part of my disguise. I also sculpt my nose and cheekbones with some specialized clay, and I use contacts to make my eyes lighter, more golden. The night we saw Ropte, it was balmy for so early in April, and I was sweating before we . . ."

There, I had it. Memories spilled past me inside her sand stream, and I saw everything as she described it and more. Her getting ready, her worry about Patrick, the sleep dart she tucked into her purse. I saw the kiss she and Patrick had shared that evening before the party. Their first, which for Noah had been long in coming but for Patrick had been a surprise.

I searched further up the stream, not wanting to intrude on their moment, even if they'd never know I'd seen it. I found Noah walking into an extravagant reception hall, greeted by lavishly dressed people dripping with expensive jewelry and reeking of perfume purchased with money that might have saved dozens of children from starvation. At least in Noah's view.

I experienced her nodding and talking and eventually being asked to sing. How she and Mari and Keene stayed close to Patrick because everyone wanted to be near him, knowing he was both Unbounded and the son of the US president. I spotted a man wearing the Hunter symbol—a silhouette of a man holding a rifle—who scowled at Patrick but didn't threaten him. Hunters would sooner kill any Unbounded than talk to them, but for the most part they were mortal and weak when not in a group. Another man watched Patrick from a distance, a sword pendant hanging from the heavy necklace around his neck. The hilt of the three-inch sword was prominent, reminiscent of a cross, the logo of Unbounded worshippers. They believed we had come to save them. I hoped they were right.

Finally there was Ropte. I saw him approach Patrick, but Noah was too far away to hear what they said. Ropte noticed her, however, his eyes catching hers and holding, but Noah dismissed him as a horny politician who looked for sexual favors when his wife wasn't looking. Knowing that Noah was Unbounded, I thought it more likely that Ropte had simply been drawn by the beauty and confidence she exuded. The rest of the evening rolled to an end without incident.

"I got it," I said, leaving her mind. "Thank you, Noah. I think Ropte likes your singing. He noticed you."

Noah shrugged. "It's hard to keep track of everyone who notices me." This she said without guile, and I knew what she meant. Every Unbounded was the focus of mortal attention, and her status as a singing sensation would emphasize that.

Mari took Ritter's vacated seat next to me. "Guess it's my turn. I talked to Ropte that night. Maybe you'll find something I missed."

"I'm willing too," Patrick said.

I took Mari's hand, aware of Patrick reseating himself nearby, while Ritter and Cort crossed the room to study the device Cort had been working on when we'd come in. Keene remained sitting on the couch where he'd been throughout our meeting, but his eyes were locked on Mari.

I was glad to see that Mari's mental shield was stronger than before her stint guarding Patrick. Because of her trouble and Jace's initial shielding challenges, I'd developed a way to extend my own impenetrable barrier to protect those I was with—mostly from Delia Vesey. Delia had also been able to punch through shields well enough that she'd exercised a reign of terror over even those who were loyal to her.

I closed my eyes and concentrated, noting that Mari was far more careful with where she began her memories than Noah had been. They started only as she walked into the house where the party was being held, clinging to Patrick's arm and smiling like a proper politician's woman. She saw everyone around her as a color that coordinated with a number that was uniquely theirs. This number was how she could find a certain person and shift to them even when she hadn't previously visited the location.

Keene followed a step behind her, and she introduced him as her brother. He still looked foreign to Mari with his red-dyed hair and very short beard, but she knew every inch of his face. Indeed, her lips had traced every . . .

The thoughts changed directions with a jolt as Mari reminded herself to focus on the task at hand instead of on Keene. She had to remain alert to anyone who might want to hurt Patrick. Jace and Cort were outside as backup and Secret Service agents watched from nearby, but she was his first and best protection. She was ready at a second's notice to whisk Patrick into the gray and back to the safe house.

Multiple people came over to chat with the man who couldn't die, the face of the Unbounded. I felt Mari's impatience at their obsequiousness and also her fury at those who treated Patrick like a monster. The Unbounded issue was still dividing America, in spite of Patrick's efforts to show everyone we were more like mortals than unlike them. People either hated us or loved us, and that only played into the Emporium's plan. Weakening America made us that much easier to conquer.

"Good evening," came a commanding voice that brought

Mari away from her dark thoughts. She stared at the attractive man before her. He was in his fifties, at least, but his light brown hair was barely graying on the temples, and his suited figure could have been that of a much younger man. His eyes were a compelling hazel that glowed with intelligence and ambition. His color number was a dark shade of red. "I don't think we've been introduced," he added. "I'm David Ropte."

"Ah, yes, Senator Ropte," Patrick said. Knowing him as well as she did, Mari heard the reservation in his voice. *Must be a jerk,* she thought. Pity when he was so attractive.

"And you are, of course, Patrick Mann," Ropte said to Patrick, "which makes this your lovely fiancée." He smiled at Mari, and despite her own reservations, she felt her mouth curve in a real smile.

"Nice to meet you, Senator Ropte," she said.

"The pleasure is all mine, I assure you." Ropte gave her another killer smile, which to Mari's disgust made her stomach flop nervously. They talked about nothing for a few moments, and then he drew Patrick aside to talk privately. Mari let them move away but kept her eye on him. She felt relief as Keene circled around Patrick's other side and gave her a nod.

Mari scanned the crowd and I with her. If I hadn't been looking so closely, I might have missed it.

"Stop," I said to Mari. "Go back to where Ropte and Patrick move off and you're looking at the crowd."

Mari did as I requested, and there *he* was again, the man I'd glimpsed in her mind. No mistake. He was in disguise, but he moved just like Jace, and his eyes . . . it was like looking at an older version of my brother. What's more, after Ropte finished his brief conversation with Patrick, he went to join the man. Swallowing hard, I released my hold on Mari's mind and opened my eyes.

"What is it?" Mari asked, taking in my expression. The

entire room had fallen silent as everyone waited for what I might say.

"David Ropte is definitely in bed with the Emporium. I mean, if we had any doubts about what Bedřich told us."

"Why do you say that?" Cort asked.

"Because Stefan Carrington was also at that party."

"You mean Triad Carrington?" Mari asked, her eyes mirroring my shock. "The horrible man who thinks you're his biological daughter? *That* Stefan Carrington? He was there that night?"

I nodded. Yes, Stefan, who'd tried to win me over while his minions attempted to murder my family.

Keene shot out of his seat. "No way. I would have noticed. Or he'd have noticed me."

"With that red hair and beard and all that makeup?" I said. "Maybe not. Anyway, he seemed to be occupied with a group of men. Ropte went to join them in a room off the main reception area. They shut the door." I looked at Patrick. "You didn't see Ropte again after that?"

"No. I didn't see him, but I didn't seek him out, either. The man is kind of strong-willed, and talking with him is a little like getting hit over the head with a baseball bat. I kept wanting to agree with him. It was odd."

Keene paced the length of the room and back again. For the briefest of instants, I recalled Mari's feelings as she looked at Keene in her memories: the rush of emotion, the thoughts of tracing his face. I knew it was her recollection, her feelings, but everything I experienced became a part of me, and I couldn't help looking at Keene differently now. "If Carrington was there," he said, "you have to believe it was about Ropte. Maybe he was making sure the man would fall into line."

"Maybe they were plotting the Burklap murders and the other kidnappings," I countered. The shock of seeing Stefan was fading, and now that I thought about it, seeing him with Ropte wasn't surprising. Of course they would be working together.

Keene gave me a weary smile. "You're probably right."

Patrick reached out tentatively to me. "Better look at my memories to see if there's more."

I was already tiring because using my ability was like rigorous exercise, and I'd need rest to fully recuperate, but he was right to be careful, especially after this discovery. For all we knew, Stefan might be at Ropte's tomorrow. I pulled in a deep breath, absorbing what I could from the air. Strength seeped slowly through each of my pores.

Patrick's shield dropped, and I didn't even have to ask him to focus. Already, I could see them walking into the party. No glimpse of Stefan. Eventually, I saw Ropte approach, saw him draw Patrick away, his grip on Patrick's hand lingering as he gave a convincing argument for opposing term limits and for joining a "group" of Unbounded that had a better plan for the world. Patrick was right that the man had something more forceful about him than the customary Unbounded confidence.

"Wait, go back," I said to Patrick. "What did he say there?"

Patrick's memories rolled backward. "He said, 'Remember how you think you are doing America a favor by teaching them to support term limits? Well, I'm telling you that limits for Unbounded are always wrong. Remember, Unbounded are not like mortals. They are superior. The group I represent has better ideas than those currently being discussed in Congress, and we want you to join us.'" Patrick laughed and shook his body as if shaking off Ropte's influence. "That's all I can recall him saying. But I'd forgotten about it until now. It was weird. Seriously. For a moment, I wanted . . ." A rush of air left Patrick's lungs. "I'm not sure what I wanted. It was strange, though."

Looking in from the outside, Patrick's fleeting desire was clear. He'd wanted to hear more about Ropte's mysterious "group." Even after the year of the torture the Emporium had put him through, Patrick had looked around and wondered, for a brief second, if Ropte was right.

"Hypnosuggestion?" Ritter suggested. "They sometimes use repetition, and Ropte said 'remember' several times."

Patrick shook his head. "I don't think so. Unless charisma is an ability, I think for the most part, Ropte is like every other politician trying to convince people to back him, except maybe more well-preserved. Anyway, I'm resistant to hypnosuggestion and a lot of other coercion methods after my time in that Emporium prison."

I discovered nothing else of importance in Patrick's memories as he greeted or conversed with most of the two hundred people who had been at the event. Though I strained to get a glimpse of the room where Stefan had been, the one other time I managed to see the door, it was closed.

I sank back into the softness of the couch, arching a brow at Keene. "Is there anything you saw that I should know about?"

He shook his head. "I wish. I thought I was careful. However, you're welcome to look."

If Keene said he didn't see anything, I didn't believe I would get more from him. I'd trusted him with my life and would again. "We'll look at it tomorrow," I said. "I'm tired."

Ritter sauntered to the couch and offered me a hand. "Let's get some rest." With his other hand he picked up his duffel.

I didn't resist as he led me down a hallway, following Noah, who went on ahead after retrieving my gear from the living room where we'd first arrived. The spacious bedroom she led us to was decorated in bold hues of brown and black. A cast iron chandelier hung from a vaulted ceiling, and the lights were on low, creating a mysterious and intimate atmosphere. But it was the king-sized bed with its plush black quilt and numerous pillows that called my attention.

I let out a breath I didn't realize I'd been holding. "It's beautiful, Noah."

She chuckled. "It's one of my favorite rooms." She left us then, promising a warm breakfast in the morning, if we were interested.

The thick carpet beckoned for bare feet, and I kicked off my shoes, burying my toes into the softness. It wasn't the getaway Ritter and I had promised ourselves, but it was better than nothing. I'd taken three steps into the room when Ritter dropped his bag with a dangerous-sounding clunk and caught up to me, lifting me into his arms.

"Finally, we're alone."

"I'm tired," I protested.

He freed my hand from my duffel strap and let it fall to the floor. "I know. That's why I'm going to help you get ready for bed." His voice was serious, but the slightest smiled tugged at one side of his mouth.

"I'm worried about Stefan being here," I said. Actually, worry didn't begin to touch what I felt. Mind-numbingly terrified, however, came close.

He set me gently on my feet next to the bed and eased off my long leather jacket. "Because of Jace."

"What if Ropte knows? Delia might have told him the truth about me. With her dead, there's no reason for him not to tell Stefan that it's really Jace who's his son."

Ritter eased me onto the bed, his hands moving over my body to find my gun, a few knives, a vial of acid. Then he removed my boots, the ballistic knife, and my backup pistol. His hand went to the button on my jeans, opening it and peeling them off me. "Jace is a big boy. It's time he knew."

"Stefan loves his family."

"He loves to *use* his family. He won't persuade Jace."

"Then he won't let Jace go unless he's in pieces."

"He'll have to find him first."

Ritter stretched out next to me, his lips trailing over my neck and up to my lips. He kissed me long and deep until I moaned softly, my arms curling around him. An instant later, Ritter drew away from me, pulled off his own shirt, and tossed it onto the floor. Instead of coming back to me, he settled onto one of the pillows, yawning. His eyes closed.

"What?" I protested, now fully awake.

He cracked one eye. "You said you were tired." Amusement spilled from the words.

I laid a finger on his chest, dragging it downward in a lazy spiral. I felt him shiver slightly beneath my touch. "I'm not tired anymore."

With a laugh, he rolled on top of me, pinning my mouth beneath his. "Good." The shield over his thoughts dropped, beckoning me inside where his desire raged as strongly as my own. "Because I know a great way to relieve stress."

All thoughts of Jace and Stefan Carrington fled from my mind.

CHAPTER 8

WHEN WE WOKE THE NEXT MORNING, LIMBS ENTANGLED, NOT a single pillow remained on the bed. Back in San Diego we'd be getting up for our four a.m. workout, but here it was nearly seven o'clock, and I felt positively lazy.

Then I remembered Stefan Carrington and what it would mean to my brother when he knew the truth. Was Jace already in Idaho, eagerly waiting for the op to be over so we could resume our conversation? Probably.

The others were already in the dining room when we appeared. I was listening to Noah's new song and was positive it would become a worldwide hit. I was just as positive I'd never be able to mimic her convincingly. But when channeling, I could fight like Ritter, manipulate data at least halfway as well as Stella, and shift like Mari. So why not sing? Still, it seemed more difficult than folding space or knowing how to cut down an opponent. Noah could hit notes that I didn't know were possible for anyone. Certainly they weren't for me; I'd tried them while Ritter was in the shower, hoping his own humming blocked out my pitiful attempts.

Stealing a piece of bacon from the mound on Mari's plate, I cranked up the volume.

Ritter gave me a sympathetic smile that told me he guessed my uncertainty. He looked more than fine in the dark suit he wore that would help him fit into whatever situation I'd find myself in—just in case. Knowing he was my backup always gave me more confidence on these solitary ops. And it was at least partially a solitary endeavor, because while the others played decoy for the politicians, I'd be the only one exposed to immediate danger. My blood raced in anticipation. Suddenly, learning Noah's song didn't seem so difficult.

Of course, I couldn't rule out the possibility a sensing Unbounded might be present at Ropte's, so I'd need to shield any mental communication I shared with my companions. Channeling Patrick was included in that because while his shield was down, he'd be vulnerable to Emporium attack. I'd have to prevent that possibility, which meant more energy, and that's where Keene came in—if I needed him. Because I couldn't afford to be completely drained in case someone caught me in Ropte's office.

Ritter, Patrick, and Mari downed more breakfast than I had the will for, chatting casually as if today were like any other. Normally, I'd join them, but lingering thoughts of my brother and his biological father made me anxious. I excused myself and went with Noah to copy her disguise.

In Noah's private bathroom that was nearly as large as my guest room and twice as ornate, she sat in front of her lighted mirror and showed me where she added makeup and face sculpting clay. "One of my colleagues in Italy makes this for me," she said. "Honestly, if it were on the mortal market, she'd make billions. It doesn't crack or fade or rip, and it looks completely real."

I couldn't even tell where it blended into her skin. "Okay,

let me give it a try." I reached out to Patrick, who was expecting me, so his shield was down. *I'm here,* I told him. *You won't need to do anything. You won't even know I'm here. At the luncheon, I'll put a shield around you when I'm using your ability. I will only need to connect with you every thirty minutes to maintain my disguise.*

Patrick made a mental response, but I was already focusing on the mirror, urging the nanites in my body to recreate my face. I'd learned that changing as little as possible was easiest to maintain. So while Noah's figure was insanely thin at the waist and her rear end prominent, we'd decided to use a flowing yellow dress she owned to mask our bodily differences and concentrate instead on my face, hair, and coloring.

"No way," Noah murmured, staring at the mirror. "Just a little flatter on the nose. There you go. Wider bottom lip." She shook her head as I obliged. "I knew someone took Patrick's place for an entire year this way, but I have to admit that part of me didn't believe someone could really not tell the difference between the fake person and one they loved. I can see I was wrong."

I did look like Noah—or the disguise she wore in public. The tiny curls of my hair extended down my back, black but streaked with lighter shades of brown and dark blond. My skin was tinted a dark brown, and I made the nanites copy Noah's makeup as well: yellow and browns on my eyes, glossy lips, lashes that were triple my usual length. The dress exposed more cleavage than I was used to, but it masked my body well enough that with the changes in my physical features, I had become Noah. I felt exotic and different. Like someone who could woo crowds.

"People really wear things like this?" I asked of the borrowed dress, raising my arms in a flutter of silk.

Noah grinned. "Obviously, which is why I have it.

Sometimes I like to make a statement. I usually wear this with heels, but you'll have to do with flats so you'll be the same height." She arose from her chair and disappeared from the bathroom, returning shortly with a pair of bright yellow sandals. "These should do. Our feet don't look too different." They weren't, and I slipped them on with satisfaction.

"So, would you like to run through the song?" Noah asked.

Not in a hundred years. "Sure, but I'm not planning on singing."

Even her laugh was music. "That's what I always say, but you'll be surprised at the ways people have of convincing you."

Noah took my hand and led me back through her bedroom to an adjoining sitting room with a computer and an elaborate sound system. "I'll cue you in." She handed me a cordless microphone, started the music, and after a few bars said, "Ready, set, and here we go."

"You'll have to drop your shield."

"Oh, right."

I slid into her mind, releasing Patrick. The nanites should be able to hold their own against my Unbounded metabolism for more than the thirty minutes I'd quoted Patrick, but it paid to be careful. Once a day was usually enough to tell my body not to eject the nanites all together, but changing my face was more complicated. Not for the first time, I wished I could channel more than one other ability at a time.

I was late coming in on the first words, "I wasn't prepared for you," but with a bit of hurry, I caught up to the rest. "You were a friend and you had my love . . . But then you stole away my heart." I was amazed at the sound. Full and rich and so . . . not me. I felt the desire to keep on singing, to close my eyes and put my heart into it.

"Louder," Noah murmured. "Go with it."

So I did. Noah hummed along, and when I finished, she

smiled. "Very nice. A little more anguish on the chorus, okay? And at the end when she gives her heart, I like to make it more breathy."

Part of me wanted to try it from the top, but my more logical side, the part that wasn't channeling the singer, remembered I had other duties. "Okay," I said. "I'll do that. But do you think it'll pass?" I gnawed off a piece of fingernail as I waited for her response.

Noah put her hand on her hip. "Honey, you sound more like that recording I gave you than I do. I'm constantly changing things. In fact, I might just add that little ripple you put in the word heart. I like it."

"Good. But I'm still hoping you aren't a big talker, or I'll have to channel you for your mimicking ability."

"Just let me know through the earbuds. I'll be ready to drop my shield. Now let's do something with those nails."

When at last I was prepared, I went out to face the others. For some time, I'd been aware of their life forces gathering in the living room where we'd first arrived. As I neared it, Patrick emerged, his eyes brightening when he saw me. "Oh, good. They want to leave now, to get into place, but I wanted to take a moment to do this." He reached for me, pulling me close and pressing his lips against mine.

"I wouldn't let Ritter see you doing that," I said, pulling away from him. "Noah should be right behind me. She was just putting away a few things."

Patrick released me instantly, looking chagrined. "Sorry, Erin. Man, I can't believe it. You really do look like her. You *are* her. You sound like you, though." He shook his head with a little frown. "Erin, did you ever think that maybe mortals are right to be afraid of us?"

"All the time. Or not us, rather, but definitely the Emporium.

That's why we're in this fight. Otherwise, I'd be on a beach somewhere sipping margaritas with Ritter."

He laughed. "Right. Me too." There was a brief wistfulness in his expression, and I wondered if he ever regretted his decision to become the face of the Unbounded. He'd been kidnapped by the Emporium, almost murdered by a woman he loved, and targeted by newly recruited Hunters who hadn't been above killing innocent bystanders. I knew I wouldn't want the job, but Patrick was one of those people who believed sacrificing to help others was not only a worthy endeavor but his duty as a human being. I was happy for whatever joy he might find with Noah.

Ritter stared at me as I entered the living room. With our connection, he knew it was me, but the transformation was apparently difficult to believe. I grinned and sidled up to him, speaking in my best Noah impersonation, which wasn't very good, seeing as I wasn't channeling her, "Hey, handsome. Want a kiss?"

"Not a chance," he said, eyes glittering. "Have you seen how scary Erin is?"

I laughed and switched to my normal voice. "Okay, Your Deathliness, what's the rundown?" We'd discussed the details at the beginning of breakfast, but Ritter always gave us a summary before we began each op.

Ritter's gaze shifted to take in everyone. "Mari, Patrick, and Noah will stay at the safe house we'll be shifting to until it's time for the luncheon. The rest of us will check out the area to see how many Unbounded are present. When it's time for the party, Cort, Noah, and I will remain outside waiting for any signals and listening in on your mics. Erin, Mari, and Patrick will go inside, and at some point, Mari will connect Cort's bypass to Ropte's security system while Patrick and Erin distract everyone. Stella will then remotely connect to the bypass and disarm or loop the security cameras. From there, getting into Ropte's computer will be up to Erin. We don't know yet if she'll need to channel Patrick to locate the information inside Ropte's network, or if at some point she can hand it over to Stella. Depends on his setup."

"Do we have a layout yet?" I asked.

"Should be on your phone." Ritter looked up as Noah and Patrick entered the room. "Looks like we're all here. Let's go."

I visually scanned the buildings surrounding Ropte's townhouse. Secret Service was already out in force, and they seemed to be doing a thorough job, even knocking on doors and checking apartments that were facing Ropte's. *Poor Patrick,* I thought. If this was the drama that filled all his visits, no wonder he looked wistful.

While Cort and Ritter did their own setup, Keene and I went for a walk in the streets. The traffic in this area was nothing compared to the rest of DC, but it was still fairly robust. A cool wind played with the fabric of my dress.

I could feel Keene's nervousness from his surface thoughts, but I didn't share his concern. In the past, using his synergistic ability, he'd made me physically lighter, stopped me from falling, helped me transport plutonium, and caused an explosion that took the top off a building. It wasn't an exact science, and I suspected he'd only scratched the surface of what he could do. This should be easy.

"I just need to reach farther," I told him. "So maybe let me see if I can channel your power so I can direct it, instead of you trying to guess what I need."

He was silent for a second before saying, "You'd better stay linked with me, then. It's not easy to keep control. I'll need to show you how."

"All right, but I don't want anything fancy. I just hope it works the way I want it to." I reached out to him, only to be met by a mind barrier that had always been strong and was now significantly stronger since his Change. "Keene, you'll have to drop your shield. Don't worry. No Unbounded are near, except the ones at Ropte's, and they're too far away right now to be a concern." Sensing Unbounded could mask their life force from me completely, but I'd be looking out for any hint of interruption, and I'd seen nothing for concern. With Keene's help, I should be able to shield us in all directions but the one we were seeking, even from unseen attackers.

His shield dropped. "Might as well run through that night with Ropte first," he said. His sand stream was already showing memories of that night, and I had to concentrate to keep up.

"Nothing, sorry," I said minutes later when the scenes rolled to a stop. Except that he was beating himself up inside for not catching sight of Stefan. "He was careful, that's all," I told him.

"Stefan is always careful." Bitterness filled his voice. "Except where others' lives are concerned. He and my father have to be made to take responsibility for what they've done."

His comment revealed a door I had to open. "What about your father? How does he fit into the Emporium's plans?" Keene and Cort's biological father, Tihalt McIntyre, was the third member of the Emporium Triad. He shared Cort's ability to see how things worked on an atomic level and, from what I understood, was the core of the Emporium's scientific research and progress.

"My father . . ." Keene stopped walking and faced me. "It's because of my father's willingness to hurt others that the Emporium has the strength it does today. Without him, they wouldn't own so many patents or businesses. And they wouldn't have been able to increase their Unbounded numbers as they have. I used to think he turned a blind eye to what they did to mortals, but I realized before I left that he knew very well but didn't care. Because to him mortals are like animals or machines."

Including his own son—Keene didn't need to say it. I could see it in his mind.

For years, we'd been playing catch-up with the Emporium's nanites, inventions, and genetic manipulations. This was in large part because of the lines we refused to cross, lines the Emporium gleefully ran over and crushed into bits with their razor-edged heels. But the knowledge and advancements that allowed them to harm so many people, even their own Unbounded, came directly from Tihalt, the brains of the Triad.

"I'm sorry," I said to Keene, who had once again instinctively pulled his shield tightly around him, this time with me still inside. I tried not to look at his private thoughts, but despite my attempt, I caught a glimpse of a woman I knew was his mother. She'd been "taken care of" years ago by his father after she'd fallen ill. Keene once believed Tihalt had done it out of compassion, but some months back he'd recognized a stark truth: Tihalt hadn't wanted Keene to be around her or to be associated with her weakness.

Guiltily, I pulled my thoughts away from Keene's to say, "I think I understand at least a little. When I'd thought Stefan was my father, the weight of responsibility felt . . . impossibly heavy, like a black mark on my family that I could never erase or atone for." A burden Jace would now bear once he knew the truth.

"I am not my father, but I did a lot of things to please him." Keene hesitated before continuing. "I don't feel I have to atone for him, but I do for my own actions. I did a lot of things I'm not proud of."

My heart ached with him. "I'm not so sure you really had a choice about your assignments, but from this point, we can only go forward. There's nothing left for us in the past except—"

"The lessons we've learned. I know."

He smiled, and in that minute I loved him every bit as much as I loved my brothers, and maybe with something more—something that might not have stemmed from our personal relationship but from Mari's mind. If my feelings for Ritter hadn't burned so much stronger than anything I'd ever experienced, this emotion I felt for Keene might have been the death of any romantic relationship for me.

Pushing the oddness away, I reached out and began searching the life forces around us. I felt Keene's shield drop again. "Okay, we'll begin searching in that direction." I sent him a mental picture of the buildings to our right. "But let's walk over to that bench under that tree, okay? We'll look a bit more natural sitting."

We walked together in step, our minds connected. "You're cold," he commented.

"A bit." Noah's flowing dress didn't offer much protection against the spring breeze.

Keene shrugged off his blazer and put it around my shoulders, and I let him because I needed to concentrate.

"Thanks." Silently, I showed him the life forces inside the building I'd targeted. "A bunch of people inside, but there are so many that it's hard to tell them apart."

"Try taking in a bit of my energy."

I tentatively dipped into the power Keene held ready, and the life forces became so clear that I could see several buildings beyond the one we'd targeted. I wasn't sure if I was so much channeling him, or if I was showing him how to enhance my ability. It didn't really matter.

The first person I looked inside was a woman late to work, hurrying to get her kids ready for school. She wasn't a likely suspect, but I released a thought near her sand stream to see if it triggered any evil thoughts against Patrick or plans to crash Ropte's party.

Normally when I spoke mentally to others, my thoughts appeared in their heads as an obvious intrusion, not as a part of their own thought process. But carefully planting a small thought near a sand stream, allowing it to be sucked inside on its own, made the thought appear to come naturally, as if it originated inside the person. Only those who had ample experience with our abilities ever suspected meddling, and even then only a sensing Unbounded could confirm the interference.

The woman was exactly what she seemed. Methodically, I passed to a widower who was planning to wrangle a dinner invitation from the new widow he'd met at a senior citizen's event sponsored by the police department. Next was a college student crashing at his parents' townhouse, wondering how he'd tell them he was failing school. Mind after mind revealed similar stories. Nothing to cause alarm.

It helped that this was a wealthier area in DC, which meant the townhouses were larger and held fewer occupants. The real worry was the apartment building one street over that rose higher than the townhouses. But this checked out too, even when we walked around the block to get a closer look.

Hours later, and after several breaks to connect with Patrick to make sure my nanites behaved, I called Ritter on my phone. "Everything checks out. We just have the final location to survey, so we're heading there now." Which was code that meant no Unbounded or anyone plotting murder in the area, with only Ropte's residence left to probe.

"We're good on this end. Don't have too much fun."

I smiled at the laughter in his voice. He knew me too well.

My Unbounded genes had definitely kicked in, and I was eager to get inside and start saving those families. "Oh, I plan on it." I hung up and texted Mari to let them know we were on our way.

We backtracked a little so we could get a good glimpse of Ropte's house without being noticed as we waited for Mari and Patrick to arrive. I used Keene's ability again, dipping into the heady power with anticipation. "Easy," Keene cautioned.

I'd forgotten we were still linked—I must have made some kind of mental exclamation. "Hey, it's not every day I could blow up something with a thought."

"Please don't start today," he returned dryly.

I laughed and pushed hard on my own ability, reaching for Ropte's house. I'd already detected some Unbounded there earlier when we first arrived, but now it was time to do a more thorough search. Any guards Ropte was going to have there should be in place by now. "I'm seeing a ton of activity. Servants. Guests arriving already. I see the same three dimmer life forces we saw earlier."

"I'm guessing that's Ropte and an Emporium hit team. But there should be at least one other team. Triad members never go anywhere without a backup."

"Oh, there they are," I said. "In back of the house. I think they're keeping hidden."

"Nothing more?"

"Not unless they have sensing Unbounded." With even more care, I began searching the townhouse again, planting thoughts and studying minds. So far, no one plotted anything more nefarious than some white lies and a couple of backroom deals that had nothing to do with Patrick or Unbounded. My anticipation increased. At some point we were going in, regardless of whether or not I caught a glimpse of anything unusual.

"Wait," I said. "I may have found something." I showed

him a dark spot in one of the rooms off the main areas in Ropte's townhouse. "It seems to move around." I released my grip on Keene's energy and it vanished. When I used his power again to enhance my ability, it reappeared.

"Interesting," Keene said. "What do you think it might be?"

"Maybe a sensing Unbounded who's hiding his life force?" I was excited that we could spot it at all. If it was a sensing Unbounded, being able to find him would be a great advantage.

"It might be something else entirely."

"What?"

Keene shook his head. "I don't know. We just need to be prepared for anything. So are you satisfied yet? I think that's Mari and Patrick pulling up."

I withdrew from his mind and handed him back his blazer. "Okay, I'm out. But I may need to examine that shadow again later."

My mic was once again hidden in my necklace, while Keene had his in a tie pin. Each of our single earbuds was wireless and all but invisible, even to those who were looking for such a thing. Both earbuds and mics were specifically designed to make it through security. "Testing," I said, after turning on my mic.

"Gotcha." Keene's reply was echoed by each of the others in turn.

"There are five Unbounded inside, and possibly a sixth," I reported. "Nothing else for alarm."

Ahead of us, Mari was emerging from a car driven by Secret Service. She and Patrick were flanked by agents. "Where are you?" Her voice blasted through my earbud, and as we moved to meet her, I surreptitiously turned down the volume on the amplifier Cort had disguised as a watch. The device also controlled which mics I could hear and who I broadcasted to, though for the most part we'd all remain connected together.

"Coming up behind you," Keene said. "Tell your friends not to shoot us."

Mari laughed and turned in our direction, waving vigorously in spite of the lone news reporter who was filming from beside a van across the street. Her red hair gleamed in the sunlight. "Oh, there's my brother and my friend. They'll be joining us."

I could feel Ritter's presence grow stronger as we approached the house. Without reaching out to him mentally, I wouldn't be able to tell his exact location, but feeling him close soothed my concern about the black shadow and evened out my anticipation. Training kicked in.

Time to step into the fire. We had families to rescue.

CHAPTER 9

MARI PUT HER ARM THROUGH MINE AS WE WENT THROUGH THE small gate and up to the townhouse. "I'm glad you could make it," she said for show. "These events are so much more fun when you come with me."

"Oh, I'm delighted to spend more time with you," I said, mimicking Noah. "Especially when you have these hunks here to accompany us." I winked at one of the Secret Service agents, who stoically looked away, but not before a slight flush worked its way up his neck. Noah had told me that she periodically teased the agents, but I had no idea it would be this fun. "I swear, one of these days I'm just going to squeeze them all over. They're that yummy."

Seeing the man's flush deepen, I laughed for real. Besides being with Ritter, I couldn't remember when I'd had any fun that wasn't related to battling the Emporium. When all this was over, I needed to find a safer hobby.

If it would ever be over.

I shrugged off the thought and glided up the cobble-stone walkway with Mari and Patrick. Keene trailed behind.

Flowerbeds looped decoratively across the small front yard, and a rare tree close to the house shaded half the area. Up close, the place didn't look much different from any of the other expensive townhouses in the area. The color of the brick, like the cobblestone, was a pale salmon that did nothing to inspire. The flurry of arched windows were beautiful, however, and had shutters on each side that were a darker color than the brick. Several tiny balconies on the third floor jutted out above the arched windows, brushing the top of the tree on the one side. The windows seemed like eyes, and the walkway narrowed as it reached the double doors, as if pushing us together, getting ready to swallow. I knew the townhouse had sold for over three million two years earlier, but you couldn't have paid me that much to live in it.

Two liveried servants opened the door, and we entered, leaving our Secret Service escort outside. I knew they had more agents in the house already, and that it had been declared safe, but I felt uneasy standing in the entry and waiting our turn to let Secret Service agents pass metal-detecting wands over our bodies.

Even inside the house, I had no sense of additional Unbounded except those five dim life forces, three of which were in the spacious room at the back of the townhouse, the other two still outside. There was also no sign of the shadow, and I was tempted to channel Keene again to find it, but I decided it was better to stay alert and take in my surroundings.

We passed an adjoining hallway that I knew led to an office where I hoped to find access to Ropte's files. The hallway was deserted for now, but plainly visible to those who were passing. I'd need to be careful when I returned.

The main hallway led to a large reception room that was alive with music, light, and conversation. Several sets of couches, already filled with people, lined the walls of the reception room. Huge windows filled one entire wall, revealing an attractive garden patio in the back yard where a tall water fountain dominated the scene. In front of the fountain, a live band had set up and was playing music. Round tables circled the fountain under a flowing canopy that warded off the sun. Almost comically, large upright heaters blasted from each of the corners of the outside dining area, ensuring that no guest would suffer from the light breeze.

I did a brief count as we entered the room and found about a hundred life forces here and outside, with more arriving steadily. A fourth of those already present seemed to be catering personnel or household employees. Without trying, my eyes landed on Ropte. He was everything I'd seen in the pictures and in Noah's head: handsome, virile, compelling. Most definitely Unbounded. He wore an expensive suit like most of the men present, his a pale tan, with a vibrant blue dress shirt and a plaid tie in shades of yellow and blue. The two Unbounded soldiers in the room were dressed similarly, one standing alone near the entrance and the other at the back door talking to an older lady sporting clumpy sapphire jewelry. I didn't need any kind of ability to know they were heavily armed. I didn't recognize them, though, from the files we had on the Emporium.

I reached out to Ritter, to send him mental pictures of the Unbounded. He had his mental shield up, but because of our connection, I could push at it in such a way that he recognized it was me. *Do you know these guys?* I asked when he let me in.

No. Does Keene?

I released Mari's arm and fell back to walk with Keene. "Know them?" I asked softly. He shook his head.

I relayed the information to Ritter and then refocused on the room. Ropte had greeted the people who had entered the room in front of us and was moving in our direction, his hazel eyes lighter in person but just as drilling. "Ah, Patrick, I'm so glad you came to my little impromptu get-together. I very much enjoyed our conversation last week."

"I'm happy to come," Patrick replied, shaking Ropte's hand. It was almost amusing, this dance they performed, since the entire reason for this event was for Ropte to have a chance to seduce Patrick to his cause. The fact that so many important senators and other politicians had dropped everything to please Ropte proved his powerful status in Congress. No way had he been able to stay off our radar without billions of dollars being spent on his behalf.

I still didn't know what role David Ropte filled in the Triad. Delia's powers had been legendary, and while Stefan was the enforcer and charismatic leader, she had wielded as much control behind the scenes. Or more. Whatever Ropte's role, I couldn't rule out the fact that Ropte might be a sensing Unbounded, despite what Bedřich claimed. Abilities always ran in families, and it was common knowledge that Delia had been trying to bring back more of the rare talents. Ropte might be every bit as powerful as Delia had been. Or stronger. Coupled with his magnetism, there might be no limits.

Maybe Ropte would become the spokesman for the Emporium, the charismatic leader who would take them into the next phase. Did that mean he was Stefan's puppet? If so, Ropte's unknown qualities only made Stefan more dangerous.

Ropte turned to Mari, complimenting her on how beautiful she looked and asking about wedding dates. Then he turned those drilling eyes on me, and I was glad he couldn't know of our real reason for being here. "Ah, Felicia West, so good to see you again. I hope you will honor us today with a song as you did last week." He bent over, drawing my hand to his mouth and kissing it.

"Oh, I don't think so," I said. "I'm sure you have ample entertainment." He hadn't released my hand, but I gestured to the band through the window, using the motion to free my hand from his.

His chuckle send chills crawling down my spine. "Ah, but there is no one like Felicia West."

"We'll see," I said lightly.

He shifted his attention back to Patrick. More people had entered behind us, but Ropte made no move to greet them. Of course, Ropte wouldn't be swayed from Patrick's side, not when this entire expensive affair had been thrown together because of him. As I watched, a beautiful, forty-something blonde intercepted the newcomers, exclaiming over them and steering them toward the door leading to the patio.

She had to be Ropte's wife—his much younger wife. Ropte's official age was fifty-six, which seemed to be more or less physically accurate. That would make him close to thirteen hundred years old. More than old enough to have learned many of Delia's tricks.

I angled away, studying Ropte as he animatedly spoke to Patrick. His magnetism was apparent, but not more so than other Unbounded men I'd met. No, his talent didn't lean in that direction. Tentatively, I reached out to him, careful to turn to address Keene so that if Ropte felt something, he wouldn't suspect me. I kept my own shield tight, reinforcing it for a potential onslaught.

Ropte's conversation continued without faltering, and he didn't start looking around, so that signaled he wasn't a sensing Unbounded. Or at least not a strong one, because I could always tell immediately when someone was trying to breach my shields. Yet Ropte's barrier was a solid black wall, every bit as strong as the best I'd seen. Even if I could break inside, it'd take me a while.

Could he have some variation of the sensing ability? I couldn't even begin to guess until I knew his lineage. Leaving Ropte for the time being, I wandered around the room, looking inside minds to learn what I could about the players. Most were fans of Ropte, their thoughts giving me glimpses of backroom deals and favors, but there were a few who regarded him with apprehension. Some of these worried about Patrick and drifted over to Patrick and Ropte, avoiding Mrs. Ropte and the Unbounded bodyguards when they tried to head them off, only to be expertly dismissed by Ropte minutes later.

The employees were particularly useful, showing me more about the layout and what I could expect when sneaking about the house. Most importantly, I learned about a second office upstairs where Ropte spent most of his time when he was home. That would be my first target once Mari planted Cort's device.

I'd barely finished surveying all the people in the reception room and was heading to the patio to get those few I'd missed, when Ropte, Patrick, and Mari approached me. With them was a woman with an enormous gray bun that was either fake or she possessed an unreal amount of hair.

"Felicia," Ropte said, "I'd like you to meet Senator Beatrice Shumway. She's from Indiana."

"So pleased to meet you," Beatrice said without releasing her possessive hold on Ropte.

I nodded at her. "Pleased to meet you too."

"The senator has a request," Ropte added.

"Oh, yes." Beatrice gave him a look of profound gratitude. "My grandniece is visiting me, and she's a huge fan of yours. She's out on the patio talking to the band members right now, but she spied you earlier and was so excited she became tongue-tied when I suggested we introduce ourselves.

She'd really love a chance to hear you sing." Beatrice's voice dropped. "I wouldn't ask, dear, except that she just got over a most dreadful bout of skin cancer, you know, and it would really brighten her day."

Noah had it right. How could I possibly refuse to sing for a young woman who had survived cancer?

"I'm sure Felicia would love to sing," Mari said, fiddling with the bracelet on her wrist. I guessed she hoped the performance would mean that she'd have a chance to plant the device Cort had hidden in the large bangle.

"Sure," I said. "I guess so." I would rather fight Ropte's Unbounded guards.

Ropte linked his free arm with mine. "Come along then. Let's get this started before the caterers announce lunch."

Beatrice snagged a glass of wine off a tray carried by a passing server. "Thank you so much, dear." She glugged the entire glass down with obvious enjoyment.

As we moved toward the patio, I saw Ropte's wife staring with open dislike at the older woman, though she had to be ten years older than Ropte's physical age. I wondered if Ropte's wife had any idea of his nature. I guessed not because if she had, she would certainly have more to worry about than Beatrice Shumway.

Outside, the caterers, who had been coming and going through another door that led to the kitchen, looked close to being ready. Some of the guests were already seated at tables, six to each small round table. Ropte strode over to talk to the band, who were delighted to have the opportunity to play for the famous Felicia West.

"Noah," I whispered, hoping she'd heard at least some of the conversation through our mics.

"Tell them it's in E flat," Noah said in my earbud.

"Okay."

I reached out to Patrick, touching his arm and nodding slightly so he'd let me channel his ability to make sure my body continued allowing the nanites to do their thing during the performance. With so many eyes on me, it wouldn't do to even partially morph back into myself.

When I had finished with Patrick, I talked to the band members, spouting stuff about chords and melody and anything else Noah threw at me. I didn't know how well they'd follow my directions, but she seemed confident.

I also noticed the other two Unbounded soldiers, who currently stood on the perimeter of the garden area, but I didn't recognize them. Keene had seen them before, but he wasn't concerned. "Those two are loyal to a fault," he murmured. "Good fighters but not great."

Ropte took up a microphone and announced my song, which brought the rest of the guests out on the patio, where they took seats at the remaining tables or stood where they could better see the band.

The music began, and this time I didn't need Noah's cue. "I wasn't prepared for you. You were a friend and you had my love . . . But then you stole away my heart." The words rang out bold and true. By the time I reached the chorus, there wasn't a single person talking.

A strange euphoria overtook me. The music, the crowd, the words. I could understand why Noah sang, why she'd never stop. She hadn't quite been telling the truth about what it did for her to be in front of a crowd. The people were riveted, awestruck. Tears fell as they perceived the agony of love that could not be, and their minds silently pleaded for more. Even the caterers and waitstaff stopped what they were doing and stared. The Secret Service agents forgot to scan the crowd. Guests who had chosen to sit on the far side of the fountain left their places and joined the others so they could see me.

My own ability drank in their emotions, turning it back again into the music. It was like a drug-induced hallucination that we all shared.

I never wanted to stop singing. I wanted to raise my voice and suck out all the emotions in the world and fill my music with them. But the end had to come. "I wasn't prepared for you. You were a friend and you had my love . . . but then I *gave* to you my heart." I stretched out the last note and whispered a refrain until the music faded away.

The crowd burst into clapping and cheers, which shook me from whatever abyss I'd fallen into. "Thank you very much," I said and stepped down from the stage, releasing Noah with a silent thank-you. As I did, the yearning to sing, to perform, vanished and I was myself again.

Good riddance, I thought. I'd never experienced an ability quite like Noah's, but I suspected it was my own ability to sense others' emotions that intensified it for me. *I should have shielded my mind from them.*

Too late now. At least I no longer wanted to perform. That was good.

Ropte took my hand. "That was incredible, my dear." I could see emotion in his eyes, still lingering from the song.

Next to him, Beatrice was wiping tears from her face. Her thoughts screamed at me as she thought about a man she'd once turned down to pursue her career. He'd wanted a family, and she couldn't stop for that, not yet. In the end, she'd never stopped. She'd never married or had children.

I pulled gently from Ropte's grasp. "I'll need to refresh myself. Could you direct me to the ladies' room?"

"Sure." He signaled his wife, who was standing only feet away. "Darling, could you have someone show her to the restroom?"

"I'll take you myself," Mrs. Ropte said. "Come with me."

I followed her through the crowd of people, who still stared at me as if they didn't know how to react. All of them wanted more.

"That was sure beautiful." Mrs. Ropte led me back into the reception room that was empty now of everyone but Mari, who nodded and smiled as she passed us on her way to the patio. I noticed Mari's bracelet was still in place, but presumably the device Cort had stored inside it was somewhere else doing its job.

"Thank you," I said.

She brought me to a door off the reception room, pausing before directing me inside. She seemed to want to say something, but thought better of it and simply smiled. "Please come out and have a seat when you're ready. They'll begin serving now."

"I'm looking forward to it." I opened the door, pitying her for the deception Ropte had enacted on her. In her mind, I saw that she suspected he'd strayed, but she stayed with him not only because she loved him madly but to save face in front of her rich, influential friends.

The bathroom had a series of stalls, some of which were occupied, and I had to wait for three minutes until the place cleared. I welcomed the delay and took the opportunity to absorb, regaining some of my strength, listening to the hum of conversation from my companions' mics as they mingled with the other guests on the patio.

"Ready phase two," I said quietly into my mic when I was alone.

"Great job on the song," Cort complimented.

"Thanks. What does Stella say?"

"Cameras on the upper floor are activated, but she's making

a loop. I'm not sure how Mari did it, but she must have found a router, because we have total control over the security and the network. If Ropte's computer were on, she wouldn't need anything more."

"So, I just need to turn it on."

"That's right. It's best-case scenario."

I'd have to thank Mari later. "Let me know when it's safe to go up."

"Will do."

I left the bathroom. Mrs. Ropte thankfully wasn't waiting for me, and the reception room was still empty, so I retraced our earlier steps to the entry hallway. There were no life forces in the immediate vicinity, but Secret Service agents and a butler still manned the front door. I'd have to find another way up to Ropte's office. I'd seen the front stairs when we'd entered, but I seemed to remember another staircase somewhere. Digging into the little yellow purse attached to my wrist with a thin strap, I pulled out my phone.

Ah, yes. The stairway was through one of the other doors leading from the reception room. I hurried across the space and stepped inside. Sure enough, at the end of a short corridor, past several doors, a narrow staircase led upward.

"We're a go," Cort said in my ear. "But Stella says his system is complicated. You have only ten minutes until the cameras go through their automatic reboot. Then it'll take her a few minutes to get control again. So hurry."

"I'm on it. Switching off the feed from the others' mics now." I needed all my concentration on getting to Ropte's office, and hearing that buzz on the patio was distracting.

The door from the reception room had scarcely closed behind me when the glow of a life force appeared, seemingly out of nowhere. I had no time to flee before Mrs. Ropte appeared on the landing.

"Ms. West?" she asked, her severely arched brows looking more pronounced. "May I help you?"

How had she appeared so quickly? I scrambled for an answer, while my mind searched the area. I saw nothing that could have caused the even temporary vanishing of her life force, but something wasn't right. Maybe Mrs. Ropte wasn't all that she seemed.

"Sorry, Mrs. Ropte," I said. "I guess I got turned around."

She smiled, though disbelief rolled off her unprotected mind in a wave. She thought I was snooping. "Well, that happens. Come along. I'll show you to your table." She turned swiftly to the door, her thoughts leaving my transgression and going to her husband and how she could make sure "that ancient slut Beatrice" didn't sit with him.

Going with her wasn't an option, of course. Not with Cort's ten minute time limit ticking over me. If I went outside, there was no telling when I'd get away or if there would be another chance.

Slipping a small pen from my purse, I flipped off the cap and closed the steps between us before plunging a dart into her neck. She sucked in a breath of air, her eyes turning to me briefly in panic before they rolled upward and closed. I caught her as she fell and dragged her to a door in the hallway. It seemed to be some sort of small privacy room, holding only two couches along facing walls. An arched window gave the narrow space light.

Gently, I laid her on one of the couches and plunged into the lake of her unconscious mind in search of the bubble containing any memory of her seeing me in this area of the house. She should wake in fifteen minutes and wonder about the blackout she'd experienced. I hoped to be back with the others before then.

"Everything okay?" Cort asked in my ear.

"Yeah, she's out."

I was about to rise when a female voice from behind startled me.

"What happened?"

I hadn't felt any life force approaching the open doorway, and the minute I turned, I knew why.

CHAPTER 10

ONLY MY TRAINING PREVENTED ME FROM SAYING HER NAME aloud and blowing my cover. Noah—or Felicia West, rather—wouldn't know the identity of the Unbounded who stood in the doorway without an apparent life force.

Jeane Baker was a null, and right now her ability was in full force—around her person at least, because I could still "see" the life forces outside on the patio. Her ability explained why I hadn't felt Mrs. Ropte before she suddenly appeared; the woman must have been close enough to Jeane that she'd also been hidden from me.

Jeane wasn't her real name, but one she'd sometimes used in a former life as a film star until Delia Vesey had taken her, used her, and finally locked her away for decades. We'd rescued Jeane, only for her to betray us once I'd killed Delia and given Jeane her revenge.

Normally, it took little effort for a null to prevent any Unbounded—or a group of them—from using an ability, but I'd learned how to shield myself and others against Jeane's nulling. But obviously, she'd made some strides since our past three months because she could hide her life force from me, if not null my ability completely. There was no doubt in my mind that she was the black spot Keene and I had detected earlier.

I strengthened my shield, pushing out at her in case she tried to target me with her ability.

"I asked you a question," Jeane said sharply. "What happened to Michelle?"

"I don't know." I feigned innocence, hoping my shock would be misconstrued as concern for Mrs. Ropte. "She just sort of fainted. I managed to get her in here." The explanation would work as long as Jeane hadn't seen me with the dart.

Jeane came forward, her movements sultry grace. Her long hair was still its natural dark brown and her eyes that bright blue. False eyelashes made her eyes pop, and the flesh-colored mole, now painted black, screamed sex appeal. She moved with the confidence of an Unbounded, but my senses couldn't verify that fact. If I hadn't met her before, I wouldn't have been able to tell anything about her—except that she apparently had no life force, and that usually only happened in the dead.

Jeane pushed me out of the way and sat next to Mrs. Ropte on the edge of the couch. She took a limp hand and patted it. "Michelle!" Next, she scooted along the edge and lightly slapped Mrs. Ropte's cheeks. There was no reaction.

Jeane being here changed everything. Everything, because it meant an association with Ropte, and I couldn't allow her to remain on the Emporium's side in their fight against us. Not when I had another choice.

I sank my second dart for the day into her neck—followed by two more. Even these three darts would only keep her unconscious for fifteen minutes; they didn't contain much sedative when compared with the Unbounded metabolism. I gave her a fourth dose just to be sure. I could see her life force now, but it was much dimmer than even in an Unbounded with a strong mind shield. Interesting that she could still partially use her ability while unconscious. In our cell, most of the older Unbounded were learning to maintain a block when asleep, but Ritter, Dimitri, and I were the only ones to be mostly successful.

I didn't attempt to take Jeane's memory. Her unconscious mind showed only a frozen lake, one that wouldn't allow tampering. It was probably why she'd hated Delia so much— Delia hadn't been able to take away the memories of the awful things she'd forced Jeane to experience over the years.

I left Jeane sprawled over Mrs. Ropte's legs and ran from the room, closing the door behind me. With a little luck, they wouldn't be found before I finished my job.

"You've only got six minutes." Ritter's voice instead of Cort's came through my earbud. "Do we need to wait for the next opportunity?" His voice was controlled, but I knew he'd felt my shock at seeing Jeane. Without knowing her identity, he wouldn't be able to understand the reaction.

"No, both women are taken care of. I'm at the top of the stairs. There are no life forces here." Unless there were more like Jeane or any sensing Unbounded, but I wasn't going to bring any of that up yet. If Ritter knew Jeane was here, he might see her as the first priority. Maybe he'd be right because Jeane was a lot more important to the overall battle than a few mortal lives, but I knew what it was like to have the people I loved in danger, and I wasn't abandoning those families. "I'm coming up on the door now."

In fact, things went almost too smoothly as I reached Ropte's office, picked the lock, and slid inside.

"Four minutes," Cort said.

Plenty of time to make sure the room was empty, sprint to

the laptop on the desk, and open its lid. The display jumped to life, and as the password screen popped up, asterisks were already appearing as Stella remotely worked on hacking the code.

"You're good to leave," Cort confirmed.

I angled the lid down until it was only an inch from shutting. Ropte might wonder about the change in position, but there was nothing we could do about that. For now, my biggest concern was what to do with Jeane. Leaving her here would expose Noah, and I didn't want to do that. It would also alert Ropte, since Jeane was obviously in alliance with him. Time to see what Ritter thought.

"Uh, we have a slight problem," I said.

"Someone coming?" It was Ritter again.

"The second woman—it was Jeane."

Half a heartbeat delay. "We need her."

I was going down the stairs now, which I hoped meant I was out of view of the cameras.

"How should I get her out?" I imagined dumping Jeane into a bin somewhere and rolling her out past the Secret Service, but I didn't think they'd be that lax.

There was a pause as Ritter consulted with Cort. Then, "How about channeling Mari's ability to shift her out?" Ritter asked.

"It took her months and Keene's help to get to that point, and I don't think I have the time to learn now. Let's be honest, I'd probably just end up a few feet down the hall." Even with an ability you had to train to be any good.

Ritter was silent again for several seconds. "Mari can't leave Patrick now. He's at too great of a risk. You'll have to walk her out."

"This is Jeane we're talking about. She'll make a scene." I reached the room where I'd left the women and dragged the door open, letting out a breath in relief to see they were still there.

"If she didn't actually see you give her the drug," Ritter said. "Maybe you can convince her someone else came in. That you need to get her out of the house because Renegades are on the premises."

"I don't think we covered acting in training."

"Noah can help," Cort said. "She's done all sorts of musical theater."

Seriously, this was what we were down to?

"I still have my pistol." I touched the plastic one I'd strapped on my thigh. Made on our 3D printer, it wouldn't be good for more than a couple shots, even with the improvements Cort had made on the commercially available models. "She won't know it's plastic." Not to mention that threatening to use it was way more my style.

"She'll know you can't carry a seemingly dead body out of Ropte's townhouse. It'd be worth being shot to get away from you."

Ritter had a point. A bullet would hurt, but it wasn't permanent. "Okay," I said. "But I need a way to convince her that the Renegades have crashed this party."

"Keene can help. He's tracking your locator and is nearly at your position. Better turn back on the feed from his mic."

I switched on his feed. "Keene, aren't you supposed to be watching Patrick and Ropte?"

"Patrick and Mari have Ropte occupied. There wasn't room for me at their table, so I shouldn't be missed for a few minutes."

I felt relief knowing Keene could help, although if Jeane recognized him, any chance we had of deceiving her would be over. But his disguise had been good enough to keep him under Emporium radar thus far, and she didn't know him well.

"There's no second exit in the front," Ritter said. "So you'll have to pass the Secret Service in the entry. We'll have a car outside when you're ready. Cort's heading to it now. But there are three more Secret Service teams that can see the front door, so you have to get her to the car before she suspects anything."

"Okay." Now that my course was set, my mind churned with ideas.

"I'm coming in," Keene said. "Don't shoot."

I was standing in front of the door, so I moved aside. "First, we need to get Mrs. Ropte out of sight. I'll tell Jeane that Ropte already evacuated his wife and that he asked you to help me get her to a car out front."

Keene looked doubtful. "What if it doesn't work?"

"I'll drop my disguise and tell her we'll cut her in three if she doesn't come with us. I can always disable the agents by the door." I'd feel bad flashing light in their minds, but I would do it.

Keene chuckled. "If it wouldn't alert Ropte to something going on, I'd almost want her to resist." He picked up Michelle Ropte and strode out the door.

By the time he returned, I'd repositioned Jeane so she was sitting on the couch. I had a syringe full of adrenaline in my hand. "She'll take a minute to become fully cognizant. Wait out there until you hear me talk to her and then come in and tell us the car is here."

He nodded, pausing for a second to gaze down on Jeane's lovely face. "Hard to believe that she's so cold inside. She has a lot to make up for."

I knew he was thinking about the innocent people killed in Morocco. "She won't get away this time." I sat next to her and jabbed the adrenaline into her thigh, the needle slipping easily past the white dress pants she wore. I capped the needle and put the spent syringe back in the sheath on my leg.

Sixty seconds later, Jeane stirred. "Oh, thank heavens!"

Linked with Noah and showing her the scene as it unfolded, I plucked the words from Noah's head as she thought them. "Senator Ropte said he's sent a car for us, but I was so afraid those awful people had done something permanent to you!"

Jeane's eyes narrowed. "What are you talking about? What did you do to me?"

"Me? Oh, no! It wasn't me. It was some people dressed all in black—a blonde with a gun, and a big guy that moved like the wind. Never seen the like! Ropte said they were Renegades or something." I gave a little sniff, which I thought might be over the top, but Noah advised it, and Jeane seemed to drink it in. "Ropte came and got his wife out of here. He asked me to stay with you until he sends my friend back to tell us a car is ready."

"You?" Jeane asked.

I lifted the gun from the couch on the side opposite her. "He gave me this." She shouldn't be able to tell the pistol was plastic unless she held it, and I wasn't about to allow that. "He said to shoot anyone who came in."

Jeane took a deep breath. "Okay, then. Where is he? Maybe I should call Ropte."

We heard running footsteps, and Jeane bounced to her feet. I followed, pointing the gun at the door. Keene's head peeked inside, followed by his entire body. "The car's coming. Come on! Ropte got his wife and my sister and Patrick. We have to hurry. Those Renegades went outside to the back yard, and we have to go before they come back in. If we can make it to the front door, the Secret Service will watch our backs. Patrick let them know we'll be coming."

I wished we really had asked Patrick to let them know to expect us.

Keene hurried out of the room, with Jeane on his tail. I followed quickly.

"No, that room is huge and we don't want to be in the open too long," Jeane said as Keene reached to open the door to the reception area. "There's another way to the foyer."

I tried to remember all the floor plans, but I didn't have Ritter's ability to remember layouts, and I hesitated. If Jeane had caught on to us, she might be leading us into some sort of trap, but if she were right, I'd much rather not risk any of the guests seeing us flee.

Keene nodded. "Show us! Hurry, before they come back for you. Ropte said I shouldn't let that happen."

Jeane opened another door and sprinted down a short hallway. At the end, it intersected another hallway that ran in both directions. She turned to the right, and at the end was another intersection leading to the entryway. She moved more cautiously now, though I could tell there were no life forces in the rooms we passed.

Finally, we reached the entryway. A servant passed to our right and paused briefly, but after seeing Jeane, she went on. Keene hurried toward the Secret Service agents, nodding at them and speaking under his breath. I caught the words *Patrick* and *car*, and from their minds I saw an image of Keene retrieving something from Patrick's vehicle. I had to laugh at the genius.

Jeane was passing them now, unable to resist flashing them one of the smiles that had seduced a generation of moviegoers. They stared and barely noticed me as I passed them, my gun hidden in the folds of my dress.

"I don't see a car." Jeane looked around frantically.

"There!" I said, pointing. It was a red sports car, nothing like the black sedan I'd expected, and I wondered where Cort had obtained it. I could see him inside, wearing a black wig with a neat ponytail.

Keene ripped opened the door and helped Jeane inside. He

gestured to me, but I shook my head. "You stay with her. I'll make sure Mari and Patrick get out."

He hesitated, and I knew he'd planned to hand me into the car and return inside. But I wasn't going to leave. If Ropte somehow discovered what we'd done, Patrick and Mari would be in danger, and since I could channel Ritter or Noah or Keene himself, Keene knew as well as I did that I was the better choice to stay behind.

"Go," he said. "Take care of her." He meant Mari.

"Mari can take care of herself." I furtively handed him the gun that I wouldn't be able to put back in my sheath under my dress before passing security. Their gazes burned into my back suspiciously even now, and agents on the rooftops probably had me in their sights. Keene grinned and swung himself into the car.

"Hurry and get in," Jeane screeched at me.

I couldn't resist leaning over, sticking my head into the car, and letting my own face seep partially through Noah's features. "Sorry, Jeane, I have to go see Senator Ropte to make sure he doesn't miss you."

"Erin!" she breathed. "No! You can't! You don't know what this means." She dived for the opposite door, but both Cort and Keene turned weapons on her. Her eyes went to mine again. "Erin, please."

In answer, I replaced Noah's features and slammed the door. Cort squealed away. I turned around and walked back to the Secret Service agents, who dutifully scanned me and searched my tiny bag, even though I'd been in full view all the time I'd been outside.

"Thank you," I said.

As I sauntered back through the reception room, I spotted Michelle Ropte coming out from the door that led to the back stairs. She was walking unsteadily, and I hurried toward her.

"Are you all right?" I asked.

"I'm just a little dizzy. I must have blacked out." She put her hand to her head and leaned heavily on me.

"Do you need a doctor?"

"No, just a glass of water."

By the time I found a servant to fetch water for Mrs. Ropte, the luncheon was well underway. Ropte barely looked over when his wife slipped into her place next to him or when I found my spot at a table nearby. Mari smiled at me, and I nodded slightly. Patrick's surface feelings shouted his annoyance at Ropte, who leaned toward him like a smiling shark, but Patrick's face was remarkably pleasant.

Minutes ticked by, taking the edge off my anxiety—or maybe it was the excellent food. Either way, no one with guns showed up, and Ropte seemed content. I studied his features under the guise of drinking the sparkling wine in my glass, wondering how a man who looked so normal, so handsome, could have been responsible for the gruesome slaughter of Burklap's family.

"Package secure," Ritter finally said in my earbud. "We're ready to move, so get out when you can."

It was all I could do to wait for dessert.

CHAPTER 11

"YOU DON'T KNOW WHAT YOU'VE DONE!" JEANE TOLD ME AS I walked into Noah's sitting room after changing from the yellow dress. I was fully myself now, though every now and then I caught myself humming Noah's song under my breath.

I gave her an insincere smile. "Actually, I have a pretty good idea. I captured the null who betrayed all of us in Morocco. And I interrupted whatever plan you were cooking up with Ropte." I just hoped he didn't connect her disappearance with the luncheon. Stella was looking to find a way to drop some hint that Jeane had left on her own, but doing so without endangering our mission to rescue the families was doubtful.

"I helped you kill Delia." Jeane rolled her neck as she glared at me, as if a camera were filming and we were in some kind of movie.

"You tried to capture us for the Emporium." I'd also seen her shoot a mortal in the back, with no remorse. There was no way I would ever trust her again.

Jeane's eyes shuttered. "Well, things have changed."

I knew that. I still couldn't see her life force, though she hadn't tried to null anyone's ability yet, which was fortunate for her. None of us had much patience where she was concerned.

"What things?" I asked. "And what were you doing at Ropte's?"

I sidled over to where she sat on the couch under the watchful eyes of Cort and Mari. I was anxious to help Ritter and Keene gather supplies for the upcoming rescue, but I was even more anxious to find out what Jeane knew of Ropte's plan.

Jeane's eyes opened again slowly. She leaned forward, her blue and white, peasant-style blouse dropping open to reveal her breasts in their see-through bra. "I'm not working for the Emporium anymore. I thought going back was the right thing with Delia gone, but I was wrong. I no longer have any loyalty toward them. Or Ropte."

I arched a brow. "Oh, yeah? Because you were in his house on a first name basis with his wife. You going to explain that?"

She sat back and remained silent.

"That's what I thought. Look, Jeane, you will tell us what we want to know, one way or the other."

"Go to hell," she muttered.

"Why don't you think about it? For now we have more important things to do."

I nodded at Cort, and he lifted a large syringe. Jeane's nostrils flared as he grabbed her hand, but she didn't struggle as he plunged the sedative into her arm. She lay back on the couch with a dramatic sigh, going limp. Her eyes fluttered closed.

"It should last twenty-four hours unless we give her something to counteract it," Cort said. "But we'll restrain her and get her on an IV to make sure she stays asleep. We can't spare any of us tonight to watch over her."

"So sad," Mari said, looking down at Jeane's still form and

shaking her head. "Why would she want to work with the Emporium? After what they did to her?"

I sighed, pushing away a pity I didn't want to feel for Jeane. "I bet she thought with Delia gone, she might be able to move up. Because the only thing Jeane cares about is herself. Let's never forget that."

Ritter came into the room, looking dark and dangerous dressed in black and carrying his customary assault rifle. Something moved inside me seeing him this way. All business. A killing machine that miraculously had found a place for me in his heart. I briefly fingered the rings I wore on a gold chain around my neck. They were always with me, except during workouts and ops where they might be a liability. This chain and the rings—the new one that was mine and the older two that had belonged to his mother and his little sister—represented Ritter's heart.

Ritter and Cort locked Jeane away in one of Noah's spare bedrooms while Mari gathered the others for our pre-op briefing.

"Stella's intel on the first three families' whereabouts was correct on all accounts," Ritter said, "but thanks to our work at Ropte's, we now have exact addresses and a location for the fourth family in Kansas. Keene and I will head our two teams. Cort, Mari, and Patrick will go with Keene to Maryland. Erin, Noah, and I will take the house in Virginia."

I was leery of using Patrick, who had little training and was a pacifist at heart, and Noah, who, despite years of good training, really had no aptitude for combat. They were better than no backup at all, but I hated dividing our forces. In Idaho and Kansas, Ava and Dimitri would also be down on personnel, but our three mortal, former black ops employees were well equipped for this kind of rescue.

"Remember, in and out," Ritter continued. "Both teams

will wait until we hear from Ava before going in. Mari, we'll depend on you to shift your family back to one of the DC safe houses, and then call Erin and arrange to do the same with our family once we're close enough for you to locate."

"Okay." Mari's eyes gleamed, and my heart echoed her excitement at the idea of saving those families. "If something goes wrong, you should just have Noah sing. Judging by the reactions of people today, we should have been using Noah all along as our secret weapon."

Noah grinned. "I'm game. Though I think Erin's ability enhanced their emotions as much as my singing ability did."

"Teamwork," Mari agreed.

"And FYI," Noah said. "Our Renegades from New York are already in place to move the families of the other politicians to safety, and the president has assigned Secret Service to the representatives themselves. Hopefully, that will prevent another kidnapping."

"If we're successful tonight, my father will also initiate an early vote with the proof we gather about these families," Patrick said. "Once the term limits and the protections are in place, the kidnappings should stop."

I hoped so. But it left me wondering what else the Emporium had planned.

"Let's go," Ritter said. "Showtime."

Mari shifted us back to a DC safe house, and from there we divided into separate vans. Ritter, Noah, and I would be heading to Louisa, Virginia, while Keene and the others drove to Denton, Maryland. They'd arrive in less than an hour and a half at a newly built farmhouse on nearly seventy acres of land. Our trip to a two-hundred-acre farm in Louisa would take two hours. Ava had reported that the other locations in Nampa, Idaho and Lawrence, Kansas were equally isolated.

"At least they're consistent," Noah said as she steered our van over the gently winding freeway. She seemed to take delight in driving faster than any other vehicle on the road. "Obviously, they want to make sure the families don't have a chance to escape to any neighbors."

"Who are the properties registered to?" I asked.

Ritter looked up from the middle seat where he was studying maps on his laptop. "According to Stella, they're all registered to different dummy corporations. Which means the properties could belong to any of the Emporium members or even the Triad themselves."

"Ropte."

"Possibly," he conceded. "In fact, they are likely his, given that the information was on his computer." He hesitated a few seconds before adding, "It bothers me that they are all so remote."

"Makes our job easier. We don't have to worry about neighbors."

"Yes, but neither do they. They'll be heavily armed. And they won't hesitate to murder the families if they think they might lose them."

"Then we'll shoot first," I retorted.

Ritter gave his first hint of a smile. "That sounds like a very good idea."

Darkness was still two hours away when we arrived in Louisa near our destination. Parking the van off the road, we climbed over barbed wire fences that were barely an obstacle and then hiked through a small forest of trees to get to the house. As I searched the house for life forces, Ritter debated with Ava on the phone whether or not we should wait until nightfall. All the other teams were in place and ready to move.

The beautiful Victorian house had strong gothic influences that resulted in a steeply gabled roof, reminiscent of a medieval cathedral. A beautiful pillared porch ran around the entire front of the house, wrapping around one side. Luscious hanging baskets of flowers decorated the porch at intervals, signaling to me that someone lived here or visited regularly. A balcony on the second floor also spanned the front of the house, and I could see yet another partial balcony on the third floor at the rear of the house. The whiteness of the building contrasted sharply with the deep green of the short lawn and the thick line of fir trees.

Ten life forces were inside the house, five dimmer than the others. Definitely shielded minds. The Georges, the family we believed was being held here, consisted of a mother and three children, ages nine, fourteen, and seventeen. That left the five shielded minds, who were likely Emporium soldiers, and another person who was unknown. Someone was in the kitchen area of the house, and I suspected that extra mind was a housekeeper or cook of some type. Probably a woman. Maybe even the person who watered those luscious baskets of flowers. Would she be aware of the kidnapping? I didn't see how she could be unaware of what had happened, and the Emporium would never allow her to survive with the knowledge once this was over. So she was in every bit as much danger as the Georges.

Ritter looked at me. "Ten," I said. "One I believe is the housekeeper, but I can get a little closer to see for sure."

"So five hostiles."

I nodded. "The family seems to be on the second floor in the room on the left end. All together. Two dim life forces are outside the room. Three dim downstairs on the main floor, and a bright one in the kitchen."

In Maryland, Keene and Cort would send in microbots to

determine the numbers of hostiles. For a moment, I worried about them, but Keene and Cort had been on far more missions than I had and they would be thorough. They also had Patrick, who could tap into their surveillance system, and Mari who could shift around inside the house and spirit the family away before the guards were even aware that something was wrong. Even so, if the distance between us weren't too great for Mari to locate me in this place she'd never visited before, I might text her to shift here and take me back to verify their count.

Thinking about it was useless. I needed to focus on the here and now and trust them to do their job. That's what Ava did with all of us.

It was harder than it looked.

"What about cameras?" Noah asked.

"Three here in the front." Ritter pointed them out. "I'll circle around to see what else they've got. Much as I don't want to wait, I think Ava is right about moving in after dark."

The custom metamaterials bodysuits were Cort's invention, made of particles smaller than the wavelength of light. The suits came from a theory he'd worked on for the past century and was finally able to implement as technology caught up. We weren't completely invisible wearing this second generation of suits, but they helped us slink around unnoticed in the trees and would be as good as invisible in the dark. Once the heat nullifiers were activated, not even radar could detect us.

Darkness came slowly, and then we had to wait more long minutes until night fell in Idaho as well. At least we were able to verify that the families weren't being moved. Of course, that did nothing to stop their anguish. Closer to the house, I could feel their emotions. Fear, mostly, but anger too. Desperation. Worry. The mother was suffering from an arm injury that sent agony rippling through her body every time she moved.

The housekeeper retired to her bedroom on the third floor, which was an added bonus to the waiting. At least she'd be out of the line of fire. Ritter would go in on the main floor and take out the three guards. Noah and I would sneak past the cameras in our suits and scale the building to the balcony on the second floor. My job would be to take out the guards, while Noah's would be to comfort and calm the family. Ritter and I would also retain a mental connection throughout the op so I could channel his ability.

I didn't worry much about Ritter as he smiled at me and left. One or more of his three targets might be mortal offspring; the Emporium seemed to be raising more expendable servants these days. Even if the three were all combat Unbounded, he'd likely shoot two of them before they were aware of him.

Pulling my metamaterials hood from my pocket, I concealed my hair and face. "Wait for my signal," I told Noah.

I sped past the camera at the left corner of the house. Even if I set off a motion sensor and someone was watching a monitor inside the house, it was unlikely they'd see me. Beneath the camera, I shot my grappling hook onto the balcony and began climbing. I whistled to Noah to follow. Even using Ritter's increased ability to see in the dark, I detected only a ripple moving across the yard as she made her way toward me.

Up on the balcony, I checked for additional cameras, but there were none. I could feel the thoughts from the mortals inside the house louder now. Mostly fear as the family sat together in a clump. The mother was singing softly, ignoring the throbbing in her arm. The youngest was asleep, the seventeen-year-old girl was crying silently, and the fourteen-year-old boy plotted revenge.

The housekeeper on the third floor was thinking about what she would make tomorrow for breakfast. *Something to please the little boy. He's sweet, unlike his older sister, who won't eat anything if their mother doesn't make her, and the angry teen boy who glares at me with hatred. Spoiled rotten rich kids. It's not my fault they're here. Really, such attitudes are the parents' fault, though the mothers seems gracious enough. But at least that little boy is an angel. So small and quiet.* He reminded her of her own son. She knelt down and prayed for his safety.

The minds of the guards were blocked, but their shields weren't terribly strong. I beat at one forcefully until it caved. With a planted thought, I could see he and his companion were combat Unbounded. No way did I want to engage both of them simultaneously. I'd have to shoot at least one, but that would end our surprise. Unless I planted another thought and sent one of them to the bathroom. They were probably bored and had eaten more food than normal while they'd been stuck here, so the suggestion should seem normal.

I turned my attention from the guards to examine the window. Ritter had already determined that none of the windows had breakage alarms, which meant they'd only trigger the alarm if opened normally. Fishing in one of the many strategic pockets of my bodysuit, I retrieved a glass cutter and a suction cup to hold the glass and began cutting.

Below on the main floor, Ritter had already cut his glass and was in position. I sent him an image of what I was doing so he'd know I wasn't ready. Not yet.

Setting the cut glass aside, I crawled in the window. We were two rooms down from where the captives huddled, close enough to shoot at the guards with my silenced nine mil. Noah had her gun out, and she looked confident, but discomfort filled her surface thoughts. I smiled at her. I didn't plan on making her use that gun.

I'd maintained the link with the guard and now released a thought next to his sand stream, a violent urge to urinate. Seconds later, I grinned as he excused himself from his companion and hurried toward the bathroom. I waited until the door shut before I signaled Ritter. *Whenever you're ready.*

Go, he thought.

Going now, Your Deathliness. His amusement at my taunt filtered back to me.

I eased open the door, aimed, and fired twice. It was easy having seen their exact position through the eyes of the guard, and my shot had taken him through the heart. Not dead because he was Unbounded, but definitely out of the picture for now.

A loud screech abruptly whistled through the house, coming from the fallen body. In the next instant, two more screeching alarms came from the main floor.

They're tagged with heart monitors, came Ritter's thought. I could see him diving to miss being shot, rolling, and lashing out at a gun with his foot.

The bathroom door opened to my left, revealing the second guard, his pants unzipped. No time to bring my gun around. I whipped my free hand out, feeling the bones crack as it sent his weapon flying. He returned the favor to my gun as I aimed, sending it clattering to the wood floor. I rewarded him with a kick to his stomach, which curled him long enough for me to slam my elbow down on his head. He was out, but I grabbed my backup pistol from a pocket near my calf and shot him twice through the heart. Another alarm began to screech, the sound emitting from what looked like a wrist watch. I grabbed his wrist, slammed it against the wall, and the noise cut off.

Noah was already moving toward the other guard to silence his alarm as I took out my phone and texted all our Renegades: *Guards here using alarms that trigger when heart stops beating.* The Emporium hadn't used this ploy recently, and it was tricky enough that it could mess up everything if taking out the guards one at a time was part of the plan for any of our teams.

The screeching cut down significantly as Noah manage to break the other guard's alarm. Ritter was still fighting the remaining guard below, but he was close and he'd silence the alarms down there when he could. I bent to retrieve my gun.

"No, stop!" I said to Noah as she reached for the door where the family was kept. I sprinted down the hallway to her and knocked on the door. "Get back from the door. We've been sent by Homeland Security to save you. Your kidnappers have been taken care of. Back away from the door. Put down that lamp."

I'd tried to keep in mental contact with the family, but with so much going on, I'd nearly missed the teen boy picking up the lamp. Only his mother's worry had called my attention.

"Please, Mrs. George. Tell him to put it down. We're here to help you." A muffled *clunk* signaled that someone was listening. Even so, I turned the knob and pushed open the door without going inside. I kept hold of my gun but pointed it down. These were mortals. No coming back if I shot them.

The entire family huddled together on a large bed, the mother holding her teen son now. I didn't see any weapons or feel intent to harm, so I nodded to Noah, who slowly moved into the room.

"Okay, now," she said, her voice singsong. "It's okay now. We'll have you out of here in no time." Tension leaked from the family.

Downstairs, I felt Ritter giving a final blow to his opponent that sent the man to the ground. He was still conscious and cursing as Ritter zip-tied his hands and feet together and went to kill the other two alarms. Blessed silence fell throughout the house.

Get them ready to leave, Ritter thought. *There's no telling if that alarm also linked to one of their headquarters. I'll go get the van. We're taking these guards with us. They'll have embedded tracking devices, but we'll take care of those on the road.* I knew why he was so determined. Five fewer that went back to their headquarters were fewer we'd have to fight later.

"Let's go," I said to the Georges as Ritter's thoughts receded slightly with the distance he was putting between us. "We have to leave now."

They began slowly to get off the bed, the mother wincing. "Wait," I said to her. I holstered my weapon. Using a knife, I ripped the top sheet into a triangle sling for her arm.

"Thank you," she said quietly.

"Be aware that the guards out here look dead," I said, my eyes going to the children, "and there's a lot of blood. But they are Unbounded and will recover." *Unfortunately.*

I picked up the sleeping child and led the way to the door. Noah put her arm around the girl, and the mother did the same for her teen son.

"Housekeeper coming," I muttered to Noah. I could feel her life force coming our way, probably alerted by the alarms. At least that would save me the trouble of going to retrieve her.

We'd nearly reached the main staircase when she came into view wearing a pale pink, floor-length flannel robe. She was plump with sparse white hair that stuck up on top as if she'd been sleeping. "What's going on here?" she demanded.

"Everything's okay," I said. "We're getting you all to safety. Please come with us."

She pulled out a gun from her pocket, even as I registered the threat. "Renegade scum! You're not going anywhere. Now all of you—get back to that room."

We retreated down the hall. "Take it easy," I said, shifting the child in my arms to remove his weight off my left hand, which was throbbing from its earlier contact with the guard's gun.

"Take it easy?" she said, her voice rising with anger. "What have you done with my son?" She knelt by the guard near the bathroom, her hand checking for a pulse. Her gun didn't waver.

"He'll be fine," I said. "You know he's Unbounded. Please let me take this family out of here. They haven't done anything wrong."

"Wrong?" she sneered. "They're mortal. What does it matter? They're nothing! They mean nothing!"

"You're mortal," I countered.

She lifted her chin. "I'm the mother of an Unbounded, so I'm different. I am revered." From a pocket of her son's black uniform, she drew a syringe of what had to be tonic, their version of curequick. She stabbed it into the man's heart and injected the mixture before rising.

"Now get back to that room!" She pointed the gun at the girl and said to me, "A shot might not hurt you, but it will this brat." The girl cringed, burying her face into Noah's shoulder. Mrs. George sobbed.

The housekeeper had to be mad. Completely and totally crazy. She hadn't used a shield over her thoughts earlier, but there was one now—stronger than most mortals could create, stronger even than her Unbounded son. I drew out my mental machete and hacked away. *Ritter,* I said, silently. *We have a slight problem.*

He'd already arrived at the van. *On my way. Stall.*

We'd reached the room, and I laid the sleeping boy on the bed. He stirred only slightly.

"Not you two," the housekeeper said to Noah and the girl. "You stay near me."

Finally, her shield gave way, and I was inside. She was thinking of her son, whom she adored more than anything in the world. She had fallen in love with an Unbounded, only to be abandoned when her beauty faded, but she'd given him five children. This son here was the only one who'd Changed, the only one who hadn't joined the Hunters to seek revenge on the man who'd sired them. This son let her be useful. He let her serve him.

I reached out to Noah and found that she'd already released her shield, perhaps hoping I would send her instructions. She had a hand around her gun. *On three,* I told her, *I want you and the girl to jump toward the wall. Make sure to shield the girl with your body.* Noah's eyes met mine in brief acknowledgment.

I stepped in front of the mother and her sons where they sat on the bed. "Please," I said.

"Stay back!" ordered the housekeeper.

I couldn't because I needed to get her far enough away from the Georges that even if the gun went off, she wouldn't hit them. If I sent a flash of light to her mind now, or if Ritter appeared from behind, her finger still might pull the trigger on her way down. The family wouldn't have a second chance.

"It doesn't have to be mortals or Unbounded," I told her. "You can choose both. There's no reason why we can't live in harmony."

"You're a liar. All Renegades are liars! Traitors to your own kind." Her face grew red as her gun hand tightened. "Well, I know how to teach you mortal-lovers a lesson. Beginning with this spoiled brat."

She pulled the trigger.

CHAPTER 12

THREE! I SHOUTED TO NOAH. NO TIME FOR ONE AND TWO AS I struggled mentally with the housekeeper for control of her gun. She'd jerked down on the trigger, but I yanked her finger up at the same time. No shot fired. Yet.

Noah jumped out of the way, pulling the girl with her, but the housekeeper didn't relent. Her face grew redder, and my energy strained. Controlling someone in this way was always difficult, and this woman had an indomitable spirit. She whirled in the direction Noah and the girl had moved, pulling harder. I pushed back. Forced her to stand still. I wondered if I'd made a mistake not rendering her unconscious immediately and risking a single shot. Too late. Flashing her mind now would take energy away from holding back that trigger, and a stray bullet might hit and kill one of these children or their mother. I'd just have to hold out until Ritter arrived.

With no warning, the woman turned her back on Noah and jerked her hand toward me. The pistol now aimed at my heart. Guess she'd identified her biggest threat.

Or so she thought.

One instant the housekeeper was standing there, the next she was falling face first on the ground, a flower of blood blossoming on the back of her flannel robe. Noah stood behind her, gun in hand, her face hard and determined. For a moment no one moved or breathed. Then the girl gave a cry and ran to her mother on the bed.

Pounding footsteps up the stairs and then Ritter was there. In one glance, he took in the situation. "Let's get them in the van."

We hurried the Georges outside, and by the time Noah had them settled, Ritter and I had the bodies of the Unbounded wrapped in blankets and ready to tie on top. "Better give that one a sedative," I told him. "The housekeeper gave him curequick."

He grinned. "Already did."

Of course he had. He produced more syringes for the agents I'd dragged out. Unceremoniously, we threw them on top of the van, secured them with lengths of rope, and jumped into the van. Noah hit the gas.

"Great job, by the way, Noah." Ritter said from the middle where he sat with the teen boy, who was looking at him with something akin to hero worship, though he hadn't seen Ritter do anything except haul out three wrapped bodies. Yeah, he'd been moving faster than was technically possible, but so had I since I'd channeled his ability.

Noah laughed. "Now that's something I never thought I'd hear from you."

"Well, I'm guessing it won't be the last time."

Noah laughed and turned on the radio. She pressed harder on the gas, and the countryside slipped by in a dark blur as the speedometer shot toward ninety.

I took out my phone, looking for a message. Ritter had texted the other teams about our successful mission after we'd taken out the guards, but as of yet there had been no response, and I didn't want to contact the others if they were still mid-op. Though we hadn't lost anyone for months, that didn't mean our good luck streak would continue forever. There were more times than I cared to count that we'd nearly lost everything.

No word. We drove fifty more miles, putting space between us and the Victorian mansion. I thought of the housekeeper, the only casualty, her life snuffed out in an instant. Would her Unbounded son mourn her at all? If he did, maybe there was hope for him at our Mexican compound, where our people would attempt to undo the Emporium's programming. If not, he'd have to pay for his treason.

Finally, Ava and Dimitri texted their success. No casualties. That meant Jace had survived to pester me another day. I was so happy that I didn't even care if that meant telling him about Stefan Carrington.

"Maybe we ought to call Mari," I said. "They might need help." I'd been pushing my thoughts out to see if I could reach her, even though she was beyond my typical range, and I felt her—maybe—just barely out of reach. My range had definitely increased since I'd worked with Keene this morning, as if we'd crammed weeks of experimenting into a few hours.

Ritter shook his head. "Cutoff time hasn't arrived. Give them a few more—"

My phone vibrated, and I saw it was Mari. "You all right?"

"Hello to you too. We're fine. Don't worry. Keene's texting everyone now, but Ritter told me to call, so I'm calling."

I met Ritter's eyes as I responded to her. "It went okay then?" Ritter looked down just as I felt my phone vibrate with an incoming text. Keene's, probably.

"Well, besides the stupid gardener suddenly going all postal on us. Jerk. We thought he'd be on our side because he was so kind to the family during the day when they were let outside to walk around a little. But, no, he's apparently one of those Unbounded worshippers. Or at least Emporium Unbounded, because he didn't have a problem shooting at us."

"Are you okay?"

"Yeah. Keene exploded a sprinkler with enough water that it knocked him over. We're fine and the family is safe. Even the gardener will live to follow the Emporium blindly another day."

"You didn't take the guards?"

"Uh, no, we barely got out of the house. Reinforcements arrived before we finished. We had to abandon our vehicle. Do you want me to come get you now? You guys are still far enough away that I can't locate any of you, but I might be able to with Keene's help. I haven't had a lot of luck shifting to GPS coordinates. Yet. You might have to drive to someplace I've been before."

I motioned Noah to pull the van to the side of the road. "You and Keene give it a try. We need to remove the trackers of the guards we captured. We're too exposed on this road; they have helicopters at their disposal."

Ritter grabbed a detector from his bag and pulled open the sliding door, shutting it behind him. Noah and I joined him on the moonlit road, but he was already jumping onto the roof of the van to find the tracking devices and dig them out with his knife. It was the best we could do on the go.

I could feel the mother's worry, so I said to Mari, "Better make it quick. They're scared."

"Searching for you now. Keene's trying to give me enough power to find you. Apparently, he was shot, so he's a little out of it." The way she spoke told me she had just learned of his wound.

"What?"

"I'm fine," Keene's voice said through the connection instead of Mari's.

A heartbeat later, Mari appeared next to me.

"I'll get our guests," Noah said.

"I'll wait here," Ritter said to me and Mari from his position on top of the van. He motioned to the Emporium agents and held up a bloody transmitter. "By the time you get the Georges settled, I'll have these guys ready to take to another safe house.

The teenage boy balked at leaving the van, so Ritter put away the knife and jumped to the ground to talk with him. This was the other side of the man I loved. The one who sang in the shower, liked dogs, and always had a houseplant. The one who gave me the necklace with the rings. He wasn't just a killer, he was a protector too.

Once out of the van, the Georges were more curious than terrified as Mari explained what was going to happen. "I just need to run this device over you to make sure they didn't put any trackers on you." Mari passed a detector wand over each of them. "Looks like you're clean."

You know I'm going to have to take this memory from them, I told Ritter.

Now still wasn't the time for the world to learn about our abilities. They were barely dealing with the idea of our extended lives. Abilities like mine and Mari's were bad enough, but if mortals suspected that Ritter and those like him were born to fight and kill, that he could determine his opponent's strength with a glance and could even predict his next movement, he'd be examined, exploited, or cut into three. We all would.

He nodded, melancholy showing in his dark eyes. Even knowing what they might to do to us, it bothered him that we had to mess with the Georges' memories.

Mari had us all link arms, and the next moment we arrived

at the large, tastefully decorated apartment that I'd seen earlier, before Ropte's luncheon. But not everything was perfect. Patrick lay on a tan leather couch, and Cort was stitching up a nasty cut in his gut. Keene observed from a nearby easy chair, looking pale. He held a hand over his upper arm.

"I *thought* he was wet from the water, but it was blood," Mari said in exasperation. "Gotta love black. Can you sew him up while I go back to help Ritter? You're better at taking out bullets than I am."

"Sure."

"Thanks." With a brief suction of air, Mari disappeared.

"We'll save the introductions for later," Noah said to Mrs. George. "Come on, let's find you some beds." The little boy was awake now, but leaned heavily against his mother.

Cort looked up from his repair work. "We'll have someone look at your arm soon, but until then I have an awesome pain-killer." He tossed Noah a packet of pills for Mrs. George, and she and the family started down the hall.

"So," I said to Keene, picking through the first aid bag near Cort's feet. "Looks like I finally get to take a bullet from you instead of the other way around."

"What's wrong with your hand?" he countered.

"It got in the way of something. Stop changing the subject." My hand already felt a lot better. I was sure I'd broken one of the bones, but the throbbing had almost stopped, and it would be better in an hour or two.

I had him lie down on the kitchen table so I had better access to his wound. "I've been thinking about Jeane," I said.

He winced as I spread antiseptic over the wound. "What about her?"

"I was never able to channel her ability. I did finally manage to block her from nulling me and those around me, but that's as far as it went."

"Because she escaped."

"Maybe." I focused for a minute on the anesthesia I was giving him, glad that I didn't have to worry about him bleeding to death or about infection. Even the bullet would be expelled eventually if left on its own, but it would take days. "She's stronger now, I believe. She's continuously nulling in the immediate vicinity of her body, and I haven't been able to penetrate that. I didn't even realize that darkness I saw at Ropte's was there until you helped me look."

"You think she could null you now?"

"Not exactly. I think extending her power to others would dilute it too much. It hasn't been that long since we went head to head. But I still would like to see if I could channel her— with you enhancing my ability."

Keene sucked in a breath, and this time it wasn't because I'd hurt him. "Oh, Erin. I don't even have to tell you how great that'd be. I had a sudden vision of you walking right into Emporium headquarters and taking them all into custody."

I laughed. "Let's not get ahead of ourselves."

"Right." He gave a sigh. "I barely have a concept of how my ability works. I can see how to give you more strength, but it's mostly guessing. I can't see how everything works together like Cort. And if you channel him, directing me how to use my power like you did in Morocco, you couldn't channel Jeane at the same time."

"Maybe we could work something out. A lot hinges on if channeling her is even possible."

"Even if you could just force her to null them for us, it would help. But the window of opportunity isn't going to be long. They'll soon realize we have their people from that facility in Texas, if they haven't already." His eyes clouded and a frown cut through his face. "Actually, now that I think about it, even if you walked into one of their headquarters and nulled all of their abilities, it would still be an almost impossible battle. I mean, it would help a lot, but we simply don't have the numbers to make it work."

I jabbed my needle into the flesh at the side of his wound, though I probably should have waited another minute or two. This time he didn't wince.

"You know it's the truth," he continued. "Our European allies have their own issues, but even if we called all of them to help, and they could come, we'd be outnumbered four to one. And that's not including the Emporium's mortal agents."

I worked on the bullet for a moment. "How many are there, do you think? Mortal agents."

He sighed. "I was with the Emporium all my life, and I wasn't even sure how many Unbounded they had. I was mortal after all, not really one of them."

The bitterness and longing that was normally in his voice when he talked about the Emporium was absent. Somehow he'd come to terms with his past—or at least the part that didn't involve his father. Maybe Mari had something to do with that.

"If I had to guess," he added, "the way they've been procreating and experimenting with genetics these past years, there are probably over a thousand mortal agents at the New York headquarters alone."

So even if we somehow nulled all of the Unbounded, there would be too many mortals to control. Ritter might be able to beat twenty trained agents on his own, but few others of us could.

I was finally able to snag the bullet with some tweezers. I dropped it onto the table. "There's a lot more blood than I hoped for. I'd better stitch you up."

"Have fun with it," Keene said with a grimace. "I know you're enjoying yourself."

I grinned. "Gotta take my fun where I can."

A short time later, I crept inside the two rooms where we had placed the families and removed their memories about Mari's shifting. For the Georges, I left memories of the van, hoping they would assume they'd slept and had been carried inside upon arriving in DC. For the other family, leaving anything would be more difficult. They'd remember Mari in the room with them and then suddenly being here, but there was nothing I could do about that. I didn't dare experiment with their memories; I was already violating them enough by stealing what I did.

Ritter and Mari joined us just after I finished. Apparently, Mari had connected with Tenika, the leader of the New York Renegade cell, and they'd shifted the captive Unbounded agents to New York for safekeeping.

"Did Ava and Dimitri encounter any problems?" Cort asked, looking up as he finished wrapping Patrick's wound. Layers of blood-drenched cloths littered the couch and floor, but Patrick was still conscious, if a little high on curequick.

Ritter frowned. "The owners of the house who were hiding Ava's family were killed."

"Jace?" I asked. If my brother had killed them, he'd need someone to talk it out with.

"No. One of the Emporium agents shot the couple after Jace managed to take the family from them. Ava was linked to the couple and saw the murders. On the bright side, there was a cook who helped Dimitri and Oliver. She shot her own Unbounded niece when she could have shot Oliver or one of his illusions instead."

"Well, at least some mortals haven't gone completely crazy," I muttered.

Ritter came over to me. I could feel the heat from his body and the response to that heat in mine. I wanted nothing more than to wipe out the day's events in his arms. "Has someone let the senators know their families are okay?" he asked.

Patrick nodded. "My dad's talking to them now."

"Any attempts on other families?"

"No." Patrick smiled. "Looks like we got them."

His words settled over me with unease. We'd bested the Emporium before, but this time it seemed almost too easy. Ritter's gaze snapped back to me, and the mirroring worry there confirmed my fear. Now we waited for the other shoe to drop.

"Let's get back to Noah's," I said. "Keene and I want to talk to Jeane."

Noah gave an encouraging motion with her hands. "Go on ahead. I'll stay here until our backup from my cell arrives to watch over the families. Two of our guys are still thirty minutes out, but one's a healer who can look at Mrs. George's arm."

"Good," Ritter said. "Let us know if you need help."

"Patrick will stay with you," Cort added. "He could use an Unbounded doctor to help heal him faster."

Mari extended her hands to Cort and Keene, and Ritter and I joined them. "I'll come right back," Mari told Noah. "Patrick should be well enough to shift to your place after he sees the healer."

Noah smiled. "Thanks."

It was time for some answers. We stepped into the gray.

CHAPTER 13

BACK AT NOAH'S HOUSE, RITTER WANTED TO COME WITH ME TO see Jeane, but although he and Keene had made up their previous differences, it wouldn't be easy for him to watch us experiment with our minds so intimately linked.

"Let me try with her first," I told him. "You'll be my backup threat."

He hesitated an instant before agreeing. "I have to talk with Ava anyway. We know the Emporium isn't going to take this lying down. But take Cort with you. He's not threatening, and if you and Keene are busy doing your thing, you'll need someone to watch your backs."

Cort harrumphed. "I'm not sure if that's a compliment or a dig at my manhood."

"When you decide, let me know." Ritter picked up the remote from Noah's couch and turned on the big screen, selecting the icon that displayed Ava's picture.

I smiled at the comradery, knowing that Ritter trusted Cort more than anyone. Maybe even more than me. They'd watched each other's backs for centuries.

Jeane was still out cold in the room, and I sat next to her on the bed. Despite her apparent nonchalance when we'd drugged her earlier, she would be angry when she awoke at how long she'd been unconscious. Far too recently, Delia Vesey had kept her in an Emporium cell for decades, headless and half rotting, only allowing enough absorption to keep two of her focus points together—her heart and reproductive system. She had lost so many years already.

Her mental block was no longer in place, as if she'd relaxed here as she'd never dared to at Ropte's. Or maybe it was the different drugs we gave her. I placed one hand on her head and my other in Keene's warm one. He was still paler than normal, but his lean face was determined. Pushing out my awareness, I found the frozen lake that represented her unconscious mind. Everything was crystal clear, bright, and more real with Keene's help. But though I could sense even the thoughts of the family in the nearest house over a mile away, no amount of experimentation would allow me to cross the ice to access her memories.

Cort watched us with interest. "It may be different when she's awake."

I wasn't so sure.

After more than an hour, I gave up. "Okay, do the honors. Wake her up." My energy was flagging, and all the absorption in the world wouldn't replace it fast enough. "We're not getting anywhere here."

Cort brought her around, and the first thing she did was lunge at him. "I'll kill you!" she shrieked. We grabbed for her arms, holding her tight. She cursed Cort, his mother, and all his ancestors and descendants. Then she started in on Keene.

"That's enough!" I said.

"It's not enough! You put me out. Never again! Just kill me! If you do it again, I swear I'll seduce every man you ever loved, including your mortal brother, and then I'll skin them alive and eat their flesh." She bucked against us.

She'd raised her barrier, but I was still inside her head, with Keene's power at my disposal. Her sand stream was readily available, the flowing thoughts presented in a language I didn't comprehend. That didn't make sense because thoughts didn't need a language. I'd been able to "listen" in on those who spoke other languages before without any trouble understanding. Drawing on Keene's energy, I sent a tiny burst of light into her mind.

She didn't grasp her head and scream in pain or faint as others did, but she stopped talking and the convulsing of her body eased. "What did you do? I felt . . . something." Her breath, once shallow and quick, was evening out.

Well, that was something at least. Maybe this experiment wouldn't be an entire waste after all. I wished I knew what she'd felt because it certainly hadn't caused her pain.

"Okay," I said softly, releasing her hands and rising from the bed, "let's try this again. If you don't want to be drugged in the future, I'm sure we can work something else out."

That promise, I think, calmed her more than anything. But the fact that my flash did affect her was no small thing.

Jeane nodded and came to a seated position on the bed, her legs drawn up Indian style under her.

Time to get down to business.

But no matter how much energy I used—and I took as much from Keene as I dared, until my body thrummed with it—I couldn't understand Jeane's thoughts. When I attempted to release one of my own thoughts into the sand stream, it crumbled and vanished before being swallowed by the flow. Jeane showed no reaction.

There was only one thing left to try. Normally, to channel someone, I simply reached for the glow of his or her ability, the certain something I sensed inside each mind. So far, it had been easy to find, saturating the entire area, part of the person's essence. Jeane's simply wasn't there, or if it was, I didn't recognize it or know how to reach it. With Keene's help, the language of her sand stream had become slightly clearer, and maybe in time I could learn it, but for now it felt like wearing a blindfold and dunking my head into water while trying to understand someone speaking a long-forgotten African dialect.

I linked with Cort and let him observe the patterns in her mind. He shook his head and thought, *If you're considering uncoding the jumble, it might be better to record it using Patrick's ability. From what I can see, she's just not compatible with us. Maybe that's why she's also barren. I think she's a screwup, an Emporium experiment gone wrong.*

I wondered what Jeane would say about his theory of her being an Emporium mistake. *Thanks,* I said, releasing him and the others. So much for my vision of confronting Stefan and nulling his ability.

Jeane smirked at my frustration. "I don't know what you're trying to do, but Delia Vesey already tried everything with me, and she didn't succeed. She couldn't control or read me. She couldn't act through me. And she couldn't stop me from plotting against her. That's why she locked me away for decades—to protect herself."

"We let you out," I reminded her.

To show her gratitude, she hit me with it then, her nulling ability, but I was ready and pushed back, extending my shield to protect Cort and Keene. "Sorry, Jeane, remember that doesn't work on me anymore." I was relieved to know that was still true.

The pressure eased as she sat back and folded her arms.

"What do you want from me? Are you going to kill me? Nah, because that's not who you Renegades are. You're weak, and that's why the Emporium will win this war."

"So you're helping them?"

The side of her mouth twitched. "What I'm doing is none of your business."

I bent over, putting my face close to hers. "Of course it's my business, and I'll tell you right now, you aren't going anywhere but to Mexico. We aren't letting you go, and your Emporium boyfriend isn't here to help you now."

Jeane flinched, and for an instant her blue eyes lost their belligerence. "This has nothing to do with Lew."

"I think it does." I drew away, glancing at the others for ideas.

Lew Roberts, the sensing Unbounded who had been Delia's assistant, was powerful enough to shield others with his thoughts and to control them. The slight, nasal-voiced man with the crunched, youthful features of an Unbounded whose Change had been forced was not my idea of a hot romance, but he'd been the one person Jeane seemed to feel any loyalty toward. Maybe she liked her men boyish.

"What happened after you were rescued by the Emporium in Morocco?" Keene asked.

"After you tried to capture us," I added.

Jeane tossed her head, and her silky hair swung over her shoulder. "I just didn't want to go back to them empty-handed. My plan, if you must know, was to take Delia's place in the Triad. Lew was going to help me. But that didn't work out, so I left."

Something in my mind clicked. "To try to take her place you'd have to be a direct descendant."

Her smile didn't reach her eyes. "That's right. Oh, don't

go all family on me. Delia was a monster, and we were so far removed that her blood barely ran through my veins. But her successor hadn't been named."

"Or so you thought."

My remark made her bristle. "So what?"

"How close was she?"

"She was my fifth great-grandmother."

Cort cleared his voice. "Ropte's also her fifth great-grandson. Did you go to Ropte's to kill him?"

To seduce him and stab a knife into his heart while he slept was more like it.

"Kill him?" Jeane's laugh was genuinely amused. "Why would I do that? We have our differences, but he's still my brother."

"Brother?" This was something I hadn't anticipated.

"Yes." She waved a hand. "He's much older, but when you have an Unbounded mother, that happens."

Cort and Keene exchanged a glance. They knew only too well since there were five hundred years separating them. For Jeane and Ropte, the difference would be double that. She'd only Changed three hundred years ago.

"Siblings aren't necessarily loyal to one another," Keene said with a drawl. "Especially in the Emporium." Cort nodded tightly. I couldn't read the sorrow in his expression, but I knew it was there. Though the brothers were on the same side now, Cort had pretended for years to feed Keene and the Emporium information about the Renegades in exchange for any information he could plunder in exchange.

Jeane clenched her fists, jumping up from the bed. "Oh, put it away," she said when I went for my gun. "There's three of you, and it's not like I have any chance of getting out of here. If you must know, I went to David for help. Since he's in the Triad now, I hoped he'd be able to do me a favor."

"Why don't you sit back down and tell us everything?" I indicated the bed. "Or if you want, I can yank Ritter from his powwow with Ava and Dimitri to see if he can convince you to sit."

She tossed her head and pushed her breasts out in my direction. "The only thing tall, dark, and dangerous would get from me is foreplay."

"Sit down," I gritted.

"Fine. But you guys sit down too. I'm sick of you all looming over me."

"Okay." I drew up one of the chairs from the small table by the window. My body met the chair with a distinct relief, and I had to bite down on the sigh that threatened to steal past my lips. Cort grabbed the second chair, while Keene settled on an edge of the bed as far away from Jeane as he could get. His expression didn't change, but that he'd sat at all told me how much his wound still drained him.

"When I found out David was Delia's chosen successor, I was angry," Jeane said, pulling her legs up to her chest. "After all, I'm the one who went through all the work to help you kill her."

"I want the trailer," I said, "not the movie."

She sighed in exasperation, but even that sounded sexy. There was a reason she had been America's sex symbol for a decade. "Okay, long story short, they held us prisoner after they rescued us," she said. "But I escaped."

"Not Lew?"

A vertical furrow appeared between her eyebrows. "No, not Lew. We had a plan, but something went wrong. I escaped alone."

I suspected she'd left him behind to save herself and later regretted it. Her attachment with Lew seemed real enough from what I'd seen between them, and in the past she'd gone to great lengths for a man. In fact, one of the reasons she'd hated

Delia so much was because the older woman had murdered her former Renegade lover.

"I went to Ropte because I thought he might be able to negotiate Lew's release," Jeane continued. "I offered him the use of my ability if he'd help me."

"Did he agree?" Keene sounded doubtful, almost mocking.

"He made me babysit that prissy wife of his." Jeane rolled her eyes before saying as an afterthought, "At least she knows how to dress."

I crossed one leg over the other, noting how the dim morning light was beginning to filter through the shuttered window and leave patterns on the black material covering my leg. "So he wouldn't help you."

"Oh, he'll help me. He just needs me to do a few things."

"I'm guessing that might take years." Or more. With how few sensing Unbounded there were, it was unlikely they'd allow Lew to leave the Emporium. Even if they couldn't force him to do everything they wished, they could use him for breeding, an irony that didn't escape me since the man once tried to impregnate me with his own genetically altered sperm.

Jeane frowned. "Maybe not. They have another sensing Unbounded. *Catrina*. A horrible little thing." She made the name sound like a curse. I was betting she was jealous.

"Ropte's older than both Stefan and"—Keene hesitated a half second before using his father's name—"Tihalt. You think he'll make a play for control of the Triad?"

Jeane snorted delicately. "Delia was older and far more powerful than David. That didn't help her. Tihalt has so much wealth and power that as long as he's willing to let Stefan control the Emporium, Stefan is too powerful to be beat. No, I think my brother has different aspirations of the political kind."

My mind churned. "He wants to be president?"

"David doesn't tell me his plans," Jeane said, "But I know for certain Stefan met with David and other politicians several times. David acts different when he's with Stefan. Acts, being the key word. Millions of dollars have changed hands."

Cort nodded sharply and cleared his throat. "Makes sense. The Triad tried taking over the presidency before with a technopath, and Ropte would be far more likely to succeed. If Ropte blocks the president's genetic testing and term limits, and convinces the rest of the Triad to back him, he could conceivably win the next election and become the most powerful man in the US, and eventually the world. Stefan and my father might trust him to do what's best for the Emporium, and maybe he will for a time. He'll definitely need help in removing the current presidential term limits and controlling the voting. But after that"—he lifted his shoulders—"anything could happen."

"Well, it's far from over," I said. David Ropte didn't have the power he needed, not yet, and maybe we could make certain he didn't succeed, regardless of the support from the Emporium. A lot would depend upon his ability and how vulnerable he was after we got rid of his henchmen.

I opened my mouth to ask Jeane about Ropte's ability when Ritter nearly exploded through the door. "Come to the sitting room," he said. "Something's happened!"

For a brief second, we took in his tightly clenched jaw and the fury in his eyes, then all of us sprang to our feet and ran past him. Jeane was last, but Ritter made sure she wasn't forgotten. He brought up the rear, and the way she hurried to catch up to me, putting space between herself and Ritter, gave me a deep satisfaction I'd never admit to.

In the sitting room, we found Noah, Mari, and Patrick staring with disbelief at the screen. A video showed flames engulfing a section of the Capitol. After several seconds, people began running from the building. *Too many,* I thought, *for this early in the morning.* Then all at once several of the people dropped to the ground without warning. There seemed to be no pattern. One woman was shot in the back and her hands flung wide in shock. Some of those who hadn't fallen tried to carry the others, only to be shot themselves.

A young woman with long brown hair appeared on the screen as the video started over. "This is the footage caught by a tourist just a few minutes ago," she said, her voice unnaturally animated. "We're playing it for you without the sound because the screaming is simply too terrifying. From what we can tell, a bomb went off inside the Capitol. As lawmakers, already hard at work even at six in the morning, hurried desperately for the exits, snipers opened fire on them." She paused and took a long breath. "We have no idea who is responsible or how many have been injured. It is also unknown if this terrorist attack comes from overseas or from fellow Americans. There are numerous snipers, apparently. Everything within a mile of the Capitol is in complete chaos. Miraculously, some people managed to help others to safety, even though they themselves were shot numerous times."

A male newscaster appeared, his gray-sprinkled hair looking too smooth for the wreckage going on in the video. "We've had confirmation that some of our nation's representatives have been hit," he said. "There are at least two fatalities and as many as ten. Our reporter is now on the scene, and in a moment we'll see if he has anything new to report. Providing he can get close enough without placing himself in danger."

"It's just awful to think that something like this can happen," said the brunette.

"Unthinkable," her male counterpart agreed.

Ritter hit the mute. "What they don't know yet," he said, "but Stella has confirmed, is that there were two other attacks outside different safe houses at the same time. Safe houses where the Secret Service were keeping two of the senators whose families we saved last night."

"No!" I said, already guessing what had happened. No wonder Ritter was so angry.

He nodded. "Both men are dead, as are the two who went to the Capitol building after their meeting with the president. We saved their families, but the men have all been murdered."

Mari groaned and jumped up from the couch, pacing with her hands clenched tightly at her sides. "All four senators? Dead?" Shock rolled off her as she forgot to block her thoughts. I braced myself against it, already reeling enough with the news. That poor little boy I'd held in my arms last night no longer had a father. Mrs. George, who'd fought her captors so forcefully that they'd broken her arm, had survived only to lose her husband.

All because of the Emporium.

"Several Secret Servicemen guarding them were also killed," Ritter continued, "but the shots centered around those senators. The bombs inside the Capitol Building—there were two—were placed to affect the offices of all four so they'd be forced to evacuate. Of course, two men weren't there, but we can assume all four have been under surveillance by the Emporium since their families were taken. Stella is sure they were the targets."

Noah took out her phone. "Some members of my cell were there, protecting the senators. I need to check on them." She walked away, putting the phone to her ear. I knew her agony. The last time something like this had happened, the New York cell had lost too many good people.

"My father is safe," Patrick said quietly when Noah was gone, "but his vote is not. The men we believe will be appointed to take these senators' places aren't likely to trust us to protect them. They'll vote with Ropte."

"This is anarchy," Cort declared.

"Exactly." Patrick laid his head back on the couch. If anything, he looked paler than when Cort had been stitching him up.

From the corner of my eye, I saw Jeane slither to the door, her gait so careful that she seemed nearly motionless. Before I could move, Ritter was there, his hand gripping her upper arm. She flinched.

"No need to be rough," she purred. Her voice lowered slightly, as if she were speaking only for Ritter to hear. "Unless that's the way you like it. It *can* be quite enjoyable that way."

He shoved her in the direction of the couch. "If you don't want to end up as a rotting mass of flesh locked in another dungeon, you'd better sit down and shut up."

Jeane flounced to the couch, tossing her dark hair in that incessant way of hers. "I'm willing to help," she said, sitting and pulling a bare foot up under her. "I only want to free Lew from the Emporium. When you look at it that way, we're actually on the same side. Though I'm not sure how wise that is, seeing as it looks like you are definitely going to lose." Her sultry laugh mocked us all.

"I said shut up!" Ritter glared at her. "I'm not asking again." Jeane folded her arms and looked away from him. I was ready to send her back to Ropte, but we couldn't do that, not now or ever.

Noah returned, a shimmer of relief in her eyes. "We've got two down. They're at a hospital now and were pronounced dead, but they'll be healing fast. Tenika wants me to go claim their bodies."

"I'll go with you," I said. I was anxious for a fight, or lacking that, something else to do.

She shook her head. "You look about ready to drop. I have the documentation, and the Emporium doesn't know they're there. I'll be perfectly safe with a new disguise." Her eyes swung to Patrick. "I think you should all stay here and get a little rest. You've been up all night, and who knows what Ava will want you to do next."

I wanted to point out that she'd also been up all night, but just that fast, all the night's work and my session with Jeane felt like a weight pressing down on my entire body. I'd pushed myself to my limits, and hearing about the senators and imagining their families' agony when they finally heard the news made it that much worse.

"I'll go as backup," Cort said to Noah. "I couldn't sleep after watching that. But Noah's right about the rest of you getting some rest. Make sure to increase your absorption rate too."

"What about me?" Jeane asked.

Noah look at her coldly. "Oh, I have a place you can wait safe and sound."

Jeane scowled. "I don't know what it will take for you to trust me again."

"Jeane," I said, "we never trusted you."

With Jeane locked up, Ritter and I left the wounded Keene and Patrick to Mari's care and retired to our room, where I flopped on the bed fully dressed. Ritter lay next to me, his taut body meeting mine along my entire side. His expression was grim.

After five minutes, I sighed. "There's no way I'm going to sleep. My mind won't shut down. We have to think of a way to stop all these murders. Because you know they won't end here."

Ritter didn't respond for several breaths and then, "The only thing I think we can do is attack their strongholds with everything we've got and with everything the president can give us."

I studied the crown molding that decorated the ceiling around the chandelier. "It'll take him too long to get approval, at least with the numbers we need, especially with Ropte and the others blocking him. Even if we manage to derail their movement enough to make a difference, it would be suicide."

Everything I'd been planning was falling apart. I'd thought, once things were settled, about taking time off with Ritter. To explore what was between us. Maybe start that family he wanted so desperately to replace all that he'd lost. All we'd lost.

He rose up on one elbow, looking down on me, his eyes holes of darkness. "I know." He brought his hand to stroke my cheek, trailing his fingers over my skin. "Once, it wouldn't have made a difference to me. I'd have everyone already gathered at their doors. I'd be at the front, determined to kill enough of the Emporium to make a difference—to stop this madness. But my mind can't seem to work out a successful scenario, and I don't want . . ." His voice roughened. "I *can't* lose you."

I reached up and grabbed his hand, squeezing it tightly. I hadn't been at this war anywhere near as long as he had but long enough that my family had been severely affected. I wanted it to be over. I wanted to have a future with this man who stole my breath and made me lose myself in his touch.

Releasing my hold on his hand, I brought my fingers to his face. I traced the slight drop at the corner of his left eye, a genetic fluke that his Unbounded genes wouldn't be programmed to fix. I pushed up through his hair, parted on the left side, and followed the strands to where the ends hung down to skim a mole on his right cheek. He pushed into my hand, closing his eyes briefly until my fingers rested on his cheek. He'd shaved before the op, but already a thick layer of beard shadowed his face, almost long enough to be soft.

"We could go away," I said when his eyes opened.

Leave, I meant. Abandon the fight and hide out for as long as we could. Let others continue the battle without us until they simply couldn't fight anymore.

He gave me the slightest smile. "Is that what you want?"

His black eyes said he'd give me anything, but choosing safety would ultimately result in his self-loathing. He was a protector, a man who didn't give up, a man who'd spent centuries fighting for mortals who hadn't known he existed, a true guardian of humanity. Taking him away before the battle was won would be changing who he was. He might be willing to give up that calling for me, but I wouldn't let him. I loved who he was now.

I let my fingers glide along his bottom lip. "We're staying." There were still my brothers and niece and nephew. We had to find a way to protect their future.

Even if it meant we wouldn't be there to share it.

"I love you," Ritter whispered. "With everything that I am."

"I know." I didn't have to say how I felt about him because I opened my mind and there it was. He was a part of me, it was that simple. And that complicated. Because I desperately didn't want to lose him either.

He caught my finger in his mouth, and his tongue felt rough as it slid over my skin. I pulled my finger and him down to my mouth, and he started kissing me. There was no slow preparation as passion and energy spiked through us. Our weapons and clothes hit the ground in record time. For the moment, we would forget the bleakness of our future, the sacrifice we would be required to give.

A sacrifice that might not be enough.

Even those thoughts drained away as Ritter lowered himself over me. There was nothing but the fire in our blood, the movement of his mouth on mine. The touch of his hand. The feel of his body moving against mine. There was no room for anything but this moment and our love.

It wasn't until later when I dozed that I had the idea, the one that might change everything.

CHAPTER 14

I AWOKE TO FIND RITTER GLARING AT HIS PHONE LIKE HE WANTED to smash it. "Ava wants us back in San Diego."

Reality swooped in. I glanced at the curtained window to gauge the angle of the light. There was enough change to see that maybe an hour had passed while I'd been sleeping. "I wonder what took her so long."

"She and Dimitri were still en route to San Diego, but she's back and waiting for Dimitri now. For all of us."

"When does she want us?"

"An hour ago."

I took my leg off his. "Well, then, let's not keep her waiting." Because my idea had been percolating in my head. It wasn't all there, but maybe with the rest of us talking about it, we could even out our odds with the Emporium a little.

"We have to wait for Cort anyway. He's not going to leave Noah until she secures her people."

"I thought I saw a little silent exchange going on between you two. Eye raising and all that."

Ritter chuckled. "No way were we about to let Noah go

alone. She's a wildly talented singer, but she's the worst fighter I've ever seen."

"Since we've trained with Oliver, that's saying a lot."

"He's not so bad. He's actually growing on me."

We showered, pulled on jeans and T-shirts, and went to alert the others. Patrick was asleep on one of the couches, but Mari and Keene were seated together talking quietly. They looked up as we came in but didn't move away from each other.

"Any word from Noah and Cort?" Ritter asked.

"They finally got the sign-off on the bodies," Keene said. "They're transporting them to the safe house where we took the families, and Mari will shift there to bring them back once they've arrived. By the way, the New York Renegade passed the families off to Secret Service because there doesn't seem to be any reason to keep them now that the senators won't be able to vote."

I hadn't thought of the Georges and the other families not being targets anymore. It was the only positive thing that had come from the past two days.

"They're taking them to government safe houses." The slight mocking tone of Keene's voice told us how much he trusted those. "But they should be safe enough."

Mari scooted forward and clasped her hands together. "So what are we going to do now? Any brilliant ideas?"

"Well," Ritter and I said together.

I turned, looking at him in surprise. He laughed, and I realized that my idea might not have been solely my own since we'd been sharing more than our bodies. I might have borrowed a strategy or two from his mind. Or he'd supplied it. Okay, it might be more his idea than mine.

"We have some ideas," I clarified. "But a lot depends on you."

"What do I have to do?" Mari asked.

Ritter shook his head. "We need to talk to Ava about it first."

After Mari shifted to the safe house in DC to bring back Noah and Cort, Keene helped her shift us back to San Diego, where Stella had shut off the electric grid to allow us through. Noah stayed behind with Patrick, who wasn't ready to go anywhere yet, but should be soon enough.

At the San Diego Fortress, everyone was still waiting for Dimitri to arrive from Kansas, but Ava and Ritter shut themselves up in the conference room with Stella anyway. Cort marched Jeane off to the holding room, and Keene and Mari disappeared somewhere together. I'd no sooner dropped my bag on the floor of my room when Jace knocked on the door, his surface thoughts screaming his worry.

"Come in," I called.

The door opened. "Got a minute?"

"Of course." I went to him and hugged him tightly.

"What's that for?"

"For being safe." I wondered if I could find a relatively safe role for him in the inevitable battle that would play out with the Emporium. But then what about Mari? Cort? Chris? I couldn't personally assure everyone's safety. Especially not the one man I wanted to live more than anyone.

I led Jace to the couch and waited for him to speak. I knew why he was here, and it was finally time that I came through for him.

"It's crazy," he said, glancing up at my large, flat-screen TV, though it was turned off. "Killing all those people." He hesitated. "I mean, sometimes I'd get to thinking that maybe the Emporium wasn't all that bad. That their way wasn't perfect, but if we just worked together, maybe more of them would see mortals as people and understand that there's room for all of us. Power and money . . . it isn't everything." He shook his head.

"But now I see that the only way they'll rest is if we're all dead and they're in control of everything. I understand why Ava and Dimitri and Ritter and you and all the others are willing to give your lives to beat them. This means something, Erin. I really understand that now."

I put my hand on his arm. "I'm glad. But you know it's not all of the Emporium. It's those who are in charge. Look at the reformed prisoners in Mexico. They have no desire to return to the Emporium. And those captives we rescued might still believe they're gods, but they only want to live out their lives hidden among the mortals. They want to have normal lives. Remember Edgel, that Emporium soldier Keene brought to Stella's house after Mexico? He had a mortal daughter he loved, and he kept her hidden from the Emporium."

"You mean the daughter he blames us for letting die?" Jace rubbed a hand through his hair, spiking it even more than usual.

"That's him." The black man had been more intent on murdering me at our last run-in, and I'd been grateful he hadn't made an appearance at Ropte's. "The point is, on some level, he knows his leaders are dead wrong."

"Then why is he loyal?"

"That, I can't say. But who those leaders are inside, and what they do, doesn't necessarily trickle down to their children or their followers. Look at Cort and Keene. They aren't anything like their father."

Jace looked at me with those blue eyes that were so much different from my gray ones. "My birth father's one of them, isn't he?"

There it was. No going back. "Remember how I found out that Dimitri was my father?"

"Yeah, yeah." Jace nodded impatiently. "The genetically altered sperm Ritter stole from the Emporium—Stefan

Carrington's sperm, it turned out—didn't arrive on time for our mother's fertility appointment, and Ava made the decision to use Dimitri's instead. I know all that, but what does that have to do with me?" Even as the words left his lips, Jace's eyes grew wide. "They saved it, didn't they? The stolen sperm."

"Back then the Renegades were far behind the Emporium in genetic manipulation. Using that sperm would give them a better chance at the child becoming Unbounded."

Jace slapped his legs with both hands and stood jerkily. "I should have known. Hell, I did know." He paced several feet and whirled around. "I'm Stefan Carrington's son? That monster?" His posture and the way those blue eyes flashed made him look like Stefan. Too much like him.

"Yes."

Jace turned again, raking his hands through his hair, stopping partway and pulling on it instead. "I knew it all along. I mean, no one ever said, but I knew. I told myself it could have been someone from the other Renegade cells, someone already dead, like with Mari's father, but I suspected he was alive—and someone awful, since no one wanted to talk about him. Now I realize I knew all along, only I didn't want to know, not really." He groaned. "Ugh, Stefan Carrington."

I stood and went to him, placing my arms around his rigid body. "It doesn't change who you are. It doesn't change everything you got from Mom or the way Dad raised us. Or how much I love you."

Jace stood still, not relaxing in my arms. "It also doesn't change the fact that because of Stefan, Grandma and Lorrie are dead. That dad almost died. That we lost good people. It doesn't change that he signed off on the death of four families."

"We're going to stop him. All of them. Ritter and I have a plan."

Jace crumpled against me then and started sobbing, his

shoulders convulsing with emotion. My little brother who was taller than me, and so much faster and stronger. A man who had learned to take orders and to think before he acted. But also a man who'd vomited after witnessing the Emporium's brutality, and who looked to his older sister for guidance.

I held him, rubbing his back and smoothing his hair until the sobbing stopped and his shuddering eased. "Thank you for telling me," he whispered.

"You needed to know." Still, part of me was tempted to knock him unconscious and steal away the memory. But it was a part of him, and I loved him enough to let him become the man he was supposed to become despite—or maybe because of—that knowledge. "I love you," I told him.

He smiled and said with a hint of his old teasing, "Then prove it. I need to work off some steam. You up for sparring?"

I most certainly wasn't up for sparring. I was tired and worried—and, actually, it sounded really good. "You're on," I said. "But I'm channeling."

He smirked. "Of course. You wouldn't be competition otherwise."

I punched him on the arm, hard enough to leave a bruise. "You're going to pay for that."

All Unbounded were trained to fight, but for those with the combat ability, fighting meant something different. My brother was no different. Though I'd trained longer than Jace and still trained as hard as he and Ritter, Jace could beat me if I depended on my own fighting skills. Only Ritter could beat him now.

When I channeled Ritter, I was a good match for Jace, but his larger size still gave him the advantage. Only when

I channeled Jace himself was I his equal. Because channeling meant I was in his mind seeing what moves he'd use before he used them. Not just anticipating the most likely move, or the responsible move, but what he'd switch up to try to confuse me. Seeing from both his eyes and my own could be a negative distraction when I was fighting someone else, but now that I was more practiced at channeling, it definitely gave me a slight advantage when he was my opponent.

I feinted with the bo staff in my hands, then carried through instead of feinting after all. Jace slammed his staff into mine, blocking every step. "Ha," he said. "I knew you'd try that again."

He didn't anticipate my next move, but he dodged just in time, rolling and coming up fighting. For several long minutes, the workout room reverberated with the clash of our staffs. Sweat dripped from my tank into my biker shorts, and hair that had escaped my ponytail clung to my wet face.

The next instant, I felt Mari, and instead of plunging forward, I stepped back. Jace lunged for me, and I whirled my staff, tapping him soundly but not painfully on the back.

"Dang it, Mari. You made me lose." Jace turned to where she was waving at us from the doorway, though she hadn't used it to find us. I'd felt her shift in.

Her face lit up. "I did? Great! Glad I could be of service. Your ego needs a little tromping now and then."

"Oh yeah? Well, you already did that by choosing Keene over me." Jace flexed. "But don't forget that I'm here if you ever need a real man."

Mari smirked. "I'll be sure to pass that on to Keene. Look, I'm only here because apparently you two aren't picking up your phones. So once again, I'm reduced to playing messenger."

"Yeah, yeah, you know you love it," Jace muttered.

Mari's widening smile showed her agreement. "Anyway,

Stella sent me to tell you that Dimitri's here, and everyone is waiting for you two in the conference room. I'll let them know you're coming." With that, she vanished.

No time to do anything but grab a towel to mop my face and neck. Jace did the same.

"Ava could have told you mentally," Jace grumbled. "Then maybe *you* would have been the one distracted."

I rolled my eyes. "Not a chance." But he was probably right.

We didn't chat as we jogged up the stairs, but as we reached the main floor, Jace touched my hand. "Thanks, Erin."

I smiled. "Anytime." His eyes were no longer red, and he seemed calm. It was worth the exhaustion creeping over me now that the adrenaline rush was fading. I reached out to absorb, buoying my energy.

When we walked into the conference room and all eyes fell on us, I was suddenly aware of the wetness of my half tank and the glistening moisture still on my skin. Keene looked amused, Dimitri concerned, and Ava impatient. Ritter's eyes met mine and turned even darker. I detected the faintest bit of regret in their depths, and I smiled, remembering how our joint workout sessions usually ended.

I was surprised to see our Emporium captives, Fenton, Eden, and Bedřich, in the farthermost chairs at the foot of the table. Bedřich's sandy hair had even been combed and the redness was gone from his eyes. Shadrack and Jeane were present as well, squeezed in on the right side of the table closest to the captives. The presence of these five confirmed that Ava and Ritter had no intention of letting them go free until all this was over. It also told me Ava wasn't as confident in our plan as she could be, and that she hoped for some additional refinements, even if they originated from an untrustworthy source.

In other words, we were scraping bottom. My earlier confidence fell a notch.

I sat in the seat next to Ritter, kitty-corner from Ava, and Jace found a seat farther down. Chris, Oliver, Cort, and even our three mortal guards were present, though these last three were standing behind the captives instead of pulling up the extra chairs we kept in a closet. I was glad to see their vigilance.

I'd no sooner settled in my seat when Ava began. "A radical offshoot from the Hunters is claiming responsibility for the murders in DC and have released a statement saying the shooting wasn't targeted, only designed to send a message against all Unbounded. The main branch of Hunters, however, deny any splinter group exists, and Stella tracked the statement to a known Emporium contact. From everything we can determine, the senators' shooting seems to have been the Emporium's backup plan all along."

"Of course it was." Ritter put in. "With the New York cell and Homeland Security agents assigned to the senators, it could have only been the Emporium."

Jace shifted noticeably in his seat, but he didn't volunteer a rash plan as he once would have. I looked to Dimitri, instinctively perhaps, for reassurance, but his expression was grim, his face unsmiling. A tremor of fear shuddered through me. Dimitri was the oldest and most experienced Unbounded in our cell. If he was concerned, we all should be. Maybe this plan would get us all killed.

At that moment, Dimitri felt my stare and lifted his dark eyes to mine. The tension on his face eased and his eyes softened. That outward sign of love allowed me to relax the grip I had on the edge of my chair. Allowed the panic to fade. Dimitri might not have been around when I was learning to skate or stubbing my toe, but I didn't doubt he had faith in me, trusted and loved me. I wanted to tell him thanks for being my father. Him and not Stefan Carrington.

"I won't beat around the bush," Ava was saying now. "The

outlook is bleak. The replacements for the lost senators will vote with Ropte, and if they don't, we could see a repeat of what happened here. The Emporium is pulling out all stops. They understand that if we win the vote, they may never achieve their goals. We've seen the desperate measures they were willing to go to in Venezuela and Morocco. Shooting our own people here at home is just one more step in their plan." She paused and looked at several of us in turn. No one spoke or moved.

"I believe," she began again, "that it has come down to this simple fact: we beat them now or never. We have never been as strong as we are now. Neither have they, but we have an advantage they didn't count on: we know the locations of all their headquarters. We have been closely monitoring these locations by satellite and in person with help from our Renegades overseas. So far there has been no unusual activity in those locations, and we're taking that to mean they haven't caught on to us yet. Either they believe their people are still with the government or they don't believe they have anything important to tell us. We can't expect that to continue. Eventually, when they don't hear from their people, they'll assume the worst. We must act now." She looked at Ritter and nodded.

"Our idea is to attack their headquarters with full guns," Ritter explained, "and eliminate, disarm, and capture as many of their people as possible. We do the same simultaneously in all five main headquarters: San Francisco, New York, England, Germany, and Norway. For now, we're not going to worry about the smaller locations they have in France, Russia, and South America. As long as we take the largest five, the smaller ones won't be large enough to stand up against us."

Cort cleared his throat, clearly wanting to speak. When Ava nodded at him, he said, "I understand what we're looking at, but we don't have the manpower. Between us and the New York cell, we're at twenty-three Unbounded and maybe ten mortals. Thirty-three against what is a consolidated number of Emporium agents in San Francisco and New York. The sixty-plus Unbounded Renegades we have in Europe may be enough to make a dent in those other three headquarters, but they will still likely experience more losses than they inflict." He paused and held Ava's eyes before focusing on Ritter. "You are my oldest friend, and I want to support you, but this is suicide. For them in Europe, and especially here in the States."

Ritter nodded, his expression without emotion. "You're right, Cort. However, we're not going to be alone. Patrick is working with his father and the military to give us backup. Without congressional approval, he won't be able to give us many troops, but there is already at least one black ops team he can commit. If we can delay a week, there may be more."

"Mortals," one of the Emporium agents mumbled loudly. "Like that will help."

I was pretty sure it was Fenton who'd spoken. The big blond man was sitting back in his seat, his muscled arms folded over his chest. "They'll die," he added when we all stared at him. "Believe me, if I thought you had a chance, I'd go up against them myself. Not to save the mortals, but to free myself from the Emporium. But using mortals . . . it's like throwing a bucket of water on a grease fire. They'll burn up, and we'll still have the problem to deal with. Plus, any delay will cost you. The Emporium *will* figure out we've told you the locations, sooner probably than later. You don't have a week to wait for more black ops teams."

"Thank you for the observations," Ritter said, his expression resigned.

He'd told me mortals were the weakest part of our plan, and that using them, even trained ones, against Unbounded Emporium agents went against everything he believed, but we both knew that without the mortals we didn't stand a chance.

Were we becoming just like the Emporium—using mortals as cannon fodder?

"Fortunately," Ava said, "we will have more Unbounded to help, and they are the crux of this plan. For years we've been sending captured Emporium agents to our compound in Mexico in an effort to undo the Emporium programming or, as a last resort, to identify those who would never reform and who needed to stand trial for their murders. It's a slow program, and many Emporium agents have been there for decades. Some were eventually tried and convicted and executed, but others learned and reformed. We got to a point where we started using a few of those prisoners to help with the newer captives. Three months ago, when the announcement was made about our existence, Tenika Vasco—she's the leader of the New York cell," she added for Fenton and the other captives, "—and I decided to allow those who had married and had children to build houses nearby and interact with the natives on a regular basis. I'm happy to say that many of these people are ready to come back to the US. Ready to help us make a world where everyone is free. There are thirty-four ex-Emporium Unbounded who are willing to fight with us against the Emporium."

I bit back worry. The last I'd heard, over sixty Unbounded were living outside the compound, and Ritter and I had hoped that many would stand with us. Still, thirty-four volunteers was better than nothing.

Cort cleared his throat and said, "Seventeen for each location here in the States. Depending on what their abilities are and how well they've been trained, I'd say our odds of fulfilling our directive just increased fifty percent."

A fifty percent chance of making a significant dent in the Emporium armor. That wasn't the only part of the plan, of course. Mari's shifting ability would be needed, not only to transport the former prisoners but also to get us inside once we destroyed the inevitable electronic grid. But now, looking around at the faces of the people I loved, I knew our plan wasn't enough. Not even if the president found more mortal cannon fodder. Fodder like my brother Chris. No, this attack still seemed more like a suicide than something Ritter should have signed off on. That he had agreed only proved our desperation.

Our only other choice seemed to be continuing our losses until we had no one left to fight the Emporium.

"Actually, we'll have to spread out those thirty-four people," Ava said, "between the five locations, based on each head-quarter size. Because if we attack only one location at a time, the others will be able to send each other backup. I think these extra soldiers will give us the edge we need, if not to win then at least to seriously impede their operation."

"You must be joking." Fenton unfolded his hairy arms and placed his fists on the table. "You can't trust those prisoners."

Ava didn't react to his derision. "If we hadn't thought it possible, we wouldn't have wasted everyone's time in sending them there in the first place. They understand the danger the Emporium has put the world in, and they have proven themselves."

Next to Fenton, Eden was flushing as dark as her many freckles. Instead of radiating cuteness times ten, the former Emporium agent was a red ball of fury. "Fenton's still right. You'll never succeed. Not with those from the prison, or the mortal soldiers. Not even if you trust them."

"I agree," Bedřich said. "Oh, you'll do some damage, and maybe it'll be enough to beat them down temporarily, but you'll lose too many people, and the next time, there won't be enough of you left to stop them."

Silence fell, and for a long time no one spoke. How could we when we knew it was the truth?

Ava's probing eyes fell on Bedřich. "Why do you say that?"

"Because you're thinking like them," the Czech said. "And they'll be ready for that. Do you imagine that they could prance in here and murder you without a fight? Even if all four hundred of them showed up at once? And a few thousand of their mortal pets? Even if Jeane here was on their side and nulled everyone's ability?" He shook his head. "I'll bet you've got so many guns and hidden traps and back doors that they'd have to demolish this whole area just to get inside, only to find you were gone once they did succeed. Isn't that right?"

Not only right, but dead on. Besides our heavy artillery, we had an entire underground network that connected into the original sewer system that wasn't reflected on any official plans. No, the Emporium wouldn't get anywhere near capturing even one of us from our stronghold.

"Well, they've planned just as well, and tripled that," Bedřich said. "Especially after Stefan's daughter here escaped from the old headquarters in LA."

Eden was nodding. "They've been busy these past months, just as you have. Your plan will only aggravate them. It will never work. And waiting to fly those reformed prisoners here or for more soldiers will completely negate your element of surprise."

They weren't factoring in Mari's ability or that I could channel her, but seeing the plan from their point-of-view made me understand that we'd already failed. We just didn't know it yet. Ropte and the rest of the Triad were going to win, and everything we did here on out wouldn't make a lasting difference. The tide had already turned and now threatened to drown us all. I couldn't breathe.

"So," Ava said, "what would *you* do in our position?" She spoke casually, but I saw anticipation in the erectness of her back. Next to me, Ritter was also at high alert.

Bedřich thought a moment and then shook his head, as

did Fenton and Eden. "I don't have a clue. I just know your plan won't work. I *feel* it. And you know what that means to a combat Unbounded. You'd be best off tucking tail and do like I plan to do once I get out of here—find a nice little out-of-the-way place and do some living before I'm forced to go back and be their slave."

"That is not an option," I said, finally unable to keep myself quiet. If Ava and Ritter's plan was to get Bedřich and the others to hand us a magic solution, it wasn't working. Our captives didn't seem to know anything to help, despite their combined years of experience and ability in combat. "What would you do if you weren't a traitorous coward who wanted to hide away while the Emporium murders half the world's population?"

Bedřich glared at me with a hint of his former wildness in his eyes, but I glared back, and eventually he looked away.

"I don't think they want to murder everyone," Jeane said under her breath. "Just the troublema—" She cut off as Jace came to his feet.

"Answer my sister!" Jace ordered Bedřich. I was proud at how controlled his voice was. More controlled than mine. Across from him and next to Stella, both Chris and Mari looked ready to explode, so at least I wasn't the only one who sat in the ashes of a perfectly useless plan.

"I don't know," Bedřich insisted. "But you go ahead and throw your lives away. It'll just buy me more time. I wouldn't have said anything, but you took us from that place, so I owed you one. It won't work, I tell you, and there's nothing to make it work." He hesitated and then added as an afterthought, "Unless . . ."

"Unless what?" Jace grabbed onto the word. Everyone in the room held still.

Bedřich ignored Jace and focused on me and Ava. "There might be a way, but it will probably still mean throwing some of you and your pitiful mortal soldiers into the fire as a distraction."

"We're listening," Ava prompted.

Bedřich leaned forward, tenting his hands on the table. "All right. Here it is, for what it's worth. When you think about it, the Emporium as a whole is not your enemy. Not even the hit teams. No, you only need to get rid of three people." He held up fingers to emphasize his statement. "Three."

"He's on to something." Fenton let out an abrupt laugh, scanning the faces around the room. "Yep, you have the right people in this room to do it."

"The right people for what?" Ritter's eyes glittered darkly in a way that made all the captives blanch.

"Why," Bedřich said, "to take over the Triad, of course."

CHAPTER 15

W E STARED AT BEDŘICH. HE HAD TO BE COMPLETELY AND absolutely crazy, even without the pieces of Delia's constructs still floating around in his brain.

Of course taking over the Triad would be the thing to do, and they were on our list of priorities once we breached their walls, but it wasn't like we could just knock on the door and make a polite request for them to turn themselves over. If Bedřich believed we couldn't get inside any of the Emporium headquarters, how could we get to those three? Ropte maybe, but not Stefan and Tihalt.

"Part of our directive is to get rid of the Triad," Ritter growled. "All of them."

"Yes, but as we've discussed, you'll never make it through their minions to get to them." Bedřich didn't quite look at Ritter as he spoke, as if trying to stay under his radar, but his triumphant grin didn't falter. "By the time you do cut them down, their replacements will just keep coming until they outweigh you with their sheer numbers. Remember, they don't care about using mortals as linings for your graves."

"Then what do you suggest?" If Ava's voice held any more ice, Bedřich would be frozen so rigidly a breath would shatter him. "That's why we've allowed you in this meeting. Because you agreed to help."

Bedřich's mocking smile faded. "The Triad positions pass from family member to family member. Not only upon death, because there have been a few—very few—occasions that Triad members have stepped down and retired. Successors are usually chosen by the Triad member before he or she retires or is killed. If they die without choosing an heir, the other two in the Triad will appoint one of the deceased's family members. Until the Triad member's death, normally only the successor knows he or she is chosen, and they hold the correct papers. Even after they prove it, they must undergo DNA tests to make sure there's a strong blood tie."

Bedřich's companions, Fenton and Eden, looked at him blankly, and I suspected that if they had ever known this information, it had been removed from their minds.

"He's right," Jeane said. "I'd been hoping Delia had died without giving anyone the correct documents, but she'd given them to David, of course."

"Why keep the successor a secret?" I asked. "Wouldn't it be better if everyone knew up front so there's no question?" I couldn't help thinking that Jeane might not have been so anxious to kill Delia and return to the Emporium if she'd known.

Bedřich opened his mouth, but it was Cort who answered. "To us that makes sense, but the Emporium is completely foreign to the way we think. If a successor was positively known, they'd need round-the-clock protection."

"From other potential heirs?" I asked.

"Yes, and from other Triad members. This was especially true with Stefan and Delia." Cort smiled at our stunned expressions. "Oh, it wasn't always this way, but it has been during my whole lifetime. One of my brothers was murdered shortly before I left the Emporium. He was my father's pick as a successor. I don't recall how I knew he'd been chosen, but in the end, he was murdered because he was my father's choice." His narrow face hardened. "It turned out to be a good thing; my brother was a cruel man. His murder probably saved my father's life because I don't know how much longer he would have waited to take his inheritance, and my father was blind to his intent." He waved a hand as if to clear his head of the images. "My father believed Delia was behind it. My brother hated Delia with a passion, and they always butted heads—unlike my father, who was content to let Delia and Stefan run the Emporium. Everyone at the time thought she was making sure she wouldn't have to work with him, but nothing was ever proven." His word choice was careful, even for him, and I wondered if he knew more than he was telling. Against my will, I felt a little pity toward Tihalt for losing yet another son.

"So I guess Triad members either want to wait as long as possible to choose someone, or pick a successor who won't knock them off," Jace remarked. No one had a response to the ugly thought.

Keene stared at Cort from across the table, an unreadable expression on his face. Power swirled around him, unsteady and erratic. I wanted to say something but didn't want to call attention to him. I was relieved when Mari, sitting next to him, angled her body slightly, as if placing her hand on his thigh. The power gradually began to subside.

"That's why you left," Keene said to his brother.

"Only the straw that broke the camel's back," Cort responded, keeping his tone light. "He wasn't the first sibling I saw die unnecessarily for a cause I no longer believed in." The brothers sat, gazes locked, and the sadness that came from their surface thoughts made me want to weep. They'd lost so much to the Emporium due, in large part, to the evil man they called father.

No more.

I could practically feel Ritter thinking beside me, despite his heavy mental shield. I could only imagine the scenarios that were running through his mind. "How," he asked Bedřich, "do you suggest we go about this takeover?"

"Well, I don't exactly know your abilities or what else you might have in place, and I doubt you're going to share everything with me, so it's hard to plan a strategy."

"Oh, go ahead, take a stab," I said, with a challenge in my voice I knew Bedřich wouldn't be able to ignore.

"All right." Bedřich motioned to Cort and Keene, and then to Jeane and me. "Here in this room, you have descendants of each Triad member. Well, in Jeane's case, she's a sibling and not a descendant, but the blood tie would still be strong enough, I'm guessing."

For the briefest instant, I thought of telling him that I wasn't Stefan's daughter and that surely Jeane and Lew had reported this to the Emporium by now. Except Jeane nodded at his suggestion, which hinted that she hadn't told Stefan the truth. Why? It didn't make sense. Delia hadn't told Stefan the truth about either my ability or my heritage because she'd wanted to use me—or my body, at least—to win Stefan over and, blood test or no, eventually take his place. But Jeane had no way to use me, and this information might have won her points with Stefan. I filed the thoughts away and forced myself to follow Bedřich's words.

"So I'd try to somehow get inside the headquarters," he was saying. "Sneaking in or blending in, not fighting or killing anyone—and then take over the Triad from within. Depending on your persuasiveness, you could force them to sign papers designating you as their successors. Or you'd figure out how to create the paperwork yourselves. The papers could be forged if you had the right access." As he spoke, his eyes kept sliding to Mari, and I had no doubt as to how he thought we might get close to the Triad once we were inside the building. He'd seen her shifting around.

"If they've already signed papers naming other successors, it'll cause a problem," Jace said.

Bedřich thought about that for a moment. "I don't think so. I've heard rumors of more than one set of papers being given out, just in case one heir is killed in battle at the same time as the Triad member. I don't know if that's true, but it doesn't really matter. Others will have heard the same thing. Your papers will be the latest and the most valid."

"So you expect at that point the rest of the Emporium will simply start following them?" Ritter's disbelief wrapped every word. "Because from what I've seen of their soldiers, it won't be that easy."

Bedřich shrugged his wiry shoulders as if to say it wasn't his concern. Eden answered for him. "Even if you just permanently kill them, you'd be further ahead than you would have been with your original plan. If it doesn't work, you could always go back to slaughtering the rest and getting slaughtered in return."

Between them, Fenton leaned forward, looking interested for the first time, if I could judge by the flush covering his pale skin. "The Triad will be surrounded by loyal people, so I expect there'll be a struggle with some of them, but given the power Bedřich claims Erin has"—he flicked his gaze over me—"she should be able to control at least some of them. And if you have people standing by to help, even better." He looked at Mari. "Tell me, can you shift other people too? And how far?"

"Don't answer that, Mari," Ritter said, and I was glad. They were still mostly our enemies, despite having agreed to help us.

Fenton looked annoyed, but his only response was to fold his arms and lean back in his chair.

There was a whole lot the captives were overlooking, most particularly, the electric grid that would keep my thoughts and Mari out. But if we could somehow *become* the Triad—that opened up an entirely new set of opportunities that didn't involve more fighting and dismembering.

Ritter had already brought up the monitor embedded in the table in front of him and was examining the plans Stella had managed to find of the San Francisco and New York locations. They were scrambled, vague, and incomplete, but he studied them with enough concentration that I knew he believed this was a plan we might carry out successfully. A plan that wasn't suicide.

Ava glanced at Ritter and came to the same conclusion. "Is there anything else you'd like to share?" she asked the captives. One by one, they shook their heads.

"But where are the Triad?" Mari said. "They used to have their main offices in LA, right? So they're probably in San Francisco now, but who's to say they aren't in New York?"

"Oh, that's easy," Jeane answered, her beautiful face looking bored. "They're in New York. After Erin damaged their building in LA, they moved the West Coast headquarters to San Francisco, but the Triad transferred closer to the action in DC. They were all there before I escaped. Except David. He stays at various safe houses that he owns."

"How can we be sure they haven't moved since you left?" Ritter barely glanced up from his screen as he asked the question.

Jeane smiled and rolled her neck, staring at him between half-lidded eyes. "Because I'll call and ask."

"You think they're going to tell you?" I asked. Her arrogance was unbelievable.

Jeane reluctantly transferred her gaze to me. "If I have something to give them, I'm sure they'll be more than happy to meet with me. With a little luck, we can get my brother there as well."

Her brother Ropte. Was she really willing to risk his life? "How?" I didn't hide the suspicion from my voice. I was on the verge of wanting to strangle her as much for the lack of clarity as for the not-so-subtle invitations she was sending Ritter. As a null, she had a lot to offer a man who might want to disconnect from an ability. That wasn't Ritter, but she still rubbed me the wrong way.

Jeane gave me the same seductive stare she'd bestowed on Ritter. "Because, I'll be taking them something Stefan's been hunting for a while: his long-lost daughter. You."

Pandemonium burst out as everyone spoke at once. "That would do it," said Bedřich, while Mari exclaimed, "Yes! We'll walk right in!" Cort nodded and said, "It could work." And "It'll be a tough sell," came from Keene. Jace's face flushed as he spoke: "She can't go in alone." Then from Chris, "Might be better to get them outside the headquarters."

More comments twisted and slid around each other, each person offering an opinion. Only Ritter, Ava, and Dimitri remained silent.

And me.

"Even without knowing you're a sensing Unbounded," Jeane continued, "Stefan will want you for breeding. He knows you're Ava's descendent, and with the right sperm donor you could have a sensing child. You're much better than the little twit he has there making eyes at Lew now."

I stared at her for several seconds before I could process her comment enough to say, "You and Lew didn't tell them I'm not a combat Unbounded?" I swallowed hard on the last word.

Jeane regarded me with wide eyes. "Honey, I never tell anyone anything unless I have to. You never know when it will become useful."

"What about Lew?"

She shrugged. "He might have said something after I left, but I'm not sure it would have come up, and Catrina isn't nearly as strong as he is, so she can't break through his shield. And it seems anyone who might have known about you had that particular memory extracted before Delia died." She gazed at the three Emporium captives. "Only they know now." About the sensing, she meant, because they still believed me to be Stefan's daughter.

Two emotions warred inside me. If Stefan didn't know for sure about my ability or my parentage, it made Jeane's idea singularly perfect. I could waltz right in. They might not trust me, but even with Lew and the newcomer Catrina, they'd wouldn't be able to break into my mind for a good long while. Stefan might not believe I'd turned from the Renegades, but Jeane was right that he would jump at the chance to have me.

That terrified me more than I cared to admit. Still, it was a real chance—and I'd take that over a suicide mission any day.

Everyone soon quieted under Ava's granite stare, but the different feeling in the room was amazing. Hope floated like protein atoms awaiting our absorption.

I had to hand it to Ava and Ritter. They'd known the original plan was weak, but they'd played it off our prisoners to create a strategy that was actually possible.

Maybe. If only so much didn't depend on me.

CHAPTER 16

AVA STOPPED THE DISCUSSION SO OUR MORTAL GUARDS COULD remove Shadrach and the Emporium prisoners, including Jeane. "No," Jeane protested. "I want to stay here. I deserve to know everything. You have to promise me that Lew will be okay."

"What about your brother?" Bedřich mocked. "Blood should be thicker than sex, even for a—" He said a word I didn't understand, but Jeane apparently did.

"You Czech pig!" She launched herself at him, her nails poised to rake his thin face.

Without thinking, I pushed hard against her unshielded mind, sending a blast of light. At the same time, our guards dived for Jeane, with no chance of separating them in time. Bedřich's hands started to rise to protect himself; he would also be too late.

A half instant before she gouged his eyes, her hands slowed and opened. She ran the inside of her fingers caressingly down his cheeks instead. "Never mind. You're not worth it." She gave a seductive laugh before turning docilely toward the door. "Take me back to my room, please."

We all stared at the change in her. Ritter's brows arched in calculation as he studied not Jeane's retreating back but my stunned face. This was twice now, so the first time hadn't been a fluke.

"All right. Let's see what we've got," Ava said after a few seconds. She waited until she had everyone's attention. "Our new directive is to capture and contain the Emporium Triad." She paused before adding, "By whatever means possible. Targeting only the Triad means we still have to get people inside, but hopefully only at one location. That also means we can do this as soon as tomorrow, which will maintain the advantage of surprise. Stella, can you show us the building?"

A holo of a New York high-rise appeared over the table. Twenty stories tall, with probably several more beneath the ground. "This is the New York headquarters," Stella said. "With everything that's going on in New York and DC, I believe Jeane's right about Stefan and Tihalt living there now. Plus, Ropte's close enough for us to lure him there in a respectable timetable."

"Impressive." Dimitri studied the building, one hand absently rubbing his chin. "If we cut off the Emporium's head, we should be able to take over long enough to set them back years, if not permanently."

Mari had a black knife in her hands and was twirling it gently. "Cut off the head. I like that." Sometimes she worried me with her knife fascination, though I sensed she was at peace with herself now, more than she had been before leaving San Diego.

Keene's gaze went from Mari to the holo. "Going in will be dangerous. We'll have to spin it just right."

"We'll also have to make sure the other headquarters overseas don't send reinforcements in case we do end up fighting more than we hope," Dimitri said. "But the way I see it, this is really our only option. That is, if we're going to act at all." There was a gentle question in his voice, but Ava met it head on.

"You know we have to."

He nodded. "I do know. I just don't like it." His stare flitted to me and away.

"Wait," said Jace. "Erin reported seeing Stefan visiting Ropte. Maybe we could lure them all to his place. There would be fewer soldiers hanging around."

We all thought about that for a moment. It was a solid suggestion, one that would certainly fulfill my wish about not walking into Stefan's den. "Stefan won't be traveling without a lot of people and talent around him," I ventured, "but it could work. Right? Especially with the reinforcements from Mexico."

"My father rarely leaves headquarters," Cort said. "And all the paperwork needed for the succession will be at headquarters. DNA, video recognition—it'll be very involved, if I know them. Still, it does seem easier. If we could somehow convince Tihalt to leave."

Ava looked at Ritter, who was staring at the holo of the headquarters. No emotion showed on his face, but the connection between us told me his mind was in turmoil. Finally, he sighed. "If we try to have Jeane turn Erin over at Ropte's, there's no way Stefan will buy it. He has enough experience to know we'll be up to something. He'll make it impossible for us."

Mari made a sour face. "Jeane did escape the Emporium and run to Ropte, so you're right that Stefan probably isn't going to trust her."

"That's exactly why this plan is only going to work if Jeane takes Erin to their headquarters." Ritter sighed and shook his head. "He'll only feel secure at his own place. We need to stroke his confidence. Even then, it's going to be suspicious. We'll have to send Erin in with a fake offer from us. Something that sounds plausible. Because Stefan's going to think we fooled Jeane into taking Erin captive for some reason. Keene's right that the spin is what will sell it."

Ava's gaze settled on my face, and I felt her probing mentally, but I kept my shields tight. At my refusal to let her in, she pushed out the tiniest breath of frustration that only Dimitri and I were close enough to hear. Too bad for her. I wasn't about to let my terror at facing Stefan stop us from trying to end this battle once and for all. "It'll have to be there," she finally agreed.

"Right. But there are a few other things we have to address." I began ticking them off on my fingers. "First, they'll have an electric grid over the entire building, and that puts me alone in there until we can cut the power. They'll have primary and backup generators like we do here. Second, we have to worry about any prison cells they may have inside that they might throw me into regardless of any spin we dream up. That means we need a backup plan. Third, we have no idea how many personal guards I'll have to deal with until you guys are able to shift in. Fourth, we need to find a way to get Ropte there."

Ritter inclined his head, and I suspected he was already far ahead of me in working out the details of my list. "And we still don't know what Ropte's ability is."

"I'll question Jeane about it," I said.

"So what happens if—when—this does succeed?" Jace asked. "Erin won't pass their blood test."

"We'll have to get around that," Keene said, "Obviously, Delia had something in mind to get around that since she planned to use Erin to take over Stefan's place. It must be possible. But I'm not totally pleased with the idea of trusting that . . . that . . . Jeane."

Mari snorted at his lack of words. "Snake? Traitor? Whore? I bet that's what Bedřich called her."

A smile tugged on the corners of Keene's mouth. "Whatever she is, she can't be trusted."

"Erin shouldn't go," Jace insisted, looking more to Ritter than anyone else. Ritter, who felt the same but wouldn't stop me because there was no other way.

"She won't be alone," Keene said. "Cort or I will be there too. One of us can go in separately for a reunion with dear old Dad." His bottom lip curled on the last words.

"As long as we interrupt their electrical shield. I can get all of us right into any room where Erin is," Mari added.

"But I'm the one you should send." Jace sat forward, hands splayed on the table. "Stefan is my father, not Erin's."

Silence fell in the room, with Keene, Mari, Oliver, and Chris looking confused. "What are you saying?" Chris was the one to ask.

Jace glanced at our brother. "Just what it seems. You know the sperm they stole didn't get to the fertility clinic in time to use for Erin—they saved it for me."

"No," Chris whispered. I knew he wanted to protect Jace from this as much as I wanted to, but there are some things from which you can't protect even those you love.

"Yes, I'm Stefan Carrington's son." Jace stumbled over the man's name. "I just found out today, but I think I've known all along."

I wanted to cry out for Jace to shut up, because he was right that I wouldn't pass the DNA tests, but sending my younger brother into that place . . . I'd rather die than let him face Stefan.

"Jace," Ava said, her gray eyes liquid and softer than normal, "you've made a good point, and certainly, you'll be there for the op, as we all will, but Stefan believes Erin is his daughter.

We don't want to take the chance of muddying the waters at this point. Her unique abilities make her the logical choice to infiltrate their headquarters. You're right that for DNA, we'll need you at some point. And I'm guessing you'll be the successor who ultimately takes Stefan's place and helps reform the Emporium."

"Mari can find me inside, once you turn off the generators," Jace protested. "Erin can come in then."

Ritter shook his head. "I have no doubt that the Emporium learned a lesson after what we were able to do the last time, and I'm betting the generators will need to be shut off from the inside. Erin's abilities will help us do that. The second she succeeds, Mari will shift you in."

Jace slumped back in his chair. "Okay, you're right." He didn't look angry, and I wondered if that meant he was as scared as I was at the idea of entering Stefan's lair.

Next to me, Ritter took my hand under the table. Though he felt cool against the clamminess of my skin, I wasn't going to let go in order to hide my apprehension from him. As our ops leader and experienced combat Unbounded, Ritter could shut down this plan at any moment, but he wouldn't shut it down, I knew, no matter how much he hated it, because this was our best chance. Our only chance.

"So Erin will go in with Jeane," Ritter said, the words heavily reluctant but determined. "Now that we're not attacking all the locations, we can use the bulk of the ex-Emporium recruits from Mexico to form a blockade around the facility. That way no one inside can run for help and no reinforcements can enter. We'll take down the electricity in much of the city, so the Emporium will only be left with generators, which, at some point, Erin will interrupt. And telephone service also needs to be taken down until we've secured the building."

Heads nodded as Ritter continued. "After we subdue the

Triad, we'll shift in more of our people. Or before that, if we have to. I'm not going to trust that they will all just fall into line when we take over."

Cort coughed gently before adding, "There's bound to be some fighting. But if we can take them over completely, it'll be that much easier to control any reaction from their other headquarters."

"So how am I shutting down the generators?" I was working through it in my mind, and all I kept seeing was Stefan throwing me into a locked room. "After all the training, I know how to bypass them, but Stefan isn't going to make it easy." I'd have to somehow overcome the guards.

"Stefan will definitely have them secure," Ritter said. "That's where Cort comes in." Everyone, including Cort, looked at Ritter blankly. "Cort hasn't played double agent since Keene left the Emporium," Ritter continued without missing a breath, "and it's doubtful they'll trust him now, but using that old cover, we should be able to get him inside. This time he'll take a few prisoners to pad his homecoming. Namely, Mari and me."

Ava's soft gasp told me this wasn't something she'd expected. Stella stopped paying attention to the holograph and started shaking her head so violently her neural headset threatened to fly off. "No. If they got their hands on a shifter . . ." she began.

"They don't know what Mari looks like." Ritter raised his voice to talk over Stella, his eyes locked on Ava, upon whom rested the ultimate decision. "Even if they've heard rumors that we have a shifter, they can't know it's Mari. She'll go in disguise, of course."

"No." Keene sat up stiffly in his chair, looking murderous. "It's one thing having her shift inside and taking backup, but going in like that . . . we have no idea what their reaction might be."

Ritter held firm. "We need to move around freely inside their headquarters. Either Mari or Erin can use Mari's ability to shift to the generators and disable them. That means getting Mari inside is the *only* way this plan has any chance of success."

"It's too dangerous!" Keene shouted, jumping to his feet. Volatile energy danced around him.

Ritter released my hand and also arose, leaning over the table on his fisted hands. "Would you rather have her storm the front doors as we planned before? I'll protect her, Keene. You know I will!" The two men glared at each other from across the table, neither backing down.

"Keene, it's my decision!" Mari tugged at Keene to sit in his chair.

He ignored her, but when he spoke again, his words were slightly calmer. "They'll put her in a protected cell. She won't be able to shift from there. After everything Erin and Delia have been able to do, they'd be stupid not to lock her up. If she goes in as a prisoner, no one will be able to use her ability."

Silence for too long, and then Cort said calmly, "I probably should have spoken up sooner, but for the record, there's no way my father will ever trust me again. In fact, he's more likely to kill me on sight, even if he could be made to believe that I was still working undercover, which I really doubt." He looked around at us, his mouth lifting in a sad smile. "I might as well tell you—it was me who killed my father's successor. Yes, my own brother. I told my father he was in danger, but he never believed I did it to save his life." He glanced at Keene as if willing him to understand. "I said before that my brother wasn't the first sibling I saw die unnecessarily for a cause I no longer believed in, but he was the first family member *I* had to kill. That was when I realized I was working for the wrong side. I never wanted to do that again."

Ritter froze, and something in his demeanor whispered of

shame. "You're right, we can't send you in like that. But we still need Mari inside. Otherwise, it could take days before Erin gets to the generator."

"I understand that," Keene said, sorrow in his eyes. "But having one prisoner showing up will be hard enough for them to stomach without throwing in a second group."

Ritter sat back down slowly, his face drawn in thought. "There might be a better way, but it means Cort and I won't be there initially to help." He paused, looking up in the direction of the wall, as if going through different scenarios in his mind.

Finally, he dragged his gaze back to Keene. "You'll be the one to go in then. I think the best way is for you to contact your father and say you want to come home. Do it before Jeane calls so the two events don't appear to be connected. Try to make him believe you're coming back for good. You've been hidden pretty much in plain sight while under their noses in DC, so he might buy that you were only with us for a short time and regret leaving him."

Keene nodded, his mouth tight as though he didn't trust himself to speak.

"My father may hate me"—Cort didn't sound too shaken up about it—"but Keene was always a favorite, or he wouldn't have led so many hit teams. Once he knows Keene has Changed, and especially about his unique ability, he'll be persuaded."

Keene's nostrils flared. "Oh, he'll be willing to have me come home, if only to do experiments on me."

"Exactly." Regret oozed like defeat in Cort's voice, and I knew he wanted Keene to do this as much as I wanted to walk through those doors.

"And Mari?" Keene asked, glancing at Mari, who nodded at Ritter encouragingly.

"I want to help," she said.

Ritter blew out a sigh. "Mari still goes in—but as Keene's

girlfriend. She'll help Erin disable the generators. Mari and Keene will be Erin's backup and vice-versa."

Keene stared at him blankly for a moment before he sank into his chair, his body relaxing. "Right. Okay. At least they'll have a slight chance of believing Mari's there because she wants to be with me. Since she's an unknown, not someone related to Cort or the Renegades, they won't have reason to watch her too closely."

"That's a great idea!" Mari said with her usual abandon. The tension seeped from the room. "I think I just might be able to get into that role."

Jace snorted a laugh. "Yeah, tell us about it."

"We could still go in," Cort told Ritter, "or get ourselves caught somehow. I might be able to talk Stefan into not letting my father kill me."

Ritter didn't speak for a long moment of internal debate that had his hands clenched on the armrests of his chair. "No. Keene's right that more of us would be too much of a coincidence. We're stretching things as they are. We'll wait until Mari and Erin can shift us inside to deal with the Triad."

"Are there any more comments? Objections?" Ava asked, looking mostly at Dimitri, Chris, and Oliver, who had been silent during the exchange. All of them shook their heads. "Okay, then we're in agreement," Ava continued. "We still need to fine-tune the details, but before that we need to discuss the Emporium headquarters in San Francisco. They will likely be the first ones to offer aid if New York doesn't go exactly as planned."

"The black ops team the president offered could form a blockade there," Ritter said. "They're well-trained and should be able to capture small groups of Emporium agents as they leave. But they know nothing about Unbounded or how to deal with them, so one of us will need to be in charge."

"I agree." Ava's attention roamed the room. Oliver sat a little taller, but her eyes landed on Chris. "You think you're up for it, Chris? You can have George, Marco, and Charles on your team, but you'll be calling the shots."

Chris blinked in surprise at being chosen. "Yeah. I can do that."

I wasn't sure how to feel about his appointment, but Chris had been training as hard as the rest of us, and he was an excellent shot. Our mortal guards all looked up to him after he'd apparently saved George and Stella's lives from an Emporium hit team when we were away on an op. At least he wouldn't have to storm the building.

"I'm hoping you won't have to take more than a dozen prisoners during the entire op," Ritter told Chris. "But there could be a lot more if things don't go smoothly. You'll need to stop them from going to New York, even if you have to shoot them down in the street."

"Without a sensing Unbounded, I'll need air support," Chris said. "I'll work with Marco and the others to figure out coverage. Needless to say, we'll try to capture them first."

"We'll get you a chopper." Ava paused for a minute, tapping a finger lightly against the table as if eager to get started. "That only leaves the other headquarter locations. We'll need to contact our other Renegade cells to see what they can do about blockades there."

"Will they agree to the plan?" I asked.

Ava surprised me by chuckling. "Since I'm only asking them to capture or delay anyone who leaves those buildings instead of demanding an outright attack, I'm sure they'll agree. They understand only too well what we're facing here. This is the battlefield. If we fail, they know they'll be next."

CHAPTER 17

AFTER AN HOUR, I LEFT THE OTHERS STILL DEEP IN PLANNING TO go talk to Jeane. She was the key to making this work, and I needed to know more of her motives before I let her call Stefan, which we'd be doing far too soon for my comfort.

"Erin, wait!"

I paused, turning in the hallway to see Jace hurrying out of the conference room after me. Looks like I wasn't the only one who needed a break. Or maybe he was going to take another stab at trying to convince me he should go in my place. I'd thought he'd backed off just a little too quickly.

"So, what did you do to Jeane?" he asked when he reached me.

I grimaced, both at the question and because that couldn't be why he'd skipped out of the meeting. "I'm not really sure. What I did *should* have made her black out, but instead she calmed down. It's happened twice now. I wish there were more time to figure it out, because I'm thinking Cort could probably decipher whatever language her thoughts are using."

"Or whatever the Emporium's done to her, you mean." Jace's frown made him look angry. "The Unbounded gene doesn't act like this. They must have done something genetic."

"Cort suggested the same thing. You're probably right. But there's nothing we can do about it now. I'd better get to Jeane to find out what more I can and to coach her about what to say." I started walking again, but Jace grabbed my hand.

"You're afraid," he said. "I feel it."

So that was why he'd followed me—my little brother knew me too well. I sighed, turning to face him. The hallway suddenly seemed too quiet, too deserted, and Jace too fragile. "Stefan Carrington is an awful man," I said, the words coming quietly because of my reluctance to speak of Stefan at all. Jace leaned forward, turning slightly so his ear was closer to me. "He tried to have you killed, and our parents."

"But?"

I sighed again. "When I first saw him, I felt how much he wanted me. Me! How much he cared for his family—all his offspring." Something stirred in my brother's eyes, but I shook my head, willing him to understand. "It wasn't what I thought. He did care for family, but only to build his empire, to expand the Emporium. I saw in his mind that he would snuff out my life as easily as he would a candle if I didn't fall into line. He only wanted me for what I could do for him." I paused, swallowing hard. "He stood there at our first meeting and pretended he hadn't ordered Lorrie's death or the attack at the house. But he had."

Anguish filled Jace's face, and this more than anything was the real reason he couldn't take my place at the Emporium headquarters tomorrow. He wasn't prepared to see Stefan as the monster he really was. "Don't think for a moment I will ever trust him, but so help me Erin, I want to look into his face. Into his eyes. I want to see for myself." He forced a laugh. "You heard what Ava said—our directive is to get them *by any means possible*. But don't kill him before I get there, okay?"

"You guys are coming in to help us get him to sign the papers. He's got to be alive that long, right?"

"And then?"

"I don't know," I lied. Surely Jace understood that we couldn't leave Stefan alive. It would be too dangerous. A thousand years in a Mexican prison compound wouldn't be enough to change his ways or pay for the lives he'd taken.

I also didn't want Stefan anywhere near my brother.

Jace's face smoothed out with my assurances. He thumbed over his shoulder. "I'd better get back there. I want to make sure I'm with Ritter when you guys shift us in." He shook his head. "He about lost it there for a moment when he realized it wasn't good planning to go in with you."

"But he *did* realize it. Ritter will always go with the plan that has the most chance of success."

"I get it." A ghost of his usual grin returned to his face.

I watched him reenter the conference room before I reached out to Ava. Her mind was open as if waiting for me. *We need to watch Jace. I think he's okay, but just to make sure.*

I'll put Stella on it. But he's a smart boy. I think he understands it has to be you.

Satisfied that Jace would be all right, I went upstairs to the holding room to find Jeane. Belying its name, the suite was considerably plush. Jeane had to share a bathroom with Eden and a sitting room with the others, but she had her own bedroom. She and Eden were in the sitting room together when Marco, who was standing guard, opened the door for me.

"I wondered when you'd come," Jeane said lazily from the love seat she was sprawled over as if posing for a magazine. Her makeup looked freshly reapplied, including heavy mascara, deep red lipstick, and black eye liner over her mole. Stella must have given her makeup with the other supplies.

"Hey," Eden called a greeting from the minibar where she was pouring herself a drink. Alcohol didn't last long in our systems, so this stuff was especially potent, but even then getting drunk was impossible. Eden's brown hair was pulled back in a severe ponytail, emphasizing her numerous freckles. She looked compellingly wholesome compared to Jeane's sex kitten act.

"I've been wanting to ask you if you thought I could dye my hair blond again," Jeane added. "Really, blondes do have more fun. Men seem to notice them more—like your man, for instance."

I was glad she'd noticed his lack of interest in her, but I wasn't going to explain that it had nothing to do with my hair. "You can't change your hair for another fifty years, at least," I said. "Especially if you insist on darkening your mole like that." Hadn't anyone told her that beauty marks had gone out of style while she'd been a hunk of drying flesh? Now most women tried to hide them.

Jeane huffed and folded her arms over her stomach. "Well, it's not my fault I can't get rid of it. My body keeps remaking it every time I cut it off."

I perched on the edge of the love seat. "A mole is not a defect," I reminded Jeane. The fact that we were discussing beauty marks when the fate of humanity was at stake made me feel ridiculous.

"*I* think it's defective." Jeane rolled her eyes. "At least it could have been black."

"We need to go over what you're going to tell Stefan." Fear gnawed at my gut even mentioning the man.

"Oh, don't worry. I know exactly what to say." She made a loose fist and brought it to her ear. "Hi, Triad

Carrington—Stefan, darling. It's me, Jeane." She batted her mascara-laden eyes for effect. "Look, I'm sorry for buggin' out on you all like that; I had some stuff to do. But I have something I think you'll be excited about." She paused before continuing. "Well, shush, now. You'll want to hear this. It's about that girl the Renegades stole from our LA headquarters. You know, your *daughter*. Well, I have her with me. No, I didn't kidnap her. I simply told her you were a reasonable man. Ha ha. Yes, of course, I'm lying. I do have her tied up. What with all those moves she can make even when I'm nulling her ability." Jeane gave a sultry laugh that hinted she was offering more than just me. "She has strong hands like her father. Now, all I want is to be forgiven. Her ancestor is sensing, as I'm sure you remember. Using her, Lew and I will help you get that team of sensing Unbounded you've been wanting. No, I can bring her in myself. Okay, see you soon." She gave a final smirk into the pretend phone and dropped her hand.

"You think he'll buy that?" I asked.

"Of course. He's a man."

I stifled my irritation. She obviously didn't know any real men. "What about Ropte? Are you willing to give up Ropte to get to Lew? What did you have in mind for that? Because he has to be a part of this or the deal's off."

"Do I have to do all your work for you?" She stuck out her glistening lips in a sensual pout.

"You sounded like you had a plan earlier."

"Well, I was thinking I'd call David and have him meet me there. But he might not come." She smoothed her hair, pretending his indifference didn't bother her. "Maybe it'd be better to tell Stefan you have information, or an offer from the Renegades for the whole Triad."

"Yeah, we've planned something along those lines." I didn't

tell her it was because we thought Stefan would suspect we'd tricked her into capturing me. "But what makes you think he'll invite Ropte? If he's got Tihalt in hand, he doesn't need Ropte for a majority vote."

"Fine. I'll call David and hint that you hold pertinent information that Stefan might hide from him. That should work. There's been tension between them lately. And to answer your earlier question, I don't believe you'll kill David. Once he learns about the takeover, he'll play ball. I've no doubt about that." She made a shooing motion with her hands. "Then you can send him off to Mexico for however long it takes him to become a good little boy."

Eden finally spoke up from the couch across from us where she'd settled with her drink. "He'll never reform. Think about it, Jeane, they have no choice but to kill him. I would."

Jeane tossed her a derisive look. "That's because you're trained by the Emporium. You don't know the Renegades like I do."

"Thanks for the vote of confidence," I said.

Eden was right, of course. If Ropte did survive the takeover, he wouldn't be heading to Mexico but awaiting trial for treason and murder. The trick would be leading him to believe he'd be all right and making him do what we wanted before he learned the truth.

I felt sick thinking about it. I'd fought and temporarily killed Unbounded many times, and a few had permanently died. Either way, killing was never easy or pretty—or my first choice. This time things were different because the Triad weren't ordinary Emporium agents. They represented centuries of pain and horror, and we needed to make sure they were never released on the world again.

"I want to go with you." Eden straightened, and her aura of defeat and worry slid like a cloak from her shoulders.

I let several seconds of silence pass before I said, "I don't think that's possible."

"I can help. I *want* to help." She held up two fingers an inch apart. "I'm this close to getting away from the Emporium and making sure they never find my daughter. If you fail, all of that's gone. I want it to finally be over. To end them—all of them."

"Wow!" Jeane crossed one leg over the other and narrowed her eyes. "Why don't you tell us how you really feel?"

Eden ignored her. "I'll fight. I'll do anything. I'll even sit in this room for the rest of my life if I have to. I just want you to destroy them and make sure they don't have information on my daughter. I want them to forget she ever existed." Her mind shield was down, and I could see she meant every word. She didn't really want to fight, or have anything to do with the Emporium ever again, but she was serious about making sure her daughter remained with the adoptive family who loved her, even if that meant Eden would never be a part of her life.

I studied the pale eyes, the upturned nose, the splay of freckles, the intense determination. In that moment, she could be any mother fighting for her young. Slowly, I nodded. "You'll have to take up your request to Ava about being part of the op, but I'll do my best to get rid of any records the Emporium might have about your daughter's adoptive family." Or any of the adoptive families.

I turned to find Jeane studying me. "What will you do when the Emporium is under your thumb?" She leaned forward quickly. "Or under our thumbs? Because I'll be right there with you as a Triad member. At least for a time." She smiled with an open mouth that showed a flash of tongue.

"I wouldn't make too many plans."

She sat back and yawned. "Oh, well. Easy come easy go."

A takeover wasn't going to be simple, not by a long shot,

and yet everything was falling into place so well that the ease bothered me. I felt a little like a puppet on a string, and that decided me. Before I went to the Emporium headquarters, I'd have Cort and Stella help me record Jeane's thoughts. I needed to know if we could decipher them.

I arose and went to the door, with both women watching me. Before I knocked to be let out, I paused and said, "Jeane, one more thing. What's Ropte's ability? I don't want to meet him unprepared."

Jeane's smile faltered for a second, the tiniest hiccup in her bright face. Then it was gone, as if she'd lost her train of thought for that smallest instant. "You know, I don't think anyone's ever said. But it's got to be big, right? Or Delia would never have chosen him."

I understood Jeane well enough to know that she would just as soon lie as tell the truth, and with little provocation. But I couldn't think of a reason she would lie now, unless she still trusted Ropte to get Lew for her—and that seemed unlikely.

"What ability did your parents have?" Eden asked.

Jeane shrugged. "Never knew my father, but he was combat. Our mother's talent was sensing. She's dead now. Long time ago."

"I'm sorry."

Jeane shrugged. "I didn't know her. I grew up in foster homes. The Emporium contacted me some years after I Changed."

I knew the rest. She had become a famous actress after stepping into the life of a young mortal, who had met with a fatal accident that I didn't believe was an accident at all. Then Delia had learned of her nulling ability and faked Jeane's death before taking her in for experimentation. Murdering the man Jeane loved—mostly because he'd been a Renegade—had come years later.

"And Ropte's father?" I asked.

One delicate shoulder lifted in a careless shrug. "Don't know. He's been dead a thousand years, and it's really never come up with David. We're not *that* close."

She was probably an embarrassment for him, especially where he was now. "Let me know if you remember anything." Something wasn't right, but I couldn't put my finger on it.

"There is one thing you'll need to be careful of once we're there," Jeane said. "That other sensing Unbounded I told you about, Catrina." The curl of her lip said everything I needed to know about Jeane's feelings for this girl. "Lew says she's powerful for one so young. If he's been working with her, she might be trouble."

"They're probably already breeding her," Eden said. "Maybe her mind will be on other things."

Jeane's face hardened. "I intend to see that doesn't happen. Lew is *mine*."

Jealousy infused every word. I couldn't read her mind, but I guessed that in a society where breeding was not only desired but required for the good of the whole, her inability to conceive was a wound she would never come to terms with. She should have picked a man with a more common ability to love.

Pity rose in my face, but she only sneered. "Save your sympathy. I *will* get rid of the girl. She has no power against me."

I nodded silently and left, experiencing an odd compassion for this Catrina.

Ritter was still in the conference room with Ava, though the others had been released for a break, and despite my desire to get rid of the Emporium, I couldn't return to the conference room. I found myself following a path that led to the dining room, looking for company that wouldn't be talking strategy.

I passed our other two mortal guards in the hallway,

returning Fenton and Bedřich to their suite after a workout in the basement. Fenton nodded, but Bedřich stared at me with something akin to hatred. I didn't blame him. I'd known Delia and what her ability made her capable of. But I wasn't her, and I wouldn't try to prove myself to him.

I paused in the dining room doorway, a smile coming to my face as I viewed the scene. Chris was there with his two children and Stella, eating a late afternoon snack. Kathy and Spencer sat on either side of Chris, their heads leaning against him. Stella sat next to Spencer, inclining slightly in his direction as if pulled toward the family, and Spencer held her hand. Stella was eating what looked like yogurt and granola, while the kids and Chris munched on grilled cheese sandwich fingers, minus the crust. Everyone had a huge glass of milk—almond milk most likely, since Spencer preferred it.

Chris reached for his glass, the muscles in his arms bulging. When had he become so fit? But something besides the muscles was different, something that took me a while to pinpoint: he was content. I'd thought for a long time after his wife's murder that maybe he wouldn't love again, and then that maybe he'd fallen too fast for Stella. That she wouldn't return his feelings because of his mortality. Stella was different too, that same contentment radiating through her. Not the sadness that had filled her after losing her husband and baby. Today they looked like a family.

Spencer made a comment I couldn't hear, and they all laughed. I smiled with them. This was what we were fighting for. This and the right to have my parents in their grandchildren's lives. For this, I'd willingly walk right into Stefan's lair.

I was about to leave Chris to his happiness when he looked up and saw me. "Hey, Blondie," he called, using the nickname I'd had as a child. He hadn't called me that in forever. "Come over here."

Spencer bounced up from the table. "Did you hear, did you hear? We're having a baby! Stella's baby is ours too!" He came running around the table, practically flying with his excitement. "It was made in a test tube, and it might be Unbounded when it gets older, but it'll still be just like a real baby. I can't wait!"

"Really," I said.

Spencer studied my face. "Aw, you already knew." But his face still glowed as he pulled me over to the table where we sat opposite Chris, Stella, and Kathy.

"Sandwich fingers?" Chris pushed their shared plate at me.

I took one. "You used to make these for me when we were kids."

"You were a kid," Chris corrected. "I was the older brother."

Spencer found that very funny. He picked up two sandwiches and pretended he was eating his fingers. Kathy rolled her eyes while the adults laughed.

Stella gave a sigh. "Break time's up. For me, at least. I'd better get back to the conference room."

Chris grabbed her hand as she stood. "You get enough to eat?" Worry creased his face, and I knew it wasn't just for Stella, but for all of us and what we were about to do.

"Yes, thanks." She bent over and kissed his forehead, her straight dark hair cascading over her shoulders and into his mouth. "Oops, sorry," she said. Chris laughed, the worry smoothing from his face again.

"You'd better take the rest of your yogurt, just in case." Kathy reached around her father for the yogurt cup and handed it to Stella.

"Thanks, sweetie." Stella circled the table, pausing to fluff Spencer's hair.

He tossed down a sandwich finger and twisted toward her, throwing his arms around her stomach, his greasy face pressed into the material of her flowing dress. "I love you, baby!" Stella laughed and rumpled his hair.

All eyes followed Stella to the door. "I hope she doesn't choke on it," Spencer said after she was gone. "It might hurt the baby."

"Shush!" Kathy hissed. But from Spencer's mind, I'd already caught the memory of a ring tucked inside the yogurt cup.

I gaped at Chris. "You're trying to propose? Now? In front of the kids?"

He looked confused. "What do you—why not now? You know as well as I do that the next few days are going to be . . . difficult. But not in front of the kids—she might say no. I was going to . . ." He trailed off, the color seeping from his face. "Oh, no. They didn't."

I nodded.

His gaze jerked to his daughter. "Kathy, tell me you didn't."

She gave him a sheepish grin, her eyes wide. "You've had it for weeks. Spencer and I thought you needed a little help."

"Help?" he repeated. "Oh, help!" The color flooded back into his face as he pushed back his chair, rounded the table in a sliding run, and sprinted for the door.

"Dad!" Spencer yelled after him. "Wait for me!"

"No, you stay here!" Chris disappeared.

"Seriously?" I asked Kathy.

"Well, it could have worked." Her smile had a bit of sadness to it. "I like seeing him happy. And Stella is so . . . I really love her."

I relented. "So do I. On both accounts. But let them work it out themselves, okay?"

She gave a soft sigh. "I miss my mom."

"I know, honey. We all do. But it's going to be all right."

"Actually, it already is. But I still miss her."

I hugged her tightly.

Ritter wants a family. I couldn't help the thought as I walked back to the conference room. He'd made no secret of it. He was ready. Was I? Only if the Emporium couldn't take them from me.

Tomorrow I would make sure they didn't.

The next hours passed too slowly but also faster than I wanted. After our final planning meeting concluded, I saw little of Ritter and the others as we hurried about our assigned jobs. After retrieving the rest of Stella's yogurt from the trash bin in the conference room, Chris ducked out to pack for his trip. Mari and Keene began transferring the former prisoners from Mexico into the care of the New York Renegade cell. Stella monitored communications, Dimitri and Jace worked on blockade plans, and Ava coordinated with New York. Ritter oversaw everything.

My job was to supervise Jeane's phone call to Stefan. The first part of the call went just as she'd shown me, but as I listened to his hard voice in my headphones, my fear grew to a fist-sized ball of lead in my stomach.

This meeting would be different from our previous one. I wasn't newly Changed, and he wouldn't try tricking me into joining his side. No, his plan would be to capture, control, and force.

Piece of cake. I signaled Jeane to end the call. The less she talked, the less chance she had to make a mistake.

"Well done," Stefan was saying. "There will be a reward in this for you when you deliver Erin in the morning. But I really think you should let my team escort you here. She's gifted in combat, remember."

"Don't worry," Jeane said, ignoring the command in his voice. "I got it covered. She has no power over me. Bye now." She pushed the off button on the untraceable phone we'd given her.

"Why didn't you ask him about Lew?" I wondered aloud.

She shook her head. "Stefan can never know that what's between Lew and me is more than a passing thing. If they suspected we were still involved, they could control us."

She was right about that. "Come on. Time to go back to your room."

When Mari and Keene arrived from New York several hours later, Mari looked exhausted, and Keene was as drained as if he'd been shot again. With Keene and Mari were four Renegade Unbounded—not former prisoners—from the Mexican compound, all combat Unbounded. Ritter had decided to send these four to the San Francisco headquarters with Chris and the black ops team. Eden had also been given permission to go with Chris, and I was glad he'd have the extra help.

"Come with me," I said to the four newcomers. "Chris is saying goodbye to the kids. I'll have him meet us in the foyer." He'd be flying his group to meet the black ops team in San Francisco, so he had to leave soon to meet them and to get his men in place before dark.

"Thanks," Mari said. She touched Keene's arm and they vanished, hopefully to somewhere they could rest.

A few minutes later, Chris appeared in the foyer with Eden and our three mortal guards, all of them wearing body armor. He greeted the four Unbounded enthusiastically before giving me a hug. "Look, keep an eye on Jace," he whispered. "This is too weird about Stefan. I have a bad feeling about it."

"I know. I already talked to Ava. But Jace isn't as impulsive as he used to be, so we need to trust him. You just be careful." I'd be doing enough worrying for both of us.

"I will. And no one from the headquarters in San Francisco will be a problem for you, I promise."

There was more to say. There was always more, but he knew as well as I did what we were walking into. Somewhere along the way, since my Change, he'd finally stopped thinking it was his job to protect me, but right now I yearned to be that little girl he'd made sandwiches for and helped tie her shoes. He'd been able to vanquish everything for me then. Today he merely hugged me again and left, taking Eden and the others with him.

As I stared after him, Ritter's arms slipped around me. Our first moment alone since this morning. "Ready?" he asked.

I'd never be ready. All I felt was dread. "Yeah. Are you okay?"

He turned me around, meeting my eyes. "You mean after I almost blew it earlier?"

"You knew about Cort killing his brother and how angry his father was over it."

"Knew and somehow forgot. And I overlooked sending Mari in with Keene because I wanted to be there with you."

I swallowed hard. "I've gone in alone before."

"Not like this."

"It'll be okay." It had to be.

Ritter's eyes were dark pools that might hide his emotions from everyone but me, but beneath the misery over his lapse in judgment, I sensed his anticipation at the coming battle. "If things go wrong," he said, "make no mistake—one way or the other I'm coming inside to get you."

Only a combat Unbounded could look at what we were going into with any sort of anticipation. Yet I found myself rising to his expectation. Maybe I *was* ready. I gave him a hard kiss. "I wouldn't expect anything less. Let's do this thing."

CHAPTER 18

WE SPENT OUR LAST NIGHT IN NEW YORK IN THE SAME HIGH-RISE safe house we'd borrowed from the New York Renegades months ago when we'd come to help them free their captives. That we'd stumbled on Jeane during that particular op and needed her now seemed ironic. Stella and Cort went right to work checking the communication system and computers in the conference room, which would be the hub of the op.

Mari and Keene were under Dimitri's care as he used his ability to help their bodies recover from exhaustion brought by the multiple shifts. They were scheduled to walk straight into the jaws of the lion in just a few hours and needed the downtime. Jeane and I would follow in the morning. For now, Jeane was in yet another holding cell, cursing that she didn't have a blow dryer.

Ritter and Ava left to meet with the New York group to help them organize the ex-Emporium Unbounded in a wide blockade around the corner building where Emporium headquarters was located. Tomorrow Ava herself would be supervising the blockade, patrolling close to the building with the former prisoners and using her ability to make sure all Unbounded in the vicinity were identified and detained. If necessary during the op, Mari would pull from the former prisoners, shifting them inside the building to help with possible fighting or to secure certain areas.

Part of the New York Renegade cell would stake out politicians and businessmen who were known Emporium sympathizers, stopping them in any attempt they might make to aid the Triad. The New York blaster, Brody Emerson, was responsible for shutting off the electricity and cell phone towers in the area. He could pull any amount of power within a certain distance into his body and send it deep into the earth. I hoped he'd learned to control it well enough that this time he wouldn't leave huge fissures in the asphalt.

Once inside Emporium headquarters, my first job—and Mari's—would be to shut down the generators so we could shift Ritter, Dimitri, Cort, Jace, Oliver, and a team from the New York cell inside. Together, we'd convince the Triad to cooperate. I'd been hesitant about using Oliver, but Ritter insisted because we might need his illusions to convince the Triad's immediate guards to do what we needed. I had to admit Oliver's skill came in handy, and he was less annoying than he used to be. Maybe.

He was plenty annoying now as he pretended to help Jace and me arrange the supplies that clogged nearly every inch of floor space in the large sitting room. I was glad Ava had left Jace behind so I could keep an eye on him, but he seemed anxious, and moving supplies around didn't expend his pent-up energy.

"Why couldn't I have gone with Ava?" Jace muttered. "At least I could have caught up with my friends from the New York cell."

"You mean Chloe?" I suspected he had a secret infatuation for her—he definitely wouldn't be the first. Like Noah, Chloe

possessed one of the beautiful abilities, and her dancing capti-
vated people all over the world.

"Of course he means Chloe," Oliver said, lifting a bag of
curequick syringes but putting them with the weapons instead
of with the other medical supplies. "She's certainly the only
one I want to see. I'm still trying to get her to show me certain
moves she learned in Africa two hundred years ago." He raised
and lowered both eyebrows rapidly several times, to tell us
exactly what kind of moves.

"Chloe wasn't in Africa two hundred years ago," retorted
Jace. "Maybe she never has been. She's originally from Holland,
you doofus."

Oliver shrugged. "That's okay. Maybe it'll be me showing
her a thing or two."

Jace snorted. "Hardly."

"That's exactly why neither of you went." I put the curequick
where it belonged. "They don't need you two fighting over
Chloe."

"It's not really a fight," Oliver said. "She likes me best." Jace
rolled his eyes, but he didn't protest, which told me there might
be some truth to Oliver's comment.

"Well, they have work to do, and so do we," I reminded
them. "You'll both see her soon enough when this is over."

I hoped.

We'd made a significant dent in the supplies when Noah
and Patrick arrived. I was surprised to see Patrick vertical.
"Shouldn't you still be in bed?" I asked.

"Naw, I'm practically healed." He stepped over a black
duffel and collapsed on a couch.

Jace snorted. "So this is what happens when I'm not on the
job." He looked at me and shook his head in mock disgust.
"Erin, you were supposed to protect him."

"Hey, I wasn't there." I moved two assault rifles from the couch so there was enough room for Noah to sit with Patrick. "Take that up with Mari and Keene."

"It's no one's fault but my own," Patrick said with a groan. "How was I to know the guy had a sword? I didn't realize it would cut right through that chair. I haven't even trained with swords yet."

I studied him critically. "So you two drove, what, four hours from DC to cheer us on? Because you don't look like you're ready for battle."

Noah laughed and perched on the armrest of the couch, ignoring the room I'd made for her. "No, he's not ready, but he will be by tomorrow. And Mari shifted us to our base in New York earlier when she brought the Unbounded from the Mexican compound, so we didn't have far to drive."

I wondered how many other side trips Mari had made. No wonder she looked so beat.

Noah stood up again, bouncing slightly. "Anyway, we have great news and couldn't wait to tell you. Brody Emerson, our blaster—you know, the one whose father is a Hunter?"

The older Emerson was not just a Hunter, but one very high up in the organization. Or had been the last time we were in New York. "Yeah," I said cautiously.

"Well, he's offering their help."

Jace and Oliver froze, each with a handful of weapons. Jace laughed. "You gotta be kidding," he said.

Patrick grinned at our expressions. "Brody's told him what's going on—meaning what *really* is going on—and they seriously did offer their help."

"They'd sooner run us through than help us." Oliver plopped onto the couch next to Patrick. "If I remember correctly, they almost cut Brody in three."

"Yeah, I can just see them mowing down all our ex-Emporium Unbounded." Jace swirled a sai in one hand. "We wouldn't have anyone left to help us take over the Emporium."

"I know," Patrick said. "And Emerson agreed that most of his people would take a lot of joy pretending to help and then turning on us, but he said there is a growing number of them who finally understand that Renegade and Emporium Unbounded are not the same."

"About time," Jace mumbled.

I grinned at him. "So, maybe you and Ritter sparing all those Hunters is finally paying off."

"About time," Jace said again, this time mimicking Ritter's voice, and we all laughed.

"Emerson did mention that some of those he had in mind have had run-ins with us," Patrick said. "He might be able to come up with as many as fifty volunteers who fit into that category. Well? You think Ritter and Ava will go for it?"

With a glance at me, Jace shook his head, but when he spoke, his words weren't exactly a rejection. "My feeling is to tell Emerson to get his people ready. But only those he'd be willing to trust with his own son's life. Even if it's only a handful. Then find someplace maybe five minutes from Emporium headquarters, and tell them to stand by. Ritter will let them know if and when we need them."

A shudder crawled up my spine and across my shoulders because Jace's solution sounded exactly like something Ritter would come up with. But if Hunters were our backup, we had truly hit bottom.

Jace smiled at me. "Maybe this is the day the world changes."

"About time," I told him with a smirk.

He rolled his eyes. "Very funny."

I wished it was already morning. I felt anxious to get started, even though that meant facing Stefan. Because maybe after tomorrow there would be no more Emporium as it was today. For the moment, though, it was a torturous waiting game.

"Come on," I said to Jace and Oliver, "let's get these magazines and the extra weapons down to the cars."

"I'll grab the medical supplies," Oliver said. Of course he would since those weighed less.

We met Mari and Keene in the hallway as we headed to the elevator. Cort was with them, his brown hair standing slightly on end and his face creased with worry.

Somehow Mari and Keene had managed to rid themselves of their red hair and the rest of their old disguises. Keene was back to his normal light brown with no beard while Mari was now sporting dark blond tresses, and she wore contacts that turned her brown eyes—which had been green for her last disguise—into a grayish blue. The blond hair looked too light to me, compared to her natural black, but Mari at least looked significantly rested. Keene, however, was still pale, and his face appeared more narrow than usual.

"I'm all right," he said, not flinching under my stare. "You're just not used to me without the beard."

"No, it's the idea of seeing our old man that makes you look like a ghost." Cort's voice was too tight to carry the joke.

"You have enough weapons?" Jace asked Keene. "They'll expect you to be armed."

Keene's hand went to his holster. "I'm all set. But Cort'll bring my good stuff. I'm not donating those to the Emporium arsenal."

We all laughed, except Mari, who frowned and began removing her arm sheaths. "Guess you'd better bring these too, Cort. I don't want to lose them. My others are replaceable." Mari wore a minimum of four knives at a time, and sometimes double that. She also had a gun, but she didn't like to use it.

"Ava and Ritter should be back in a bit," I told them. "We're just taking the weapons to the vans."

"I can't believe this is finally happening." Mari leaned against Keene for assurance. His arm snaked around her.

I thought Jace might make a comment about Mari getting into her role already, but he closed the last foot between him and the elevator, punching the button. "Tomorrow it'll be a whole new world."

Down in the cavernous underground parking beneath the building, we divided the duffels between the five vans our group would be stashing around the Emporium headquarters, so our troops could restock as needed. The vans could also be used to hold any Emporium prisoners we might take during the op. Metal rings were embedded in the van at intervals for the purpose of securing any captives.

I was turning from throwing in my bags when Jace hit against me, knocking me partially inside the van. Before I could protest, he had zip-tied me to one of the metal rings. "I'm sorry, Blondie," he said. I could feel his regret in his surface thoughts, but his voice was thick with determination.

My heart thudded against my rib cage. "Jace, what are you doing?" I reached out to his mind but found his shield a tight, swirling black. Shoving my free hand into my pocket, I pressed the panic sequence on my phone that would alert all our Renegades that there was a problem. The phone in Jace's pocket began buzzing.

"Don't be angry," he said, tossing the phone into the van and backing away. "This is probably the only chance I'll have to meet him. I know what 'by any means possible' implies. I need to do this."

"Jace, no! He'll never let you go!" I drew out the imaginary version of my machete and hacked on his mental shield. If I could get through, I could make him stay. I didn't want to flash light to his mind for fear of doing permanent damage, but I could control his body for at least a short time. Maybe by then Oliver would have found us and could free me so I could channel Jace and fight him with his own combat ability until someone arrived to help.

"I know what you're probably trying to do," Jace said. "But we've been working for months on strengthening my shield. I figure I have at least three minutes before you break through, and that should be enough time to get beyond your reach."

"Please," I said. Why hadn't I seen this coming? I'd never imagined Jace would do this to me. Try to sneak away, yes. Or maybe fight Oliver, who we'd privately appointed to shadow Jace until tomorrow. But never to lock me up and leave like this.

"Don't worry. I won't ruin the op," Jace continued, ignoring my plea. "I'll tell Stefan I spotted Jeane talking to you and that when you went missing, I suspected she'd take you to him. I'll tell him I wanted to meet him and that you told me all about him. With so many years passing and so many things that can happen, Stefan should believe there was enough of his stolen sperm for both of us. It'll work, and we'll be there together. You won't have to face him alone."

"You can't do this!" I hacked harder with the machete. "It's not only about you. This will hurt everyone!"

"No, it won't. Go talk to Ritter. He'll tell you I'm right. And when this is over, I'll still be your favorite brother." With that, he dived into a small car next to the van, started it up, and squealed across the parking lot, heading toward the garage door that began opening onto a ramp leading up to the street.

I slammed harder at his shield, but as he left, it became harder to maintain contact. My one stroke of luck was that the garage had no electronic grid to keep me from following him. *Almost there,* I thought, grasping after him. *Slam! Hack!*

Slam! As if from far away, I heard my phone emit the vibration pattern I'd assigned to Ava's number.

Jace slipped farther away. He must be breaking every speed limit to put so much space between us this quickly. I kept him for one block, two, and even a third. All the other thoughts from the crowds of people he passed threatened to break through the connection I had with him, but somehow I clung on. Yet the farther he went, the less impact my machete had on his shield, until I finally let the weapon disappear and simply held on to him. Two breaths later, his presence abruptly cut off.

Tears ran down my face. I wanted to weep and cry and swear and pound Jace's face, but instead I reached for one of my knives and began hacking away at the tie on my wrist. The plastic had thin lines of metal reinforcing it—Cort's special design—and I hadn't begun to make progress when Keene and Mari appeared with a soft *pop* near the stairwell and ran to the van. Cort and Dimitri were close behind, bursting from the stairwell like water from a high-pressure hose. Only Stella remained upstairs, and she was probably monitoring the garage with cameras through her neural headset. Some part of my mind was glad she wasn't willing to risk her baby—not after what happened last time.

"What happened?" Mari asked.

I dropped my knife and faced them, my hand still tied. Hope ran through me. Mari could find people's locations even farther away than I could trace thoughts. "Find Jace. He's gone to Stefan. We have to stop him!"

Placing my free hand on Mari's arm, I shut my eyes and reached out for her mind. Her thoughts immediately flooded me as her shield dropped. "Keene," she whispered. At once, I felt Keene's power pulsing, plenty for both of us to use.

But Jace was nowhere.

"Reach for the street in front of Emporium headquarters," Keene said.

I saw in Mari's thoughts that visiting the headquarters had been another side trip they'd made earlier, partly by car, as they'd scoped out the location so she could fix it in her mind.

In the next instant, the street was shimmering around us. Mari pushed out her mind through the connection and so did I, using both her ability and my own, and drawing from Keene's power. Nothing. In fact, a very big nothing met us where the building stood, though we could plainly see it with our physical eyes as Mari folded space. All around, thoughts from the people in the buildings next to it assaulted me, but within the Emporium headquarters, I felt nothing.

"He's nowhere," Mari said.

"He can't be inside yet. He hasn't had time."

"Keep looking," Cort said. "Pull all the locations you've been to near here."

Mari nodded and pushed on, with me clinging to her mind, trying not to think the worst. One by one, the places she'd visited materialized before us, and I sent my thoughts through the fold in space, searching for Jace.

After a long while, Mari shook her head at me sorrowfully. "I'm sorry. Earlier when we got here, he was asking how I felt not knowing my father, if it bothered me that I wouldn't ever meet him. I told him I'd always thought he was some nameless sperm donor, and I hadn't ever thought about having a relationship with the guy. I didn't know he was a Renegade who'd been killed until just a few months ago. Jace didn't like my answer. I should have known he was upset."

I remembered how Jace had leaned toward me in the hallway back at the Fortress, as if trying to drink in any knowledge of his father. He hadn't bought my promise to keep the man alive. Of course his ability would have told him that "by any means possible" left too much to chance when dealing with a member of the Triad.

The garage door opened, and a van careened down the ramp and across the parking garage, screeching to a stop before us. Ritter jumped from the driver's seat, and Ava from the other side. Her phone was in her hand, but my phone was no longer vibrating with her call.

"What happened?" Ritter barked.

"Jace is gone." My voice sounded like broken glass crunching beneath my feet. I opened my mind to Ava and pushed my thoughts at Ritter, letting them see for themselves.

Ava's mouth pursed so tightly she appeared to have aged decades. "Any trace of his location?" she asked Mari.

"No," Mari whispered.

Ava was tapping on her phone. "Can't find his signal. He must have deactivated his transmitter."

Ritter leaned into the car and finished freeing me with a snip of wire cutters he pulled from an interior pocket. "Where's Oliver? Isn't he supposed to be with Jace?"

"Oliver!" Mari snorted.

"It wasn't his fault." Dimitri's voice made us all look around. I hadn't even noticed him after Mari and I began searching, but apparently he'd been looking for Oliver, who now leaned on him heavily. One of Oliver's eyes was reddened and fast growing a bruise that stood out on his dark face like a spill of oil on concrete. His short, tightly curled hair had a heavy brush of gray on one side, as if he'd slid over the dusty floor. Given his expression, he'd probably done just that.

"I'm sorry," Oliver said, and for once his arrogance wasn't showing. "I didn't see it coming."

"He was knocked out behind that van." Dimitri indicated the farthest van with a wave.

"You won't find Jace," Oliver said. "He had those devices in the car, the ones he and Cort took from the hospital where the Emporium was trying to hide Patrick."

"The portable electric grid!" Mari said. "That explains how he could disappear like that."

I knew it was my fault. "I didn't see this coming at all. Jace seemed okay with everything." I slammed the back doors of the van shut and started kicking the concrete pillar next to it—again and again until my booted foot ached. "Stupid . . . idiot . . . kid." I wasn't sure if I meant me or Jace.

Ritter put his hand on my arm, and I turned into him, burying my face in his shoulder. His hands ran through my hair, but for once they brought me no comfort.

"He's an adult," Ava said. "This is no one's fault but his own. Short of locking him up, we couldn't stop him."

I pulled away from Ritter's shoulder, my head feeling as if it weighed a hundred tons. "Whatever his feelings about Stefan, he shouldn't have endangered the op!" I retorted, wishing that was the only reason I was angry. "We'll have to abort and figure out how to get Jace back." It all seemed too impossible. When I did catch up with him, I was going to kick him to the next state. Then I'd never let him out of my sight again.

"Maybe we don't have to abort," Ritter said.

I recoiled from him. "What?"

"Depends on how he explains his presence once he's there."

Against my will I repeated what Jace had said about telling Stefan he was looking for me and that Jace wanted to meet him. "It doesn't matter how he spins it," I concluded. "Stefan's never going to let him go, and with Jace there, he can use us against each other. I won't be able to do my job."

I waited for Ritter to tell me I was right, that we had to abandon the plan and focus on retrieving Jace, but he only looked shaken as he dragged his gaze from mine to Ava. "If Stefan buys it," he told her, "it should work. Maybe it'll even be better than just sending in Erin and Keene and Mari—we can never have too much backup. There's no doubt that Jace will play his part perfectly, since it's mostly true."

"No!" I punched his arm hard enough to hurt my hand, but Ritter didn't flinch as his head snapped in my direction. "His Deathliness just doesn't want me there without a combat Unbounded!" I accused. "He never did. He's *glad* Jace did this. But we can't just carry on the op as if nothing has happened." As if my brother didn't matter. "We have to get Jace out of Stefan's reach, or I won't be able to do anything against the Triad."

When Ritter spoke, he used a hard tone he rarely used with me anymore—not since we fell in love and got married. "Are you saying you won't do the op? Because there is no one else." He closed the step between us and put his hands on my upper arms near my shoulders. "If you want to help your brother, you have to go through with the plan. If you want to take over the Triad, we have to act now. There's no other way except the frontal assault we all decided was suicide. You were willing to have Jace participate in that. How is this any worse?" He shook me once, but gently, almost a caress.

"Fine!" I pulled away from him, knowing he was right but furious at him anyway because there was no one else to be angry at.

Except Jace, who wasn't here. And myself.

Ritter nodded and turned to Keene and Mari, who watched us with dismayed expressions. "It's time for you two to leave. You have everything you need?"

"We each have a couple bags," Keene said. "To make it look like we're planning to stay awhile—not that they'd let us leave anyway. The bags are still upstairs."

"Cort and I will get them." Ritter motioned to Cort.

Cort looked relieved, and I knew that was exactly why

Ritter had asked. It never got any easier saying goodbye, and this way Keene and Cort's farewell would be shorter.

Ava waited until Ritter and Cort left before saying to Keene and Mari, "When you get there, try to find a way to contact us. Post that last signal phrase we gave you if you see him."

"Jace will know enough to pretend not to recognize you," Dimitri added. He had a hand on Mari's arm, helping her regain her strength, and I was glad since she looked drained again.

I didn't share his confidence, not after what Jace had done.

Ava moved to my side, her arm slipping around me. "It's going to be okay."

"No, it's not okay, and you know it."

"I'd bet each of our people against any three of theirs," Ava said. "Jace is no exception."

Ritter and Cort returned with the bags, transferring them to Mari and Keene. Without any signal between them, Mari and Keene nodded at us and shifted, vanishing from sight. They would appear in another safe house and from there make their way to Emporium headquarters.

I hoped I would see them again.

Ritter looked at Cort. "Are you and Stella ready to record Jeane's thoughts?"

I was still furious at him but also relieved at his suggestion. Working on Jeane's mind would keep Cort and me from thinking too much, at least tonight, about what we'd lost.

For the next two hours, I studied Jeane's mind and passed the patterns to Stella, who recorded them on a computer so she and Cort could decipher them. Jeane wasn't happy about it, but she didn't try to null me again or keep me out.

Afterward, I wandered upstairs to the room I shared with Ritter. He was already there, and for a few torturously long minutes, we didn't talk except to discuss what we would take with us on the op the next morning. Ritter would bring all his usual accouterments and also my guns and knives and the new sword so he could pass them to me when Mari and I shifted him inside.

I couldn't carry any obvious weapons, but since my ultimate cover was that I'd fooled Jeane into thinking she was capturing me, going in with no weapons at all would seem out of place. So I planned to take weapons built into jewelry and hair accessories, things Jeane might overlook. Their people would find them, I was betting, but at least I'd appear to be a real combat Unbounded. If I managed to get something past their security, so much the better.

Finishing my short list, I dropped to the couch and stared blankly at the wall. Ritter left his weapons and sat next to me. "Jace isn't so different from you, you know. Remember how you took off to confront Delia alone in Morocco?"

I brought my gaze back from the nothingness to glare at him. "This is *so* different. Jace doesn't have a snake in his head. He wasn't in danger of killing us all if he stayed."

"We only defeated Delia because we were all together. We'll do that again with the Triad." He tried to take my hand, but I yanked it away. "Erin, I know you're not mad at me," he tried again.

"You're right. I'm furious," I growled. At him and all the Renegades for not fixing the Emporium problem years ago. For waiting until Jace and I were born to finally set it right. For putting my brother's life in danger. "We don't have any idea what's really going to happen tomorrow. We should be rescuing Jace tonight."

"And how do you suggest we do that?"

"We go in. We get a presidential order to search the place. We negotiate. I don't know!"

"What about taking over the Triad?"

A sob escaped my throat. "I don't care about the Triad!"

Faster than I could ward him off, Ritter grabbed my hands and pulled me to him. "Stop, Erin. Please. You're right that we don't know what will happen tomorrow. We can't change what Jace has done, so shouldn't we be making the most of tonight?" His voice spoke of deserted beaches and lazy nights with no thought of the Emporium. Of children's laughter.

"Let. Me. Go."

"No."

In the next instant, we were kissing and tearing our clothes off. There was no time for words. I wanted this man of mine, who made me so furious and happy and right with the world, even when it was falling apart.

Yes, I was going to hold a grudge at his stubbornness, and because of my own guilt at letting Jace leave, but I was also going to say my goodbyes. Just in case. Our lovemaking was different this time, more urgent, more passionate. I could only pray that wasn't a sign of something horrible looming in our future.

It wasn't until much later when I awoke in the middle of the night, half crushed by Ritter's weight, that I realized I hadn't channeled Stella's ability today—or Patrick's—to make sure my body allowed the nanites to do their job at preventing ovulation. In fact, my body had probably ejected the nanites altogether. After tomorrow, it wouldn't matter. One way or the other.

CHAPTER 19

THE NEXT MORNING, JEANE AND I WERE OUR WAY TO EMPORIUM headquarters in a taxi driven by a disguised Cort. Jeane called Ropte, examining her nails with apparent disinterest as Ropte questioned her about leaving his house yesterday. He shut up all too quickly when she told him she was with me and where she was heading. After trying to talk her into taking me to his house instead, he told her he'd see her soon and hung up.

Jeane's brow furrowed. "He's never offered to send a helicopter for me. And that was before I said you had a message from the Renegades. Apparently, David is very interested in you."

The idea worried me more than I wanted to admit. "Are you sure you didn't tell him about my ability?"

She gave me a flat stare. "I think I'd remember."

Cort dropped us in front of the Emporium building, and Jeane preened in the mirrored surfaces of the double glass doors as we waited to be let inside. Despite my lack of sleep, I looked rested, thanks to my increased absorption. Jeane looked stunning, even for an Unbounded, and I wondered if she'd taken such care of her appearance because of Lew or if she still had some other plan involving Stefan Carrington.

My hands were zip-tied in front of me, and Jeane carried a gun, which she was serious enough about keeping on me that if I'd really been a captive, I might have had a problem getting away.

I felt a momentary panic and an urge to flee. I hadn't told Ritter I loved him after our fight, not even after our night together. When I'd awakened, he'd been downstairs discussing last-minute details with Ava and Dimitri, and all I'd done was scowl at him and everyone else. I hadn't hugged him goodbye, and he hadn't pushed me. His Deathliness knew me too well.

I regretted all of it now, especially the shuttered look in his eyes.

One of the doors opened, not by a secretary but by four guards armed with multiple guns and swords in back sheaths. One of them I recognized: Jonny Carrington, Stefan's son and my supposed half brother. I'd had two run-ins with Jonny, and I liked him despite his blind loyalty and the fact that he'd once shot Ritter. He had a lesser variation of the combat ability that allowed him to move faster than even Ritter, but without the other advantages. Because of his forced Change at eighteen, ten years ago, his projected life span was only four hundred years, something he was privately bitter about. Even so, he was always grinning, and today was no exception.

"Hey, Erin," he said. "Good to see you again."

I nodded. "Jonny."

The guards patted us down, stripping us of all jewelry and anything else that was suspicious, including a hairpin that had no value even as a lockpick, much less as a weapon. After we were deemed weaponless, they marched us to a room where they cut my bonds and made me lie down on a padded surface, which slowly fed into a circular machine.

"She's clean," announced the female technician a short time later.

"Of course she is," Jeane said. "You think I'd bring her here with a Renegade tracker still inside her?"

"You're next," said the technician.

Jeane rolled her eyes and sauntered to the padded surface, stretching luxuriously as if lying down on a massage table. She was completely dark to me at the moment—no life force at all—so her ability was active, though she wasn't trying to null our guards. That told me she was out of her comfort zone; she'd been far more relaxed back at our safe house.

While she was sucked inside the machine, I studied the three guards with Jonny. All of them were Unbounded, probably gifted with combat, and physically in their mid- to late-thirties, which meant they had several centuries of experience—far more than Jonny's hundred-plus years. One woman and two men. I reached out to their minds and found strong shields, but nothing like Lew's or Ropte's. Or Jace's, for that matter. I was sure I could get inside.

On the other hand, the technician was mortal, though young enough that she might still Change. Her surreptitious glances at the female guard and her occasional surface thoughts told me she longed to be just like her.

From there, I sent out my thoughts farther into the building. There were hundreds of life forms, some actively moving and others seated closely together as if working in cubicles. As I did more tallying, I realized there were not just hundreds but over a thousand, nearly every one of them dimmer than usual, which meant their minds were shielded, be they mortal or Unbounded. I was glad we hadn't gone through with the frontal assault because even the mortal technician was armed with a gun at her hip and the bulk of a sword under her white jacket.

I wondered if they had a nursery here like in the LA safe house. Probably. I checked to make sure that none of the few unshielded minds belonged to Mari, and I was glad not to find her because it wouldn't be safe to go unshielded here. I could still find her; it would just take longer.

And Jace. I couldn't think about him without a pain in my chest.

Jeane had no tracking devices either, but that was quickly remedied when the tech injected us both in the arm with what I assumed was their own tracking device.

"Are we done yet?" Jeane drawled. She was making eyes at one of the guards, who ignored her steadfastly, though I sensed an interest. She should be careful because I didn't think Lew would appreciate the competition. Providing he was still alive.

"Come," said the oldest-looking guard, who seemed to be in charge. He was Asian and shorter than the other three men but wider. Jonny showed the way while the other three took up positions behind us. I had a déjà vu feeling as they marched us across a foyer to an elevator where two more Unbounded stood guard. This building was eerily similar to their old headquarters in LA, from the guards and cameras to the classy paintings and gray color of the walls.

To my surprise, we didn't go up to the twentieth floor, where Jeane told me Stefan should be waiting, but stopped on the thirteenth. I arched a brow at Jeane, who misunderstood my signal. "It's just another floor. We don't believe in superstitious nonsense here." To the guards, she added, "I'm supposed to take her to Triad Carrington. He knows we're coming. We have no reason to cool our heels here."

The Asian inclined his head. "This is where Triad Carrington told us to take you." Next to me, Jonny smirked.

Once more, they took up formation around us. Here the decor had changed from upscale business to professional killer.

Weapons of all sorts were embedded into the walls, protected by glass coverings, interspersed by violent, bloody paintings depicting Unbounded Renegades being sliced into three. Both the weapons and the paintings spanned the epochs, from warriors on horseback to men in business suits. Mortals were portrayed as servants who knelt to worship their Emporium gods.

Rage built inside me. So many lives lost.

Finally, we came to a set of nondescript double doors that were open wide. Two additional guards stood to either side and motioned for us to enter. We did, but the guards accompanying us remained outside. Through the doors, we found a vast gym, half of which was covered in mats and the other half with exercise machines. Mirrors covered several walls, but on the others hung more scenes of decapitation and body-severing.

Despite all the space and the hundreds of people in the building, the room held only two life forces. As we walked over the wood floor along the edge of the mat, my eyes went to Stefan Carrington, my supposed father, who stood barefoot, a black bo staff in his hands. He was tall and well-built, and his hair so blond it masked any gray. His face was tanned, with fine lines around magnetizing eyes the color of the sky on a hot, brilliant day—Jace's eyes. Instead of the suit he'd worn on our previous meetings, his chest and six-pack abs were shirtless, and his workout shorts emphasized the muscles in his thighs. The hair on his chest was also blond and again showed no gray. I couldn't pinpoint a physical age for him, but he'd lived at least a half century.

"There you are," he said, passing his staff to his companion and striding over the mat. It was only then I recognized the other occupant of the gym. The tall man with ebony skin and ultra-short black hair was Edgel, an Unbounded soldier who had loyally served the Emporium his entire life. He'd worked under Keene when he'd been a team leader, and then became his own team leader under Delia. Now he was with Stefan.

As Jace had so recently reminded me, Edgel blamed us for his daughter's death. I was betting Stefan had never discovered that Edgel had hidden a mortal daughter from the Emporium and had once come to us to save her life. It was something I might be able to use against Edgel, if I had to.

Edgel met my stare without sign of recognition, zero surface feelings registering on my awareness. I was tempted to break through his shield. I'd done it before.

I turned my attention back to Stefan, who was the more dangerous man, even if only because he commanded Edgel and others just like him. Killing machines. Unlike Edgel, surface feelings radiated from Stefan, including a real pleasure at seeing me—or more likely at having me under his control—but nothing important escaped past the black walls encasing his mind. The last time we'd been together, I'd felt more of his inner thoughts, and I bet I had Delia's betrayals to thank for his added strength.

"Triad Carrington," I said.

He laughed, the lines on his face giving him more character than age. "Oh, that's priceless. Though I suppose the formality is in keeping with the choice you made the last time you left."

"People change."

Stefan chuckled. "Oh? Are you the prodigal daughter, hoping for forgiveness?"

"I haven't done anything that needs forgiveness."

His smile faded. "Neither have I."

"Oh, Stefan, give her a hug," Jeane said with a laugh. "She *is* your daughter after all."

Stefan's face froze as he turned to her. "Hello, Jeane. I hope you'll excuse us. Erin and I have a lot to talk about." He rotated in Edgel's direction. "See that she's secured in her old quarters."

Edgel nodded and stepped forward, laying Stefan's black bo staff and his own red one on the mat and taking Jeane by the arm. "Really?" she asked Stefan. "You said I would be rewarded for bringing her. Is this about me leaving before without your permission? I did come back. I just needed time to think."

"I just want to have a private reunion with my *daughter*. We won't need your ability here."

Jeane drew her lips into a sexy pout and stared over my right shoulder. "You're not even going to allow me a moment to say hello to Lew?"

Her statement sent a blast of fear coiling through my gut. Of course Stefan would have the Emporium's pet sensing Unbounded here to probe me, just as Stefan had used Delia the first time we'd met. Lew couldn't enter my mind without alerting me, and even then that wasn't a fight I'd lose easily, but what Lew might have told Stefan was another thing altogether.

Lew stepped partially from behind a weight machine, releasing the power that had masked his life force. He was as thin and curly-haired and feminine as ever, his young-looking face slightly crunched. He appeared to be in his late teens, which put him at around a century or so old, but beside Delia and me, he was the strongest sensing Unbounded I'd ever heard of, his shield nearly impenetrable, even for me. I was grateful Jeane had seen him, though I wasn't sure how she had. I wondered if Stefan's other sensing Unbounded was here, or if he felt one was enough.

Lew and Jeane regarded one another without any sign of the emotional connection between them. I couldn't help but think of my last moment with Ritter because on the outside we would have appeared exactly the same.

"You can catch up later," Stefan said.

Jeane regarded him through slitted eyes. "We'll do that."

Not wanting to give Stefan any kind of satisfaction, I gave

Lew only one glance before refocusing on Stefan. "He isn't needed here," I said, tilting my head in Lew's direction.

"Maybe not." Stefan wasn't convinced, and I hadn't expected him to be.

Without so much as a wave at Lew or me, Jeane turned and let Edgel lead her across the gym, walking with her hands clasped on his black-clad arm as if leaving had been her idea. Stefan and I watched her in silence. When she reached the double doors, she looked over her shoulder and said, "Please let me know when my brother arrives."

"I wasn't aware that David was coming." Stefan's frown seemed to indicate the news wasn't welcome. Apparently, Jeane hadn't been lying about the tension between Stefan and Ropte.

"Oh, I'm sure he's just concerned about me. We are very close." Jeane stepped through the doors.

It was just us now, Stefan and I. Well, and Lew, who didn't count. I wished I could ask about Jace.

"My technician says you came in with eleven potential weapons," Stefan said, his gaze lingering on the door where Jeane had disappeared.

"Twelve." I reached into my mouth and removed the tiny plastic envelope I had under my tongue.

"Let me guess—acid."

"Poison," I corrected, cracking an insincere grin. "You need to hire better people. Or buy a bigger machine."

Stefan's only response was to pick up the staffs from the floor and toss the red one to me. It felt smooth in my hands and perfectly balanced. "We missed this the last time you were here. I thought we'd start with it in case we're interrupted again." His tone promised there would be no interruption.

He'd know in a minute that I wasn't a combat Unbounded unless I channeled him or one of the guards outside the door. Breaking through his shield might take more time than I had right now, so the guards were a more promising choice, but the guards might not have personal knowledge of Stefan's strengths and weaknesses. With my smaller size, I'd need that to impress him.

"I've heard rumors about you, Erin Radkey." Stefan spun his staff above his head in a series of complicated drills. "I want to know if they're true."

"Rumors about what?"

"About your ability." He laughed at my feigned surprise. "I do have some informants, you know."

Not enough, or he wouldn't need this tender father and daughter heart-to-heart.

"I'll let you have the first strike," he added.

All fine and good, except I wasn't ready. My dilemma was quickly solved as Edgel, having passed Jeane to the guards at the door, returned. Imaginary machete out, I banged on Edgel's shield. He and his shield were familiar to me—I'd broken through before. Still, it might take a while, and Stefan was waiting.

Edgel 65890V. The thought came like a blip from my subconscious, from memories that had become a part of me, but yet weren't familiar. Something from someone I'd channeled or examined. No, that wasn't it. This memory was a residual from those Delia had downloaded into my mind. Maybe it was a code to break through his shield. I'd never heard of such a thing, but it was possible.

Edgel 65890V, I thought at the man, batting the sequence into his shield with my machete like a bat hitting a ball.

Nothing.

Stefan motioned to me with a hint of impatience. I toed off my black loafers and slowly unbuttoned my green blouse, dropping it to the floor, glad I'd worn a workout bra underneath and stretchy pants.

Fortunately, Edgel hadn't improved as much as I had over the past months. The tiniest hole appeared, allowing me entrance. I stepped onto the mat, pulling Edgel's ability to me. Uttering a loud cry, I ran at Stefan with a head strike. He blocked easily and tried a hook, his favorite move, according to Edgel's mind. I slammed it away with a side stroke, hurling past him and throwing a punch with the staff. He thrusted, which I blocked before attempting a low strike at his calves.

Stefan was extremely fast, but not as fast as Ritter or Jace, and he didn't know my style as Edgel knew his. Side, head, knee, nothing was out of bounds. Neither of us held back. I knew the slightest wrong move would mean I wouldn't be conscious today to take out the generators. We clashed hard, the staffs quivering with our rage. Sweat dripped from my brow and beaded on the bits of hair that escaped my ponytail.

He landed a tiny hit to my shoulder, but that left him open to a sweep, which he barely avoided by jumping higher than any mortal could. I laughed for the sheer joy of the fight. He was a worthy opponent. I gave another thrust, whipping the staff up and around, barely missing my own collarbone when I brought it back to my shoulder.

Lunging forward, Stefan tried a powerful head strike. *Not holding any grudges,* I thought. My genes begged to end this. To end him. I dodged, waiting a heartbeat until his staff was just right and then slamming his staff and hooking it up and away. The staff went flying.

Or should have. Instead, Stefan held onto the staff, bringing it around to slam into my stomach. The air whooshed from me, followed by intense pain. He raised his staff again for what should have been a killing blow but stopped a foot from my head.

He barked a laugh. "Not bad."

I couldn't answer. All I could do was to stand there, gasping to find breath. He must have held back with that last punch because however much it hurt, I was pretty sure my ribs weren't broken. At least I wouldn't be spending the next hours unconscious somewhere. I had to admire his restraint.

Stefan gestured for Edgel to take my bo staff. Both men closed on me, and I felt a momentary panic until Edgel strode away. "Why are you really here?" Stefan asked.

"Because," I puffed, "Jeane betrayed me once again. I'm sure you know she was with us in Morocco."

"Ah, but only because she hated Delia. Do you really expect me to believe that Jeane bested you?" He snorted. "You can't fight like that unless you've trained hard enough to beat the average Unbounded. Jeane's vicious, but even if she'd nulled your ability, you could have beaten her without raising a sweat."

Finally, air seemed to work its way back into my lungs. "So I used Jeane. I'm here to discuss a deal."

He rotated and started toward a stack of towels on a shelf against the wall. I scooped up my blouse and followed, pain grabbing somewhere inside my chest. I purposefully allowed the space between us to increase, keeping hold of Edgel's mind, just in case. Stefan was like an exotic animal, and I didn't know if at any moment he might turn and rip me apart.

"Fortunately, we don't need anything from you or the Renegades." He swept up a towel and dabbed at the sweat on his face. "But I can use more sensing Unbounded. Your grandmother's genes might be strong enough in you to help us with that."

I ignored that. No way would I be his breeding machine. "That's it? You don't even want to hear my offer?"

He smirked, his handsome face becoming threatening. "Unless you've all decided to give up the fight, or move to, say, Africa—no, that's too big—maybe Cuba. Yeah, we could let the Renegades have Cuba." He dried off his neck and bare chest before tossing me a clean towel. "Okay, give it to me. What are Ava and the rest of your Renegade friends offering?"

My fake offer was a complete cease-fire—but only if they agreed to stop killing mortals. Part of that involved creating a focus group to compose a treaty detailing mortal rights. I had comprehensive suggestions about who to have in the group and ten basic rights to which every human should be entitled, but it was all make-believe, because we could never trust any promises the Triad might make.

Edgel approached us with a glass full of amber liquid and handed it to Stefan, who downed it in one long pull. Must be scotch. It wouldn't give him much of a buzz, but I remembered he loved it. "Another," he said to Edgel before looking at me expectantly. "Well?"

I shook my head. "I can only present my offer to all the Triad members. Sorry, *Father*, but that is my directive."

The skin around his eyes crinkled with his amusement. "I could make you tell me, *Daughter*." His gaze went past me to where Lew still presumably waited.

"With your pet there?" I let my disgust show on my face and in my voice. "We've met before. He can't break me."

Stefan's blue eyes wandered over my face. "There are many ways to break a person."

"I would kill him first." I meant it. Lew and I still had unresolved business. "But at present, I don't have anything to hide from you or him. The offer I have is genuine. For the whole Triad."

Stefan's nostrils flared and danger ignited in his eyes. "I *am* the Triad. Tihalt does what I say."

"And David Ropte?"

"I guess Jeane told you he took Delia's place. Well, make no mistake, he's no more than a pawn. He and Tihalt both do what *I* say. For now, he's exactly where I want him to be."

Could he be telling the truth? Or trying to make his position seem stronger? Either way, I certainly wouldn't disabuse him of the idea that Jeane had been my informant. "What about his ability?"

"I'm sure Jeane filled you in on that too."

"Actually, she didn't remember what his ability is."

Stefan shrugged, apparently not finding that as odd as I did, that Jeane wouldn't know her own sibling's ability. But it bothered me. She must have lied.

"Hypnosuggestion has never worked on me," he returned with increasing irritability. "Or pheromones, or any of those gifts. You tend to develop an immunity over the years."

"So it was you who ordered the hit on Senator Burklap and his family."

Stefan leaned close to my face. "It's all part of the plan. We won't wait anymore. Once Ropte's in place, we'll only be a few steps away." He was right, of course, which was why I was here. But something was off with his statement.

Releasing Edgel's mind, I concentrated on Stefan, pushing at his shield. "Then you'll be interested in what I have to say." If I stalled here chatting with him long enough, I might find the chink in his armor—or make my own. But now layering Stefan's own mental shield was a spinning black barrier that I recognized as belonging to Lew. *Little weasel getting his revenge, no doubt.* Belatedly, I realized I was fortunate he hadn't thought—or hadn't bothered—to protect Edgel earlier, or I would have been forced to channel one of the guards instead.

I rubbed the towel Stefan had given me over my wet face, hiding my frustration. A drop of sweat drizzled down my back. "Now, if I can just freshen up before Ropte arrives . . ."

Stefan studied me for what seemed like a lifetime and then nodded. "Edgel," he called, raising his voice, "please escort my daughter to her room. Take Lew with you."

Edgel reached us and handed Stefan another glass of amber liquid before meeting my eyes. Hatred burned there. I knew it was because of his daughter, and it made me sad that he blamed Renegades for a problem the Emporium had caused.

Still no word about Jace, and I was tempted to sever Lew's protection of Stefan and attempt to invade his mind anyway. But Lew would know, and there was no telling how loyal he was to Stefan. From the way Stefan acted, I didn't think Lew had spilled my secrets—or at least not the ones that counted. He must have his own agenda.

"Thank you," I said to Stefan, tossing my towel into the tall, plastic-lined bin where Stefan had discarded his towel.

Stefan's smile held a hint of regret. "Maybe you will find we're not so bad here."

Not likely. Especially when I remembered the terrified expression on the Georges' faces. I chose my words carefully. "Hopefully, we can come to an arrangement all Unbounded can live with."

"Our goal of Utopia can be a reality, Erin," Stefan said.

"The problem is, one man's Utopia can be another man's hell."

"Touché."

I went with Edgel willingly, trying not to think of how he wanted me dead. Lew followed a half step behind, his presence oily and stalker-like. It still evaded me what Jeane saw in this boy-man.

So, Lew pushed at me, the communication seeping past his impressive shield. *Why are you really here?* The thought hung between us, not penetrating my mind, but there for the taking.

Why haven't you told Stefan about my ability? I countered.

Jeane told me not to.

Do you do everything you're told? I shouldn't provoke him, but I couldn't resist.

A flare of anger let me know I'd hit a sore spot. His pale brown eyes flashed. *Giving Stefan more power is not my goal.*

Well, at least I'd learned something from him. Even so, I was relieved when we arrived on the next floor and Edgel opened a door for me by placing his hand on a palm reader. "Thank you," I said. He didn't meet my gaze.

"Tomorrow, I'll need to see her in my lab," Lew said in his nasal voice. "I have the Triad's approval." With that, he turned and strode away—or tried to. It looked more like mincing to me.

Just as I'd thought. Stefan was all courtesy in my face, but in the end he only cared about one thing: building an empire with everyone under his complete control. Jeane would never forgive me for what I would have to do to Lew if I was still here tomorrow and he tried to carry through on his threat.

"What is it with that boy and his obsession with me?" I said, not really expecting an answer.

Edgel stared after Lew. There was no expression on his face, but a sense of puzzlement filtered from behind his mental shield. Obviously, he wasn't aware of any Triad order. Either he simply didn't know about it, or Lew was overestimating his position.

Or maybe Lew's permission hadn't come from Stefan.

I was relieved when Edgel didn't reply but waited silently until I went inside and then locked the door behind me. Scarcely glancing at the small studio suite, except to verify that no one else was inside, particularly no one who was masking a life force, I pushed thoughts of Lew and Edgel from my mind and dropped to the couch.

Time to get to work.

CHAPTER 20

SEARCHING FOR MARI WAS NOT A SIMPLE TASK. WHILE EXAMINING, one by one, the shielded Unbounded in the building, I had to be careful to keep my own protection strong in case of a mental attack. I started with this floor—the fourteenth—because it seemed likely they would put all guests on the same floor. I was wrong.

I found Mari and Keene on the seventeenth floor. They were together, which was good. I'd detected no sign of Jace.

Since it was past time for me to contact Mari, she would be concerned over my delay. In fact, I could feel nervousness radiating from her surface thoughts. Concern mixed with boredom and claustrophobia—she always felt claustrophobic when she wasn't free to shift. Her shield would be easier to breach than Keene's would, but even then it took me a good ten minutes. She'd be excited to know it was that strong. I suspected Lew could still get through her shield, though, and that made me uneasy. For now, there was no sign of him in her mind, but I wasted no time in placing a second layer of protection around us both now.

Mari, I said.

Relief flooded me—Mari's relief. Something had happened.

Finally. Mari said. *Can you come to me? Channel my ability. But you need to check for cameras there before you shift. They have them everywhere here, even in the bathroom.*

I arose and made my way to the door leading to the bathroom. There, I tugged off my shoes and flipped my blouse up over the camera near the mirror before turning on the water in the large stone-encircled shower and stepping inside. The shower was large enough that I wasn't immediately drenched as I channeled Mari's ability and shifted.

They were waiting for me in a bedroom that smelled like smoke. One of the curtains covering the barred windows was scorched. Besides that, the room looked upscale, much nicer than the studio I'd been given. Someone was more pleased to see Keene return to the Emporium than Stefan was that I'd come.

Mari hugged me, sending pain throughout my chest and stomach. I was glad she hadn't seemed to notice the bruises that were already appearing. "Ugh, your clothes are all wet." She stepped away quickly.

"Not as wet as they were forty minutes ago. Stefan decided to test my combat ability. Fortunately, Edgel was there, and I channeled him." I tilted my head toward the scorched curtains. "What happened?"

Keene grinned, and Mari laughed. "A bomb exploded," Keene answered at the same time Mari said, "Oh, Keene was just making sure all the surveillance devices were gone. He fried pretty much everything electronic in here and in most of the living room."

"It's not an exact science." Keene rocked back on his heel, hands in his pockets. He didn't look much better than he had last night. "I confronted my father about it, and I don't think they'll try to put them back. They can still see the entrances."

Mari noticed my concerned examination of Keene. "Tihalt kept him up all night doing test after test. I told him Keene needed to rest, but he ignored me. That man is insufferable. It was all I could do not to sink a knife into him. He still treats Keene like a kid."

"To him, I am a kid," Keene said mildly. "I endured the tests only for what he could teach me." He stared at Mari as her blond dye job began to lift up around her, as if it had a life of its own.

"Stop that!" Mari smoothed down her hair. "He's only doing that because he's too tired to change the atoms in anything else."

Keene sat on the edge of the bed, looking close to collapsing. "Actually, I'm changing the atoms in the air. I know how you women are about hair. I wouldn't dare touch your hair in case your head burst into flame or something."

Mari rolled her eyes and continued talking to me. "Tihalt had him levitating practically everything—including himself!"

"You might say I can fly." Keene gave me an impish grin. "And I don't need pixie dust. It's still hard determining what the reaction will be, though. I sent a desk through one of his walls. Oops."

I was betting it hadn't been a mistake.

With a soft *pop!* Mari disappeared from next to me and appeared near the bed. She pushed Keene onto the pillows. "Get some rest!" she ordered. "I'll fill her in."

"Fine." He threw an arm over his eyes with a sigh.

Mari was back to me in the next second. "You see Jace?" I asked her.

"No." Her head swung back and forth. "We haven't seen practically anyone except a few guards and Tihalt."

"Not even Stefan?"

"Nope. I don't think he knows we're here."

"That's odd. Why would Tihalt be keeping it a secret?"

"He was probably too excited about his experiments," Keene said from the bed, pulling back his arm and opening his eyes. "But he did hint at some inventions he was working on and hadn't shared with anyone, not even the Triad. It was weird because he didn't used to hide anything from Stefan, at least."

"Anyway, we have news from Ava." Mari drew me a couple feet away from the bed, which was pointless since Keene could still hear us.

"How?"

"We used a scrambled phone, that's how. Keene still has at least one friend here. We had Stella check to make certain we could scramble the call further just in case the friend wasn't so friendly." Mari leaned toward me, her eyes flashing. "Stella and Cort discovered something about Jeane—her memories have been tampered with."

"Really?" Ava had told me stories about Unbounded being able to change memories instead of just extracting them, but no one really knew if the stories were history or only a legend. I'd assumed it was related to sensing or a variation of the ability, if it even existed.

"Yep. Stella and several other technopaths have had Renegade servers all over the world working to uncode Jeane's thoughts." Mari glanced toward the bed to make sure Keene was still resting. "They haven't really had a lot of luck yet, but a Renegade in Ukraine figured out the memories had been tampered with."

"What do you mean tampered?"

"Someone layered new ones over the old—perhaps using a supposedly extinct ability called mnemokinesis, or memory manipulation. The mnemo ability for short."

Unbidden, a memory came to my mind from those left by Delia. *Mnemos can erase, change, absorb, or transfer memories—others' or their own.* Mnemokinesis was a variation of the sensing ability, or a mutation that allowed additional power. Delia had known a mnemo in her youth, and over generations, Delia had learned to mimic part of the ability, which had eventually resulted in the memory transfer she'd attempted with me. However, she'd never achieved full use of the ability. Still, by mixing generations of sensing Unbounded with the science ability, she'd managed to create . . . Unfortunately, there was a gap in the memory before another kicked in. Delia was furious that she didn't have control over the mnemo. *But there is more than one way to get around that.*

In an instant, the memories were over and I was aware of Mari continuing. "But the Ukrainian thinks this looks more like a raider changed Jeane's memories—a raider's a weaker variation of a mnemo—because the memories weren't erased, just overlaid. The old memories are still underneath, but the brain can't recall them. If whoever tampered with Jeane had extracted the memories before putting in new ones, the Ukrainian doubts we'd be able to detect anything. He almost missed the tampering as it is."

"So is that what makes Jeane's mind scrambled?"

"Ava and her experts don't think so. The untampered stuff is still scrambled. She's just different."

"Who would do such a thing? Could it be Ropte? Stefan let it slip that Ropte's ability is hypnosuggestion, but maybe he's wrong."

Mari scrunched her nose. "How could he be wrong about that? He would have seen him in action, I'm assuming."

"Well, Stefan hasn't figured me out, so I'm just covering all the bases. Jeane didn't seem to remember anything about Ropte's ability, which I think is strange."

"Or she was lying."

Right. I turned and began pacing the room, trying to piece it together. Something didn't add up. Why would anyone care about changing Jeane's memories? "If only we knew what memories were changed."

"They're working on that," Mari said. "If they get a translation, Cort theorizes that you could channel a technopath and 'read' her memories. The guy in Ukraine also thinks he might be able to rig Stella's holo program to show us at least a few images—if they can crack the code. It's difficult because her brain doesn't seem to work like anyone else's."

They could theorize all they wanted, but ultimately that meant for now we were on our own. "So what could Jeane know? Maybe she told Stefan more than we think. He was definitely questioning my ability."

"But he doesn't know you can channel people or break through shields, right?"

"Didn't seem to, but I didn't share much of that with Jeane. I never trusted her."

"Anyway, Jeane's a null," Mari said. "It shouldn't be possible for anyone to replace her memories."

"You sure about that?" Keene asked from the bed, sitting up abruptly and swinging his stockinged feet to the thick carpet. Ignoring Mari's frown, he continued. "In Morocco, Erin managed not only to block Jeane from using her ability on her but also to protect all of us from Jeane. Erin couldn't in the beginning, but she figured it out."

He transferred his gaze to me. "And we all saw how docile Jeane became in the conference room. I thought it was a coincidence the first time at Noah's house when we were questioning her, but obviously you *can* use your ability on her when you're past her shields or she's not blocking. You just don't understand her language, so you can't sense her thoughts. If you can affect Jeane without understanding her, then why not whoever overwrote Jeane's memories?"

I stared at him for a full ten seconds. He was right, of course. I *had* influenced Jeane, and I could protect against her nulling and see her thought stream even when she was exerting her ability. But I was different, or so I'd thought. No one else that I knew, including Ava or Jeane's boyfriend Lew, had been able to do that.

Looks like things had changed.

"I guess whoever did the tampering could have done so when Jeane wasn't blocking," Mari mused. "Anyway, they theorize that Jeane's memories had been newly recalled before being plastered over with the new ones. So maybe they were talking and—"

I reached the window and turned sharply on my heel. "What about that new sensing Unbounded Jeane told us about—Catrina, wasn't it? Memory manipulation is a variation of sensing, but if she did it, she's not a regular sensing Unbounded. She'd be stronger. *I* can't replace memories."

"Any sensing Unbounded can learn to take memories," Keene said. "So she wouldn't necessarily be stronger. They weren't erased, they were replaced."

"Probably because she didn't know which ones to take, not if she can't decipher Jeane's mind any more than I can." I scowled at Keene, wishing he were Ritter so he could tell me what this might entail on a defensive level. "This is bad, guys. If they have someone who can change memories, what's to stop them from changing ours? Or anyone's?"

"Our shields?" Mari offered.

Right, our shields. But would those really protect us? They didn't stop me for the most part, given enough time. And not understanding Jeane's thoughts hadn't stopped whoever tampered with her mind. "That might work if it's mental, but what if it works by sound like hypnosuggestion? Or touch?" Even my mental connection was enhanced by touch.

Keene shrugged. "Shields don't work very well against hypnosuggestion. I don't know about touch, but you might have to shield our bodies like you did in Morocco."

My anxiety cranked up a notch.

"I'm more worried about how this relates to what's going on in Congress," Keene added. "It seems strange that a popular president could lose so much ground, but it makes more sense now, knowing someone with this ability is running around. Memories are basically knowledge, and if they have the ability to 'raid' memories, they can change politicians' minds to make them think they believe something else, or have different alliances within the senate. Or even plant memories to make it look like President Mann is an idiot."

"But why kidnap those families or murder the senators?" I asked. "Why not change their memories instead?"

"Maybe it's not an ability?" Mari ventured. "Maybe it's technical, a program, or even hypnosis."

I restarted my pacing. "I'm guessing Stella's doing research on it, but didn't Dimitri have anything to say? He's probably heard something about mnemokinesis in the last thousand years."

"Dimitri's only heard the same rumors we have," Keene said. "And it's going to take me time to get another phone to find out if Stella's uncovered anything more. My contact isn't under suspicion, but she has to be careful."

"She?" Mari asked.

Keene flashed her a grin. "Jealous?"

"Not a chance—unless you've suddenly developed the ability to lie." He'd drifted away from the bed, but Mari pushed him back toward it. "Now rest while we install the relay switches on the generators, or you'll be useless when Ropte gets here.

With the kind of distances we're talking about, we don't need you to help us shift."

"And let you have all the fun?"

Mari glared at him. "Don't you go all macho on us. This is our job. You're here only because of your dad."

"Wait a minute." I pulled my mind from its preoccupation with Jeane and the mysterious raider. "Look, neither of you has to go anywhere. I'll take care of the generators."

"You'll need a lookout," Mari protested. "I can shift away if there's a problem. I even brought a couple of Cort's bodysuits for us."

Keene looked surprised. "What? You know Cort's going to kill you, right? We don't want to hand them that kind of technology."

"Oh, well." Mari gave an unconcerned shrug. "They didn't take them from me, so we're probably in the clear."

The last thing I wanted was for Stefan to know about Mari or suspect that we were connected, especially with a mind-sucking raider lurking around. But her coming with me had been part of Ritter's plan, and I knew better than to second-guess his skills. Besides, I desperately wanted to search for Jace, and the sooner we planted the relay switches, the sooner I could get to that.

Keene started to speak, but I shook my head. "Just her. You look ready to drop. You'll only be a liability." Funny how he could increase our abilities but not fix his own exhaustion. Or maybe he just hadn't figured it out yet.

He raised his hands in surrender. "Don't get yourselves caught."

"We won't." I looked again at Mari. "Did you get what we need?"

"I did," Mari said, going to a drawer. "Tihalt's lab is exactly like Cort's, only ten times the size. Really, it's ridiculous. After

I told him my ability was adding numbers, he pretty much ignored me, so while Keene kept him busy, I explored. Tihalt tried to order me back here at one point, but when Keene said he'd go with me, Tihalt let me stay."

Mari retrieved a length of wire, a roll of black electrical tape, wire cutters, several screwdrivers, and some tightly rolled-up blueprints as long as my arm. "How did you get all this from the lab?" I asked.

She pulled up her wide-legged pants to show compression stockings that reached to her knees. "Stuffed in these. Believe me, it wasn't easy. Those plans were the worst. I would have just shifted with it, but we hadn't disabled the cameras in here yet."

"Nice. It'll save time not having to get the location of the transfer switches from someone's mind. What about the relays?"

The most important element of our plan was the four dime-sized relays that she carried inside the metal buttons on one of her jackets. If we needed more than those four, we were going to be scrambling, but we could make new relays if we had to, even if it delayed our plan. Cort assured us we could find all the necessary parts in his father's lab.

"One of the guards took both our bags into their security office when we came in," Mari said, stuffing the tape, wire, and wire cutters into a purple sack stamped with a yellow daisy. "You know, before they fed us into that imaging machine? I faked a desperate need for the bathroom, and while I was there, Keene caused a distraction so I could shift back into the room to snatch the jacket. They didn't even notice when I emerged with it over my arm."

"If they'd known about your shifting, they would have locked you up inside a shielded cage. So Jeane didn't tell them that either."

"Well, she didn't know I was coming." Mari made a face. "And if she did tell them about me, I'm disguised enough." She twirled a finger through a lock of dyed hair. "I still say she's hiding something."

"Yeah, but does she even know what?"

Mari shrugged and didn't answer. Instead, she fished in the drawer and pulled out a syringe. "I took a couple of these too—their version of curequick. You look like you need it." Her eyes dropped to my bare stomach, where the bruises had darkened considerably.

I glanced toward the bed. "Keene probably needs it more than I do."

"He's had three."

"Oh, thanks." Taking the syringe, I shot the thick liquid into the flesh around my ribs, wincing at the prick. I really hated needles.

Mari unrolled the plans, revealing not one but several sheets of paper. "How do you even know these are for this building?" I asked.

She laughed. "Easy. The dimensions. I saw the building from the outside, and I just *know* how large it is, how much space it takes up. Unless they have another building exactly like this one somewhere, including the lobby and security room and Tihalt's lab, it's this one."

"Could you shift us to the generator room?" Maybe her experimentations with coordinates would be useful here.

A grimace stole over her face. "I could try, but these plans don't give me nearly enough information spatially. It would be too easy to come out somewhere we'd be seen. Using my new method of folding space, we could take several glimpses downstairs before we found where to shift, but I'd rather reserve the energy—I have no idea how much effort it's going to take to get the others inside safely. However, the plans do show us where to start looking for someone near the generators who can provide you with a visual link—"

"And we can use that link for a simple shift through the gray." Seemed easy enough, and it wouldn't take much energy on my part.

"Exactly." Mari dragged a finger down the plans, one floor to the next. "There are so many floors, it gets confusing, but basically, each paper has about three floors. So here's the lobby, and the generators are two floors under that. Half of each of the two underground floors is also a parking garage. Looks like they have three generators intended to supply energy to different sections of the building. The transfer boxes are there." She stabbed a finger at a line that represented a wall.

"Great. If the setup is anything—wait." My concentration broke as my mind registered a warning. "Looks like a life force is approaching that apartment they locked me in." The life force was moving closer and closer to my door. At my words, Keene sat up again from the bed, his brow furrowed. Keeping my hold on Mari, I shifted.

Back into the shower. I tugged off the rest of my clothes and began washing for real. The water was a tad too hot, but it felt comforting on my strained muscles. Soaping down my hair and body in record time, I turned off the water, grabbed a towel from a hook, and wrapped it around me. The life force I'd seen was already inside my room, and I prepared for battle.

To my surprise, a tiny, sweet-looking young woman stood in the middle of my apartment, her arms full of clothing. She had dark strawberry blond hair, the kind I'd always thought of as being orange, and a splash of pale freckles warmed her face. Her spaghetti-strapped tank and short shorts made her look about seventeen. She wasn't much taller than my twelve-year-old niece and probably weighed less.

"Hi," she said, raising the bundle in her arms. "Triad Stefan asked me to bring you clothing. He said you didn't pack much."

"Thank you." I took the clothing from her and dumped it on the bed. "Who are you?"

"I'm Catrina Silvaski." Her words had a slight lilt I couldn't place, like an accent that hadn't quite been eradicated. So this was the sensing Unbounded Jeane had vowed to get rid of. Why hadn't she come in hiding her life force, especially if Stefan suspected my ability? Or maybe he didn't suspect anymore after our bout.

Catrina looked sweet and young—but definitely Unbounded. To be this young, her Change must have been forced, yet she didn't have the typical crunched facial features, so maybe I was wrong. Unless the Emporium had perfected the process. I didn't want to think about that or how many lives they'd sacrificed to make it happen. Too many didn't survive the process.

Her appearance told me little about her, but the probing at my mind told me much more. She felt like a tiny fly hitting my shield. Maybe the rumors of her strength had been greatly exaggerated. Unless she was a mnemo variation. I arched a brow. "Is there something else?"

She opened her mouth and then shut it again just as quickly. Suddenly a thrust of her mind jabbed into my mental shield, driving a volley of pain into my head. I pushed back, but only to strengthen my shield, careful not to let her know I'd felt her attack. She watched me with unveiled interest in her pale green eyes. "Your shield is very strong. Stronger than Lew's. That's unusual."

"So you're a sensing Unbounded."

She dipped her head in agreement. "I was told to come in here and pick your mind. I have better luck sometimes than Lew in breaking down mental shields. Probably because many people—well, most people—don't like him." She shrugged her slight shoulders. "But I guess I failed."

"Are you sure you tried hard enough?"

Again the shrug, but aloud she said. "Definitely."

She was lying. I felt it in her surface thoughts. If she was letting those escape, she either didn't suspect anything or she knew my true nature and was toying with me.

"I'll have to try again," she said, "probably after they inject you with drugs, but I've never been able to get through Lew's even then."

I could see more questions in her eyes, but for whatever reason she wasn't voicing them. She strode forward, her hand reaching for my arm. I stepped back, avoiding contact. "Don't touch me."

If she was the mnemo or raider, even a shield over my entire body might not hold up to a physical touch—and I couldn't risk such a protection now, because only sensing Unbounded could extend mental shields beyond their minds, and she'd instantly perceive my actual ability.

"So you know touch increases my gift."

"My grandmother is sensing."

"Your fifth great-grandmother."

"That's right. You guys *murdered* my real grandmother."

Something passed over her face in a wave. Was it regret or satisfaction that she'd rattled me?

"You touch me and I'll kill you," I said.

She took a pace backward. "I didn't know about your grandmother. I'm sorry."

I wanted to ask her about Jace, if she'd stolen his memories. But I still wasn't supposed to know he was here. "Was it really Stefan who sent you?"

She nodded. I wanted to rip into her shield and delve into her mind, but I couldn't or she'd feel me every bit as much as I felt her. She'd also have a chance to get inside me that way. Not a large one, but still a chance. Better to focus on keeping my shield strong. I hoped Jace's shield had held if she'd attacked him.

"You are like your brother," she said softly. "I couldn't get through his shield, either. Lew will try soon."

"My brother? He's here?" I thought my simulated surprise was pretty good, but Catrina gazed at me with an amused expression. Strangely, it didn't feel like she was mocking but rather admiring me.

"Apparently, he heard you were taken by Jeane and came here to rescue you. He arrived last night. Surprised everyone. We had a DNA test done, and Jace *is* Triad Carrington's son. Looks like he's had two prodigal children come home."

"Where is Jace?" The words came out choked instead of confident.

"I don't know." Her eyes drifted briefly up to the ceiling. "He's fine, though. After your meeting with the Triad this afternoon, I'm sure Triad Carrington will allow you to see him." A frown appeared on the narrow lips. "Oops. I think he wanted that to be a surprise."

I didn't get it. I was almost sure she was the person who'd tampered with Jeane, but why had she come here alone if she didn't intend to force me? Or was I already forgetting something I held dear? I pulled out my mental machete and searched my mind, prepared to do battle, but there was no trace of Catrina or anyone else. Just me.

I had to trust myself. "Thank you," I said, "for telling me about Jace."

Catrina smiled, and for a moment she looked older. "My pleasure."

She'd taken a step toward the door when my next words stopped her. "Are you related to Delia Vesey?"

"Delia?" Catrina turned. "Thankfully, no. I come from another line. I mean, all sensing Unbounded probably originated from the same person four thousand years ago or whatever, but Delia wasn't my direct ancestor. In fact, I was living in Russia until a short time ago. I was sent here after Delia died—my people refused to send me before then. Delia was, however, very involved in our breeding. I think that's why they hated her so much."

I couldn't blame them, but it was interesting to know she had family. That might mean the Emporium had more sensing Unbounded than we'd guessed. "How long ago did you Change?"

Her smile this time was more childlike. "Well, I grew up among Unbounded, but I've only been one myself for six months. You?"

"Not much longer. Seven months ago, I'd never heard of Unbounded."

I wanted to ask if she'd volunteered to be forced or if she was older than she looked, but I didn't want to pity this childlike woman who was probably the biggest danger to me since Delia.

Her pale eyes danced. "Your brother asked, and I bet you want to. I don't mind telling you. I'm nineteen, the youngest person ever to have Changed without being forced. It just happened. But many of my ancestors Changed early. It's a family trait we kept secret for as long as we could."

I wanted to know if it was Delia they'd tried to hide it from and, if so, how the Triad had uncovered the secret. "I bet Tihalt's been testing you nonstop."

Her smile widened. "Not since I learned to break through his shield." She laughed and resumed her journey across the carpet. So she wasn't a puppet, at least not the way she was supposed to be.

I didn't want to like Catrina, but there was something appealing about her. Maybe it was partially because Jeane disliked her so much.

Or had Catrina *made* me like her?

I hated this.

As soon as the door shut behind Catrina, I reached out to Mari. *Let's get this done. Ropte will be here soon. The relays need to be in place before then.*

CHAPTER 21

MARI AND I STOOD GAPING AT THE THREE HUGE GENERATORS. They were as large as dump trucks, and stood one after the other, gleaming with bright yellow paint. They were attached to massive, equally gleaming metal vents that umbrellaed each generator like a silver cloud. Ritter had trained us on the schematics of numerous generators after the last time we'd had to deal with one, but seeing these enormous things up close was a little daunting.

"I bet they'd only need one to power this entire building," Mari whispered, her voice muffled by her metamaterials hood. She needn't have whispered. I'd mentally followed one of the guards to the generators, and he'd been inside this cavernous space alone when we'd shifted in. If there were cameras or mics here, he hadn't been aware of them. He was in a corner now, unconscious after a little fast work on my part. I'd have to deal with his memories before long.

The three six-foot metal transfer boxes were located exactly where Tihalt's plans said they would be in the room, but in case of doubt, block letters stamped on the bare cement above the boxes read TRANSFER CONTROLS. These boxes were what made it possible to use either outside power from the city or power from the generators, transferring between the two systems as needed. Leading from the boxes were thick wires that sent electricity throughout the entire building.

Ignoring the outside control buttons on the transfer boxes, Mari dumped the contents of her bag and went to work loosening the screws on the first panel. The good news was that we'd brought plenty of relays. "Thank you, Cort," I murmured.

"If only someone would invent a better screwdriver," Mari growled through the first screw she already held in her mouth.

Our targets were the wires that connected the batteries in each generator to the transfer switches located inside the metal boxes. In the case of a power outage, the battery provided the electricity for the transfer switch to sense the outage and automatically turn on the generators. Placing one tiny relay on each incoming wire would give us the ability to cut the electricity to the switch and interrupt the power generated by the fuel in the generators. In that case, it would switch back to outside current—which should be down—giving us control over the building's power and its electric shield.

After stripping the wire, we used the wire from Tihalt's lab as a bypass, wrapping each end over the bare surface of the stripped wire several inches apart, making sure the contact was good before cutting the original wire. No alarms came from the generators, so the bypass was doing its job of completing the circuit. Then we spliced the relay into the original wire, once again completing the circuit before removing the bypass connection.

"Easy peasy," Mari said, looking almost cheerful.

We separated to complete the other two transfer boxes, double-checking each other's work when we were finished.

If anyone looked inside, the small relays appeared almost as if they belonged. But no one would have any reason to open the boxes until the power went out, and even then they should first attempt to use the outside controls or check the generators for problems. If the power outage lasted long enough, someone would eventually realize the transfer switches were the reason, but we hoped to have the generators back on before they even got to this room. We'd need less than a minute to bring Ritter and some of the others inside.

I took out two more tiny plastic envelopes like the one I'd given Stefan. A drop from each packet on the screws assured us that no one would be removing these panels without some heavy drilling. Stefan really needed to hire better people.

Now for the Unbounded we'd left lying in a corner near two stacks of medium-sized crates. I shifted over to him, and Mari followed, her suit making her almost invisible in the dim light. He was unconscious, but his mind was still partially shielded. Laying my hand on his cheek, I hammered through his shield and passed down into the lake of warm water. For a time, I studied the memory bubbles. Was this how a mnemo worked, except by changing the memories instead of removing them?

I reached out to the memory bubble that showed the guard reeling as I stepped out from behind some crates and punched him twice in the head. If I could just replace that with him hitting his head on something, it would be far more effective. But the bubble vanished as I touched it like they always did when I extracted them. So much for that idea. I opened my eyes and arose.

Mari had been busy while I was occupied. She'd pushed one of the crates onto the floor near him, and another now teetered on the edge. With any luck, he'd assume it had fallen on him and wouldn't report his blackout. If he did report it and Lew examined him, Lew might be good enough to detect my tampering.

Without speaking, we shifted back to Mari's suite where we found Keene pacing the room. He looked better with the short rest and the curequick running through his veins, but not yet fully recovered.

"Any luck?" I asked him. I'd been watching our apartments and had seen a life force come to his door, but it hadn't entered.

"My contact says everything's in lockdown mode. No one can leave or enter—except Ropte, who they're expecting. We can't get another phone right now."

"A lockdown actually works into our plans," I said. "Especially once we're in place. Until we have this building secure, we don't want anyone trying to get past Ava's blockade to help them."

"Any problem with the relays?" he asked.

Mari shook her head. "Everything looks great." She removed the tiny remotes from the remaining buttons on her jacket and handed one to each of us. "Press and hold for as long as you want the generators to quit." I peeled off the back paper and stuck the remote behind my ear.

We stared at each other, and I said, "They won't cut the power until sixty minutes after Ropte arrives. Now we wait."

To preserve my strength, I did my waiting in my own small suite, lying fully dressed in my original clothing on the surprisingly comfortable bed. In order to catch Ropte's arrival, one part of my mind lingered on the lobby and on the floor leading to the rooftop where they had a helipad. I knew he wouldn't come alone, so I just had to be aware of a group of life forces arriving. At that point, I'd alert Mari, and she could begin a countdown with her internal clock. What took far more effort was extending my shield around Mari so we could leave our connection open.

Waiting was torture. I felt Ritter's absence like an ache, as if I'd left an arm behind. Being separated from him by the electric grid surrounding the building made me crazy.

Instead of focusing on that loss, I combed upward through the floors, trying to find my brother. Jace was nowhere in the building, not even on the lowest floor, but I did find a gap on the top floor that made it appear as if half the level didn't exist. Only another separate electric grid could do that, and it made sense for Stefan to use the new technology in his private quarters, especially to protect him while sleeping. Catrina had seemed to indicate that Jace was somewhere above me, and I had no reason to trust her, but maybe Jace was there.

Time clicked on. I kept my eye on the ornate clock on the wall, breathing deeply and absorbing until I felt my energy at full strength. Even the pain in my chest was completely gone. No one disturbed me. I wouldn't have eaten anything they might have brought, to prevent being drugged, but their neglect worried me.

I found myself thinking about Edgel and the odd numbers attached to him in my mind. I went after the memory now, searching in the depths of my subconscious where I kept those pieces of Delia. They hadn't given me much, except the occasional tidbit of knowledge, but maybe this was important. Or maybe it was only a code between Edgel and Delia, long in disuse and no longer valid.

Jeane stared up at me, horror in her eyes. "No. No!" Her voice rose to a scream. "I hate you! I hate you! I will kill you for this. I swear it!"

"You knew the rules, Jeane. He was a Renegade. He's dead; it's over. And if you won't help, I no longer have a use for you."

Jeane cringed away, trying to hold in her sobs, turning to Lew, whose embrace was the only thing keeping her upright.

"Clean her up." Delia's voice held no compassion. "I want to try another insemination. Yours this time. If we could create a sensing Unbounded with the ability to null, we'd be invincible."

I gasped for air as the memory vanished. Not the one I'd been searching for. I knew Jeane had been abused, but experiencing the utter lack of compassion Delia had shown her was sobering. Had Delia always been this way, or had it happened gradually over the centuries of loving and losing people she cared about?

More troubling was the next thought: if I lived as long as she did, was I fated to become like her? She'd once told me that was my destiny.

No. I wouldn't believe that. I had Ritter. I had my brothers. I had the Renegades. I cared. These were memories that weren't mine, however real they felt. I would ask Ava to remove them when this was over. I'd beaten Delia in life, and I wasn't about to let her steal any more of my happiness in death.

With relief, I felt my attention pulling in another direction. I had no idea how long I'd been caught in Delia's memory, but Ropte had just arrived with four other life forces.

Begin the countdown, I told Mari.

Ropte had been in the building thirty minutes before Edgel and two other Unbounded male soldiers appeared at my door. I was glad Edgel was there in case I needed to channel him before Ritter arrived, or until I found Jace. Each soldier wore an additional knife at their belts along with their normal guns and swords. I wasn't sure what that meant. Were they expecting trouble or just trying to impress someone?

We marched to the elevator in silence, with me hacking away at Edgel's mental defenses. At least Catrina was nowhere to be found.

"So where is my brother?" I asked Edgel as the elevator closed on us.

His dark, angular face showed no emotion, but I was already in his mind, and I felt his surprise. "What are you talking about?"

"Catrina told me he was here."

A slight widening of his nostrils would have told me little, but his mind registered fear. Of Jace? Of Catrina? Of my knowing Jace was here? No, the fear was definitely of Catrina. I wondered if she'd breached his shield or if he simply and finally understood that his mind was not the sanctuary Delia had led him and the others to believe all these years. That would explain why Stefan now shielded his quarters.

The elevator was fast, the numbers changing as we hurtled upward. "So, where is Jace?"

Edgel's mouth finally cracked, as if pried open with a crowbar. "You'll have to take that up with Stefan."

"Don't you mean Stefan and David Ropte?"

Edgel didn't reply. A bell dinged, and the elevator door slid open on the nineteenth floor.

The two Unbounded guards standing outside it stepped back, and Edgel gestured me out. He kept pace with me while the other two guards who'd ridden up with us followed several feet behind.

Edgel needed to loosen up. Of course, he wanted to kill me, and that might be why he was so communicative.

"Has Jeane seen her brother?" I pushed. "Ropte seemed

very interested in meeting with her when they talked this morning, and strangely enough, she seems to care about him." Or at least enough that she wanted us to put him in prison instead of killing him.

My comment again surprised Edgel. From his thoughts, I caught a glimpse of Ropte's face, the handsome features contorted in bloodlust, a sword in his hand. A woman was screaming. I was pretty sure the woman was Jeane. What had happened between her and Ropte? I needed to know.

My curiosity stuttered to a halt as I felt Jace. I'd stopped looking for him, but now he filled my senses. He was here, somewhere close. I reached out to him, but his shield was tight. *Good boy,* I thought, but of course he couldn't hear. There seemed to be a few life forces near him—no, under him, rather. He must be on the floor above us.

Edgel turned a corner before stopping at a wide door guarded by three men, where he ignored the handprint reader and knocked. A slight rustle, and the door was opened, not by a guard but by Catrina, who was now dressed in tan business slacks and a patterned silk blouse. I should have known she would be here. Lew probably wouldn't be far behind.

Inside the room, four long couches faced each other in a square, with three feet of open space at the corners. An oversized coffee table, also square, sat in the middle of the couches, where cups and a pot of steaming coffee lay on a tray. The wall on the same side as the door held a large screen, while the opposite had north-facing, floor-to-ceiling windows. The right wall boasted an impressive display of swords that looked only too real, and against the left wall, a well-stocked minibar offered a variety of refreshments. At least twenty feet of bare rock floor separated the couches from the bar and the windows, with less than half that on the two other sides of the couch arrangement. Black pillars filled each of the four corners. It seemed a strange place for a battle, but here the fate of the world would be decided.

Catrina smiled and shut the door behind Edgel and me, leaving the other two guards outside the door. I was glad I'd released Mari for the moment, or Catrina would surely have noticed the trail of my shield as it snaked downward to Mari's location.

Wait. Had I still been connected with Mari at my first meeting with Catrina? I couldn't remember now.

Catrina reached out to Edgel and me, and we both shrank from her touch. Her smile dimmed as she motioned for me to precede her farther into the room. Edgel remained near the door, and I felt his relief at the increasing distance from Catrina.

As I guessed, Lew was present, and also Jeane, sitting across from each other on the couches. Stefan leaned against the bar, and Ropte stood by the windows, staring at dark clouds gathering in the distance, the gray on his temples more pronounced in the light. Next to Ropte was one of the bodyguards from his luncheon, and I decided that the three men in the hallway must be the others who'd accompanied him. Tihalt was nowhere in sight.

Stefan came toward me, swirling a cup of amber liquid in a glass. "Thank you for coming, Erin." He smiled graciously, the perfect host, exuding confidence and a magnetism that was strong even for an Unbounded. I was glad he wasn't my real father and that I'd glimpsed inside his mind on our first meeting and knew his heart. If I hadn't, I might want to believe.

"You're welcome." I didn't try to hide my irritation. "What are they doing here?" I looked over at Jeane and Lew. "My message is for the Triad."

Stefan's eyes hardened, and his face lost some of its welcome. "Jeane will be leaving before our meeting." He glanced across the room at Ropte and then back at me. "Her brother wanted to check on her welfare. However, both my sensing Unbounded will be present. We have to be sure, you know."

I wasn't about to open my shield for either of them to check the veracity of my statements, but we'd get to that later. "Where's Triad McIntyre?" I asked. Tihalt had to be a part of our group for our coup to work at all. If he was buried in some lab with hundreds of soldiers between us, that might be a problem, even with Mari's ability.

"On his way. But while we wait, let's get to the introductions. I don't believe you've met David Ropte." Again, his gaze went to the man by the window, and this time Ropte turned to regard us with hazel eyes that today seemed calculating.

"No, I haven't had that pleasure."

"David," Stefan said, angling his body toward the windows, "meet Erin Radkey."

Ropte came forward, his hand outstretched in greeting, but Catrina shoved a cup of coffee in my hand, coming so close to touching me that I shied away. Some of the hot coffee sloshed over the cup onto my skin.

"Nice to meet you," I said, dabbing with the napkin that had come with the cup. Ropte frowned and dropped his hand. I felt a rush of emotion from him, but I didn't know what it meant.

"Would you like a scotch instead?" Stefan's mocking grin softened the hardness in his eyes and reminded me of Jace.

"No thanks," I said.

Stefan drank the contents of his glass and crossed to the minibar to pour another before rejoining us. "Are you sure? I thought you might want to toast our pending victory. That's why you're here, isn't it? To concede the battle and offer the terms of Renegade surrender?"

"Not even close."

Stefan's grin vanished, and he barked a laugh. "Whatever you've come here for today, you have to know you won't be leaving us. Not this time." His hand ran down my arm in an unmistakably sexual way, his eyes slipping over the curves of my body. "Believe me, we have a place for you."

What?

My world tilted. He'd touched me before, but never in that manner. He might be an evil murderer, but he wasn't into incest. "I would think," I said acidly, "with the shared genes between us that I would be afforded more respect."

Stefan chuckled at my expression, and Ropte laughed with him. "I admit we share a common ancestor with the Renegades, but make no mistake: we won't let any of you stand in our way."

I knew then that someone had told him he wasn't my father. Jeane? Lew? Jace? I knew my brother would rather die than give me up, but if Catrina had tampered with his memories, he might have been deceived enough to betray me. Or maybe Stefan had taken my DNA from the bo staff after our fight—I didn't know if that was possible.

I floundered, feeling sick to my stomach. Did they know about my ability too? But, no, unless they had learned I could channel, they couldn't know—and how would they even think to ask that question of Jace?

Jeane arose from the couch, where I'd spotted Lew shooting glances at her—tender ones that had his heart written all over them. Stefan would be blind if he hadn't noticed, and my bet was that Stefan hadn't gotten to where he was by not being observant.

"Oh, Erin," Jeane said, moving with her customary swaying gait, "you don't have to worry about uniting with the Emporium. My brother will make sure you're treated well regardless of what you decide." She put her arm around Ropte, who returned the gesture. They looked good together, more like a politician and his young trophy wife than brother and sister.

Stefan's eyes turned angry as he stared at them, but within a breath he turned those ice blue eyes in my direction again. I kept my mouth shut and waited for the other shoe to drop, for him to say Jeane had told him everything. For them to throw me into a shielded cell and disrupt all our plans.

I'd never free my brother. Or see Ritter again.

Instinctively, I checked my connection with Edgel, planning to use his ability to determine everyone's threat level in case I had to fight. I guessed Stefan was the greatest challenge, but Ropte's guard could be just as dangerous. Not to mention whoever was altering memories.

What I saw in Edgel's mind froze me.

He was sickened at the way Jeane held on to her brother. He remembered how she'd cried after Ropte had come home with her lover's blood on his hands. Delia's orders, but Ropte had carried out the deed. Edgel had been with him that day as a witness, and when they returned with the report, Jeane's cries had made him feel regret. Cries that reverberated in his head for years afterward.

Yet here she was clinging to her brother and smiling.

If Edgel's memories were correct, I would expect Jeane to null Ropte's ability and kill him instead of asking for favors and babysitting his wife.

Edgel wasn't the only one upset. Lew was now on the edge of his seat, his jaw locked and his eyes angry. His shield reached across the space separating him from Jeane, enveloping her body entirely, as if to keep her apart from Ropte. Whatever Jeane currently felt—or thought she felt—for her brother, Lew didn't share the feelings.

The tampered memories! Hope flared through me because maybe Jeane hadn't given me up. Maybe no one had.

Yet someone had definitely been tampering again, someone who didn't want Stefan to remember he had a daughter. Why?

I released a thought into Edgel's sand stream, causing him to remember this morning and also the last time he and Keene had brought me to Stefan. What I found make the fear inside me grow. He had no memory of me ever being considered Stefan's daughter, and I could see that the sands holding those memories were a different color, the grains layered with a shimmering translucence. I reached my hand in to touch them, thinking maybe I could pull the glow off.

Edgel jerked around, bringing his hand to his head. He stared at Catrina, scowling. His shield bucked at me, and the next minute I was thrown from his mind with the violence of his reaction.

One thing was clear: any safety I might have been afforded as Stefan's biological daughter had ended. In light of Catrina's presence, they didn't really need to keep me alive for breeding purposes, either. I wanted to panic, but I knew what Ritter would say: "The lie got you inside. That was all we needed."

My eyes snapped back to Stefan. "I did come here with an offer." Silently, I reached out to Mari. *How much time left before the outside power goes off?*

Eighteen minutes, thirty-three seconds. I plucked the thought from her head, giving her a quick thanks.

I could do this.

"But first, as much as I appreciate the coffee, I'd rather have tea." I turned and crossed to the bar where a stack of cups and a basket with tea bags sat next to thermoses of hot water. "Tihalt is on his way, isn't he? You did say that he was."

Under Ropte's stare and Stefan's amused smile, I filled a cup with heated water and plopped in a tea bag. At least it couldn't be poisoned. I dumped in a package of sugar as well, and then another, and stirred slowly before cleaning up the discarded packets. Eyes and silence followed me as I crossed the room to the farthermost couch where I could see the door and, with a little luck, reach the weapons on the wall behind me. Catrina had already settled on the couch opposite, so I was as removed from her as I possibly could be.

"So we begin negotiations?" Ropte said. To my annoyance, he sat kitty-corner on the couch next to me, his back to the window. His leg brushed Lew, who scooted away, leaving no doubts how he felt about the man. Lew's tension didn't leave even when Jeane sat next to him. Ropte's guard took up position directly behind Ropte's couch.

"Then we'll excuse you, Jeane." Stefan said, the only one besides Edgel and the guard who was still standing.

Ropte shook his head. "You have your two sensing Unbounded; I'd like Jeane to remain with me to protect my interests." Ropte's eyes landed on Catrina as he spoke.

Stefan's mouth pursed. "Very well, she may stay. But her ability won't be necessary."

"Only as a deterrent," Ropte agreed.

Stefan glanced toward the door. Too late, I saw Edgel open a panel and turn a switch. At once, glowing red lights emerged from holes set at intervals in each of the black pillars, casting a red grid pattern over the walls, ceilings, and floors. They ran under the couches and coffee table, perfectly aligned to avoid the legs. At once, the life forces in the building vanished from my mind, except for those in the room.

Immediately, I recognized the technology that had given birth to the portable grid.

Whatever link I had with Mari was gone. I was completely alone.

CHAPTER 22

ALONE. No way to signal Mari to set off the relays and bring everyone inside. I could try triggering the relays myself once the city power was cut and hope Mari noticed and began shifting our people inside, but would my transmitter work past the grid?

Ropte smiled at my discomfort. "Not what you expected, is it?"

"I'm not sure what you mean, but these lights are distracting." I set my tea untouched on the coffee table and waved my hands at the red lines crossing the walls and ceilings. Red crisscrossed my feet as they met the floor, cutting off some of the line, but the overall grid remained strong. The color lent a macabre haze to the room.

"Distracting but necessary." Ropte sat back. "Delia told me what you are. I don't know why you're here, but I suspect you have some kind of ridiculous plan, which I refuse to allow you and your misguided allies to carry out. Get used to this room because you are never leaving it—or one like it."

Stefan stood behind the couch where Catrina sat. "You're

not making sense, David. What's going on here? You have one minute to explain, or *you'll* be the one I throw into a dark cell. She's *my* captive, and I will determine what happens to her."

"I'm saying she's a sensing Unbounded. That's why I requested the grid for the meeting." Ropte's tone held barely concealed derision. "If you weren't so blind, you would have noticed it before. She's not here to offer a deal, she's here to take you down, to put herself in your place." Ropte's eyes again met mine. "It's what I would do."

Stefan's hand went to the gun he carried at his back. "Impossible. Oh, I've heard the rumors, but she's definitely combat. I tested her when she arrived."

So he did remember something from our meeting this morning. My initial panic was fading. When Mari couldn't see my location, she'd quickly realize that something had happened. Regardless, this grid should go off for at least a second or two when the outside electricity was compromised, and I'd be able to tell her to proceed without me. After the generators kicked in, she could set off the relays and shift Ritter and the others here.

"She has two abilities then," Ropte said, "because Delia told me she was the strongest sensing Unbounded she'd ever come across. She had big plans for her, which was why she kept it a secret. Unfortunately, Delia's plan failed."

Stefan glared at me. "Is this true? Have the Renegades found a way to breed in multiple abilities?"

My muscles bunched as I readied to defend myself. I had no doubt this would get ugly fast. "He hasn't told you everything," I said to Stefan. "Ropte and Delia were plotting to take over the Triad, and from what I've seen here today, I suspect he still plans to get rid of you and take control of the Emporium. Do you think you'll be any use to him once he has what he wants?"

I didn't know if what I was saying was true, but why else had Ropte waited until now to tell Stefan about me? And then there was the matter of the changed memories.

Stefan's gaze flicked to Ropte and back to me again. There was fear in that single look, and I wondered if Stefan had the same thought. "Are you a sensing Unbounded?" he demanded.

"What I am is your biological daughter," I said.

Ropte barked a laugh, but Stefan held my gaze. "Explain."

"Near the time of my conception, Renegades stole genetic material from your lab—your genetic material. You tagged the canister so you knew where it went, and you sent someone to retrieve me when I Changed, but I escaped. Now you have no memory of that, and apparently neither does Jeane." I didn't spare a glance in her direction. If she did remember, she was on Ropte's side and wouldn't help me. "There have to be records somewhere that show the truth."

Ropte's nostrils flared. "Impossible!"

Stefan rotated in his direction, staring down at Ropte. "Oh, but it is possible—I've just learned I have a son from that event."

"My brother Jace," I said. "Weren't you going to let me see him after this meeting?"

Stefan took a deep breath, confusion in his eyes as they rested again on my face. "I was going to have him . . ." He broke off, as if wondering why he would have allowed Jace to meet me. He looked at Edgel, still standing near the door. "Have you heard any of this?"

"She must be lying." Edgel gave me a dark glare.

Ropte laughed. "She can sense your thoughts, I tell you. She breaks down shields like Delia. You can't trust anything she says."

"Yet I do have a son. And he did come looking for her."

"Renegade lies." Ropte arose, his fists clenched at his side.

His guard's hand rested on his gun. "I will take responsibility for her. I'll get her tamed. I know how to break people like her."

I really hated him.

"No hypnosuggestion now," Stefan shot. "I want to get to the bottom of this. If there's any chance she's as powerful as you say, do you really think I'll hand her over to you?" He took a step around Catrina's couch, moving past the coffee table in my direction. He was still several feet away, but towered over me. I'd have to break through Edgel's shield to fight him, but with the other guard, Ropte, and Edgel himself here, I had no real chance at winning.

Catrina stared at me with her mouth partially open. Her shield completely enveloped her now, and I extended mine to my whole body as well. No use trying to hide what I was from her any longer. Without backup, I'd need the shield to stay alive.

"Okay, then," I stalled, calculating the effort to catapult myself over the back of the couch. Maybe I could make it to the swords on the wall. "I have proof. Delia ordered Ropte to kill Jeane's old lover. It took Ropte at least two attempts, but he succeeded. Jeane swore she'd never forgive him, but she doesn't remember that now. Someone has tampered with her memories."

Jeane gasped. "No! That's not how it happened. David tried to stop it. I-I—"

"Ask Edgel," I said. "He knows."

"She's right," Edgel and Lew said simultaneously.

Jeane's eyes showed pain. "No, no, no," she whispered. But there was doubt in her voice, doubt that made me think about the many tiny memories attached to that single, traumatic event. Maybe whoever replaced her memories wasn't good enough to find and replace all of them.

Ropte looked at Jeane. "Who're you going to believe?

Besides, no one can replace memories. This is just another Renegade trick."

"Actually, memories can be manipulated," Catrina said, her soft voice cutting through the harsh silence.

I'd been waiting for her to speak, to confirm Ropte's accusation about my ability, and this shocked me. "Is it you?" I asked her. "Who's behind you?" My bet was that she was working with Ropte.

Whatever Catrina's response might have been was lost as Ropte leapt to his feet, reaching for his gun and setting off a chain reaction in the room. Edgel pulled both his sword and his gun. Stefan drew his gun, moving backward away from the couches, closer to Edgel. I jumped over the back of my couch, the mental version of my machete banging at Edgel's shield. Ropte's guard, gun in hand, edged closer to me around the back of my couch, as if to prevent me from reaching the swords on the wall. Lew and Jeane hurried away from all of us to crouch in the corner between the windows and sword wall, his shield spread out to protect them both. Only Catrina remained sitting on her couch, her green eyes wide and interested, her face calm and unafraid. Her shield looked almost silver now.

At that moment, the overhead chandeliers blinked off, barely noticeable in the light coming from the huge windows, and then only because of the lingering clouds. *Yes!* Our Renegades had cut the outside power. I should have a moment to talk to Mari before the generators kicked in.

I reached out, but the red lines of the grid were still in place, except around our feet, and I could feel nothing beyond the room. *The columns have internal batteries,* Catrina sent to my surface thoughts, and I wondered why she bothered.

Two seconds later, the overhead lights flickered back on, signaling that the generators had kicked in. My chance was over. Even if Mari triggered the relays, I wouldn't be able to reach beyond this room to let her know what was happening.

Ropte was watching me, plainly gloating over my dismay. I recovered my expression and hacked harder at Edgel's shield. I was in! Still, getting out of here was a long shot, unless I could convince Lew and Jeane to work with me. I glanced in their direction to see them both staring murderously at Ropte, their hands tightly locked.

"Check to make sure the building hasn't been compromised," Stefan barked at Edgel. "I want the guard tripled and all soldiers ready for battle. Send an alert to the entire building."

So much for our surprise. I'd blame Ropte and that stupid red grid, but Stefan probably would have checked anyway.

Edgel jumped to open the panel near the door, bringing up the cameras on the huge wall screen. He talked briefly into an intercom inside the panel before facing Stefan. "All areas secure," he reported. "But there is a power outage in the neighborhood. Phone service seems to be out as well."

Stefan whipped his head toward me, his lips twisted in contempt. "You'll have to do better than that."

With all the guns in the room, I needed a weapon. I'd have to mentally control Edgel and his gun until I could find something to fight with, regardless of how much energy it would cost me. I only hoped Mari and Keene could get backup here before I ended up permanently dead.

"I don't know what you're talking about," I told Stefan. "I think you have bigger problems right here. Someone tampered with your memories. How much else have they changed?"

A series of short beeps made everyone look toward the door. It opened to reveal Tihalt McIntyre drawing his hand away from the handprint reader. With him was Keene. I schooled my face not to show relief that I had at least one person for backup. I hoped Mari used the relays soon. If she could bring Ritter anywhere inside, he'd find his way to me.

Tihalt was older than I remembered, his brown hair darker and heavily washed with gray. His narrow face, slim build, mocking green eyes, and even the way his body screamed exhaustion reminded me of Keene. "I see you started without me," Tihalt said without emotion.

"What's he doing here?" Stefan jerked his head at Keene, still aiming his gun somewhere in the direction of the coffee table—closer to Ropte than to me, I noted with satisfaction.

"This is my son, if you will remember. He's back to stay. He Changed." No mistaking the pride in Tihalt's voice, a pride that highlighted the disappointment and abuse he'd heaped on Keene when he was only a mortal. "His talent is synergy. He might be the most powerful Unbounded ever."

"He's a traitor!" Stefan countered. "I will not tolerate him here."

"Oh, but you *will* tolerate your own daughter, whose loyalties have long been decided?" Tihalt's lip curled in a sneer. By all accounts, they'd always presented a united front, but any warmth between them was completely missing now.

"My daughter," Stefan murmured. He blinked, his face straying briefly in my direction.

Tihalt snorted his impatience. "Well, what has she to say? I'm assuming she's the reason you're all pointing guns at each other."

"We've a mnemo here," Stefan said in a deceptively soft voice. Murder laced through the words. "Or a raider. Someone has apparently messed with my memories. Would you know anything about that?" Stefan's gaze transferred to Ropte. "Are you working with him? Is that why you've been withholding your recent inventions?"

"Don't be insane," scoffed Tihalt.

"I told you, it's got to be her!" Ropte pointed at me. "She's messing with our heads."

"Call the guards," Stefan barked at Edgel.

I didn't know if the guards were for me or Ropte. *Oh, no you don't.* I pushed hard at Edgel, keeping him from the buttons inside the panel. Terror spread through him. His eyes rolled toward Lew, but Lew wasn't looking in his direction. Edgel met my gaze and shuddered. His mind revolted, but I clung on, not allowing him to push me out or signal for backup.

Ropte fired at me, his pistol bucking slightly in his hands. He didn't miss—or wouldn't have if I'd remained where I was. Using Edgel's speed, I was near Ropte's guard now, my foot popping up to smash the gun from the man's hand. The guard turned and pumped his fist in a hook, catching me on the side of my head. Pain reverberated in my ear and jaw.

If only their mental shields weren't so strong, I'd flash them all with light and end this. For now, there was nothing to do but fight on.

Another shot came from Tihalt's direction, and the bullet bounced off my shield, the momentum slamming into me. My body skidded backwards, my head smashing into the drywall with a sickening *whack!* Blackness mottled my vision. I heard one of the displayed swords clanging to the floor as I slid down the wall. My control over Edgel wavered.

Edgel 65890 V. Delia's memories crowded in on me, bright and glowing in the darkness of my mind.

"Kill her!" Ropte commanded.

I watched from Edgel's eyes as Ropte's guard readied a blow that would probably keep me down for the count. Ropte sprinted from the couches to pick up the sword that had fallen, its gleaming edges no doubt sharp enough to permanently finish me, as his gun could not.

"Edgel 65890V!" I screamed, giving in to the memories that weren't mine. What did I have to lose?

My sight returned, and I steeled myself as Edgel brought up his gun and fired. A bloody spot appeared in the middle of Ropte's guard's forehead. Blood and brain matter splattered behind him onto the weapons hanging on the wall. Drops hit my face.

Banging on the door sent echoes reverberating in my head as Ropte's other three guards and the two Edgel had left there tried to get in. The two men by the elevator would probably be with them now, alerted by the shooting, and they would warn others. Just me and Keene against all of them. How did a perfectly good plan go so wrong?

The lights hadn't gone off again to signal that Mari had triggered the relays and begun shifting people inside, or at least not that I'd been able to notice. Nothing to save us. There wasn't even time for me to beg Jeane to null everyone—and even if she could, what use was that against their guns and swords?

Ropte fired at Edgel repeatedly, but the soldier jumped over the couch nearest him and landed on top of the coffee table, inexplicably unscathed. Ropte fired again, and his last bullet tore into Edgel's neck. He fell back, his pain knifing through our connection, but his heart beat on. Ropte laughed and lifted his sword over me. I lunged at his feet, knocking him off balance, and he stumbled back, momentarily losing his grip on his sword.

"Help me!" Ropte shouted at Lew, who cowered in the corner behind him. "Or you'll never have her. I'll kill you both!"

Another shot ricocheted off one of the black corner columns, sending me diving for cover. Tihalt's weapon again. Keene was grappling with him now, and I heard the *clunk!* of a gun as Keene pushed Tihalt back. Stefan started toward them, but Keene glanced over at him, and Stefan tripped, his feet tangling together. Keene was rewarded for this by a slam from his father that spread him onto the carpet.

Regaining his footing, Stefan pointed his gun at Keene's sprawled form. He fired, but the bullet shot toward one of the huge window panes instead. Glass shattered onto the carpet or disappeared outside. Stefan shot again and again with the same result, but the bullets went less far now, as though Keene was tiring.

Tihalt brought something from his pocket and closed in on Keene. "You *are* a traitor," he sneered.

I dodged Ropte's next swing, still channeling Edgel, who was somehow holding on to consciousness, then lashed out, kicking Ropte's knee. His sword slashed toward me, hitting into the wall and sending pieces raining down. From somewhere in the hall, I heard machine-gun fire—that door wouldn't hold out those guards for long. I needed to get past Ropte to one of the swords on the wall.

I became aware of Edgel's gun rising from between the couch and the coffee table where he'd fallen. Shakily, he aimed at Ropte. A second later, Edgel's head exploded as Lew fired a gun that was suddenly in his hands. Abruptly, my combat ability vanished. I was on my own, with only my training to save me. I sprang to the side, barely ducking away from Ropte's blade. More chunks of drywall scattered to the floor.

The next hit caught me on the top of my arm, and even though my shield was tight and the blade didn't pierce my skin, it felt like being bludgeoned with a baseball bat. I needed to put some space between us—now. I jumped back. Ropte lifted the sword again.

"AAAAAAA!" The horrible scream pierced the air, and for a second, everyone looked around to see where it came from. In that instant, Jace dropped from a jagged hole in the ceiling, passing through the red crisscrossing grid and slamming into Stefan, sending his gun clattering away. I reached for Jace and found his shield gone. A dangerous gamble with Lew and Catrina there, but exactly what I needed.

Channeling his ability, I jumped onto the couch and pushed off it past Ropte toward the wall with the weapons. Lew fired at me, but I was quicker. Grabbing a sword, I sprang away from the wall to confront Ropte, positioning him between me and Lew. From Jace's eyes, I got a glimpse of Keene, back on his feet now. Tihalt faced him with an odd-looking sword in his hand, one that glowed with light. No, it *was* light. Had to be a laser of some sort.

Even as I watched, Tihalt slashed at Keene with a horizontal strike. Keene jumped up and out of the way a breath before the light touched him. Instead, the laser sliced cleanly and deeply into the wall with a power that could easily sever a man in two.

I swung at Ropte and he blocked. He might not have the combat ability, but he was powerful and well-trained, and I was tired from my efforts with Edgel. I feinted a jab and tried to twist his sword away, but he held on. With each crash of our swords, I slammed at his shield. If I could just get inside.

More machine-gun fire came from the hallway, accompanied by screaming.

Stefan and Jace were evenly matched, exchanging blows so fast the motions were blurred. But in the next instant, Stefan had a knife in his hands. "Stop." He waved the knife in front of Jace, his face twisted with fury. "I don't want to hurt you, but I will."

"Really?" mocked Jace, his mouth curving into a smile. "Because the only reason I'm here is to kill you."

"Go ahead and try, *whelp.*"

I pulled my attention back to Ropte, finally hitting him on the arm. Blood dirtied the pale blue of his sleeve. "Lew!"

Ropte screamed, but every time Lew tried to shoot me, I danced around Ropte.

Then Lew altered his trajectory, aiming at Jace. I pushed out my shield toward my brother—hard. But I was too late. The bullet hit the middle of his back, and he fell forward onto Stefan's knife.

Jace! I felt the hot pain of the knife at the same time he registered that it hadn't hit anything vital. Neither was there any sign of blood on his back. It was then I felt the other shield over his back. Not mine. My eyes ran to Catrina, who stood alone by the broken windows, her small face concentrating on Jace.

She'd protected him?

Lew pulled his trigger again, but he was out of bullets. I parried another swing from Ropte as Jace pushed himself off the knife, shaken but not beaten. He punched Stefan in the face, and something cracked so loudly, I heard it across the room. I lunged at Ropte again.

If Catrina was helping Jace, maybe she wasn't the mnemo. Or maybe she just liked him. Either way, we had a chance, at least as long as the door to this room held. We could still turn off the red grid in the room, trigger the relays to shut down the generators, and shift our people inside.

The gunshots in the hallway had lessened but still came at intervals. Miraculously, the door held.

"Damn you!" Ropte spared a moment to slash out at Lew, who shrank away, his shield deserting Jeane as he enhanced his own protection. "Grab a sword. You're trained like the rest of us!"

"Don't listen, Lew!" I countered. "He'll never, ever let you or Jeane go. I know you hate me, but it's him you need to fight!"

Ropte's laugh resounded in our ears. "We have over a thousand soldiers here. Do you really hope to get out of this room alive?" He jabbed at me before taking another swing at Lew, his sword rebounding off Lew's shield. "If you don't help me, Lew, I'll make sure you never see Jeane again."

I pressed the advantage of Ropte's distraction, sinking my blade into his shoulder.

Ropte backpedaled. He grabbed Jeane's hand and threw her between us, but he didn't let her go completely. He held her hand tightly as she tried to tear away. "Remember Kennedy? I never hurt him. Never! I love you. I wouldn't do that. Remember how you think you hate me. It's not true. I'm your favorite brother. Remember, you would give your life for me. You would fight for me."

Something in his words clicked. *Remember . . .* he'd used the same word with Patrick when he'd asked for his support. *He's the one changing memories,* I thought. *Not Catrina.*

"Leave her alone!" Lew jabbed in another clip, his gun wavering uncertainly on Ropte.

"Not me, you idiot!" Ropte leaned to the side as I tried to reach him around Jeane. He parried my thrust. She sobbed but was no longer trying to get away.

Lew aimed again at Ropte and pulled the trigger, but Jeane was already in motion. She launched herself in front of her brother. The bullet crashed into the left side of her chest, and Ropte pushed her at me as she fell. I barely stopped myself from accidentally burying my sword in her stomach. Lew gave a bleak cry and scuttled across the floor to pull her to his chest.

Time to finish this, I thought. Ropte retreated toward the windows as I lunged.

The splintering door cut off all thoughts of success. Guards piled into the room from a dark hallway. There seemed to be far more than the seven I'd expected.

Dark hallway? I glanced up to see that the lights in this conference room were also off, though with the fighting and the light from the window, I hadn't noticed. The screen that had once held images from the security cameras was black.

Someone had activated the relays—and maybe left them off. What that could mean for us, I could only hope.

A bullet from one of the guards slammed into my chest, ramming me again into the wall. My shield held, and I bounced off the wall, bringing my sword against Ropte's, hooking his sword up and away from his grasp, leaving him wide open. Too bad we'd need him later. Rejecting the urge to slaughter him, I turned my blade flat and slammed it into the side of his head. He crumpled to the floor and stayed down.

I turned back to oncoming guards. There was no way past them. Jace had jumped away from Stefan and was battling three guards at the same time. Blood drenched his chest. Next to him, Keene slammed a few heads together. Tihalt wielded his laser, accidentally slicing through a guard as if he was nothing but air.

Bullets flew into me. One pierced my shield, ripping up the surface of my arm to my shoulder. Pain made me want to vomit. Keene threw a guard into a man that was targeting Jace. Stefan picked up a fallen guard's gun.

We weren't going to make it.

And then I felt him come through the door.

Ritter.

CHAPTER 23

GUARDS WENT FLYING AS RITTER BURST INTO OUR MIDST. CORT and Dimitri immediately followed him. I had no idea how they'd gotten inside the building or how long they'd been here, but they already looked worn, as if they'd fought their way down a hallway full of Emporium soldiers. Ritter didn't carry an assault rifle, and the only way he'd have abandoned it was if he'd run out of ammunition. Maybe that explained the repeated gunshots I'd heard.

Had Ritter fought his way into the building after all? If Ritter had fallen back to one of the alternate plans, where were the New York Renegades and the ex-Emporium Unbounded? I'd even welcome Oliver—we could use one of his illusions about now. I still felt nothing beyond this room, so I had no idea what awaited us in the hallway. Or how many we'd lost.

I couldn't think about that now.

Ritter looked once in my direction, taking me in with hungry eyes. *I'm okay,* I thought to him, but his shield was too strong for me to get through without expending energy

I didn't have. But he'd be able to see I was fine, despite the shallow furrow up my arm that drenched me with blood.

Even as I had the thought, his shield opened a crack, and I was in. I saw his invitation to channel his ability, and also felt his agreement when I suggested I stick with Jace in case he needed backup. Jace had been on ops before, but not like this. Not with his father trying to kill him. Besides, Ritter would fight better if he weren't so closely linked to what I was doing; his protective urge where I was concerned might distract him.

There was no time for a reunion. More Emporium Unbounded were pouring into the room after them. At such close quarters, guns had mostly been abandoned in the fear of hitting a comrade. Or they were kicked away by opponents. A female Emporium soldier threw down an empty pistol. Knives and swords flashed. The two Emporium soldiers nearest me had drawn their swords, but when they saw our reinforcements and no one behind me, they reached for their guns instead. I dived between them, coming up fast and bashing one in the neck with my sword. He hit the ground before drawing his gun. The other man blocked my next swing, but not my kick at his groin, which gave me an opening to thrust my sword through his middle. I'd never really understood the appeal of swords before, but I did now. They were so very deadly.

I whirled to face two more combatants, trying to pierce their mental shields at the same time. If I could flash light into their minds, I could even the odds a little. But they were at full alert, and like Stefan and Ropte, their shields were strong. Until I could get somewhere away from the fighting, where I didn't have to concentrate on staying alive, I wouldn't be able to break through.

I rammed my sword into one guard, but he clutched it as

he fell, and I had to let it go or be skewered by his comrade. Backpedaling as fast as I could, I was relieved when Cort took out the guard, his sword sinking deep into the man's side.

A few more Unbounded came through the door, one heavily wounded. He took only a few steps before collapsing to the ground. The others plunged into the battle.

"Erin!" I turned to see Ritter fighting his way toward me. Only two men separated us when he took out another sword from his back sheath—my sword—and tossed it to me.

I grabbed it in time to slash at another opponent. Over the man's shoulder, I spied Tihalt struggling to his feet after an apparent fall. Keene was turned away, finishing off another attacker, when his father raised his laser to slice across Keene's torso. Keene would never move out of the way in time.

"No!" Cort shouted. He lunged at Tihalt, pushing his brother away. The laser ripped through Cort, severing his head from his neck. For a moment, I thought I was seeing things because he looked exactly the same, but then his body started to crumple and his head tipped. Tihalt grinned, his face covered in gore, his eyes glinting with triumph. He was already slashing down with another thrust that would severe Cort's remaining two focus points. Three parts severed. There would be no coming back from that.

I threw back another guard and rushed toward them. Keene caught himself and turned, his mouth open in a silent scream. Down came Tihalt's laser.

The light pierced Cort's body, carving through it with the same ease it had shown before.

No!

Grief rose up to meet me, along with another guard. I feinted and slammed into him, my sword piercing his heart.

Power pulsed around Keene, and Tihalt slammed backward against the wall, his head twisting violently to the side. Keene raised the sword in his hands. Tihalt cursed him, blood and spittle flying from his mouth. Keene sneered at him as his sword cut through the man's neck as effortlessly as the laser had, driven by his ability. He raised the sword again.

I pushed another soldier aside. "We need him!"

Keene turned and looked at me, his eyes dilated and his face rigid. "No, we don't. This ends here." He brought the sword down through Tihalt's torso, severing it completely.

I looked away in time to see Mari hovering in the hall by the doorway. My grief over Cort turned to an aching numbness as I saw her. She was alive! Mari slipped a knife between the ribs of a soldier at the door and stepped through, her life force burning with welcome. Completely unshielded.

I reached out and shifted next to her, lunging for the panel holding the controls for the room's electrical field. I slammed my fist into it, and the red web in the room vanished.

All at once, I felt them—more than a hundred life forces crammed into the wide hallway on this floor, locked in the ancient struggle for life.

"So many," I whispered.

Mari looked at me, her face pale and haunted. Streaks of red ran down her cheeks, and her pants looked as if she'd wiped blood from her hands repeatedly. In her mind, I glimpsed how everything had gone wrong. She'd set off the relays and shifted Ritter and a few of the others into Tihalt's lab one floor below. They'd fought their way up here, but soldiers already filled this hallway, with more coming behind them. They'd continued their desperate fight, protecting Mari while she shifted more Renegades inside the building. She'd made trip after trip, bringing everyone she could: Ava, members from the New York cell, the thirty-four former prisoners. Those were the life forces that now struggled in the hallway against the Emporium hit teams.

All along, Mari hadn't known if Keene—or any of us—still lived.

"Keene," she whispered.

I thought it was a question, but she vanished and appeared across the room, startling two men attacking Keene. In front of them, Ritter and Dimitri stood back to back, battling a ring of Emporium soldiers. Jace was near the couches, once again clashing with Stefan, but another guard was interfering, wearing Jace down. He looked beaten and resigned, and his mind raged with fury and terror.

Don't think about Cort, I told myself. *Focus on Jace.* I headed toward him, dodging around the soldiers fighting Ritter, slashing two of their legs as I passed. Stefan turned as I approached, beating me back with his sword.

"Are you really my daughter?" he growled.

"You'll never know," I sneered through the numbness encasing my heart, "but I would rather die than have you as a father."

"I can help with that." He sliced hard, risking his hands to twist away my sword as he'd done in our earlier bout. This time I held onto it, bringing it down to block him. He lunged for me again, but channeling Mari, I shifted behind him. Both hands on my hilt, I smashed my elbow into his head. He collapsed. I hit him again to make sure he'd stay out.

Jace dispatched the other guard, but two more escaped past Ritter and came up to meet him. There were fewer opposing soldiers standing now, and Ritter and Dimitri were pushing them toward the door. By the time Jace and I managed to fight our way free, they had all disappeared into the dark hallway. Agonized screams and cries met my ears.

I ran to the door and into the hall. It wasn't as dark as I'd first thought, and my eyes readily adjusted, but it seemed impossible to believe the mounds of bodies clogging up the hallway—far more than the hundred life forces I'd detected earlier. Many were full of bullet holes and only temporarily dead or passed out, still retaining faint life force glows. But far too many had been slaughtered. Permanently dead. One woman I recognized from the New York cell: Francis Bennet, a summoner, who had recently given birth to a baby after we'd freed her from an Emporium prison. Her head lay next to her torn body, her short blond hair askew, her muddy, almond-shaped eyes forever closed.

I also recognized Jonny Carrington, my supposed half brother and Jace's real half brother. He would no longer have to worry about his short life and not measuring up to those with the full combat ability. He'd never have to mourn again the woman he'd loved who hadn't survived the forcing experiment.

Seeing the devastation, I didn't know how anyone could continue fighting. Yet what other choice did we have? Near the elevator, a group of our people led by Ava blocked the stairs and the elevator. More clumps of people fought along the corridor.

A soldier leapt up to confront me, stepping on the pieces of Jonny in his eagerness. Bile filled my throat as I brought up my sword, my feet sticking on the bloodstained floor.

Where was Ritter? Why couldn't I feel our connection? He was just . . . gone. The numbness in me spread.

I swung and ducked and swung again. The line of soldiers seemed never to end. My shield took two blows that would have flattened me, if my opponent hadn't been as weary as I was. I was making stupid mistakes, not ones I should be making still connected to Jace, no matter how thin the thread between us. My muscles screamed with fatigue.

Finally, I spotted Ritter battling two huge men down the corridor. Two more rose up to join the fight against him. Dimitri was nowhere to be seen.

And Cort. Oh, Cort! He was dead. Truly and permanently. I couldn't wrap my mind or my feelings around that. Had Ritter seen? He would be devastated. Maybe that's why he was fighting like a maniac, mowing down the enemy like a scythe through wheat.

I slammed aside a soldier and started in Ritter's direction. But the soldier came back at me, and I had to fight him off again. A cut from his blade told me I'd let my shield drop. I tried to put it back up, but my mind was slow to react.

Then it happened. Over my opponent's shoulder, I saw a sword from one of Ritter's assailants slice hard into Ritter. He staggered and fell, taking a bunch of them with him.

"No!" I screamed.

I forced my attacker back with my sword and my mind, which shattered his mental barrier. Taking advantage of the breach, I flashed light into his unprotected mind and he crumpled.

Another took his place. There were too many bodies separating me from Ritter—and far too many swords around Ritter for him to survive. But I had to get to him. I wouldn't let it end like this. We'd come too far. I reached for Mari, hoping to channel her ability, but I couldn't find her. I could only feel Jace through our tenuous connection.

Why couldn't I feel Ritter? I could always recognize his life force—feel him even if our minds weren't connected. All I felt now was that horrible numbness that seemed to fill my entire body. I wanted to give up, to lie down on the ground and curl into a ball.

Ritter! I screamed silently, searching for him. If I could feel him, I would know it was okay.

Nothing.

I shoved forward, only to be pushed back. I lost my grip

on my sword. Then Dimitri was there, touching the man from behind with his healing hands that could also kill. The soldier collapsed. I grabbed for my sword, but there were no new opponents. Standing behind Dimitri were a dozen of our Renegades, some quickly finishing their last battle, while others stared with the same disbelief I felt.

Just like that, it was over. No more Emporium guards came through the stairwell or elevator. No one was still standing except Renegades.

"Ritter?" I asked Dimitri, wilting against him.

He shook his head. "We were separated."

"I can't feel him." *Just like I can't feel Cort.*

A hand touched my arm, and I turned to see Ava. I hadn't even felt her coming. "Erin, this was only their main contingent. Someone down there will be gathering a second wave. We have to go through with the takeover. And fast."

I remained where I was. Something whispered that if I moved from this hallway, a part of me would stay behind forever, and I'd only be half alive. Was this what happened when a sensing Unbounded lost her mate? Agony finally burst through the numbness, all enveloping. I pushed Ava and Dimitri's hands away.

"Erin," Ava said, unyielding. "We haven't lost this yet, but we have to calm the people below."

"I have to find Ritter," I said.

She searched the hallway for a moment. She didn't have my connection with Ritter or my mental strength, so I knew in this confusion she wouldn't be able to tell one person from another. Yet for a moment, I let myself hope. Then she said, "I know."

I could see her sadness. The pity for me. But how could she be so calm?

Oh, yes, I knew how. Over the years, she'd buried too many babies, and also husbands she'd loved. She'd lost them and continued living and fighting and loving. So would I.

"Wake Stefan and Ropte," I said, the words barely audible through clenched teeth. "Get them started. I'll be right there."

I staggered on—alone, I thought, until I realized Dimitri was with me. His hand reached out to mine and held on tightly. Warmth tingled through my body as he used his ability to find my wounds and increase the healing process. The horrible ache in my shoulder subsided, but not the agony in my heart.

My goal was the knot of men sprawled in the hallway where Ritter had gone down. I could see a few life forces glowing, though so dimly as to be almost nonexistent. Other lumps showed no glow. We found Ritter lying on two unconscious men, the neck of one clamped tightly under his arm and his legs scissoring the other. Three others were on top of him, two bleeding from knife wounds to the heart.

Dimitri and I each pulled off a man. I gave a strangled gasp of relief.

Ritter's life force was one of those still glowing, despite the ugly gash severing a fourth of his torso. His head was still firmly attached. However, I still couldn't feel the essence that was him. Had someone damaged him mentally?

Tears stinging my eyes, I pulled off the remaining soldier and lay next to Ritter, reaching my mind toward his. There he was. I could feel him now that I was touching him, even through the emotions that threatened to crush my heart.

While Dimitri held his hands against Ritter's wound, I fumbled through Ritter's pockets to find his emergency curequick. "This is bad," Dimitri commented.

I didn't know how Ritter had survived here alone, until I looked at the last soldier I'd pulled off Ritter. His face was different now, slowly morphing from an Emporium soldier into Oliver. Our illusionist wasn't much of a fighter, but he had fought, and he certainly had chosen a great disguise.

"Oliver?" Dimitri asked, keeping his hands on Ritter. "Looks like he managed to hold onto the illusion for a time even after losing consciousness. I'm impressed."

"Don't tell him," I said. "He'll never let us forget it."

Dimitri chuckled. "Maybe you should get back to Ava. Ritter's breathing, but it might be a while before he awakes."

Ritter's eyes suddenly came open as he growled, "Cut the racket, would you? I was just taking a little break."

The lights chose that moment to come back on, so either Mari had reset the relay switches, or someone below had broken into the transfer boxes and fixed them.

I gave a laugh that might have sounded more like a sob. "No time for rest," I told Ritter. "We have a takeover to finish."

CHAPTER 24

B Y THE TIME WE GOT OLIVER SQUARED AWAY AND RITTER doctored enough to get back to the conference room, all the Emporium dead in the room had been cleared. Only Tihalt and two unfortunate mortal Emporium soldiers had been permanently killed in that conference room. The other twenty Emporium soldiers who had fought there would recover, including Edgel. Lew and Jeane would also survive, but something had happened when Lew shot Jeane. His shields had vanished, and his mind was now empty. Ava didn't know if he'd ever recover.

The New York Renegades and the former prisoners were now clearing the corridor, using the other meeting rooms on this floor as makeshift hospitals. So far, forty-one mortal Emporium soldiers and twenty-three Emporium Unbounded had been permanently killed in that hallway, but at least sixty more would survive.

The Renegades had suffered far less damage overall, due in large part to Ritter's strategy and Mari's shifting. We'd permanently lost three Renegades from the New York cell, including

Tenika's second-in-command, Li Yuan-Xin, whose combat ability had been legendary and who had always been kind to me. Five more had fallen from the thirty-four former prisoners who'd fought with us.

And Cort.

Cort, whose passing had numbed my heart so deeply that I still couldn't feel my connection with Ritter unless I touched him. In fact, I could no longer detect anyone's thoughts without touching them, except Jace, to whom I still clung.

"You'll recover once the shock is over," Dimitri said, his hand on my shoulder still sending healing into my body. "Losing someone this way, and then that scare you had seeing Ritter go down . . . it's too much." His voice became so thick, I could barely understand the words. "It's too much for all of us."

"I don't want to forget Cort."

"You won't. We never forget." He opened a large vial of curequick and added, "Drink this. The faster you heal, the faster your shock will wear off." I gulped down the sweet mixture, welcoming the buzz that chased down my throat and slowly spread throughout my body.

Feeling Ritter's stare, I looked down at him where he sat on the couch by the wall of swords, swathed in bandages, his eyes burning with a hurt that dug into me as deeply as my own. That he didn't reach out his hand told me he understood our shared grief was a burden neither of us could take right now.

"Let's finish this," he said.

I nodded. "Okay."

Ropte and Stefan were conscious and seated on separate couches to keep them from attacking each other. Someone had found them clean shirts and roughly bandaged their wounds.

"Just don't let Ropte touch you," Catrina warned, walking over from the minibar where she'd begun setting up a makeshift office. "That's how he can change memories. It's the only way, though, because he's a raider, not a mnemo."

I remembered how she'd handed me the coffee when I was about to shake Ropte's hand. She was being equally helpful now, making sure Ava had every access to the computers and the Triad's passwords—a good thing because I didn't know if I could enter an unblocked mind, much less force my way through any shields.

"Why are you helping us?" I asked her.

She smiled, her eyes straying to Jace, whose wounds were being sewn up by Keene. "Because I saw in your brother's mind that everything my family has heard about the Renegades is true. I grew up watching the Emporium use my family's abilities in the name of good, and I wanted to believe, but when I Changed I learned the truth about the corruption that drove those lofty goals. When my mother tried to leave, Delia and Stefan killed her. Today I am finally taking steps to avenge her and every Emporium agent who has ever believed the lie."

"You're a traitor!" Ropte spat.

Catrina's head turned in his direction, slowly and deliberately. "Not to the human race, I'm not. And I might be Unbounded, but I'm still every bit human. Besides, you're the one who stole Stefan's memories. The one who planned to steal Erin's memories and place her in the Triad in Stefan's place as your puppet. You and Tihalt planned it together. I saw it in his mind."

During most of Catrina's conversation, Stefan had remained expressionless, but now his face twisted with hate toward Ropte. "So that's why he'd never give me the laser weapon," he snarled. "He was planning a coup."

Ropte shrugged. "We needed it to subdue your soldiers."

"And I suppose he helped you go against my orders to kill those senators. This is all your fault!"

"Those senators were resistant to me."

"You're just not that good, are you?" Stefan mocked.

"I made you forget your supposed daughter."

"I told you killing them would draw too much attention." Ropte sneered. "Your way took too long."

"*My* way didn't make Renegades interfere. I would have put you in the White House."

"And then I still would have killed you!"

Stefan tried to launch from his couch at Ropte, straining at his bonds, but Ava shoved him back down. "It doesn't matter now. It's over. You'll sign the documents passing your share of the Triad and all your Emporium holdings to Jace. Ropte, you'll do the same for Jeane."

"Actually,"—Catrina waved the tablet she was holding— "Stella's been able to get into Ropte's Emporium database with the codes I took from his mind, and it looks like Jeane is already his successor."

"*She's* the best you could do?" Stefan mocked Ropte. "An infertile woman? What a great legacy. How is she going to find a successor?"

Ropte stared him down. "It was only until I found someone better. At least I knew she wasn't going to stab me in the back."

"I guess altering memories has its advantages."

Ava cleared her throat. "If you two are quite finished," she said, "I'd like to get started."

Stefan shifted his gaze to Ava, his eyes telling everyone how much he'd love to wrap his fingers around her neck. "What about Tihalt?"

"You know how it works better than I do. You and Ropte will both sign an agreement saying that he wanted his newly returned son to fill his place." Ava's voice skipped on the word son, and I knew she was thinking of Tihalt's other son. The one we didn't yet have time to mourn. "If Tihalt's real successor shows up, we'll deal with him then. We may not be able to change memories, but we can remove them."

"It'll never work," Stefan growled.

Keene looked up from where he was finishing a last stitch on Jace's arm. "Tihalt never made public appearances. At least he never did when I knew him. He left all that to Stefan. He even communicates mostly over email with his department. So maybe for now, we can pretend he's still alive, and I'll start showing myself around here to get people used to seeing me again before we publicly transfer the title. That way we won't have three new Triad members at once."

Ava thought about it. "That's sounds reasonable."

Stefan had the gall to laugh. "It won't work. My soldiers will be up here before the hour is out." He gestured to the feed from the security cameras, which had been restored with the generator power. We could see Unbounded suiting up all over the building, and a crowd gathering on the floor below. "It's going to make the bloodshed you've already experienced nothing more than an appetizer."

Ava showed only confidence. "As long as we have you, they won't dare come in with too much force."

"My real successor is in London." Stefan's smirk deepened. "He won't take this sitting down. Make no mistake. Even if you succeed today, tomorrow he'll be here with an army."

"Exactly," Ropte said. "His heir has everything to gain if Stefan is dead. He won't mind murdering everyone up here, including Stefan."

Stefan scowled. "The only one of us he'll be murdering is you."

"There will be no reinforcements," Ava said. "We did have to break our blockade when we shifted inside, but a group of Hunters took our place. Even if reinforcements come, they won't get past them."

"I'm going to drink your blood," Stefan promised.

Ava sighed in exasperation. "Somebody gag him. Gag them both. Until we're ready to record the video footage to send downstairs."

As Jace and Mari jumped to do her bidding, Ava drew me aside, close to where Cort had been cut down. I avoided looking at the blood that soaked the carpet, but memories of him assailed me. Especially memories of a particular restaurant he'd taken me to when I'd first Changed, and how he'd told me about his château in Paris and promised to take me there.

"Stefan's right," Ava said, her back to our prisoners, her voice stretched to a breaking point. "We need to calm those people downstairs. We're too vulnerable here. I'm thinking a succession announcement will have to wait a week—or more. We'll get it all signed today and move Stefan and Ropte and all the wounded guards out of here, but for right now, it's better to have Stefan announce that his son has been returned to him and with his help, they were able to overthrow a Renegade plot. Catrina says they have speakers and video screens about every twenty feet throughout the entire building, and in every work station and private residence. They should all hear his message."

I chewed on my lip as I tentatively sent my mind downward to the gathering masses. Dimitri was right—now that things had calmed down, I was already regaining some control. "I don't know that it'll work—no matter what we tell them. The panic coming from below is strong."

"One of the soldiers had a battery-powered radio, so they know a little of what was going on up here."

"Then I'm guessing those soldiers will start coming up those stairs within twenty minutes. If they receive backup from the other headquarters, we'll be in big trouble."

Ava shook her head. "That shouldn't happen. Reports

are already coming in from the other headquarter locations. Someone here did manage to get out a call for reinforcements, but so far anyone leaving the other buildings has been turned back inside or taken prisoner by our people."

"Chris?" I asked.

"Stella said he's taken fifty-two already. The rest have stayed inside. But whoever has taken control below is bound to hatch a plan if we don't send out instructions from the Triad."

Across the room, Mari clapped her hands. "Wait! I know what to do. It's Noah. We need Noah!" Everyone stared at her, but she vanished, appearing next to Ava. She lowered her voice so Stefan and Ropte couldn't hear. "Or rather, we need Erin channeling Noah. Together they can calm them down. All those speakers they have should easily spread the emotion Erin can put into the words. It's not like a recording or anything."

Ava snapped her fingers. "It's worth a try. Where's Noah?"

"Helping Stella and Patrick with communications," Jace said from behind me, moving so fast I hadn't noticed his approach. "But the electric grid around the building is back on."

"Can we disable it up here without shutting off all the electricity?" Mari asked. "And we'll need to have Stella turn off our grid over there."

"I'll take care of this one." Jace shifted the assault rifle he'd appropriated from somewhere and stalked up behind Stefan's couch, grabbing him roughly by the neck. "Hey, old man, I need some codes from you." He looked over to where Catrina was printing documents. "We'll need computer access too." She hurried over with her tablet.

Ava pulled out her phone. "I'll let Stella know we need Noah ready."

Mari tapped her foot impatiently until the grids were shut down in both locations. Then she disappeared and returned less than two minutes later with both Noah and Patrick. From the couches across the room, Stefan and Ropte stared in shocked surprise at Mari's ability to shift others, but it didn't matter what they saw now.

"I know just the song," Noah said to me. "It was inspired from a speech by Mother Teresa. Not her words exactly, but the same sort of thing: brotherly love, living in peace, helping one another. You get the idea. I'll teach it to you. I brought the music. But first you have to look the part." She lifted a bag containing the same outfit I'd worn at Ropte's. "Mari took us back to my place for this, and it's why I brought Patrick and more nanites, so you can channel him first. It was in the paper that you were at Ropte's, and some of them will recognize you—me—in this outfit." She shook her head with a little laugh. "Whatever."

"Let us know when you're ready," Ava said, her voice easier now. "I'll have Stefan make a public statement on a recording. Ropte too. We'll try to get a shot of them sitting on the same couch without killing each other. If they won't behave, Patrick will have to fake being Stefan."

"I haven't been able to study his mannerisms," Patrick said, "so I wouldn't be able to do a thorough job at becoming him, but why don't we do a pre-announcement first? I could do that much, and just seeing Stefan alive and letting his people know there will be a more lengthy announcement soon should buy us time to record one that will satisfy them."

"Good idea. The camera is that way. Make it brief. Have Catrina actually make the announcement. Maybe you can pretend you're on the phone in the background." Her voice lowered. "Record it first. Catrina seems trustworthy, but we can't risk anything at this point."

Patrick nodded and moved off, pulling out a portable neural headset.

Ava raised her voice and signaled Jace. "I'll need your help with Stefan to provide an incentive to say what we need him to say—exactly the words I choose."

"My pleasure," Jace said. "I'm sure Ritter will offer pointers, if I need them."

From the couch, Ritter laughed. Our eyes met, and emotion rushed between us, briefly stirring our connection. This time it didn't hold only grief. The tightness in my chest eased ever so slightly.

"Wait!" Jeane, who had apparently regained consciousness under Dimitri's care, chose that moment to stagger to her feet. Her hair was knotted and bloody, her eyes wide with shock. For once, there was no sign of the playful sexiness she normally portrayed. Shaking off Dimitri's hand, she stumbled inside the square of couches to stand in front of her brother, the coffee table rubbing at the back of her calves.

"Fix it," she demanded. "I heard what everyone says you did to me, but my mind remembers it another way. I want back the truth."

His response was muffled, and she leaned forward, yanking out his gag. "I said fix it!" She leaned over, extending one hand to where his hands were securely tied and resting in his lap.

He hit her hand away. "I can't fix it, you nitwit. I just ask you to remember how it was and then I tell you how I want you to remember it. There is no undoing anything. You could have nulled me while I was speaking. Too bad you were too stupid."

"Then I guess I don't need you." A light shot out from her other hand, arcing across Ropte's neck. Ritter jumped to his feet and over the huge coffee table, but wasn't able to reach her before she'd waved it across Ropte again. Not twice, but three or four times. She appeared to have every intention of continuing her strikes until Ritter grabbed her from behind and wrenched Tihalt's laser from her hand.

Ropte didn't make a sound. And he never would again.

Ava swore under her breath, and in all the time I'd known her she'd never cursed. "Will you ever think of anyone but yourself? We need him!"

Jeane shook her head. "Not really. People here barely know him. Remember, *I'm* his successor, and they do know me." Her contented, blood-streaked smile chilled me. "He said it would only be temporary until he chose someone better. I guess he was wrong. His legacy—and Delia's—end with me."

On his couch, the gag still in his mouth, Stefan was laughing.

Ava nodded at Dimitri, who'd come up behind Jeane with a syringe of sedative. Jeane turned at Ava's motion, and the fear returned to her eyes. "No," she protested in a small, breathy voice. Her shoulders slumped as all the fight drained from her body.

I took the three steps separating me from Dimitri and placed a hand on his arm. "She's suffered enough. Let her stay conscious—just tie her up in another room. Take Lew too." The man's sightless stare was unsettling, reminding me of Cort's eyes in those seconds after his death.

Ava nodded at Dimitri. "That's fine. We may need her anyway after we announce she's Ropte's successor."

Twenty minutes later, Ava's video was ready. Catrina and I had worked together to get Stefan to look natural, with Jace waving Tihalt's laser occasionally near Stefan's feet for encouragement. After a rapid cleaning and splicing by Patrick, the clip lasted only two and a half minutes but appeared genuine.

In the recording, Stefan appeared briefly with a cleaned-up Jace and assured everyone that the Renegade rebellion had been squashed despite the shifter the Renegades had employed to infiltrate the upper floors. "She is in custody now with the rest of her comrades," Stefan said. "My son, who has recently Changed and joined us, was instrumental in capturing her."

He raised a fist. "We are invincible as always, and soon we'll have many shifters of our own."

Stefan paused before dropping the "terrible" news of a Triad member fatality, and here a hint of his gloating showed through despite our best efforts. "However, David's official successor, Jeane Baker, is safe and will take his place as soon as the customary documents are examined by the department heads and DNA testing by doctors is complete. But you all know Jeane," he added with an empty smile, "and we look forward to her future contributions to our organization."

He finished by promising to bring Jace to the lower levels later to officially introduce him around. Of course, if we ended up doing that, it would really be Patrick looking like Stefan, but Ava felt that promising a physical appearance would ease more tension, even if we didn't follow through for a few days.

Jace took over the rest of the video, introducing himself and spinning a yarn about how he'd come to train under his father's tutelage. He wrapped up by announcing that he'd brought with him a special visitor who was famous on every continent. Then he introduced me as Noah.

At that point, we switched to a live feed. As I sang into the microphone, the words and music blasted over every speaker in the building, and my face—or Noah's—appeared on every screen on every floor. I sang of peace and love. Of family and the human race. Keene enhanced my efforts, and I pulled on his proffered energy, imbuing his sadness into the notes.

My eyes strayed to Cort's blood on the carpet. He'd be proud of what we'd accomplished here today. Proud that he'd saved his brother's life when for five hundred years he'd been helpless to save any of his other siblings from the monster he called father.

"It's working!" Mari whispered, pointing to the monitors.

"They're going back to their desks and jobs and whatever else they were doing before the call to arms went out. Look!"

"Three department heads have asked to meet personally with Stefan," Catrina put in, tapping on her tablet. "I scheduled a meeting for tomorrow, and they seemed okay with that. So I hope Patrick will have studied Stefan enough by then to pass their examination."

No doubt there would be more who questioned. We'd have to slowly weed out the troublemakers and place the former prisoners from Mexico in every department as new "managers." That some of them were known in the Emporium from before their capture should make it easier for them to spot trouble brewing.

In the end, where fighting and negotiation had failed, Noah's supposedly useless, beautiful ability, not meant for battle but for inspiration, convinced everyone and won the day. I hugged Noah tightly. Maybe if we'd bred in more abilities like hers, we could have finished this battle a century ago.

Catrina came up to me after I was myself again. "You do have multiple abilities," she said, touching my arm. "I didn't know that was possible."

She must believe I was also a technopath because I'd changed my appearance using the nanites. "Something like that," I told her. Now wasn't the time to explain channeling, not until all the Emporium headquarters were secure and we were sure about where she planned to go from here.

She leaned closer. "Erin, there's something wonderful inside you. Can't you feel it?"

The comment was strange, but no stranger than others she'd surprised me with today. I decided she was still talking about my channeling. Maybe soon I'd see if she could learn how. With the way Jace's eyes lingered on her face, I had a feeling we were going to be seeing a lot more of each other.

Warm sand stretched for miles on end with no one in sight. Ritter and I were completely alone. We'd had a busy month with Cort's funeral, Chris and Stella's wedding, and, yeah, that little matter of taking over the Emporium. We were still working out issues on that.

With Stella and Patrick sifting through the Emporium databases, uncovering centuries of plots and government interference, we were making headway with our changes. Slow changes that we'd accomplish hand in hand with the mortals to find a peaceful co-existence.

Stefan hadn't officially retired, but he'd been transferred to Mexico, where he was under constant sedation after an escape attempt. He was alive only because we might need him, but I suspected that wouldn't be for long. I was glad he was far away from Jace, who was quickly filling Stefan's public role with the Emporium. That everyone liked Jace and few had liked Stefan made his job easier.

Ironically, our biggest problem, besides extending new directives to all the Emporium headquarters and deciding when to announce Stefan's retirement, had been Jeane dying her hair blond again, painting her beauty mark, and trying to seduce every male in sight. She was no one's idea of a leader, and her antics caused more than a little trouble among the guards. She offered to step down so she could spend the rest of her days shopping and tending a near comatose Lew, but as she had no posterity, and never would, we had no immediate way of replacing her. Triad succession rules would have to change—and soon. Our experts were still decoding her brain, but Catrina and I thought we might eventually extract her false memories. In the meantime, it was a full-time job keeping her out of trouble.

Someone else's job right now. A week ago, Ritter and I had finally escaped to the tropical island Cort had left us in his will. "He always teased me that he would honeymoon here," Ritter told me. "But he was married several times, and it never worked out."

We could talk about him now, and it was a relief to share memories. Ritter had far more than I did, of course, but I had a few he didn't know about.

The sun sat low enough in the sky that the heat was pleasant and the humidity bearable. The occasional wispy cloud and seagulls winging through the air provided the only variety in the endless blue sky. We'd been swimming, not in the ocean this time but in a small pool formed by a waterfall and surrounded by luscious palm trees. We'd left the pool to dry in the sun and soak up some rays.

"It's tomorrow the others are coming, right?" Ritter lifted himself up partway on the blanket and put an arm over me. His head blocked out the sun.

"Yeah. Mari's bringing everyone after lunch."

He heaved a sigh. "With Chris and his kids here, we'll have to put on clothes."

I laughed. "I miss them."

"Clothes or the kids?"

I rolled my eyes. "Shut up and kiss me, Your Deathliness. Tonight's our last night alone."

"No, it's only one of the first." But he obliged me, lowering his mouth to mine and covering my bare legs with his.

He was wrong. Because I'd discovered the something wonderful Catrina had seen inside me—the tiny spark that meant life. Ritter would soon have a new op to plan, which was in some ways more frightening and exciting than anything we'd been through together. I wanted to tell him more than almost anything, but I wanted one thing even more: a few more hours as the center of his world. Because in a few months, we'd never really be alone again.

Tomorrow we would celebrate. Ritter would pick me up and spin me around and laugh like a madman. He'd put his mouth to my stomach and talk to our child. In another month or two, he'd start asking me to relay messages and begin designing workouts for children. I couldn't wait.

Instead of deepening the kiss, Ritter drew away, his face growing serious and his black eyes searching mine. "Where do we go from here? I've fought them so long. I never really thought about what came after."

"We make sure nothing like the Emporium ever happens again."

Something akin to relief chased across his face. "The only way is for Unbounded to continue monitoring. We have to protect all our people."

I liked how he said "our people." From here on out, there were no more Renegades or Emporium, or even Unbounded and mortals. They were all our people.

Together, we would go into the future and discover what it held.

THE END

NOTE FROM THE AUTHOR

THANK YOU SO MUCH FOR GOING ON THIS JOURNEY WITH ME. *The Takeover* is the final installment in the *Unbounded* series—at least for this generation. (There eventually may be a few more spin-off novellas.) But I have other series in the works, and I hope to see you again in their pages. Meanwhile, if you missed learning how Mari developed her ability to shift with other people, please read *Lethal Engagement (An Unbounded Novella)* to catch up on her story. Thank you!

TEYLA BRANTON

TEYLA BRANTON GREW UP AVIDLY READING SCIENCE FICTION AND fantasy and watching Star Trek reruns with her large family. They lived on a little farm where she loved to visit the solitary cow and collect (and juggle) the eggs, usually making it back to the house with most of them intact. On that same farm she once owned thirty-three gerbils and eighteen cats, not a good mix, as it turns out. Teyla always had her nose in a book and daydreamed about someday creating her own worlds.

Teyla is now married, mostly grown up, and has seven kids, including a four-year-old, so life at her house can be very interesting (and loud), but writing keeps her sane. She warns her children that if they don't behave, they just might find themselves in her next book! She's been known to wear pajamas all day when working on a deadline, and is often distracted enough to burn dinner. (Okay, pretty much 90% of the time.)

She loves writing fiction and traveling, and she hopes to write and travel a lot more. She also loves shooting guns, martial arts, and belly dancing. Teyla also writes romance and suspense under the name Rachel Branton. For more information, please visit http://www.TeylaBranton.com.

9 781939 203670